Lost Boy

THE LOYAL BOYS BOOK 3

CHARLI MEADOWS

SYNOPSIS

I'm lost to the numbness. Can his love make me feel again?

Fallon

Being alone is nothing new. I've been abandoned by everyone. Now, I have absolutely no one. I might even prefer it that way. All I really need is a guitar and my thoughts.

Just shy of my eighteenth birthday, I'm forced to move across the country to live with my uncle in California. He's the head basketball coach at Acadia Lake Prep, the new private academy I'm attending. Ryder Cruz is his star player.

He makes me question things about myself and what I want. Things I've never once considered. The oversized and enthusiastic jock is always around, insisting I smile and laugh with him. But it won't work. It can't. The painful memories and regret I carry are too strong. I'm not sure I'll ever feel again.

Ryder

Basketball is great. So are my friends. Dad. My little sister Sofie. I'm team captain, and I'm taking us to State.

It's easy to forget that nothing is ever as it seems. I fight my demons with smiles and awkward jokes, but things are starting to pile up. Pranks between my guys and the rival public school, issues with my mother, and a secret I can't tell anyone. A truth that holds me in its grasp. I can't risk the team or my college acceptance—my *future*. Can't risk my dream.

I'm gay. And no one can know.

It wasn't as hard to keep this close to my chest until Fallon Rivers showed up with his big, sad eyes and bright blue hair. I'm not sure I can continue hiding who I am. I *need* this boy to smile. To talk to me. I need to spark some life back into his soul.

He doesn't realize my dad and his uncle are partners, but he'll find out soon enough. Sleepovers happen almost every weekend. And now that he's here and staying for good, I guess he'll just have to get used to my presence. Because I'm determined to make him feel again and maybe even free myself along the way.

Lost Boy is a 90,000-word friends-to-lovers gay romance. It is book three in The Loyal Boys Series, a collection of standalone, contemporary M/M romances. You can expect opposites attract, forced proximity, hurt/comfort, steamy first times, and a supportive found family. This novel is intended for 18+ readers and contains explicit scenes, mild violence, language, and bullying from outside sources. See Author's Note for a full list of Content Warnings.

AUTHOR'S NOTE

Thank you so much for continuing *The Loyal Boys* with me. It really means a lot that you're here for book three! *Lost Boy* is once again a standalone but has similar themes of love and loyalty to *Cali Boy* and *Bad Boy*. Fallon moves to a new town for his senior year, attends a private school, and meets the golden retriever jock Ryder Cruz, forever changing his life. There's a little bit of violence and a lot of trauma, grief, and healing. I have included a list of content warnings if you want to know what to expect.

These boys mean so much to me, and I can't wait to share their story!

Content warnings: Language, explicit sexual scenes (both MCs are eighteen), mild violence, underage drinking and drugs, bullying (outside of the MCs), homophobia, parental loss (off page in the past), parental neglect (off page), grief, anxiety, and depression.

PLAYLIST

Available on Spotify

Seams by INTRN
Blue by Kayla Rae
Darkside by Vwillz
No, I'm Not Ok by Yung Bleu
High Enough by K.Flay
Wicked Games by The Weeknd
The Freshman by The Verve Pipe
Shirt by SZA
We Go Down Together by Dove Cameron, Khalid
sAy sOMETHINg by Lil Yachty
High For This by The Weeknd
Peter Pan Was Right by Anson Seabra
Lavender Haze by Taylor Swift
Luv Me Again by PnB Rock
Little Do You Know by Alex & Sierra
Maroon by Taylor Swift
Underneath It All by No Doubt, Lady Saw
Midnight Rain by Taylor Swift

all the kids are depressed by Jeremy Zucker
Sad Beautiful Tragic (Taylor's Version) by Taylor Swift
LTW by Kid Ink
Sitting In Fire by MASN
Strike (Holster) by Lil Yachty
Photograph by Ed Sheeran
Snooze by SZA
Creep (Acoustic) by Jada Facer
Stitches (Acoustic) by Jada Facer, John Buckley
Chemical by Post Malone

DEDICATION

To those who may feel lost. . . There's always someone who sees you.

CHAPTER ONE
FALLON

The air vent rattles loudly while I sit in an uncomfortable plastic folding chair outside my new social worker's office, staring blankly at the ceiling, waiting for whatever happens next.

I wasn't listening.

I don't even *care*.

I can guarantee I've lived with worse. Mom never knew how to pick nice guys. Not since Dad died. Her drastic decline was startling enough for twelve-year-old me to feel partly responsible. I guess I wasn't enough to make her happy. Not only did I lose my father—my hero—I lost Mom too. To drugs, alcohol, and her less-than-stellar taste in men. Anything she could find to forget the pain. And I'm starting to understand the need to block it all out and shut down. Because fuck my feelings. I'm not sure if they're even there anymore—

"Fallon."

Torn from my negative thoughts and the overly exciting ceiling, I glance down and make eye contact with my Uncle Joel. I haven't seen him in three years.

Not that he didn't try.

I only have a decent hoodie on right now because of the Christmas money he sent me. Money he *always* sent me. Every birthday. Every major holiday. And every summer before school starts. Without fail. He's not a bad uncle; I just ignore his texts half the time and all his phone calls.

What can I say, I'm a shitty nephew.

Lost and broken. I'm just not interested in this world. Nothing and no one appeals to me.

His brows furrow, creasing the skin in between, when he takes in the nasty bruise blooming around my eye. Social Services placed me in a group home after Mom got arrested, and well, they didn't like the silent kid with half a head of hot pink hair too much.

"It's fine," I say quietly, dodging his touch and avoiding the outstretched hand reaching toward me. We haven't even talked since I texted a *thank you* for my Christmas present. He doesn't need to touch me.

"What happened?"

"Nothing," I mumble, voice rough with disuse. He also doesn't need to know all of my business.

Uncle Joel turns his concerned eyes to Ms. Gail as if she'll be the one to supply him with any information. She takes a deep breath before heaving out a loud sigh, like being my social worker for all of twelve hours has been such an inconvenience to her and caused undue stress and headache.

Can't blame her, I guess. It probably has.

"This young man won't talk to anyone. He won't tell us what happened or who hit him. His careless indifference is concerning." Ms. Gail purses her lips at me, creating even more tiny lines around her mouth that her bright red lipstick seeps into.

Like I just said, it was nothing. They won't listen or care, so what's the point in trying again?

I don't answer.

She huffs this time, crossing her arms somewhat aggressively before speaking about me as if I'm not sitting in the hallway, like a criminal waiting to be booked, instead of a kid with nowhere to go.

"His mother was arrested for drugs and—"

"Yes. I know. Thank you," Uncle Joel says in a clipped tone, cutting her off firmly yet not unkindly.

I'm not even sure what else she got locked up for. It could be any number of things, really. I'm not up for guessing.

Ms. Gail's impatient eyes dart to me, brimming with disappointment and annoyance.

Don't care.

Once she's had her fill, she turns her back to me, addressing my uncle again like I'm not right behind her.

As if I'm something irrelevant. Inconvenient. And possibly even incapacitated.

I'm not.

At least not right now.

Might be later, though. I have some weed tucked in my front pocket, and I'm hoping this *civil servant* doesn't try to shake me down before I get to my uncle's car.

I can hear Ms. Gail droning on and on, but I zone out, focusing now on the interesting pattern of dots on the speckled vinyl floor.

"Fallon."

My uncle's deep, authoritative voice filters into my ears again, alerting me that it's time to pay attention.

"Let's go home. I have everything I need."

His eyes are soft as he peers down at me, yet his jaw is

tense. Contrasting. I could write about it. Poems. Lyrics. Different thoughts. I keep them on paper and floating in my head. A way to silently voice things I wouldn't otherwise speak out loud.

"Let me remind you, Mr. Rivers. Fallon turns eighteen in a week. You have no obligation beyond that."

It's true. She's not lying. But Uncle Joel doesn't seem to like her statement.

"Fallon is my nephew. *Family*. We'll be leaving now. Thank you for getting in touch with me, Ms. Gail. But I won't be needing any future advice or phone calls. Goodbye."

She huffs again before looking over her shoulder, pursing her lips, and pushing her glasses up her nose.

What-the-fuck-ever.

I didn't do *anything* to her. Except exist.

"Carry on then, Mr. Rivers. I have a busy caseload." She spins on her heel and, thankfully, doesn't spare a second glance.

"Do you have more things for us to get?" He eyes my belongings curiously.

Mom lost the house after Dad died.

We lost a lot of things.

"No."

His frown and the creases between his eyebrows deepen, but Uncle Joel isn't old. He was my dad's younger brother and probably isn't even thirty-five yet. His brown hair is short on the sides, longer on top, and styled neatly. He has black-framed glasses, but the man is no nerd. He is *jacked*. I was always intimidated by his size as a kid. He's at least six-foot-four and clearly works out regularly. I don't have the energy for such things, and I'll be lucky if I ever make it to five-nine. Hope he doesn't expect us to bond over sports, either. That won't happen.

"Well, are you ready to head out, then?"

If he insists.

"Okay."

"I got in late last night, crashed at an airport hotel, then came here first thing. I'm so sorry, Fallon. I left California the second Ms. Gail called me. Are you sure you're alright? Do I need to take you to a doctor to get checked out?"

It's just a black eye.

"I'm fine," I mumble, uncomfortable by the care in his tone and the earnest look in his bright blue eyes that remind me of Dad. I glance down quickly and pick at the black nail polish that's been chipping away for the past week. I've just been too tired to do anything about it. Then Mom's arrest happened, the group home, and now this. Not sure I even have nail polish remover anymore.

"If you're positive, Fallon." He sounds unsure.

I give him a single nod in acknowledgment. I'm tired of talking.

He leans down to grab my bag without asking, squatting so we're at eye level. "Why didn't you tell me things were this bad, kiddo? And I don't mean in the last week since your mother's arrest. I mean, in the last three years."

Why is he asking this kind of question *now*?

Here?

"Didn't wanna bother you," I mumble, continuing to pick at this shitty nail polish I found at the dollar store.

Uncle Joel came around the first two years after Dad died, but I haven't seen him since I was fourteen.

A giant, calloused hand stops my fidgeting, and my eyes automatically dart up, startled by the touch.

"You're never a bother. *Ever.* We're family, Fallon. And I

shouldn't have let three years pass without checking on you in person." The sincerity in his tone is jolting.

He stands, slinging the giant, overstuffed army duffle bag over his shoulder. I found it at the thrift store down the street from our trailer park and could fit my entire wardrobe in there. It's pretty heavy.

Uncle Joel's voice softens even more. "I can see I'm overwhelming you, so we don't need to get into anything more. Instead, I thought we could stop and get a bite to eat before we headed to the airport. We have time. IHOP maybe? You still like pancakes, right?"

He's remembering the phase I went through when I was eight. Mom and Dad entertained it, letting me eat pancakes for one meal a day for over a month, as long as I had a fruit on top and a vegetable on the side.

"Yeah," I murmur in response instead of telling him it's been years since I've even had a pancake. Mom stopped cooking, and we never went out.

"Brunch it is," he says, smiling in that teasing, younger brother way he always did with Dad. I have to fight the surge of *feelings* attempting to well up and burst out like a geyser that's been dormant for years.

It won't.

I finally stand and slip my ratty old backpack over my shoulder, following Uncle Joel. I ignore the probing eyes of half a dozen social workers hiding and judging from behind their cubicle walls like cardboard fortresses.

Hunched over the table, I take another huge bite of pancakes, swallowing after a couple of chews. Then I shove a whole piece of bacon into my mouth, flicking my eyes up to catch my uncle staring at me with concern. Or maybe confusion?

Whatever. I'm hungry.

I ignore that he's not eating his own food, just watching me, and take a big gulp of orange juice. Those assholes at the group home kept fucking with my food. And there was never much beyond peanut butter and jelly at home with Mom. Cereal and milk on the good weeks.

Like I just said, I'm fucking hungry.

"Fallon. . ."

He needs to stop saying my name like that. . . like he *pities* me.

I don't need it.

I ignore Uncle Joel and polish off my bacon and sausage before returning to the pancakes.

By the time I'm done, he hasn't even finished half his food.

"Bathroom," I mumble and slip out of the red vinyl booth toward the back. I take a side exit instead, leaving the door cracked so I don't get locked out, and pull the tiny stash box from my front pocket.

I grab my last joint and light it up before chucking my lighter and little metal tin into the dumpster next to me. I'm about to fly from Philadelphia to California. Can't keep this shit. I need to smoke it and toss it.

I lean against the rough brick exterior and rest my head back, closing my eyes. I inhale deeply and hold it, letting the smoke work its way through my system and do its job. Numb me.

Just as I release my last hit and stub the cherry out with my boot, the side door creaks open, and Uncle Joel sticks his head out, immediately spotting me.

"Fallon. You okay?"

"Fresh air," I say, lying. It smells like sewer and garbage and exhaust out here.

"Well, I just paid the check if you're ready. I'm excited to get you settled in. I think you'll like it. I'll tell you more on the flight." Uncle Joel props the door open with his thick forearm and nods toward the restaurant, indicating for me to get back inside.

I duck my head and slip past him, thankful he didn't catch me getting high. Hopefully, the already shitty fumes out here hide the smell of weed on me.

CHAPTER TWO

FALLON

The flight was long, and Uncle Joel talked a lot before I could slip my headphones on without being completely rude. He informed me of the private high school I'll attend, where he's a gym teacher and the head basketball coach.

As his dependent—if only for a week—I get to finish my senior year at this prestigious academy full of kids who probably won't understand me. Or even like me. And classes start on Monday. *Tomorrow*.

Uncle Joel said his partner has a son and daughter who go to my school, and the three stay over a lot. I already knew my uncle was gay. It's just something I've always known. Dad never cared, and I sure as hell don't either.

At least they don't actually live with Uncle Joel. I'm not ready for the whole blended family vibe. And I can't say I'm completely thrilled about the prospect of other people being in my personal space after living in that shitty group home for a few days and living with Mom's shitty boyfriends for a few *years*. But like Ms. Gail said, I'll be eighteen soon. Maybe it's better if I'm just alone.

I climb into the SUV Uncle Joel left at the airport, gently shut the door, and buckle up as he reverses. "I can leave next week. After my birthday. You won't be on the hook for me anymore." It's the most I've spoken to him since he picked me up in Philly over seven hours ago. Judging by how high his eyebrows just jumped up his forehead, he might be a little shocked.

Uncle Joel clears his throat and regains his composure, pushing his thick-framed glasses up his nose. "Fallon. Thank you for expressing that. I'd like you to continue to feel like you can open up to me as we get to know each other and I gain your trust. Because there will be a lot more time, kiddo. You're here to stay. And you *will* be getting a nice birthday dinner to celebrate. With presents. No ifs, ands, or buts about it. You're here to stay, buddy."

"Thanks," I mumble, relieved he doesn't actually want me to go. I can fight him about the birthday party later. I don't want anyone celebrating me. There's nothing to fucking celebrate. I'm alive another year, and yet I just don't care.

We park at the shop across the street, and Uncle Joel turns toward me with a big smile. "Alrighty. Now that that's settled, let's run into the store real quick. I don't know about you, but I am beyond jet-lagged."

I'm sure he is. Two cross-country flights in two days will do that to a person.

He's a great uncle, but it's yet to be determined if I actually deserve him. We'll see, I guess.

We hop out of Uncle Joel's lifted Bronco, and I nearly faceplant, unused to such a drop. Luckily he's on the other side and doesn't see me stumble. Big vehicles and my height don't exactly mix.

The little bell above the door chimes as we enter the airport-adjacent drug store late on a Sunday evening.

Uncle Joel hands me a red plastic basket. "Go pick out what you'll need day-to-day. Shampoo. Deodorant. Body wash. Everything. Okay?"

I take the basket from his grasp but don't respond, so he ducks his head until he's more at my level. "Okay?" he repeats, and I chew on my lip ring, unsure how long the current toiletries I have in my bag will last.

Not long, probably.

I nod. "Yeah. Thanks," I manage.

"Good." He places his hand on my shoulder and gives me a firm squeeze. "I've got a few things to get myself. Meet me in the candy aisle when you're done?" And then he grins widely before turning around to grab his own basket and disappear into the aisles.

After ten minutes, I have everything I need, including nail polish remover and a new bottle of onyx black. But I stand in front of the shelves of colorful hair dye. Half of my head is hot pink and half is black, but my natural hair color is dirty blond. I grab a new box of black dye but hesitate in front of the neon pinks and reds.

"You could switch it up. Start new," Uncle Joel suggests from where he just snuck up next to me.

I drop my hand and scan the selection of colorful options. My eyes land on a blue—deep and bright and perfect. I reach for it.

"Good choice. I like it."

Me too.

"You have school in the morning, and you can ride with me. You'll have to wear regular clothes until we get you fitted for your uniform. Since this is all so last minute and under special circumstances, the headmaster approved it, and we put a rush order on the tailoring."

I was already going to stand out with the bright-ass hair. Doesn't even matter. I grab a box of color remover and drop my last items into the basket before following Uncle Joel to the candy aisle to grab fuel.

He's just so. . . happy and smiley.

Was he always like this?

I can't remember. Emails and voicemails don't quite portray this innate. . . *kindness.*

But it's just candy. Even though I'm a little thrilled to choose what I want when it's been so long since I've had the option. Not that I tell Uncle Joel that. It'll only make him feel worse, and he's not a bad person. I know bad people, and he ain't it.

We make our selections and check out, leaving in a hurry, ready to get *home.* To my new house here in California.

I'm startled out of sleep when my bedroom door opens loudly and abruptly. I shoot up in bed, familiar with this dance, ready to hop out and defend myself. I was so exhausted I must have passed out, despite being in a new environment.

"Shit!" The loud shout turns into a hushed whisper. "Dude. I'm so sorry. Lemme just, I'll just. . ." The giant silhouette illuminated by the hallway light retreats quickly, shutting the door silently like he doesn't want to wake me. Even though I'm sitting straight up, my chest heaving involuntarily.

Fuck.

That must have been the boyfriend's son.

I close my eyes and attempt to clear the confusion and vulnerability away, taking a deep, calming breath. I scrub a hand over my face.

I don't like *anyone* bursting in while I'm asleep.

Commotion out in the hall has me flopping back down and hoping whoever's out there doesn't take this impromptu wake-up call as an open invitation to come and say hello. I glance at the glowing red numbers on the alarm clock and note that it's nine pm. Guess I'll be up all night now. I know better than to mess up my sleep schedule, but this unexpected jet lag has thrown me and my body for a loop.

After Uncle Joel and I stopped for toiletries and something to eat, we drove another hour north from the airport to Acadia Lake.

It was dark when we pulled up, but the landscaping lights illuminated Uncle Joel's well-maintained, two-story home with flower pots on the front steps and a wooden porch swing. A real home. One that he obviously takes pride in. Not the rundown trailer I lived in for five years that smelled like stale cigarettes and booze.

Loud giggles and that same deep voice seep through my door, slightly muffled, so I slip my headphones on to tune it out. I grab my notepad and a black Sharpie before lying down and scribbling out whatever lyrics filter into my brain. I wish I still had my guitar, but Mom's boyfriend sold it last year to pay for their habits.

I hum along to the beat and just write without thinking. It doesn't take much for me to get lost in the lyrics and melodies in my head, and before I know it, three hours have passed. Now, it's midnight.

I crawl out of bed in my black flannel pants and no

shirt. The hardwood is cold against my bare feet as I pad over to the plastic bags from the drugstore. I grab the little caddie Uncle Joel insisted I get and fill it with my shower things, including both boxes of hair dye.

I stick my head out of the bedroom door and peer into the dark, deserted hallway. Uncle Joel told me his partner and kids were coming over for a late dinner but not to feel pressured to come downstairs and meet them if I was tired. There will be plenty of time for that later.

So I didn't.

Now that I know they're gone, and it looks like my uncle is in bed, I sneak down the hallway to the bathroom and slip inside, locking it behind me just in case. I set my supplies down and stare at myself in the mirror.

A black eye and smudged eyeliner outline a lifeless blue-gray stare. My dirty blond roots are starting to show—my half-pink, half-black hair isn't maintained. It's nearly chin-length, too, and in complete disarray. My lips are full, but my cheeks are slightly hollow. A silver hoop hugs my bottom lip perfectly, encouraging me to chew on it every time I remember it's there.

I probably look like a mess, but as always, I can't find it in me to muster up the energy to care.

I'm numb.

The way I want to be. The way I strive to be. I'll pour feelings into my words and lyrics, but I don't want to actually *feel* them.

It makes no sense. And I'm fine with that.

My stomach growls loudly, but I can't help myself to someone else's food without asking. I can wait for breakfast.

I get busy on my hair instead, re-dying the black before stripping the pink and switching to neon blue. While my color sets, I take off my chipped nail polish and re-paint them with the new, long-lasting black.

Guess I'll wear a black hoodie and black jeans tomorrow. I don't have many options. I actually wish I had the uniform now.

An hour later, my hair looks sick, threatening to pull a smile from me for once. There's nothing I can do about the black eye, but I'm happy with this small upgrade.

I amble down the hall, freshly showered and newly painted, ready to crawl back into my bed and write down the melodies swirling around in my head until I fall asleep. I need to be ready to roll out of bed in a few hours for my first day at Acadia Lake Preparatory Academy.

A dark shadow hovers over me at the lunch table, where I'm sitting, minding my own business. Uncle Joel walked me to the front office, where I signed in, gathered my schedule and books, and had an otherwise uneventful first morning at my new school. I looked forward to a quiet lunch, reading over my latest lyrics, before starting Advanced Music Studies. The one class I've actually been a tiny bit excited for.

"Hey. Can I sit here?"

I glance up and eye the behemoth standing in front of me from behind my curtain of blue hair, wondering why he's asking this on my first day here.

This guy has to be at least six-three and over two hundred pounds. He has curly brown hair that's long on top and shaved on the sides, with a few golden highlights woven in. His bright eyes are a strange, olive green color and stand in stark contrast against the tan, sun-kissed skin tone, as does his brilliant, way-too-happy smile.

I subtly close my notepad and lift a shoulder. I don't own this table. I stop staring at the oversized boy in front of me, duck my head, and stab a bite of the salad I added to my plate of pizza in an attempt to be healthy and balanced now that I have the option.

The table jostles as he slips into the attached seat and sets his tray down in front of me. I peek from under my lashes and see that he has some sort of meatloaf, mashed potatoes, green beans, two slices of pizza, and a large pudding on the side.

I can't help it.

My head and my brows immediately shoot up in surprise at the massive amount of food on his plate.

He must not know what it's like to be hungry. Or maybe he does. Often. It's got to be hard to keep a body that size fueled properly.

He chuckles at the obvious expression on my face.

"I'm six-four, play basketball for hours a day, and run two point five miles. I'm fucking hungry, dude. A lot."

If I wasn't numb to everything. If it was before. If it was five years ago. I might have smiled. I might have laughed.

But it's not. And I feel like a pillow is pressing down on my face, suffocating me with regret and painful memories. Even through the numbness, there's an echo of hurt and a shadow of harsh truth. And there always will be.

The spark of happiness I felt a moment ago dies, and I know my face falls, if only by the slight cinch in his strong brow. He's wearing a typical letterman's jacket over the same preppy uniform as the other students. The same preppy-ass uniform I'll be wearing in a few days.

I lean to the side and glance behind him. There's a table

of what appears to be popular kids laughing and smiling in our direction, and I finally understand what this is.

Laugh at the new kid. The poor, orphaned emo kid. The kid with half a head of blue hair.

It's too easy, really. There are a lot of choices to single out. I can hardly blame them.

"Name's Ryder. You?" he asks with another beaming smile.

CHAPTER THREE
RYDER

"Fallon," he replies in a low mumble, darting one last look to the open cafeteria behind me before returning his cool blue-gray eyes to mine. I already know his name. I already know a lot, actually. Coach Rivers isn't just my basketball coach; he's my dad's boyfriend.

I like to think it's all because of me too. They started dating my freshman year of high school when I made the varsity team, and Coach took me under his wing, instantly earning brownie points with the old man. Dad's twelve years older than Joel, but they've never let that, or the fact that he's my coach, affect their relationship.

Fallon lowers his eyes back to his salad and stabs at it. "Your friends are laughing," he states in a quiet, bored tone. Very matter-of-factly. I search his face for any trace of anger, fear, or annoyance. Something. Anything. But he gives me absolutely nothing. He's a blank slate, showing no emotion.

I twist in my seat and catch a glimpse of Cole and Jamison, indeed looking like assholes right now. But they're actually really great guys. All of my friends at the academy are.

"They're just horsing around, making bets on whether I can get you to sit with us."

"Why?" He sounds suspicious.

"Why not? I don't see anyone else around for you to sit with. You don't want to eat alone, do you?"

"Yes."

"*Ouch.* You wound my pride, Blue."

Joel warned me he doesn't talk much. That I'd have to try hard to be his friend, and it may not be easy. It's okay, though. I can put in the work for him. He also warned me that Fallon got into a fight in the group home he stayed at for a few days before Joel was contacted. So the dark bruise surrounding his left eye doesn't shock me too badly. Although, it definitely pisses me off.

Fallon is small. Even seated, I can tell he's probably under five-ten. Anyone who would hit a guy smaller than them just because he looks like an easy target is a bully and a coward. I'm not a fighter—I'm a ballplayer—but the thought of someone hitting him has me clenching my fists tightly.

"It's Fallon," he says softly after an extended pause.

He doesn't like the nickname?

"Yeah, but your hair is just so fucking blue, dude. It's awesome, by the way. So, you sure you don't wanna come sit with us? 'Cause if you don't, I'll just stay here and keep you company; it's no biggie. I don't mind either way."

Joel is like family to me, and Fallon is his nephew. I'm staying if he's not ready to meet my friends. I'm definitely not leaving him alone at lunch on his first day.

He takes a deep breath, his smaller frame heaving with effort as if he's exhausted.

He needs to eat more too. I push my pudding toward him. "The tapioca here is bomb, dude. Try it."

I can't help but grin as he chews on his lip ring in indecision. And my smile only grows when his eyes dart to my mouth and stare for a moment too long before dropping back down to the pudding in front of him.

"Thanks," he mumbles.

Score!

I really wanted that pudding, it's definitely bomb, but Fallon needs it more.

I thought my somewhat corny, yet very friendly, gesture might earn me a small smile or even a twitch of the lips. It doesn't. But that's okay. I got a *thanks* instead. There's plenty of time to earn one from him later, and I have a feeling it'll be special.

He switches from the salad to dessert, and while he's enjoying the best pudding known to mankind, I see if it'll help coax some answers from him.

"So, what classes do you have next?"

Instead of answering, he leaves the spoon in his mouth and reaches under the table, digging in his front pocket. He pulls out a wrinkled half-sheet of paper that's been folded five times, sets it on the table, and slides it toward me.

Jesus. He really doesn't want to talk to me.

It's fine. I'll get through to him. I know I will. Eventually.

I unfold the paper and see that he has Music next, followed by AP Statistics, English Lit, and gym.

"Sweet, dude. We have the last two classes of the day together." I fold it the way it was and slide it back toward him. When he reaches for the paper, I leave my hand and let our fingers brush purposefully. His nails are painted a shiny black, and his skin looks creamy and soft.

Fuck. No. Shit.

I pull my hand back fast, ignoring the weird flip my stomach just did.

"I have basketball practice most days except on Fridays. Maybe we could hang out after gym?"

I'm taking a risk here, asking that so soon. But he looks like he needs a friend, and Joel confirmed he did. I also need to figure out how and when to break the news to him that his uncle and my dad are dating.

I could see him clearly when he jolted upright in bed last night, but I know I was nothing more than a darkened silhouette and a whispered apology. Unrecognizable as myself.

After stuffing the schedule in his pocket, he darts those detached eyes back to mine before looking down at his food. He picks up a piece of pizza and mumbles, "Why?" before taking a big bite.

Okay, this is good. He's eating and talking. He finished half of the tapioca impressively fast too. I can answer his questions.

"Have you seen the town? The lake? The mountains? We could camp or hike or swim. My friends and I do something outside almost every weekend."

"Not really my thing."

"None of it?"

He shakes his head, shaggy blue and black hair swaying in front of his face.

"Not even going into town? We could just get ice cream if you're more low-key."

He peeks at me from under his lashes and chews on that lip ring again, daring me to stare.

"'Nother time," he finally mumbles before eating his

pizza. Everything he says is laced with a bit of melancholy, like he's given up, and it hits me right in the heart.

"Okay. Sure." I won't push him. I can try again later. I accept his answer and sit with him instead. Silently. Eating my own pizza and meatloaf while the cafeteria buzzes around us.

He scoops up a bite of tapioca, and I can't help but watch him slip the sweet treat into his mouth and pull the spoon out clean, dragging it against that fucking piercing and tugging on it. He notices me too. Staring at him. But he thinks I'm eyeing the pudding, not his edible-looking lips.

Fallon pushes the bowl across the table, nodding toward the unused spoon on my lunch tray. Okay, well, I do love pudding. I pick up the spoon and enjoy a big bite of my favorite school dessert.

I close my eyes and moan a little, forgetting where I am for a moment. When I open them, Fallon's blue-gray gaze has widened and twinkles under the fluorescent light. I know he's practically smiling at me.

I'll fucking take it.

We finish our lunch and pudding in silence until the bell rings, and I get a quiet "See ya" before he slips out of his seat and heads to Advanced Music Studies. I remembered. Because I memorized his entire schedule just now. I know two spots I can ambush him on the way to his morning classes. I can't wait until lunch to see him every day; it has to be sooner.

Fallon seemed more awake in English, actively following the lesson as we reviewed the last three chapters in Mary

Shelley's *Frankenstein*. He was the first one to hand in his pop quiz. Guess he's read it already, then.

Unfortunately, class is too fast-paced to talk much, so I didn't get to do much more than stretch my legs out and brace my feet against the back of his chair. Just reminding him I was there.

But now, in gym, we have plenty of time to hang out and talk.

Cole shoves my shoulder. "Enjoy your lunch with emo boy, Ry?" He laughs, but it kinda pisses me off because I know that Fallon has been through some shit. Not what, exactly. But nothing good or he wouldn't be coming to live with his uncle, who's only thirty-one.

"Cole, don't say that, bro." My tone is serious, and my friends aren't assholes, so he instantly drops the grin and agrees, no problem.

"Of course, my bad, Ry. Didn't mean anything by it. I actually think the hair and nails and the whole vibe are pretty sick. I'm surprised the headmaster is allowing it, though. And no uniform on top of it?"

He's being nosey, and although he's not an asshole, he likes to *talk*. Too much sometimes. I give him a look because he *knows*. He holds his hands up and mouths *sorry* before walking away to talk to some of our other teammates just as I spot Fallon emerging from the locker rooms. He must have gone to Joel's office to find a uniform that fits and, I guess, change there.

"Yo, Fal, over here!" I shout across the gym and watch his cheeks turn slightly pink before he ducks his head.

Right. Oops. Not the smartest move.

My other best friend, Jamison, chuckles next to me.

"Shut it," I say playfully, nudging him with my elbow.

"You're into him." It's not even a question. He just

knows. He always knows everything. If I need to talk, it's with Jamie. He's the only one I've come out to. Not even my dad knows, as fucked up as that may seem.

Basketball is too important to me, and I can't risk it. My dad wouldn't want me to hide, no matter what, but as good as his intentions are, I don't need that added stress. Especially after the way my mom treated him when he came out. Jamie silently supports and listens. That's what I needed.

I stare straight ahead at Fallon crossing the gym but answer Jamie.

"I just met him."

He chuckles again. "That doesn't mean anything."

Fallon has his head down, blue and black hair obscuring those steely eyes. His gray T-shirt fits him snuggly, which means it's probably a small, and his short-as-fuck maroon shorts show off pale, slim legs. Tall athletic socks are pulled up to his calves, and the same black Chucks he's worn all day complete the look.

He joins Jamie and me, not saying a word. But at least he came over here. I make eye contact with Joel from across the court and give him a slight nod, letting him know I got Fallon.

He's Coach Rivers when I'm at school. We don't blur the lines. I fall into step when he blows his whistle, and we jog over to start our warm-up.

Class passes quickly, and Fallon is surprisingly nimble and athletic. He doesn't try that hard or put in too much effort, but he does enough to look like he's participating. Can't say that I'm too into volleyball either. Besides, I have basketball practice after this; I need to save energy.

As we walk back to the locker rooms, Fallon veers off to Joel's office before I can even think of a reason to see him again this afternoon. He'll catch the bus and leave for the day after this. If I didn't have basketball, I'd drive him home.

Joel said Fallon doesn't mind taking the bus. He's used to public transportation. But the problem is. . . I didn't get to tell him my dad and his uncle are partners. I'm coming over for dinner. And I'm spending the night too.

CHAPTER FOUR

FALLON

"You," I somewhat growl out. My voice isn't used to this much strain on a daily basis.

What the hell is he doing here, ringing my doorbell and standing on my front porch with that giant, dazzling fucking smile of his and what appears to be an overnight bag.

I hear more car doors slam, and my eyes flick into the darkness behind Ryder. An even larger shadow and another half the size emerge, and things start to click into place as they stroll into the soft yellow glow emanating from the front porch light.

No.

Fuck.

A younger girl, maybe fourteen, and a man in his forties make their way up the steps until they both stand next to Ryder, all three with matching, radiant smiles.

They're too happy.

Just like Uncle Joel.

I don't understand it. Not sure I've ever felt that.

I prop the screen door open with my bare foot and rub

my arms; it's too cold to stand here in just a T-shirt.

Ryder notices and frowns at the movement. "Let's get inside." Then his bright eyes dart to mine in surprise. "Uh. I mean, this is your house now. We can come in, right?"

He's funny. But I don't laugh. Not sure I can anymore. The numbness takes it all away. The bad and the good.

"Of course," I reply before letting him grab the door and hold it open for his dad and little sister.

As soon as we're in the warmth of the foyer, the man turns to me.

"Fallon, it's so good to meet you," he enthusiastically declares before giving me a big bear hug with my arms pinned to my sides.

"Dad. No hugs. Not everyone's a hugger," the girl chastises, causing her dad to chuckle and release me from the awkward embrace.

She's right. I'm not a hugger.

"I'm Sofia," she says, introducing herself with another gleaming smile.

"And I'm Alejandro, but please just call me Al," her dad says.

I glance at Ryder, expecting him to say something, even though we met at school today.

He didn't bother to tell me he's the boyfriend's son.

And that means he was the shadow in the hallway last night too.

Sneaky.

I narrow my eyes on him.

What's he playing at?

He rubs the back of his neck, looking sheepish.

"Talk later?" he whispers, flicking those pale olive-green eyes toward his dad and sister.

I nod. I'll listen, and he can talk. Explain himself.

Uncle Joel takes this opportunity to come bustling out of the kitchen with his own smile lighting up his face.

I don't fit in.

I don't smile.

This isn't good.

This won't *last*.

"Al! Honey, how are you?" he inquires, kissing his partner on the lips before he even replies. I glance away, giving them their privacy.

Sofia leans into me, whispering conspiratorially. "You'd think they wouldn't be such fans of PDA at their age, but you'd think wrong. *Gag*, Dad! Joel!" she shouts, giggling and walking further into the house. She plops down on the leather couch in the living room and switches the TV to Netflix, completely making herself at home.

"Sofie, you know you love me, darling!" Joel shouts back. "Especially when you find out what's in the oven!"

She squeals on the couch, her curls bouncing right along with her. She has the same brown hair as her brother, with golden highlights woven throughout. The same green eyes and tan skin too.

They're both objectively very attractive.

"Sweet! Joel's famous chicken pot pie," Ryder calls out, passing me and plopping down next to his sister.

"Almost as good as Abuela's tostadas."

"It's true," Ryder supplies, grinning widely.

He's extremely handsome. And tall. A lot taller than me. Half a foot. Or more.

These aren't thoughts I usually have.

I don't *care* what people look like.

I'm not interested.

Ever.

"Fal! Come over here! Wanna start a new show

with us?"

He's so friendly and nice. I'm not used to any of this. And now that I know he's *the son*, I feel like maybe I could trust him. But I can't make a decision like that on day one.

So, for now, I reluctantly trail over to the couch and sit at the far end, away from the siblings, tucking my legs under me and curling into the corner.

I'm wearing comfortable dark gray joggers and a hoodie. Ryder is wearing something similar, except his hoodie is white and his sweats a light gray. A really light gray. An obscenely light gray. If such a thing is even possible.

I dart my eyes away, confused as to why they're lingering *there* in the first place.

Uncle Joel and Alejandro slip into the kitchen, smiling and laughing at each other, sipping glasses of white wine.

This just can't last. I don't fit.

I'll tear it all apart. Ruin their family. Their happiness.

I zone out, not listening to the sibling's chatter, even when Ryder tries to nudge my leg with his hand.

I've never had any streaming service, so I don't know what's on. I have nothing to contribute to the conversation.

After several minutes, the talking and scrolling stops. Some action movie plays, and I close my eyes, giving in to the warm, blissful atmosphere of the house and letting sleep steal me away.

Sometimes I sleep too much, and sometimes I don't sleep at all. It's not a good balance. I know this.

Subconsciously, I feel myself burrow my bare feet under the large, warm thigh next to me, but my brain doesn't fully know what it's doing. I recognize the feeling of a soft blanket being pulled off the back of the couch and draped over me. I snuggle deeper into the warmth and smell of fresh laundry, curling in on myself but keeping my toes under the body next to me.

Clueless about how much time has passed, I'm completely startled and jolted awake when Uncle Joel shouts, "Dinner's ready!" from the kitchen.

I sit bolt upright, eyes wide and locked on Ryder's concerned ones. My chest is heaving, pulse pounding.

It's unreasonable.

Definitely not an appropriate response to being informed that dinner is ready. But everything is changing and everything is new.

I squeeze my eyes shut, trying to calm my strained breathing. A big hand settles on my thigh, squeezing gently to get my attention.

"Look at me, Fallon."

Not sure I can right now. Emotions are creeping up, along with the panic.

"I know you're freaking out, but I got you. Open your eyes." I automatically listen to him. Something fierce yet soothing is in his tone, and it cuts through the panic. He slowly reaches out, giving me plenty of time to object.

I don't.

Ryder cups the side of my face. "Listen to me, Fal. It's just you and me right now, okay? Take a deep breath, yeah?" He talks to me like we've known each other for years.

I listen. I have no choice. He's the only one here. The only one helping.

"Good. Now, another." He's so patient and considerate and caring.

Who the fuck is like this?

It's been a long, long time since I've felt such a tender touch, and as my breathing finally settles, my eyes flutter shut. Embarrassingly enough, I nuzzle my nose into the palm of his hand.

"Fallon. . ." he whispers, and *fuck*, what am I doing? *What the hell am I doing?*

"Boys! Food's ready!" Alejandro shouts from the kitchen, and I jerk back, letting the blanket slip off me as I jump up and rush out of the room to compose myself before dinner.

I duck into the small hallway bathroom, lock it, turn the loud-ass fan on, and lean against the door. I'm freaking out all over again, and not from being startled out of sleep this time.

No, this time it's because of whatever the *fuck* that was.

I've never been interested in anyone. *Ever*. Guy or girl.

But. . . Ryder's touch. His *care*. . . *Fuck!*

My belly does this weird somersault all over again just thinking about it.

I don't like it.

Getting a grip, I do my business and head for the dining room. I'm not exactly looking forward to the four happy faces that await me, yet I'm not dreading it either.

They're good people. I know this.

I slip into the empty seat between Uncle Joel and Ryder. It's clear it's meant for me. Sofia and Alejandro are on the other side, no one sitting at the heads of the table like an asshole.

I like that.

"I didn't dish up your plate, Fallon. I wasn't sure how much you wanted," Uncle Joel says from next to me.

He knows I don't like to talk much, so he points at the largest piece, and I nod, looking down at my nails while Uncle Joel serves me a massive amount of steaming chicken pot pie and salad on the side.

Once everyone has a plate full of food, we dig in. I add a gallon of ranch to my salad and devour it while the pot pie cools. I hate the feeling of a burnt tongue. It's weird and uncomfortable. I shudder thinking about it.

My Coke is ice-cold, and the carbonation tickles my nose as I chug half of it. Next, I scoop up a huge bite of pot pie, nearly moaning as the flavors burst across my tongue. This is homemade all the way. None of that frozen crap. Actually, I like the frozen kind too. Not gonna lie.

I don't stop until my plate is clean, only slowing down for a few drinks in between. When I'm done, I subtly and silently burp into my shoulder before settling back in my seat to relax my stomach.

I will never take food for granted.

Ever.

I glance up to find four sets of eyes staring at me in various degrees of concern, amusement, and maybe a little awe.

"What?" I say roughly, folding my arms across my chest defensively.

I'm tired of all these emotions leaking out of me today. I don't care what people think. This isn't me.

Alejandro is the first to speak up. "Nothing, mijo. Just glad you enjoyed the food and made it through the inhalation process safely and securely without any obstructions. I would hate to have to give you the Heimlich on our first meeting."

There's a beat of silence before Sofia bursts out laughing. "Dad! Stop it!"

"Yes, Al, don't tease Fallon. He doesn't know our humor yet." Uncle Joel turns to me, blue eyes careful and sincere. "He's just teasing, Fallon."

"Yeah, dude. Don't worry about it. I know this shit is

bomb. Just like the tapioca at lunch." Ryder winks at me, and my stomach does that stupid thing again. That flippy thing. "Don't pay attention to my old man's corny jokes. You'll get used to them soon enough, no matter how shocking they can be when you first meet him."

"Yeah, Dad. Tone it down, please!" Sofia says, giggling from across the table. Alejandro just beams from ear to ear, peering around the table at his family. And maybe that even includes me.

These people are so nice, and I'll say it again.

Who the fuck is like this?

I remember Dad being kind and thoughtful, and I guess Mom was nice *before*. But it was never quite like *this*. So fucking positive and expressive.

I feel uncomfortable.

I really hope there's dessert to distract me.

As if reading my mind, Ryder jumps up, ignoring his half-eaten food. "Come on, I'll show you where Joel hides all the good ice cream."

"Hey! So, you're the one who's been eating all my double chocolate chunk!"

Sofia places her small hand in front of her mouth, pink glitter nails sparkling in the warm overhead lighting, and giggles more.

Joel gasps in mock outrage, clutching his chest. "You?! My little Sofie? Eating my special ice cream in secret?"

"Sorry, Joel, but I'm not the only one. Who do you think showed it to me?"

"Sofia, cariño. That was our secret," Alejandro whines to his daughter.

"Let's go," Ryder whispers to me while his family continues to tease and enjoy themselves over dinner.

Probably like normal families do. I'm not sure. This is unfamiliar, uncharted territory.

I slip out of the chair and follow Ryder into the modest, modern kitchen with sage green walls and dark wood cabinets. He walks over to a deep freezer tucked into the far corner, partially obscured by the massive wine rack on the wall and the wet bar beneath it.

"Sorry, my family can come on a little strong sometimes. They're just really outgoing and don't think about the fact that others may not be too. But everyone really likes you, and we just want to make you feel welcome. In our own weird ways, I guess?"

He's perceptive.

God, why does he have to be so understanding?

This isn't good for the fucking roller coaster ride my stomach has been on today. I don't like amusement parks, and I definitely don't like that my stomach flips upside down and inside out because of this smiling boy with the curly, sun-kissed hair and flawlessly tan skin.

He opens the top, and I lean forward, peering into a freezer full of ice cream, popsicles, and frozen cookie sandwiches.

"I got drunk and ate way too many Oreo ice cream cookies once. Recently actually. There was no denying that I found Joel's secret hoard. I told him it was a few of my friends too, so he wouldn't know I actually had the munchies and fucking devoured the whole box on my own." Ryder grins wide, showing me all his teeth, and I just stare, silently transfixed.

He reaches in and grabs two, tossing me one. "These. They're addicting," he jokes, but my mind is fixated on one word.

Munchies.

CHAPTER FIVE

RYDER

"**Y**ou smoke?" Fallon mumbles from under his curtain of electric blue hair, the dark half facing away from me, like the dark side of the fucking moon. Mysterious and unknown. But damn, do I want to get to know him better.

He tugs at the wrapper before opening it, sliding the cookie up and taking a huge bite.

"Sometimes. At parties or if friends have it. You?" I ask him in return. He probably wants to know for a reason, and I'm guessing the answer is yes.

"Yeah," he mumbles around his mouthful but doesn't elaborate any further.

He continues to eat his dessert with a detached, almost vacant look in his blue-gray eyes.

I'm not going to acknowledge any of what happened before dinner. Nope. Nothing.

I can hold back. That's not the problem at all. I can wait for him. I can be patient with his friendship. Patient for his trust. I won't say anything to him about the fact that he burrowed his freezing cold toes under my leg while napping on the couch, freaked out at Joel's shout, nuzzled my palm, ran to the bathroom in panic, and devoured his dinner like a starving man lost in the woods for a week with nothing but protein bars and rationed rainwater.

I won't say a word. He doesn't need me to point any of that out.

"There's a party on Friday at one of my teammate's houses. He usually gets some bud for the weekend. We. . . could hang out after gym class like I said earlier? Here? It would be even more low-key than ice cream on the boulevard. See?" I motion toward the Oreo cookie in his hand. "We're already having ice cream together anyway. Let's up the ante to pizza on Friday. What do you say?"

"Just us?" he mumbles.

Fuck, why does that question do something for me?

"Yeah, dude. Just us."

"Okay," he says quietly, glancing up at me and shoving the rest of the ice cream into his mouth. His cheeks puff out slightly, but he has no problem chewing it. Those intense-as-fuck eyes stare back at me, the black liner and his pale skin making them pop even more, before darting down to the Snickers ice cream bar in my hand, then off to the side, staring at nothing.

He's so small.

"Want another?" I ask, holding out my choice. I can get another. It doesn't really matter. We all know where the ice cream stash is. We just like to tease Joel and act like it's his big secret.

Fallon needs it more than me. He can have five of each if he wants, and I know Joel feels the same way. I shared a look with him and my dad while Fallon was inhaling his dinner. It was concerning, and everyone at the table felt it.

Joel told me Fallon's been through some tough times. I

mean, of course he has. Why else would he have to move in with his uncle? I know his dad, Joel's brother, passed away five or so years ago, and he feels like that may have been the catalyst. Although, he still can't fully understand the Fallon that he sees before him today. And Joel feels guilty about that. He hates seeing his nephew like this. And he especially hates that he didn't know about it for so long.

Fuck. I hate it, too, and I only just met him today.

It's fine, though. He's here now, and so am I. I'll make him smile. No doubt. It's my new mission in life.

Fallon silently takes the second ice cream and mumbles a "thanks" before heading back to the table, leaving me standing here. I stare after him, wondering what the fuck happened to him and if he'll ever tell me.

Standing in front of the mirror, brushing my teeth in the dark, I'm not startled when Fallon walks in unannounced and flips the light on. I left the door cracked open with only the nightlight on, like no one was in here, in hopes that he might do just this—unintentionally join me.

"Oh. Sorry," he says roughly, quietly.

Fallon turns the light off and backs out of the bathroom, gripping the doorknob tightly as he pulls it shut.

I yank the toothbrush out of my mouth and spit. "Wait. We can share. Here." I flip the light on and scoot over, allowing him space in front of the sink. "Room for two." I wave my toothbrush around like some sort of magician.

He walks in and sets his little bathroom caddy on the counter. Cute. Definitely don't say that out loud, though.

I stare at him in the mirror as we brush, unable to stop myself. I'm still wearing the gray sweats from earlier but took off the white hoodie and my tee. I like to sleep without a shirt, sometimes even without pants. But that wouldn't be appropriate considering I have to sleep on the couch when we stay over now that Fallon is here and living in the second guest room.

We alternate who spits like we're already in sync with each other. I get an itch on my chest and scratch it, accidentally brushing over my nipple.

I make an involuntary noise. Not exactly a groan. Definitely not a moan. But maybe a little. . .

I skim my nipple *again*, humming and causing Fallon's eyes to dart up and lock on mine in the mirror.

We both freeze. Cease the cleaning of teeth. Pause.

His intense stare, the blue hair, the touch of make-up, the lip ring. *Everything* hits me. It hits me harder than it's been hitting all day. And all at once too.

My dick twitches in my sweats. Involuntarily, of course.

Fuck.

Traitorous bastardo.

The fleeting hope that Fallon doesn't notice dies quickly when those deeply serious eyes jump down to my crotch and widen a fraction.

He noticed. There's no way he didn't notice. I'm not small. *Anywhere.*

I have no clue if he's gay or what. I don't assume anything just because of the eyeliner and black nail polish. But I definitely know he's not emotionally available. That's a given.

I decide to play it off. Here goes nothing.

"Sorry. Just an automatic response to stimuli. I've always been into nipple play."

There's a pause, like at dinner. But it's a lot longer this time, and no one else laughs or breaks the awkward silence.

Fuck.

I ruined it.

Scared him off.

Frightened him!

There's a snort next to me. A sardonic, you're-an-idiot-but-a-lovable-one kind of snort. I think.

I turn away from the mirror and peer down at him, in awe that he just sort of, maybe somewhat, laughed. Whatever. I'm definitely counting it.

Fallon is at least half a foot shorter than me as I gaze at his vibrant, electric blue hair. It's so freshly dyed that I can't tell his natural color.

He spits, rinses his toothbrush, and grabs his caddy, turning away from the mirror. He darts his eyes to mine and stares for a beat before quickly flicking my other nipple roughly.

"Unhh!" I sound like a bad porn star with that terrible, high-pitched moan. It's obscene, over the top, and not quite appropriate for the situation. But I wasn't lying, exaggerating, or even joking when I said I enjoy nipple play.

I thought it would be funny, so I made a joke out of it instead. And it worked because I think I see a twitch of a smile on his pouty lips before he strolls out of the bathroom, completely unbothered by our exchange while I'm about to bust a fucking nut.

My cock fills up after Fallon leaves, hardening all the way from the tiniest flick of his finger against my nipple.

It's sick. It's twisted. I know it is. But I lock the door, turn the sink on full-blast, and aggressively rub one out to really, really inappropriate thoughts of Joel's nephew and my new, intriguing friend.

God. Who jerks off to a sad, lost boy?

It's the norm to ride to school together when we stay over. So, I'm in the backseat of the Bronco with Fallon while Sofie sits in the front, talking Joel's ear off. He loves it, though. Girl talk, he calls it.

I hadn't seen or spoken to Fallon since last night until he climbed into the car late and mumbled "morning" to everyone, promptly leaning his head back and closing his eyes. He wasn't at breakfast, which, judging by the way he ate lunch and dinner with such fervor yesterday, is a little odd.

Fallon's stomach growls loudly next to me as if on cue, but he doesn't react. Fuck, I'd be whining and complaining and hangry by now. Joel and Sofie can't hear us back here, too busy lamenting the temporary disbandment of her favorite K-pop group, so I try to get his attention.

"Hey."

He doesn't respond.

"Fallon."

Nothing.

I lean over and gently place my hand on his shoulder, rubbing down his arm, then back up again. I don't want to shake him; that's an asshole thing to do to a person when they're asleep. I already know how he reacted to a shout. I won't scare him.

I continue to rub his arm softly. He's wearing another black hoodie with black jeans again. Still the only one in the entire school not wearing a uniform.

"Fal," I whisper directly into his ear.

Jesus, he's knocked out. We just woke up too. He's going to have a rough day.

"Fallon," I say a little louder this time, adding pressure to my touch. It works, and he doesn't freak out.

His lashes flutter, and his eyes slowly open. He turns his head, still resting it against the back of the seat, and peers up at me with sleepy, half-lidded eyes outlined in black. "Hmm?"

"Hmm?" I repeat. Because I forgot. I. . . Um. . .

My eyes dart down to his mouth, and I'm transfixed. His lips have a sparkle to them.

Fuck. I think I like it.

I clear my throat awkwardly, focusing back on his sexy, sleepy stare.

"Are you wearing Chapstick. . . with a *shimmer?*"

Oh. Goddammit. *No.* That is not what I wanted to ask him. *Shit.*

He sits up then, blinking rapidly as if clearing the cobwebs from his mind. "Yeah. And?"

He sounds defensive, and rightfully so. That sounded rude and judgmental even though it was anything but. "Oh. It was just an observation. No biggie." I try to play it off. *Fuck.* I hope I can play it off. He doesn't need to know I'm really fucking into it.

I need to see those sparkles on my dick.

I swallow thickly, forcing the lust-fueled thoughts down into the pit of my stomach.

Fuck.

He narrows his eyes ever-so-slightly, then rests his head back and closes them again.

Well, that was a fail. But I'm nothing if not persistent.

"Psst. Fallon."

He cracks one eye open, and I can't stop the smile tugging at the side of my mouth.

"Your stomach growled like an angry fucking chinchilla."

He closes his eyes, but I get a full response.

Score!

"What the hell is that?" he mumbles in a sleep-groggy voice.

And I'm all too eager to answer him. "Oh, they're these cute little fluffy things, but they're complete assholes when they get angry. Make this loud-ass noise. Sofie used to have one. Mr. Two Chins."

"Hmm," is all he responds.

"Here," I say, nudging him with my granola bar and orange juice. I like to have a second breakfast, not unlike a hobbit, but I'm willing to share with Fallon. He needs the energy.

He sits up fully now, once again mumbling "thanks" and taking the offering, devouring it in less than five minutes.

By the time he's done, we're parked in the staff lot, and Joel and Sofie are already out and on their way to Aspen Hall after a quick goodbye. I have a key to Joel's Bronco so we don't need to rush. Sofie just likes to gossip with her friends, and Joel has to get ready for his first gym class of the day. I also let him know this morning that I have Fallon's back. He doesn't need to worry about him at school.

"Ready?" I ask, and Fallon nods, so I hop out and jog around to his side as he attempts to get out of the lifted vehicle. He stumbles, but luckily I'm right there to catch him. I wrap my arms around his smaller body and pull him to my chest so he doesn't hit the pavement.

Oof.

"I got you," I whisper, letting him slowly slide down the front of my body and press against my dick.

Shit.

I swallow roughly and release him, brushing his hoodie off like he's five years old and got grass all over himself. I clear my throat, trying to let the awkwardness kill my semi.

"Sorry. Big drop," he mumbles, and I burst out laughing like it's the funniest thing ever.

"Yeah, dude. Take it easy next time. Or I could get you a step stool," I tease, seeing if I can pull a smile from him that way.

He narrows those steely eyes on me, but I see the quirk in his lip, and I will fucking take it!

I hold my hands up in mock surrender. "Kidding."

My smile is wide and earnest. I couldn't wipe it off my face if I tried.

CHAPTER SIX

RYDER

I constantly wonder what Fallon's doing—if his ride home on the bus went okay—and wish he was watching me on the bleachers instead.

When Joel and I get back to the house, I drop my things by the door since I know I won't be staying the night.

"I'll order some pizzas for dinner. Tell your sister and Fallon, please," Joel says as he trails down the hall toward the kitchen in search of my dad.

"Get pineapple and green peppers, please and thanks!" I shout as I head in the opposite direction, snickering at his mumbled disgust over my fruit and veggie pizza. He'll still order it. Joel is awesome and loves Sofia and me like his own.

I climb the modest stairs with the soft beige carpet runner so different from the ridiculous grand staircase at home. I honestly prefer to be here, and I know Dad does too. After he came out and Mom left so negatively, the house became an empty shell, and no one wanted to be there. We all like it here with Joel and now Fallon, too.

Mom left five years ago, and Dad and Joel bonded over

mutual trauma in a local support group, reuniting when I made varsity. Joel was dealing with the death of his older brother, and Dad was still processing the ugly divorce with his wife and her bitter attitude toward him coming out and finally living his truth. As if I'd ever feel comfortable talking to her about *my* truth after how she treated Dad.

I don't even care about me, though. I can handle her not being in my life. I have, just fine. But no sixteen-year-old boy should have to take his crying twelve-year-old sister to the drugstore for stuff for her first period. I did, though, and still do every month. I know the brands she likes without her having to ask. They just appear in her room every month.

Along with chocolate. Lots of chocolate. We don't have to talk about it, and she doesn't stress about it. Dad knows I have it handled, so he doesn't worry either. It's just what big brothers do.

I hover in the doorway of my old bedroom, Fallon's room, watching him with Sofia unnoticed.

"Fallon! You're supposed to let the girl win! Don't you know that?" Sofie whines like she always does when we play video games.

It might work on him because he's new to this, and Sofie hates to lose. But he doesn't listen and continues to annihilate her character in *Mortal Kombat*, ending with a nasty fatality. Sofia screams.

"Fallon! *Ohmygod!* You just tore my spine outta my body by my head! *What is that?*" she cries dramatically as if she hasn't already seen it happen a hundred other times.

"Sofie. Chill," I say, laughing as I stroll into his bedroom and plop down on the bed, squishing Fallon between us.

"Ew! Ry! You stink, and you're all sweaty! Get off of Fallon's bed and go shower! So rude!" she huffs, backing out of the game and scrolling through the other choices. I told Joel to keep my PS5 in here for Fallon. I have one at Dad's house anyway. I figured any dude would like it, and I wasn't wrong. He's pretty good.

Ignoring my somewhat annoying little sister, I talk directly to Fallon. "Your uncle said we're having pizza tonight, so we could order Chinese on Friday before the party. You like sweet and sour chicken? Beef and broccoli? We can get whatever. Think about it. And don't worry about the party," I reassure him. "My friends are cool, and I'll stay by your side."

"Okay, you big, lovable dork-of-a-big-brother. Go cleanse your mind, body, and soul, would ya?"

Fallon snorts, and I roll my eyes at her.

"I like Chinese," is all he says, but it's progress. And by Friday, I'm sure we'll be having full, deep-as-fuck conversations.

"Cool," I agree casually, although I'm so fucking excited to hang out with him all night Friday. Cole's parties are always a good time. "I get next round when I'm out of the shower. Me versus Fallon," I say, pushing up from the bed, realizing I might actually smell like a locker room.

Our arms brush, and my bare skin tingles. I stare at him for a beat too long in front of my little sister. "I'll be right back," I mumble in a low voice, and he sucks his bottom lip into his mouth, chewing on that silver hoop that's been tempting me nonstop.

"I'm gonna call Katie," Sofia declares, standing up and dropping her controller on the bed. She turns to Fallon first. "Good game, sir. I'm no poor sport." And then she bows before spinning on her heel and strutting from the room.

"Don't eat all the pizza, big bro," she says on her way past me.

Fallon doesn't say anything, just continues to sit there.

"Still wanna play when I get out?" I ask, just to make sure he's not tired or something.

He nods, but I'm going to start needing more of a response pretty soon.

"Yeah?" I question, just to get him to answer.

"Yeah."

"Cool. See ya in ten." I sniff both pits. "Make that fifteen," I say teasingly with a giant grin.

Fallon snorts again and even shakes his head this time.

Hell yeah! I'm growing on him. I know it.

I leave Fallon's room and head straight to the bathroom, eager to get back and play video games with him.

I left my bag downstairs, but I'm pretty sure I still have some sweatpants in the dresser in Fallon's room. I meant to clear out the bottom drawer but forgot to do it. And now it's paying off.

I knock lightly before I push the door open, walking into his room with just a white bath towel wrapped low around my hips.

His eyes do a double take and scour my body, and I have to bite back my grin. I'm dying to know if he's gay, but I wouldn't ask. Not yet, at least.

"Think I still have some sweats I meant to clear outta here." I cross in front of the TV to the dresser next to it while Fallon plays some RPG. I squat down and pull the mostly empty drawer open, grabbing an armful of things and standing back up, realizing too late that I don't have a hold on my towel with my hands not free.

It falls to the ground, and I show my ass to Fallon. I'm

talking full-moon, butt-ass, no underwear, dick hanging between my legs, *bare ass.*

I hear a sharp intake of breath and quickly drop my clothes to grab the towel and wrap it securely around my waist before confronting the shocked boy behind me.

"Whoops," is all I say, looking sheepish. At least he didn't see my dick.

His normally tired, half-lidded eyes are wide open, and his mouth is slightly agape.

"Sorry, dude." I try again. "At least it wasn't a full frontal, *amiright*?"

That does it, and he snorts again, rolling his eyes and giving me the closest thing to a real smile I've seen yet.

Fucking score!

"Let me slip these on, and then you can catch this fade in 2K. How does that sound?" I'm teasing him again; he's probably good at basketball games too.

Fallon smirks a little more, and I bet I'm right.

Two games later, and we're tied. It's pretty cool to have a friend that can keep up. My actual teammates are shit at video games.

I turn the PS5 off and can't help but notice the jittery energy of his hand. It's unusual for his normally stoic self.

I try not to stare, but he catches on and tucks his hand under his thigh. We're still relaxing on top of the covers, his simple navy blue plaid bedspread neatly made. "You okay?" I whisper.

His steely eyes dart to mine, peeking between his vibrant blue hair.

"What? Of course I am." His voice is quiet yet rough, and he sounds defensive, so I back off.

"Cool."

He scrambles off the bed, and I let him, my eyes tracking his movements.

What is he doing so urgently?

He digs through his backpack like he's desperate to find something. He pulls out a small green notepad and a thick black pen. A Sharpie.

Fallon climbs back on the bed next to me, but this time, he's angled away so I can't see the notepad. His foot taps out some rhythm, his sock making a soft thumping noise against the comforter. He chews on that silver lip ring while he frantically scribbles as if he desperately needs to get whatever is in his head onto physical paper.

I turn my attention to the TV and start a solo game of NBA 2K23 for extra practice, leaving Fallon to do his own thing as we wait for this slow-ass pizza. We can chill and enjoy each other's company in silence. I'm cool with it.

The rest of the week flies by, and we stay at Dad's house, so I don't see Fallon except for lunch, English Lit, and gym. I need more than that. Private time with him is a must, a priority, and I'll get exactly that tonight.

I slam my locker door shut, ready to get out of here and start the night. Fallon still doesn't have his uniform after a full week of school, and I have no idea why. He wears black every day, his neon hair the only splash of color. Well, that and the pink shimmer on his lips. Lips that I want to kiss and suck on and see wrapped around my cock.

Fuck. . . I'm distracted again. Staring at him again.

After a few days of hiding out in Joel's office, he started changing with the rest of the class. I've tried to keep my eyes off him, not wanting to be a creeper and alert the other guys to my interest in him or dudes in general. Well, except for Jamie. He already knows.

Peeling my eyes away from Fallon seems to be a feat far too great for me to overcome.

Fallon's creamy, pale skin is flawless and smooth. His muscles are lean, and there's not an ounce of fat on him. He's a little thin and on the shorter side, but everything about him does it for me. His size included.

I want to pick him up, throw him over my shoulder, and toss him onto the bed. Experience new things together.

I've never hooked up with anyone. Guys or girls. I'm fucking horny.

"You're doing it again, dude," Jamie's even tone warns from under his breath. "Be careful."

Right. The staring. It needs to stop. I shake the lusty thoughts from my brain and finish putting on my school uniform so we can leave for the weekend.

"Trying," I mumble under my breath.

I can't let my attraction to him mess up basketball. I just can't. But would it? I just don't know if colleges or even the NBA would accept it.

I grab my backpack, and Fallon, dressed in all black again, grabs his. I throw my letterman jacket on because it's winter, and even though this is California, we aren't far enough south, so it still gets cold.

Fallon hasn't been wearing anything but a hoodie over his T-shirts, so I think a trip to the mall is in order.

Joel told me it's Fallon's eighteenth birthday tomorrow, and he wanted to throw him a party, but Fallon apparently spoke to him the other night. And when I say spoke, I mean three words. "No party, please."

Joel agreed, although I could see the disappointment on his face when he told me about it. He and my dad love planning parties. Joel may be a jock, but he's pretty gay too, and I like to tease him about his certain interests. He loves it, though, and it's all in good fun.

"Ready for home?" I ask, slipping my arms through the straps. "Joel's staying late to do paperwork so we can take the Bronco. My dad will pick him up later. We just need to grab Sofie."

"Yeah," he mumbles, his head down and thumbs looped into his backpack straps. I don't let his lack of enthusiasm bother me. It only makes me want to try harder.

"Alright. Let's venture deep into the depths of the catacombs where the evil spirits and succubi known as freshman girls reside." I smile widely and stare down at him. Waiting.

I'm corny. I know it. He knows it. But he peers up at me, and I see the twitch of his lip before he shakes his head and leaves me behind in the locker room, grinning after him like a complete idiot. Jamie chuckles behind me, probably laughing at my lack of finesse and game.

Whatever.

The little smile that tried to break free was all that matters to me. It's a step toward Fallon's happiness, and after only one week, I'm already rooting for him.

When we get to Fallon's place, we split up to tackle our homework and knock it out before the weekend. We've always done it like this. Dad encourages us to get business out of the way so we can truly focus on the fun.

Dad has a string of restaurants in LA and San Diego called Jandro's that do really well. He's recently been able to leave them in the hands of his management, allowing for more family time and a lot more *Joel* time. They're constantly leaving on mini weekend trips, and they trust me with Sofie while they're gone. It's no different tonight. They can trust me with Fallon too.

They're taking Dad's small private plane, a Cessna TTx, down to LA to check on one of his newer spots in West Hollywood. Dad got his pilot's license three years ago, proving he could do another thing he always wanted.

Joel said they'll be back before we even woke up in the morning and that he has quite a few surprises to try to make Fallon smile on his birthday. And talk.

Fuck. I wish he'd talk to me. After a week, I thought I'd be further along than this. But I won't give up on him. Like I said, I've made it my duty to get him to smile.

I may be a jokester and a jock, but I take my responsibilities very seriously.

CHAPTER SEVEN

FALLON

I fell asleep on my bed with my lyric notebook open next to me, like always. I never fucking learn. I don't realize until it's too late. Until I wake up to Ryder sitting on the edge of the bed, his eyes wide and his mouth slightly open, caught red-handed. As if he stopped himself from saying something really shitty. Something they all say. Anyone who's ever ripped my notebook from my hands and read my words aloud scornfully and disrespectfully. And by anyone, I mean half of Mom's boyfriends.

What is this bullshit?

You think you'll ever be anything more than trailer park trash like your mama?

You're not good enough.

These words are pathetic.

Man up.

Weak.

Pussy.

I swallow the bile threatening to work its way up my throat and grab the notepad from the sheets, closing it roughly and shutting the harsh slashes of black Sharpie off from the world.

No one needs to see that. I don't want anyone to. It's just for me. But I'm an idiot if I think this overgrown puppy won't accidentally overstep his boundaries. They always do —fucking puppies. You can't even be mad at them. They're too cute and too loyal. Ryder is no different.

But my depression doesn't care. I lash out.

"Why are you in my room?" I growl in an agitated whisper. He's in my fucking bubble, really.

My hands start to shake, and I grab my notepad, walk over to the desk, and drop it on top. He doesn't need to see which drawer I put it in. Or which bag. Or if I hide it under my pillow like a pre-teen girl. That's my business, not his. I'm getting a little angry at the puppy because he's not answering.

I spin around and brace my hands on the edge of the desk, clamping down hard.

"Why are you in my room, Ryder?" I say louder, clearer. More with the voice I had before I stopped talking.

He perks up at the sound of my full voice, and his lip starts to twitch on one side.

The puppy's tail is wagging.

"I wanted to see if you were ready to order Chinese food. Sorry, but we have to feed Sofie too. She's going to eat with us."

I like that he doesn't ask me. He shouldn't. That's his sister.

"Of course," I reply. "Of course, she'll eat with us."

His smile is wide and blinding. All teeth.

I can't remember the last time I smiled that carefree. Or if I ever have.

I hope he doesn't ask me what he may have seen in my

notebook. I shut it too quickly to see which page was open, but none of it is good. Absolutely none of it. Some of it was written on my worst days, the loneliness, regret, and painful memories swallowing me whole. This tiny book has a lot of pages, and I only write down what *has* to come out. It's not good.

I glance down at the miserable little notebook in question, then back up at Ryder.

His smile drops a little, and he looks at me with sympathy. With pity. And it makes me lash out again. It makes the dark side show. The demon in me that writes those depressing lyrics no one will ever hear me sing.

Fuck! It's too much.

I run my hands through my hair, roughly tugging on the tangled strands.

I need to be numb again. Ryder makes me feel. I don't know if I like it.

"I need something."

"What?" he asks, although he definitely heard me. My voice is deep and raspy for my size, and it comes back to me when I'm around him.

"I saw the bar downstairs. All the alcohol. My uncle won't miss it." I sound confident, but I squeeze the desk behind me harder so he doesn't see the tremor in my hands. The anxiety, the depression. Sometimes I can't block it out. Sometimes I need something to help me.

"So, you're talking now?"

"No."

"Sounds like you are."

I narrow my eyes at him and grip the wood even harder until I feel like my nails will rip off.

Why is he pushing me?

Does he even realize it?

"Order whatever. I'll eat anything."

I push away from the desk and stroll toward my door, feeling angry and unlike myself.

"Fallon, wait."

I freeze but don't spin around.

"There will be plenty of weed and alcohol at Cole's party. Don't drink here, around Sofie."

His tone is firm, and I can respect that, but it doesn't mean I can't swipe a bottle for my room later.

"Got it."

He can tell I'm in a mood and doesn't try to joke like he normally does. I respect that too.

I leave him in my room and head for the bar in the kitchen anyway. He can't tell me not to. I won't drink in front of Sofie. I can agree with that.

I grab a Gatorade from the fridge and dump it, rinsing the bottle out and discreetly filling it with a little of each of Joel's whiskeys. It's a trick I learned from my friend Dex back in Philly. His old man would beat the shit out of him if he caught him stealing his booze, so he never gave him a chance and just took a little from each bottle. I know Joel wouldn't do that, but I don't need him looking at me differently. I need something to numb the pain and the memories. Something to help me sleep later.

I tuck the bottle into my oversized hoodie pocket just as Sofie walks into the kitchen.

"Hey, Fal! Do you like sesame beef or chicken?"

"Both," I answer honestly. "I mean, either."

She doesn't miss a beat, and her energy is infectious. But I need to get this alcohol out of here before Ryder catches me.

"Okay. Well, let's get honey chicken. It's similar but different. And then sesame beef. Ryder can get whatever the

heck he wants. Probably something with cashews. Bleh."
She flips her glossy brown curls over her shoulder, the
golden highlights catching in the light. "Oh, and I want an
egg roll. You?" She turns those light green eyes on me,
waiting patiently and expectantly. I've never had a little
sister before, and this feels oddly like such.

"Yeah. Definitely. I'm starving. Thanks, Sofie."

It's the most I've given her, and she knows it. She beams
from ear to ear. Her beautiful smile rivals her brother's, but
I don't look at her the way I look at him. And it confuses me.
I've never really been into anyone, but I didn't think I'd be
into guys when the time came. I'm not sure how I feel
about it.

Do I even like girls?

Did I *ever* like girls?

Fuck. My chest feels tight, and I chew on my lip ring
nervously. Now is not the time to think about this or to
spiral.

Ryder walks in just then and eyes me, then the wet bar.
I keep my hands in my oversized pocket, praying nothing
sloshes around. I'm getting hot, my body heat rising, and
my skin overheating in this hoodie and tight jeans. A light
sheen of sweat breaks out across my forehead and my
upper lip.

I hope he doesn't notice.

It's starting to feel like something is tied tightly around
my neck, suffocating me.

I need a break before dinner. Need to be alone.

"Lying down for a bit. Headache," I mumble, walking
over to the fridge to grab a water bottle and head back to
my room now that Ryder is out of it. I lock it behind me and
press my back against the wood, exhaling a defeated breath
and closing my eyes.

His face flashes before me. His friendly, kind, smiling face. And he's so fucking handsome that I think I know there's no dilemma at all.

I'm gay.

And I think I want Ryder Cruz.

Still overheated, I hurry to my desk and set down the Gatorade bottle of liquor. I rip my hoodie off, leaving me in my tight black Jimi Hendrix T-shirt that's two sizes too small.

My stomach grumbles in protest, but I grab the bottle of alcohol instead. I can handle it. Sofie won't know. I need to fill the hollowness in my chest with something, and right now, it's this grab-bag whiskey.

The burn is unpleasant, but it always is, and at least it's something. I drain a quarter of the bottle and cap it back, tucking it far under my bed before taking my pants off and climbing inside, letting the alcohol warm me and sleep take me.

I hear the doorbell ring but don't move. This is the most comfortable bed I've been in since we had a house and Dad was alive. And that nap was not long enough. The alcohol is still making me dizzy and clouding my thoughts. I'm cozy and content now, in a numb, sleepy fog. I'm not thinking about how Uncle Joel and everything here reminds me of Dad, coupled with these new *gay* feelings—

"Food's here, dude! Chow time!" Ryder yells from downstairs, his loud, clear voice echoing off the walls in the hallway, not allowing me to miss it, even though my door is shut.

My stomach growls louder, and I know I need to eat. I really am hungry too. I whip the covers back and hop out, wavering on my feet, realizing I'm a little drunker than I thought.

Great.

Golden Boy is going to notice for sure.

I grab my skinny black jeans with the rips down the front and shimmy into them, pulling them over the swell of my ass. I leave my shirt on because I don't have many and don't need to waste another, even for a party tonight. I'll just wear this.

I don't care.

I stop in the bathroom to do my business and wipe some of the smeared eyeliner from under my eye, careful of the bruised skin on one side.

I'm ready for this black eye to go away. I don't need the added attention. At least my uniforms are supposed to arrive on Sunday, so I won't have to spend another week standing out in all black. I finger-comb my blue and black hair as best I can and head downstairs.

Ryder and Sofie are laughing and smiling at the table when I walk into the dining room. There are about ten Chinese food containers set out and an empty plate and chair next to Ryder, with Sofie on the other side.

I slip into my seat quietly before Ryder can tell I'm unsteady.

"Fallon, the egg rolls are sooo good," Sofie mumbles around a mouthful of food. She swallows the lump and takes a drink of lemonade. "Sorry. We were starving and couldn't wait. That was my first bite, though. You're not late. Here." She shoves the container of egg rolls at me and pushes a little packet of sauce across the table.

I can't remember the last time I had takeout Chinese food. Especially all of these options. I grab my egg roll and scoop up decent-sized portions of what Sofie and I picked out, but I eye the chicken dish covered in broccoli and cashews. I haven't tried that before, but it looks good.

Ryder notices but doesn't even say anything. Just adds a scoop of white rice to my plate and a huge scoop of his cashew chicken. I try that first and end up devouring the entire portion before touching anything else.

"Nice, dude. This and Kung Pao chicken are my favorites. It has peanuts instead and is kind of sweet and spicy."

I nod, agreeing that would be good too.

Sofie giggles, nearly choking on her egg roll.

"You okay?" Ryder asks like he's two seconds away from jumping across the table and giving her the Heimlich.

She nods, taking a drink of her lemonade and laughing more. "Sorry. You guys just. . ." She trails off into more giggles. "You just really like nuts."

There's a beat or two of silence.

"In your mouths!" she shouts and then erupts into peals of high-pitched laughter with her head thrown back as she tips onto two legs of her dining chair.

Ry's chair scrapes back from the table as he stands abruptly. "You little shit!" he yells back, and I'm not quite sure what's happening. I've never had siblings.

Her chair drops back down, and she hops up too.

"Ry! Don't! I'm too full! Please don't!"

I'm drunk and confused and just keep eating, watching the show in front of me.

Ryder chases her around the table.

"Don't! I'll throw up egg rolls all over you! They have shrimp in them too!" Ryder visibly shudders but doesn't stop, easily snatching his little sister up and tickling her relentlessly. She squeals and pleads, and he stops after less than a minute.

"Don't say the word *nuts*, Sofie. If another guy besides Fallon heard that, I'd have to beat them up."

Sofie giggles at that. "You don't beat anyone up, Ryder!"

I can believe that. The golden boy is always happy.

"Doesn't mean I won't or I can't. Now let's eat. Fallon and I have a party to get to."

"I'm coming to Cole's too! Jenna and Katie were invited by juniors, and they're bringing me."

"No way, Sofia. You're fourteen. You are not going to a party with a bunch of eighteen-year-olds, and Jenna and Katie shouldn't either."

"Okay, Dad."

I don't miss the flash of hurt that tears across Ryder's expression, and neither does Sofia. I don't know where their mom is, but I know they have a nice father. Still, it must be a sore subject in the family.

"Sorry, Ry," she mumbles, lowering her head, her brown curls covering her face.

"It's fine, Sofie. Just finish dinner, yeah?"

"Yeah," she agrees, and they sit down, and we eat quietly. Even though the numbness is taking over, I can feel the shift in the mood.

"We can play *Mortal Kombat* tomorrow, Sofie," I tell her, not liking it when she's sad.

She darts those pale green eyes up to me, smiling softly. "Thanks, Fallon. For sure." And then she grabs a little round ball of dough rolled in sugar crystals. "Chinese donut?" she asks, and I take it from her, stuffing the entire thing in my mouth and humming at the taste, making her giggle.

Ryder is smiling when I glance at him out of the corner of my eye. He hasn't noticed I'm drunk or mentioned that he knows it's my birthday tomorrow. This food is also delicious. Maybe tonight won't end up being so bad after all.

CHAPTER EIGHT

RYDER

Fallon is drunk. He can't fool me. Even though he barely talks, I don't miss the glassy sheen to his eyes, the waver in his steps on the way to the table, or the slight smell of whiskey on his breath before we started eating.

After we clean up, Sofie informs me she's going to watch Netflix in her room and read. She looks disappointed, and I hate that, but there's no way a freshman girl needs to be at Cole's party. And now I feel a responsibility to watch her two friends while we're there.

Great.

Once she's left and Fallon and I are walking down the hallway toward the living room, I grab his arm, pausing before we get there. I crowd his back and lower my lips to his ear. "I know you're drunk. Don't deny it. I told you not to drink in front of Sofie," I nearly growl, causing his body to shiver. I'm a happy-go-lucky guy who likes to joke, but I also need to be taken seriously.

Fallon shrugs away from me. "I'm not drunk. Get off my case."

"Yeah. But you were drinking."

"So. It was in my room. She didn't see or notice." He folds his arms across his chest and raises his chin.

Oh. I see. It's like that.

Fallon got some liquid courage. Better keep my eye on him tonight too.

I stalk forward until he's pressed completely against the wall, hovering above him with my height and peering down into his stormy ocean eyes. His arms pressed against my chest.

"I told you not to," I repeat, and he pushes against me.

Fallon swallows roughly, reverting to his silence, and I worry I lost him when I was just starting to get through to him. Get him to talk, show me who he is.

"Don't do it again," I tell him, my eyes zeroing in on the silver hoop he's always chewing on.

I'm staring again, and Jamie isn't here to tell me to stop.

"Okay," he whispers. My eyes dart to his, but I can't quite see them all the way.

Without thinking, I reach up and swoop a lock of blue hair back with my fingers, tucking it behind his ear.

Shit.

Why did I do that?

"Couldn't see you," I whisper back and watch his Adam's apple bob as he swallows thickly. I don't think I'm the only one affected by our close proximity.

I can't get enough of him.

The tension between us ebbs and flows. His aura is intoxicating, and I want so badly to push through the fog surrounding him and find him. Pull him out and to the other side with me. Bring him *home*.

Shit.

Got deep. Too fucking deep.

I step back before my semi presses into his stomach and ruins the night. "I'm going to grab my bag and get ready in the bathroom. I can meet you downstairs or. . . in your room?" It's his choice.

"My room," he answers shyly, and we separate. He heads upstairs while I grab my gym bag and use the downstairs bathroom.

When I open the door to Fallon's room, he's already completely ready and lounging on his bed, playing *Mortal Kombat.*

He's wearing the same ripped black jeans, but his T-shirt is solid black this time, with holes all over it, and a blue and black buffalo plaid flannel tied around his slim hips. His blue and black hair is wet and shaggy, uncombed and hanging in a mess.

Fuck me, he looks good.

"If Sofie saw you right now, she'd say you were cheating. You're not allowed to practice and get better when she's not around. It's against the rules," I tell him.

"Whose rules?"

"Princess Sofia," I answer in all seriousness. Doesn't he get it by now?

Fallon snorts, and I almost see a smile.

Fucking score!

Maybe Sofie is his soft spot too.

"Wanna head out early? Cole always has good food, and I like to eat it before everyone else touches it."

"We just ate," he states, sounding confused.

"Yeah, but my body is big and already digesting it, so I should probably eat before I start drinking, ya know?"

He snorts again, and I smile, warmth blooming in my chest whenever he gives me something. I might spontaneously combust if he actually smiles, becoming a burnt patch in Joel's recliner and another unsolved mystery.

I check my phone. "Uber's here. Let's go."

I grab my thick letterman jacket as we head out the door, and Fallon slips on a worn-out jean jacket with more holes. I don't say anything, but we need to fix this. I'm taking him shopping for his birthday. Store or online. His choice.

"We're leaving, Sofie! Set the alarm, okay?"

"Okay! Bye!" she hollers back from upstairs in her room. She's never done anything like sneak out or lie, so I trust her to stay home. She's old enough that Fallon and I can leave her alone and go to a party. We have a security system. It'll be fine.

We pull up to Cole's mansion, right on the lake. The spotlights are on, showcasing the nearly all-glass exterior mixed with natural wooden beams and sharply angled steel architecture. The privacy screen is off, and we can see inside the elaborately decorated home built into the lakeside cliffs. Acadia Lake is beautiful, and Cole's house is one of the biggest lakefront properties.

His parents are criminal defense attorneys and represent some pretty nasty people and pretty big cases. I'm actually a little terrified of them and tend to stay away unless they're out of town like they are now when Cole throws his ridiculous ragers.

Fallon is pretty street-smart. I think. I'm sure I don't need to warn him to be careful at a house party. Even though it's Cole's house, we can't always control all the drugs or alcohol brought in. And I bet some of our rivals from Jefferson High, the public school across town, might show up. The pricks are always starting shit, trying to haze us. They spray Silly String on our cars, toilet paper our houses, and somehow bleached half the teams' jerseys last month. It was a shit show, that one.

These parties get crazy, so I don't plan to leave his side because of his size and because he doesn't talk much and tends to check out. That makes him an easy target, especially for pricks at Jefferson like Seth Nelson.

Ever since eighth grade, when I dunked on him, he's had it out for me. He's grown a lot since then and nearly rivals my height, but I can still dunk on his ass, and he's mad about it.

"Thanks, dude," I tell the Uber driver and hop out, Fallon following suit.

Cole leaves his door unlocked for these parties, so we walk right in and help ourselves to the food just as the catering service sets it out.

"Cruz! You can't even say hello to a guy before chowing down on his buffet?" Cole shouts, cackling at his own innuendo.

I just roll my eyes, turning to dap him up and mumbling a greeting around a mouthful of guacamole.

"Hey, Fallon. 'Sup?" Cole asks, and I peek at him out of the corner of my eye as I load my plate with different dips, finger foods, and a small cup of ice cream.

Fallon just nods his head in greeting, not saying anything out loud. Cole darts his eyes to me but doesn't say anything, either.

A million questions are running through his head, but he won't get the answers. Not from me and definitely not from Fallon.

"Jamie here?" I ask before dipping a chunk of

cauliflower into ranch and shoving the whole thing into my mouth.

"Yeah, he's in the kitchen."

Fallon follows me, opting not to eat anything since we ate dinner not too long ago.

I find Jamie leaning against the kitchen cabinets, his tall frame dressed in fitted dark jeans and an indigo button-up that complements his golden brown skin. His short black curls shine under the bright kitchen lights, and I can tell he just got a fresh edge-up after school.

"Looking sharp, my friend," I tell him, doing the special handshake we've done since seventh grade.

He runs his hand along the side of his head, turning to show me the swirly line with the heart looped through. It's slick.

"Nice, bro."

"Cruz. The ladies love it, I'm telling you," he teases casually, giving me a blinding white smile with a small wink. He's definitely popular with the girls at school, but he treats them right and has had two serious girlfriends during our time in high school. His break-ups end well too. Jamison is just a nice fucking guy.

"I know they do, bro. Trust me." I flick my eyes to the blonde chick at the other end of the kitchen island, hovering by the liquor bottles and coyly checking Jamie out.

He tips his head back and laughs, excusing himself to talk to her.

"Hey, Blue." I don't know why I say it when he told me not to. It just slips out, but it feels right on my tongue none-theless.

Fallon narrows his eyes but doesn't comment.

"Want me to make us drinks?"

"Sure." He boosts himself up on the counter next to the refrigerator, folding his legs and sitting cross-legged as he watches me with an intense expression in his steely blue eyes.

He took his jacket off and laid it over the back of one of the barstools so he's in just the tiny black T-shirt again. His pale skin peeks through the holes, teasing me with glimpses of his soft flesh.

I don't let his stare distract me. I'm used to being watched and under pressure, my every move scrutinized. The basketball court doesn't miss a thing. Even on the sidelines, you always have to be aware. And the way I'm staring back at him wouldn't go unnoticed.

I focus back on making two strong mixed drinks and hand Fallon his as I polish off the rest of my food. He's still sitting cross-legged on the counter, like a little blue-haired, sparkly lipped magical creature. Then the front door opens, and I hear loud, obnoxious laughs and hollers.

Great.

The Jefferson High douchebags. Just what I needed. Before I can tell Fallon to hop down and leave the kitchen with me because they are undoubtedly here to get wasted, Seth, Rich, and Dustin come strolling in with cocky smiles and shitty attitudes.

I wanted to have fun, not deal with these assholes. I don't know why Cole continues to invite them to these things. His parties should only be for Acadia Lake students. These guys are always up to no good, and I don't trust them.

"Cruz. 'Sup, pussy?"

God, Rich is such a tool. I cannot stand him. Seth has been my arch-nemesis and rival since middle school, while Rich and Dustin are always annoying.

"Eat a dick, Lopez," I tell him.

"Nah, I bet that's more your taste, Ry," he says patronizingly and pats me on the chest as he strolls by and opens the refrigerator door next to Fallon.

"The food is on the buffet, and the drinks are on the island," I tell him firmly without actually saying to stay out of the fridge and back away from Fallon.

"And who's this pretty little girl?" he says like a complete asshole and raging homophobe when he finally notices Fallon. Not that I even know if Fallon is gay! But I'm gay, and I'm fucking offended by this tool every time I see him.

"Shut up, prick," I say defensively, showing my cards like an idiot.

"Oh. Oh, I'm sorry. Are you sweet on her?"

His misgendering of Fallon is boiling my fucking blood.

He has on nail polish, eyeliner, and lips that fucking sparkle. That's it.

Not that it matters.

But this prick is being an asshole and digging at me on purpose. I'm not a fighter, but I step forward. Fallon hops down, and Seth walks over, trying to clear the tension, even though he's a dick too.

"Rich, enough. Leave Cruz to whatever weird shit he's into. Another man's kink is none of our business, m'kay?"

Fallon grabs his drink from the counter and strolls out of the kitchen, not acknowledging any of the hate and not waiting for me.

I'm glad.

"Listen here, cunts. It's just me and you three. I'm not scared. Come at me if you want to. But don't disrespect my friends. And Dustin, stay the fuck away from Sofie. I'm tired of telling you."

"She here tonight?" he asks like a moron. I stalk toward him, ready to grab his T-shirt, but Seth interferes.

"I'm not 'bout to be accused of jumping you, Cruz. Three on one, your ass would be bleeding out, and we'd be off the team. I'm sure that's exactly what you want, but it's not happening."

I keep advancing until I'm in Seth's face now. "I'd like to see you try."

"Ry. I got this," Jamison says cooly, strolling into the room and stepping up to my side, Cole not far behind him, flanking me.

Seth slips away laughing, and Jamie squeezes my shoulder reassuringly, whispering low. "Go find Fallon. Don't worry about these tools. Cole and I will handle it."

"Yeah we will. And give this to Fallon for me." Cole slips me a little baggie of weed and a blunt wrap.

I nod and back up until I'm far enough that they can't grab me. I snatch my red plastic cup and storm out in search of the boy with the shimmery lips. I need to make sure he's okay after what they just said.

CHAPTER NINE

FALLON

The numbness won't let the hateful words seep in. I've heard them all before, so I just casually hop down and leave the negative environment. Something I used to try to do around my mother and her shitty boyfriends but didn't always succeed in. I can leave right now, though, so I will.

I'll find Ryder later.

I freeze at the entrance to the large living room. The furniture is pushed aside, the rugs are rolled up, and teenagers fill the space.

My heart rate picks up a notch, ricocheting around in my chest like a loose cannon and making the anxiety creep back. Maybe someone outside has some weed. The thought spurs me on, and I turn toward the back porch in search of a blunt.

The second I step out of the house and onto the back deck warmed with space heaters, I'm instantly hit with the pungent, skunky aroma of good bud. My eyes dart to a group of kids sitting under an umbrella table and passing something around. My social anxiety makes this hard, but I push through and wander over, accepting the blunt when they offer it to me.

It sparks and hisses when I pull deep, and I cough into my elbow, taking a quick second hit before passing it back to the kid with bright copper hair. I'm not sure it tasted quite normal, but I thank them anyway and walk around, enjoying the fresh air and the sounds of the lake lapping at the shore down below. I let the high of the weed take me away and numb every worry and memory that threatens to pull me under.

I might have enjoyed myself tonight in another world or maybe another dimension. I close my eyes, letting my senses experience what my emotions won't.

"It's beautiful, isn't it?" Ryder's earnest voice washes over me, and I open my eyes to silver moonlight streaming down and his olive green eyes staring at me, *not* the view.

I swallow thickly. Was he saying *I'm* beautiful? He couldn't mean that could he? Those assholes just made fun of me and called me pretty. I know Ryder wouldn't do that, but still.

"It is," I agree. "Cole has a really nice house."

I stare off into the distance again. I can't see the other side, and it feels like I'm staring into the ocean.

"Here." Ryder shoves his hand into his pocket, pulling out a small baggie of weed and a wrap. "Cole said to give this to you. On him."

"Thanks," I mumble, not admitting that I'm completely stoned. I pocket it for later, and gaze into oblivion.

The night is dark, but the moon is high and bright. The twinkling stars, unobstructed by city life, reflect off the calm, gentle waters of Acadia Lake. The massive body of water is surrounded by tall redwoods and steep cliffs.

Ryder seems lost to his own thoughts, until he turns to me abruptly. "Hey. Ignore those assholes, okay?"

"Okay," I respond. I already did, but Ryder is upset, so I let him continue.

"What they said is bullshit. Don't ever listen to that and don't ever let it bring you down."

He's so passionate I can hardly tell him I'm numb most days and don't feel anything.

"You are pretty, though," he blurts out.

My eyes widen in shock before he quickly corrects himself. "I mean, you're really attractive, Blue." Ryder runs his hand through those thick, soft-looking curls.

My breath hitches at his words, unsure where we're going to take this, but knowing if and when we do, it can't be on Cole's deck in the middle of a party. Even as drunk and high as I am, I know this. My dick pulses in my pants just thinking about it. So, when Ryder leans into me, his bigger frame crowding my smaller one into the railing and his lips nearing mine, I dodge him and slip under his arm.

He would regret it later when it ruins basketball for him.

Is he even gay?

"I need some water," I declare, slipping back into the house and into the throng of inebriated teenagers dancing and partying. The beat of the music threatens to break through the haze and make me feel again. My fingers twitch with the need to write something.

I'm seeing double, and I can't find Ryder. I trail my hand along the wall, knocking into the picture frames and decorations, as I stumble down the upstairs hallway, searching for a place to rest.

This isn't good at all. I'm not sure if I picked up the wrong drink, or someone slipped me something when I wasn't looking, or if I'm just this fucking drunk right now.

It doesn't feel normal, though. Maybe the weed was laced. The funny after-taste from the blunt comes back to me, and I'm sure that's it.

This is different from the numbness. This feels like sedation as I trek through quicksand, desperate to get to the other side.

My eyes are heavy as I push into what I think is an empty bedroom to lie down and gather my spinning head, but someone's already in there. "Sorry," I mumble, slowly backing away and looking down so I don't accidentally see anyone hooking up.

There's a small muffled whimper and some rustling that sounds like a struggle. My eyes instantly dart up, and I strain to bring the image before me into focus.

"Sofie?" I ask, my drunk and high brain unsure if I'm hallucinating. The quiet cry I get in return spurs me into motion, and I rush the guy pressing her to the wall and clock him on the side of the head with the textbook I grab from the desk as I run by. She slips away and scrambles behind me, grabbing onto my T-shirt.

This guy is way bigger than both of us. I'm not even much taller than Sofie.

"Sofie! Get Ryder, now!" I holler at her over my shoulder, trying to snap her out of the shock.

The distraction is my downfall, and Sofie's eyes widen just as I turn right into a nasty sucker punch to the side of my head. I stumble sideways, the force of the unexpected blow knocking me into the wall with a heavy thud. My legs give out, and I slide down, unable to hold myself up anymore. Sofie screams, and I think the sound might haunt me until the end of time.

"Get Ryder," I tell her again through my darkening vision, but she's sobbing.

"Dustin. Stop it, please. Don't hurt him. You're drunk. I said I'll go out with you!"

"Like hell she will," I sneer through bloody teeth to the wannabe sexual predator above me. My mouth tastes like copper, and I'm losing focus.

"Sofie, please," I beg, and I know she finally listens when I hear her heels tapping as she runs out of the room and down the hall to her brother.

Dustin chuckles menacingly, his dark eyes unfeeling. "I'll pop that beautiful little cherry, eventually," he slurs cruelly, squatting down and getting right in my face. "After I take all of her other firsts too. We have a date planned."

"You're disgusting," I tell him, then gather all the bloody spit in my mouth and launch it directly into his face, landing right on his cheek.

"Freak!" he shouts, rearing back and kicking me in the ribs.

The air is forced out of my lungs in a sharp burst, and I wrap my arms around my center. My diaphragm is frozen for a moment, the force of the blow paralyzing my breathing.

After what feels like an hour, but probably not even three minutes, I gasp for breath. My lungs greedily take heaving gulps of oxygen as Dustin laughs down at me.

Once my body is functioning properly again, I glance to the side, away from his ugly face, and see the glowing red numbers on the nightstand, alerting me that it is now twelve-sixteen in the morning.

"Happy birthday to me," I say out loud to no one.

"You're demented," he sneers, but I don't give a fuck. The numbness is taking over, leaving a void of nothingness, and I welcome the darkness when he pulls his fist back and lets loose his fury.

"You just beat up Coach Rivers' nephew, dumbass," a voice scolds. Cole maybe.

They must not know *why* he beat me up. What I walked in on.

Where's Sofie? Is she okay?

I try to say the words aloud, but I don't think I succeed. Everything is fuzzy. Fuzzier than normal.

"Jamie. Get the girls. Now. Jenna is passed out in the bathroom; you'll have to carry her. They're all hiding out there in Cole's room."

I can hear Ryder's voice now, but I can't open my eyes as I'm jostled against a hard chest. I moan, unable to stop the pained sound from escaping my lips.

"Shh. You're okay. I got you, Blue."

It's useless to fight against the nickname right now, so I just whimper again and nuzzle into his warm pec, letting oblivion take me again.

The next time I wake, I'm in the back of someone's car, and Ryder yells at them to rush to the hospital. To go faster.

Is he saying that because of me?

He can't be saying that because of me.

Oh, God.

"Is Sofie okay?" I ask in a panic, sitting up quickly and adding a head rush to the mix.

"Whoa, whoa. Lie back down, Blue. She's fine, thanks to

you. She told us what happened, Fallon. It's you that's got us worried. You probably have a concussion, and you passed out. Wouldn't wake up. Scared the shit out of me."

Ryder is in the middle seat with my head in his lap as I peer up at him. He sweeps my hair out of my eyes, running his hand lightly over my forehead, swallowing roughly.

"I passed out because I'm drunk," I inform him.

"At the exact moment of impact when a fist struck you in the face? That seems like a really odd coincidence and completely unrelated at all," he deadpans.

I can't right now.

"Ryder. My head." I rub my forehead gingerly. It hurts.

Did I get punched there too?

"Sorry, Fallon. But you need a hospital."

"I don't have insurance," I mumble.

"What?" he asks, like he's never heard of people without health insurance.

"Does your uncle know?"

"I don't know, Ryder. I moved in a week ago. My head," I moan.

Why is he making me talk now of all times?

I can't handle it.

"Dad will pay for it," he declares without calling or asking his father.

A trip to the emergency room without insurance will cost thousands of dollars. I'm not Alejandro's nephew; I'm just his partner's unfortunate responsibility.

"No."

"I'm worried about you," he whispers.

Sofia must hear him.

"Me too, Fallon. Please get checked out. This is all my fault," she sniffles, and I can't handle it.

I sit up to see her better, Ryder grumbling the entire way.

"Sofia. This is not your fault," I tell her earnestly. The seriousness of what just happened to her—to me, to both of us—hits me hard.

"It's not, Sofie. I'm gonna murder him for touching my little sister and for what he just did to Fallon. Dustin Flynne is a deadman." Ryder pops his knuckles, and Jamie agrees from the front seat where he's driving. Sofia's two friends are passed out and strapped to the bench seat next to him.

Ryder and Jamie are good guys. Trustworthy. But they can't ruin basketball over this guy.

"I think the blunt was laced with something, and that's why I passed out," I tell them.

Sure, I got punched in the face a couple of times and bit my tongue, but I don't have a concussion. I'm pretty sure.

I meet Jamie's eyes in the rearview mirror, and he nods.

"You don't actually believe him? Do you, Jamie?" Ry asks in outrage. "Get on the highway and go to the hospital downtown. Now, dude."

"I'm taking Katie and Jenna back to Katie's house. Kelsey's home and will take care of them. He said he's fine, and I believe him, Ry."

"He got punched in the face and passed out! Are you all insane?!"

"Calm down, Ryder," Sofia chimes in. "It's been a long night. Let's just go home. Please."

At his little sister's plea, I know he'll give in.

Sighing deeply, Ryder leans back, resting his head and staring at the ceiling. I study the column of his throat for a beat too long before his hands grab for me, steering me back down until my head is in his lap again. I don't protest.

I feel safe here as he runs his long fingers through my hair, soothing me.

"Don't fall asleep, Fallon." His tone is firm, and my eyes shoot open, locking onto the pale green gaze above me, transfixed by his concern for me.

"M'tired," I mumble in protest. My face hurts too.

"I can keep you awake," he mouths and winks. The Ryder I've come to know is back. The jokester. I snort at his innuendo, wincing as I clutch my side.

Ouch. Shit.

His teasing smile turns into worry once again.

Guess we'll see, Golden Boy.

CHAPTER TEN

RYDER

I've never been so terrified as I was when Sofie came running to me in tears, screaming about Fallon and Dustin and tugging on my hand to follow her upstairs. I burst into the bedroom to find six-and-a-half-foot-tall Dustin on top of Fallon with his eyes closed and blood smeared across his face.

Jamie and Cole were seconds behind us, grabbing Dustin and hauling him away so I could scoop Fallon up and run to Jamie's truck. I can deal with Dustin later after Cole does.

Sofie told all three of us he wanted to make out with her. She changed her mind once they got to the bedroom, and Dustin was too drunk to realize. He's been after Sofie the entire year, and half of that is just to mess with me. Throw me off my game so they can win the championship. It won't happen. Either thing.

Sofie begged us not to tell Dad and Joel. She said nothing happened, and he couldn't get into trouble for trying to make out with her anyway. That she thinks what he did isn't that bad really pisses me off. It makes me even angrier because Mom should be here to explain these things to Sofie. She should have a mother to confide in, not just a big brother and a dad.

I hate it for her, but I can't think about that tonight. Sofie is safe, and Fallon is too. Jamie dropped Sofie's friends off, ensuring Katie's older sister had everything under control. I know she'll take care of the girls, so that's one load off.

We pull into Fallon's driveway, and Jamie shuts the engine off so I know he plans to stay the night. He won't leave this all to me; he's worried about Sofie and Fallon too. I trust him with my sister completely, to care for her like I would.

She had too much to drink after sneaking out and coming to the party when I told her not to. She hates being left out, but it wasn't safe for a fourteen-year-old girl, and tonight proves that.

Jamie gets out and shuts his door quietly, walking around and scooping Sofie up from her side of the vehicle. She's over a foot shorter than him and curls up in his arms like one of the little kittens she still likes to wear on her pajamas. "I got her, dude," he whispers. "You can trust me."

"I know," I tell him. It's not a question in my mind. He loves my little sister like his own, and she loves him. They disappear inside after I use the app on my phone to disarm the house alarm and open the garage door.

"Blue. You ready?" I don't know why the nickname is coming out so much tonight, but I can't seem to stop.

"Yeah," he mumbles, sitting up from my lap with his eyes barely open. It's been hard to tell if he's sleeping or not, but he assured me he was awake each time.

I hop out on my side and run around, helping him before he tumbles to the ground.

He's kind of a mess.

Fallon stumbles three times before I get impatient that he's not in bed with his injuries being attended to. I scoop him up, and he doesn't even protest as I walk up the stairs to his room.

I kick the door shut behind me and lay him gently on the bed, scanning his body for any injuries.

Fallon curls up on his side. His chest rises and falls steadily, small puffs of air leaving him as he hovers on the edge of sleep. I roll him to his back, and he lets me, still out of it.

"I'm going to take your shirt off now," I inform him, giving him a chance to stop me as I reach for the hem.

I gently peel it off as Fallon lifts his arms. His eyes are half-lidded from the drugs, booze, and possible concussion as he stares at me. I climb onto the bed fully, hovering beside him on my knees. My hands reach down, lightly resting against the pale skin of his belly, causing little goosebumps to break out across his skin.

He's so small my two hands nearly span the entire width of his abdomen. I could grip his hips easily, controlling his body effortlessly. Fuck, I want to know what that's like.

I shake the lust-fueled thoughts from my mind because he's lying injured in front of me. His lean, toned abdomen is so tempting, even with bruises blooming on the soft flesh where it looks like Dustin punched him.

That worries me a little.

"Does this hurt?" I press lightly on his stomach, his muscles jumping under my touch.

He shakes his head no.

"Did he punch you here?" I ask, skimming his ribcage

with my fingertips and noting the dark red splotches already turning purple from where flesh met bone.

He shakes his head no again, and I narrow my eyes. He hasn't lied yet, so why would he start now?

"Kicked," he clarifies, eyes barely open.

I grit my teeth at the casual way he says this, my jaw pulsing with the pressure. I scoot up higher on the bed and lean in to inspect his face more closely. He doesn't have a split lip, thankfully. He must have bit his tongue, though, and his previous black eye looks darker and a little swollen.

It's not too bad, but he needs ice.

I brush his hair back from his face, telling him this.

"I'll be right back," I whisper gently.

And then I lean down to kiss his forehead. I have no idea why I do it, and I can only hope he's too drunk and high to remember it.

I jump up, rushing for the kitchen in search of snacks. Not even five minutes later, I'm back with ice, drinks, snacks, and a chocolate cupcake with bright blue frosting. I set my goodies on his desk and walk the cupcake over to him, sticking a candle in and lighting it.

"Happy Birthday, Blue," I tell him, licking the frosting off my finger after he grabs it.

I'm going to take care of him tonight. Especially since he got beat up on his birthday, defending my little sister's honor. I prop two pillows behind him, helping him sit up. "Lean against the headboard while you eat that. I'll rest a bag of ice on your ribs, and you can hold one to your eye after you're done. You don't want that swelling shut."

"Mm'fine," he mumbles around a mouthful of cupcake. "You don't have to bother with me."

Bother with him?

Why would he say it like that?

"You're on some unknown substance, drunk, high, possibly concussed, and it's your birthday. You aren't a bother, Fallon. I'm worried about you." I say this again, trying to make him understand. Seems like he hasn't had anyone care about him in a long time, which makes me sad for him and the little boy who lost his dad too young.

"Okay," he agrees, and I climb onto the bed next to him, setting a towel over his stomach and placing the bag of ice on top. I watch goosebumps erupt across his sensitive skin and glance away, the urge to touch him riding me hard.

Fallon finishes his birthday treat while I flip through my Netflix list until I find a mindless comedy to zone out on. A million thoughts race through my mind, and I can't turn them off.

Light snoring comes from next to me, and I realize I spaced out so much that I let him fall asleep.

Fuck!

"Fallon, wake up."

No response.

"Wake up," I say louder.

He doesn't move a muscle, and I freak out just a smidge.

I hover my ear over his bare chest to check his breathing.

The steady rise and fall of his chest and the rhythmic thumping his heart stall my rising panic. I sigh in relief and drop my head to his heart, lying there for a moment, relishing each and every breath. The feel of his smooth, warm skin and the alluring smell of him that's uniquely Fallon. A mix of fresh laundry soap and something sweet and fruity. Strawberries maybe.

He's intoxicating. Better than a drug.

"What are you doing?" His chest shakes my head when he speaks.

"Making sure you're still alive. You went to sleep."

"You went to sleep first," he counters, and maybe I did. I spaced out, at least.

"I'm fine, Ryder. Really. We're both tired; let's just sleep. You can stay," he adds in a vulnerable whisper.

He sounds like he's starting to sober up a little.

"Okay," I agree, and we maneuver under the covers.

"I'm taking my pants off," he declares boldly, breaking some of the tension.

"Oh, thank fuck, dude. I can't sleep in jeans. The thought of waking up with a zipper imprint on my dick doesn't appeal."

"Has that happened to you? Sounds like it's happened to you," Fallon responds cheekily, and I wish I could see him better, but we've already turned the TV off. The only other light is from the hallway nightlights shining under his door.

"Fuck, dude. It has. Do not recommend." I laugh lightly, and we both wiggle and shuffle around until I hear two thunks of our jeans hit the bedroom floor.

We lie still for a moment, shirtless and in our underwear, and we haven't even kissed.

I want to fix that tonight.

I roll to my side and stare at the dark outline of his profile, reaching out to skim my fingers along the ridges and valleys until I get to his mouth. I let them hover over his lips, feeling his breath coming out in little short puffs.

Is he worked up?

The thought, even the possibility, starts to get me hard. I touch the pillowy-soft flesh of his lips and trail my fingers over the silver hoop I've been dying to taste.

"Do your lips hurt?" I ask.

"No," he responds, breath hot against my touch.

"Damn," I tease. "I was gonna kiss them better."

Fallon whimpers, and the sound gives me the consent I need to press my mouth to his. The feel of his plump lips and that cool metal held against my own spurs me on. To experience what I've so desperately wanted to experience with him. I plunge my tongue deep, tangling with his and kissing him how I've dreamed of since we met.

Fallon scrambles to his knees, never breaking the contact between our lips. I help maneuver him on top of me, encouraging him to sit down with a firm grip around his small waist. It's sexy as hell.

Holy fuck.

"Fallon," I whisper into his mouth. "You okay?" I need to check on him. He doesn't voice things out loud on his own.

"Yeah. Fine," he responds, out of breath. I nuzzle my face into the crook of his neck, inhaling his scent and rubbing my skin against the slight sweat on his overheated flesh.

"You getting hot for me, Blue?" I ask him, wishing I could see his face but settling for tasting his mouth instead. I squeeze his waist more firmly and slide his body down until he's resting over my dick instead of my abs.

"Sit," I instruct so he has no room to be shy. Fallon listens, whimpering as he lowers to my lap, only the soft cotton of our underwear separating us. And I'm hard, like offensively hard. It's ridiculous, but I can't stop now, and I know Fallon doesn't want me to. I press my hips up and grind my cock into his.

"Ride me, Fal," I tell him, running my hand down his waist and grabbing hold of his hip, helping him rock against me. I feel his erection graze my own, and we groan at the new sensation. It doesn't take more than a few fumbling thrusts before we get into a steady rhythm that's both of our undoing.

"Ryder," he whimpers. "I. . . I'm going to come." He's grinding against me harder but keeping the same even tempo.

Oh God, he's so fucking hot. "Come then, come for me on your birthday."

Fallon's body obeys, and he buries his face into my chest as he comes hard, crying out as his dick pulses against mine, triggering my own release. My hold on his hip tightens, possibly adding another mark to the many that already decorate his body, but I can't stop myself. I grit my teeth and come harder than I ever have.

Holy fuck.

We're panting, sticky messes when we come down from the orgasm high. That was incredible, and I *need* to do it again.

"Shit. Blue."

"I know," he murmurs into my chest, and the cool scrape of his lip ring against my nipple causes me to hiss out and thrust into him again.

"Fuck. Can you suck on my nipple? I need to feel that lip ring. *Please*, Fallon."

I'm not above begging. Clearly.

"Unghh!" I shout obscenely, and Fallon quickly slaps a hand over my mouth to stop the porn star moan from exploding out of me as he continues to suck and lick at my nipple. He drags his lip over the tight little bud, and I shiver as his piercing tugs on my sensitive flesh.

"Stop, or I'll need to come again," I tell him in a breathy rush.

"Do it, then."

I hesitate. "Uh. . ."

As much as I want to, I don't think we should go any further than making out and coming in our underwear together.

"I need to take my sticky boxers off," Fallon insists, but I can see his glassy, half-lidded eyes because of the moonlight peeking through the open curtains. He's fucked up, slipping into the abyss, and I'm worried he'll regret it.

He stops licking my nipple and peers up at me. "Can I come again too?"

The earnest question catches me off guard, like he's asking to tag along to the movies with my friends and me, not if he can take his underwear off and nut bare-skinned against me.

I can't give in yet.

"Fuuuuck," I groan. He's going to be the death of me.

CHAPTER ELEVEN

FALLON

"Rise and shine, birthday boy!" Uncle Joel shouts, and I crack one eye open as he comes bustling into my room with a tall stack of pancakes and a candle.

Is this breakfast in bed? That actually exists? People do this for other people?

He's too loud, and it's too early. I can hardly remember what happened last night. My head is killing me. I groan and blindly reach for a pillow, covering my face and possibly attempting to smother myself. Birthdays haven't meant shit since Dad died. I was lucky if my mother even remembered and bought a cake and a card. Those were the good birthdays.

"Fallon, don't be grouchy. You're eighteen now. That's something to celebrate. *You're* something to celebrate."

His words punch through my shield and hit me right in the gut. I don't like it.

"I am not a proponent of *it's my party and I can cry if I want to*, so sit up and enjoy your favorite breakfast food and blow this candle out before you collect more wax than butter."

Uncle Joel tugs the pillow away, the cool, cotton pillowcase slipping through my fingers easily.

I'm tired. It's one of *those* days. Doesn't matter that it's my birthday.

"Fallon!" he gasps, quickly setting the breakfast tray on the end of the bed and perching next to me. He even has a little vase with a daisy in it.

I don't deserve a flower.

Uncle Joel reaches up to touch my face, the tender flesh of my cheekbone aching.

Memories from last night flood in. The party. Drinking. Smoking. Sofie. *Fucking Dustin.* Then. . . *holy shit.* We. . . Ryder and I. We. . .

I wiggle around, hoping my morning wood goes down fast. I definitely don't regret any of it. I just wish I had a clearer head for it.

Maybe he'd want to do it again?

Sober.

I don't know if I can ask him that.

"Fallon, what happened?" Uncle Joel's stern tone cuts through the headache and lingering fog. Sounds like it's not the first time he's asked that. It makes me uncomfortable.

"Nothing." I don't feel like talking.

Uncle Joel sighs heavily and grabs the tray from the end of the bed. Guess he already blew the candle out for me.

"Well, I'll grab you some ibuprofen. I want you to have a good birthday. Regardless of what happened last night."

"Nothing happened."

"That's what Ryder and Jamison told me," Uncle Joel says with creased brows.

I glance away, unable to maintain eye contact, when the

easy lie slips off my tongue. Uncle Joel's been nothing but kind to me, and I can't even be truthful with him.

"They're camped out in the living room, by the way."

An unusual torrent swirls in my gut at the thought of them sleeping in the living room together. It reeks of *jealousy*, and I don't like the feelings that Ryder is making me endure.

I prefer the numbness.

"But you forget, Fallon. I work with teenagers for a living. I know when I'm being bull-shitted."

My tired, surely bloodshot eyes pop open a little wider at his use of a curse word. I don't normally know what to say, and right now is no different, so I just pick up my fork, saw off a chunk of fluffy pancakes, and mumble out *thanks* before shoveling it into my mouth.

Uncle Joel sighs again, and I know I'm probably riding a thin line. He could ask me to leave now. It doesn't matter that I'm still in high school. I'm eighteen, and he can tell me to fuck off. "Should I leave?" I blurt after I swallow the mass of pancakes in my mouth. He'd be better off without me. Less hassle. Less to worry about.

"What?" he asks in complete confusion, his brows creasing behind his dark-framed glasses. "Leave?"

"I'm an adult now." Do I need to remind him? He's the one who just brought me a stack of pancakes with a candle on top.

His bright blue eyes soften, and I try not to lash out at the pity I see shining back at me in his caring gaze. He has too much concern for me. I don't deserve it.

"No, Fallon. That's not happening. The wrath of Sofie and Al can be too much for one man to handle. Please, nephew, don't even think about doing that to me. You are staying. We all want you to. It's not an option. Okay?"

I glance away, then back to him, feeling uncomfortable again. "Okay."

"So, I don't want to hear you ask again. Alright? You're not going anywhere. This is your home. Forever."

I don't know what to say, so I just nod and continue eating until it's all gone. I glance up and catch the big smile on his face when he sees my empty plate.

"I'm going to get you that ibuprofen now." Uncle Joel leaves with the empty tray, and I close my eyes, leaning back against the headboard, drifting off.

"Psst. Blue. Got your meds, dude. And some water." I hear a clunk on the table beside me and peek one eye open. Ryder's long slender fingers retreat from the glass dripping with condensation. My eyes travel up his tanned, muscular forearm to his firm biceps and his nipple showing through the giant cut-out arm hole in his T-shirt. His baseball cap is on backward, and his curls are sticking out of the hole in complete disarray. I chew on my lip ring, taking in the golden boy in front of me.

Yeah. I'm gay.

Doesn't really matter to me what I am. Guess I'd just like to be happy. Eventually.

Ryder catches me staring and doesn't miss a beat. "You like these bad boys?" he teases, flexing his bicep and letting it bulge obscenely, his light brown skin stretching taut over hard muscles. I feel my cock jump under the covers.

He gives me a ridiculously sexy wink and then licks his own bicep in a way that only Ryder Cruz could make endearingly hot. I can't help but snort and maybe even smile a little.

"Score!" he shouts out loud, startling me a little. "That was a smile. You smiled. I made you smile on your birthday! And there's more where that came from too."

He's persistent, and he's probably right too. Because here I am, not even two seconds later, wanting to smile again.

But I don't.

Ryder notices. "Take the pain pills, and you'll feel better, Fallon. Come downstairs when you're ready. We all got you presents, and you can choose anything you want for dinner. I'm gonna text Georgie to make you an ice cream cookie for dessert."

I groan and rub my head, wondering how I could possibly be so tired if I was passed out all night.

"I'm thinking Oreo ice cream and a classic chocolate chip cookie. It's the best combination."

"Huh?"

What is he even talking about? Oreos again?

"It's two giant pizza-sized cookies with a layer of ice cream in between. A giant ice cream cookie. Our family chef, Georgie, makes them every year for my and Sofie's birthdays. I don't even remember if there was a time before birthday cookies."

He's so serious it's a little outrageous, and I snort, earning me a dazzling smile.

"Let me get out of here before Sofie finds out you're awake. She's been asking for you all morning. We've been a little worried, Blue," he whispers.

"I'm fine. I told you that. See? Wasn't wrong." I gesture to my body tucked in bed and propped against the headboard.

He eyes me, unconvinced. "You remember things from

last night, don't you?" He looks vulnerable and unsure. Unlike his normal, playful self.

I don't like it, so I quickly reassure him. "I do. And I don't regret any of it. Do you?" Now I'm the one to sound insecure.

"Of course not. It was incredible. You're incredible. Unbelievable, really. Can I give you a proper birthday kiss?" He's unguarded again, but I like it this time. "Just a quick one." He glances over his shoulder at the open door behind him and then back to me.

I nod, always short for words. Ryder leans forward and presses his mouth to mine before pulling back slightly, swiping his tongue along my lip ring, and playing with it. I groan at the pull on my sensitive flesh, leaning forward after him, begging for more.

I grab his cutoff and pull him toward me, sealing my mouth to his, branding him with a red-hot kiss. Ryder runs his long fingers through my hair, getting tangled in my bedhead. It doesn't stop him from taking control and angling us just right to devour my mouth how he pleases. We pull apart when we hear people downstairs laughing and talking.

"You taste like syrup, and you smell like strawberries," he murmurs, nuzzling his face into the crook of my neck. "So fucking sweet." I'm seconds away from pulling him on top of me and demanding he ride me, just the way I did last night.

I want to drag him as close to me as I can until his warmth cocoons me and shields me from all the bullshit in my life.

I... what?

I actually just want to come.

He bites at my earlobe, and I shiver, the tremor making

its way from my scalp to the tips of my toes, causing my dick to pulse and thicken. "Go get ready," he whispers directly into my ear. "It's your birthday, and I'm not the only one who wants to celebrate you."

His words cause my heart to warm a little. The emotions I've been allowing myself to feel are new and different. It's been a while since I've felt this way. I'm not sure I'm ready.

After a quick shower, I wipe the mirror with my hand, clearing away the fog to see my reflection. I use what's probably Sofie's comb, part my hair along the color split, and comb out all the tangles, leaving it to dry in a smooth, straight sheet. I use black eyeliner and my favorite strawberry shimmer Chapstick. Before I left my room, I grabbed my go-to outfit—my extra-small comfort tee has a few holes, especially around the neck. I pair it with my favorite black jeans that have been washed and dried so many times they practically feel like pajamas. The holes are natural, and my right knee is nearly separated from the top of the pants. I didn't wear these to school, but it's my birthday, and I want to be comfortable.

I leave the bathroom and drop my things in my room before heading downstairs for more food.

"Fallon! Happy Birthday!" Sofie shouts before hopping up from her spot on a giant pillow around the coffee table. Jamie must have gone home, but everyone else is playing a card game with snacks in the center. I could get down with that. She runs over to the bottom of the stairs and tugs on my hand, steering us around the corner where no one can see us.

"Are you okay?" she whispers into my ear as she hugs me tightly. I swallow past the lump in my throat and wrap my arms around her small frame for a second. I'm barely bigger than her but four years older, and she's worried about *me*? After last night, I don't think I'll be able to stop worrying about *her*.

"I'm fine, Sofie. Just needed to sleep it off. Are *you* okay?" I emphasize the *you* because she needs to realize something. "What Dustin did isn't okay. And I don't want you going out with him. Promise me, Sofie."

"He was just drunk. He wouldn't do anything, but I don't want to go out with him now that he hit you, and I told him that." She crosses her arms in front of her chest and scrunches her brow in determination.

That probably just made me a bigger target for those assholes at the public school. I don't even play basketball or do drama and gossip, yet here I am at what feels like the center. I try not to think about it on my birthday and silently make a plan to sneak away and enjoy the weed in my backpack. No way in hell I won't be having a birthday blunt.

"Fallon?" Sofie's eyes sparkle with concern as she rubs her hand up and down my shoulder. It sounds like she might have said my name more than once. But this isn't unusual for me.

"Yeah?"

"I said I promise I won't go out with Dustin. I already promised Ry, and I'm making it to you too. Okay? What he did was. . . really scary."

I'm not a hugger, but this family is forcing me to feel and do things I don't normally do. I pull Sofie back into a tight embrace. She's only fourteen, and I hate that she went through that. I don't give a shit about myself. I barely felt it, anyway.

"I'm sorry," I tell her, unsure what else to say.

"Let's forget that douche canoe and celebrate *you*. Come on." She grabs my hand again and tugs me the rest of the way back to the living room, leading me to a giant blue jean bean bag large enough for two or three adults.

She plops down, giving me no choice but to land next to her and sink into the soft foam beans, causing her to giggle. I feel my lip twitch as I resituate myself to see what I need to do to win the Starbursts and cheddar Pringles.

"I'm done. Dad won't quit cheating," Ryder says dryly, tossing his cards onto the coffee table.

"Mijo! I'm insulted. I do not cheat." Alejandro places his neatly manicured hand over his heart, looking rightly offended.

"Mentiroso," Ryder mumbles under his breath, and I have no idea what that means, but hearing him speak Spanish like that makes my dick twitch.

"Ryder! I heard that."

"I know, Dad. I'm taking my snack choice because I should have won and because of your lies. Fallon can have that, plus one for his birthday."

It's like he could read my mind. I don't hesitate to reach forward and grab my haul, instantly peeling back the top of the Pringles and popping a stack of three into my mouth. I'm starving.

"You just had birthday pancakes," Joel says in astonishment.

"Do the appetites of teenage boys really surprise you anymore, my love?" Alejandro turns his amused eyes to me. "What do you want for your birthday dinner, Fallon?"

I pop more chips into my mouth and think.

"Anything," Uncle Joel insists.

"Steak," I answer because it's really the only nice food I know, and they look like they're expecting a nice choice.

"And anything else? Baked potato? Fries? Broccoli? Lobster?"

"All of it," I answer honestly if he's offering.

Sofie giggles, tearing open a bag of peanut M&M's. "You should come stay at our house sometimes. Georgina, our chef, would love you. Ry only ever wants chicken fingers or cheeseburgers."

"And pudding!" Ryder defends, causing everyone to laugh and maybe pull another little smile from me thinking back to that first day at lunch when he insisted I eat his tapioca.

"I saw that, Blue," he whispers into my ear.

I knew that sliver of joy breaking through the haze wouldn't go unnoticed by the golden boy. Of course he'd see. I'm trying not to let any defensiveness or resentment I've built up from my past affect my future with this family I seem to have found.

"I already texted her to make an ice cream cookie for Fallon," he declares proudly.

A chorus of praise rings out, and I'm pretty excited to try this birthday dessert.

Uncle Joel pulls his phone out. "I'm thinking we order in from the new steakhouse on Fifth Street. I'll check out the menu."

"Now isn't the time to take risks on a new restaurant. We need amazing food, guaranteed, tonight," Alejandro adds.

"Dad's a restaurant snob," Ryder whispers to me.

"Let's go to our house for dinner, then!" Sofie says with excitement. "I'll text Georgie that we want surf and turf with different potato options, some broccoli, pudding, and maybe an actual cake too. Since that's probably what Fallon is used to on his birthday. We can't deny him his own traditions." Her pink sparkly thumbs fly across the screen, and there's no time to argue, even if I had the energy or desire. "Sent. It's happening. Birthday party at our place!"

I don't miss the look that Ryder and his dad share, as if it's unusual for her to be excited to go to her house. I don't want to crush her spirit by telling her I don't want a party. Don't *deserve* a party.

Sofia grabs the remaining snacks, shoving them into her hoodie in massive handfuls until the pockets bulge. "Y'all are too old for all this candy anyway. It'll go straight to your asses!" she hollers as she scurries toward the staircase, giggling the entire way.

My smile threatens to break free completely, but the numbness stops it.

"Sofia Eleanor Cruz!"

"Sorry not sorry, Dad!"

And then a door slams shut before promptly reopening. "Oops! Sorry! Didn't mean that!" she calls downstairs. The door clicks shut quietly, then opens again ten seconds later. "Georgie says dinner will be ready at six sharp! But to come much earlier!"

The thought of all the food I requested being handmade just for me gets me excited for this dinner. I just need to find a way to sneak my birthday blunt before we go or take it with me.

"When do you want to leave?" Uncle Joel asks me.

"Whenever," I reply, decisive as ever.

"Oh, I need to ask you something about class," Ryder blurts. "Can we go to your room for a minute?"

I stare at him for a moment too long. He nods to the

side, indicating that I should follow him. I finally get my legs to work and trail after him upstairs.

"We'll leave in an hour! Pack a bag, Fallon!" Uncle Joel shouts after us.

I guess we're having a sleepover at the Cruz residence tonight.

I shut my bedroom door behind us. Ryder strolls over to my closet, grabbing a brand new gym bag with our school's athletic department logo imprinted on the side and tossing it to the bed. "Pack light, just some clothes. You can borrow my toiletries and stay in my room. I have a king-sized bed, but I still have my old bunk beds in the corner that I never got rid of. I blame Cole and Jamison. They won't let me." Ryder's smile is so charming and wide that I have to glance away, my skin prickling with new sensations and unfamiliar desires.

Bunk beds?

Strange at eighteen, but I've slept on way worse.

"Okay," I agree. "Can I smoke at your place?" I'm counting on the fact that it's my birthday and this is all I've asked for.

"Sure, dude. We have a few balconies with killer lake views, and we sort of live out in nature."

"Acadia Lake?" I ask, somewhat interested. I haven't seen the town's namesake yet, and the fact that Ryder's house is near the water makes me nervous. I don't know why he'd like me if he's that wealthy.

"Yeah. We've lived in that house my whole life. No one wants to be there anymore, though, not since Mom left."

Ryder clears his throat like he didn't mean to let that

slip, but I don't press him about it because I sure as hell don't want him asking about *my* mom.

"We have a fire pit in the backyard, a dock, two jet skis, and a speedboat."

I eye him speculatively. All that, yet he hates to be there? His mom must be shittier than mine to ruin a place like that for him. "Nice" is all I can manage at the moment.

Ryder gives me his easy-going smile, always cool, calm, and collected. Full of happiness and joy. He's sunshine and light, but I'm just darkness. The miserable, trap-you-in-it's-clutches type of dark that people avoid. He doesn't need me. None of them do.

I open my desk drawer and reach in the back, grabbing the eighth Ryder gave me at the party and the pack of blueberry haze blunt wraps. I shove the contraband into the inside zipper of my shitty backpack from home.

My notepad and Sharpies are already inside. I like to write with more than just black, and I got a new rainbow pack at the drugstore the other day. Blue is my second favorite, but there's something extra satisfying about the severe lines of thick black ink that really allow me to pour the pain out, leaving only numbness in its wake. The weed helps too. Alcohol. Anything really. I try to stick to music, though. Words. Because I *cannot* become my mother.

I'm lost in my head, not paying attention until a tall, strong body crowds me from behind, pressing his full length into my back and curling around me to whisper into my ear.

"I didn't really come in here to help you pack, Fallon."

Ryder wraps his arms around my torso from behind, hugging me tightly with my arms pinned to my sides. He buries his face into the crook of my neck, breathing deeply.

"Mmm. Fucking strawberries."

I shiver involuntarily at the feel of his breath tickling my sensitive skin. His full lips press into the tender flesh where my neck meets my shoulder, kissing and licking and sucking.

Fuck. It feels good. And that's part of the problem.

Ryder tries to make me *feel*.

I don't want to feel.

The past. It haunts me.

But I push it away and let the pleasure take over instead.

I drop my head back, allowing him to devour my neck, probably leaving more marks on my pale skin. My chest is heaving, and my lungs are demanding more oxygen. I'm dizzy as Ryder spins us, backing me into the wall and settling his knee between my thighs.

"What—" I don't get a chance to finish my question, and I can't even remember what it was going to be. Ryder gently lowers his mouth to mine, careful of my injuries, and kisses me tenderly. He slides his hands down my waist, gripping tightly, and flashes of last night pop in and out of my brain as he guides me to rock into his leg, cupping my jaw with his other hand.

I'm not used to this sexual stuff with guys or girls, but my dick is beyond hard right now as I grind into his thick thigh. I can't turn it off around Ryder. He gets me so worked up. Feeling brave and bold, I slip my hands under his cutoff and slide them up the hard ridges of his abdomen.

"You like that, Blue? Like touching my body while you get yourself off? Use me and make yourself come."

"Fuck. Ryder," I whimper, and I don't whimper. Ever.

What is he doing to me?

A sharp knock on the door halts all movements as we freeze.

"Hurry up, you guys! I'm ready to show Fallon my room!" Sofie whines from the other side of the door.

I can't help but snort. I've never had a little sister, but the massive cock-block that just occurred makes me wonder.

"Does that happen a lot?"

It's like he reads my mind when he answers, and Ryder gives me what I really want to know.

"I don't hook up with people."

People?

"Me neither," I tell him.

"Good." His hypnotic eyes bore directly into me, putting me in a trance. "We can pick up where we left off later. At my house." Then he leans down and presses his mouth to my ear, causing goosebumps to erupt and a shiver to run through me. "I'm excited to show you my room too." Ryder releases me from his leg and the wall, and I nearly slide to the floor. My knees are weak and shaking.

I don't know what's happening to me, but I know we're both going to have the worst case of blue balls at my birthday dinner.

CHAPTER TWELVE
RYDER

Fallon again devours his dinner, Georgie looking on with pride and admiration. He's so tiny, yet he just inhaled an entire filet, a lobster tail, and tried some of every side, including her weird little meat pies.

"I'm glad yer enjoyin' yerself, Fallon. It's nice for my culinary expertise to be appreciated by young folk every now and then. This one over here only eats children's food." She hikes a thumb to her left, pointing at me. Her long white braid rests over her shoulder like it always does when she's not cooking.

"Hey! I just ate a steak and a baked potato! Right in front of you. What the heck, Georgie? You're gonna side with all of them now? I see how it is. I'll remember it too."

"Don't take that tone with me, lad. And don't forget I know ye wet the bed 'til ye were ten."

"Georgie!"

How can she play me like that?

"That was fucking cold."

Sofie bursts out laughing, and now I'm regretting

inviting Georgie to join us for dinner, even though she *is* part of the family, and she *did* make everything.

She's like another grandmother to us. Abuela lives in Southern California with Aunty Marie, Dad's little sister. They live close to the border, near Mexico, where my dad's side of the family is from. We don't see her every day, so it's nice to have Georgie around to cook and help with things. When she's not being an asshole, that is.

I glance next to me and check to see if there's any way Fallon didn't hear that. Sometimes, he's in his own world, so there's a slight chance. But no can do; the sideways pull to his mouth and the slight tilt to his tempting-as-fuck lip ring tells me he's trying desperately not to smile or maybe even laugh at me.

Fuck. I wouldn't care if he laughed at me if it meant I could hear the sound. He barely speaks; I can't even think of what his laughter would be like. I need to know.

"Don't worry, Fallon. I won't drink too much before bed, but you can take the top bunk, just in case."

There's that awkward silence again that loves to happen in this household for some reason. Especially at family dinners, holidays, first meetings. . . important things like that. It must be a Cruz family tradition. *Swear to God.*

My sister comes in for the save again when a loud peal of laughter erupts from her lips, along with some tears.

"Joking. Obviously." Do I need to state the obvious? Fuck. It's obvious, right?

Fallon snorts, and I only hear it because I'm right next to him.

Sweet relief washes through me. I was once again convinced I fucked it all up, ruined what I thought was a growing friendship and maybe even more.

"How are you captain of the basketball team? You are

such a dork, Ry!" Sofie teases warm-heartedly. It's not like it's the first time I've heard that.

"Captain?" Fallon asks quietly from next to me.

"Yeah. Why? You didn't know?"

My family is still laughing at me and chattering away while Fallon speaks to me in our own little bubble.

"No. Guess not." He lifts one shoulder, idly pushing around the sad remains of Georgie's boiled bacon and cabbage that no one *ever* wants to eat. Not even Fallon.

"The big 'C' on my letterman jacket stands for captain," I inform him.

"Hmm," is all I get before he sets his fork down and leans back, folding his arms across his chest. I peer down at him, waiting for more. "Didn't notice."

My jaw ticks. I can't help it. Not because he didn't know I was captain. I don't give a shit about that. He seems completely and purposefully oblivious to his environment and those around him. Like he doesn't want to get too close. Doesn't want to *feel*. And that bothers me.

"Present time!" Sofie shouts from across the table, jumping from her seat and leaving her plate behind.

"I don't think so, missy! Come take yer plate to the sink and help clear the table. It was a group effort to make this mess, so it'll be a group effort to clean it. I'm off the clock as of six p.m. I'll take an espresso while yer up too. Thanks."

Sofie heaves a loud sigh before coming back and helping us clear the table, then using her favorite machine to make various lattes and espressos for everyone. She wants to become a barista at the local coffee shop downtown when she turns sixteen.

"Okay, that's done, and Sofie's right. Presents!" Joel exclaims giddily, a huge smile splitting his face. The pure joy emanating from him at having his nephew here and getting to celebrate his eighteenth birthday is endearing as fuck. Dad reaches over and squeezes the back of Joel's neck. I glance away at their display of affection.

Joel always has such a sincere, youthful attitude. I know it's one of the things that first drew my dad in. I also know my mom hates it even more that the man he left her for is thirteen years younger. It's the cherry on top of her shit sundae, but I can't feel bad. Not after the way she treated Dad.

The things she said to him, in front of Sofie and me five years ago when Sofie was only nine, can't be repeated. I can only hope she doesn't remember because it's seared into my brain for all time, taunting me with the harsh reality that I can never tell my mother my truth. Who I really am and the life I will eventually live. Well, after basketball.

Fuck, though!

The idea of waiting until my basketball career is over to come out publicly is becoming less and less appealing the more I'm around Fallon. It's getting harder to pretend I'm not gay. Harder to pretend I don't want to take Fallon out on a date. And the hardest to pretend the situation with Mom doesn't bother me. I'm so pissed at her. For all of us.

I shake my head, brushing my curls back with my hand and rubbing my brow. Why the fuck am I thinking about this shit right now? My breathing picks up, and my neck breaks out in a cold sweat.

Everyone's getting up from the table. I see their lips moving, but I can't hear them. I blink rapidly, trying to clear the darkening edges of my vision. I can't get enough oxygen, and my heart is beating too fast.

A small, warm hand grabs mine and steers it to his chest. I can't read lips, but I can read *his* right now.

Deep. Breaths.

Like I told him.

I watch his chest, feel the rise and fall, and close my eyes. I focus on breathing when Fallon does.

After a few minutes, my heart no longer feels like it's going double its speed, and I blink my eyes open slowly.

"Thanks for that. Did anyone see?" I ask awkwardly, rubbing a shaking hand across my forehead and down my face.

"No. They had already left."

Oh, thank fuck.

"I'm sorry, dude. I don't know what that was."

"Panic attack," he states matter-of-factly.

"Huh?" I don't get those.

He eyes me wearily. "You've never had that happen before?"

"No," I say, answering truthfully.

His voice gentles, the slightest emotion seeping in. "It's okay, Ryder. It used to happen to me a lot and still does sometimes," he confesses. I wonder if he's thinking about what happened on the couch. "What were you thinking about right before?" The look in his eyes is anything but probing. I swallow thickly, unsure if I should answer that question or not. Especially now, on his birthday.

I want him to open up to me so I can learn everything about him. I need to gain his trust, his loyalty. "My mom," I whisper, nearly choking on the word and hating myself.

"It's okay," he says again, earnest and understanding, nearly causing me to wince. "You don't need to tell me about it right now. I get it, okay? Believe me. I get it." His last words are sardonic, but they're not aimed at me.

We clearly have more in common than we even realize. And I think we both see that now as we sit at the dining room table, staring at each other, both a little lost.

"Let's go open your gifts, Blue," I say, wanting to change the subject and steer his birthday back on track. This isn't about me. This is *his* day. And *fuck* does he deserve to be celebrated.

When we walk into the living room, Joel, Sofie, and my dad shout *Surprise* at Fallon. They're all standing around a giant lump with a blanket over the top and a bunch of shiny wrapped gifts.

He doesn't react much.

"We didn't want to box it up or wrap it," Joel says, explaining why it's under a throw.

"And it's not a kitty! Unfortunately!" Sofie adds in, unhelpfully.

I shake my head, ignoring my little sister's strangeness and constant fixation on wanting a cat. It can't be healthy.

"Come in, boys. Fallon, we have lots for you to open!" My dad ushers us in, and we plop down on the loveseat together. Dad hands him a small box wrapped in shiny blue paper with a big silver ribbon tied on top.

"I wrapped that!" Sofie exclaims proudly. She really is good at wrapping gifts.

Fallon glances up and looks at her behind his curtain of blue hair. "Nice."

"Open it!" she insists.

He delicately and politely opens the gift, never tearing the paper too much. Inside is a brand-new iPhone 14. His eyes dart over to mine, wide and possibly freaking out inside. Okay, definitely freaking out inside.

I try to make it not a big deal because it really isn't to

someone like my dad. "Sweet, you have the newest model. I'm waiting two more months to upgrade."

"Me toooo! And I'm dying with the old model. I swear it's so slow," Sofie whines.

"Wow. Thank you. It's too much, though, really," he says, leaning forward and placing the phone on the coffee table separating us from the overstuffed gray couch my dad, Joel, and Sofie are piled on.

"I don't deserve it."

His words are soft and hesitant, but we all heard them. There's another awkward silence, so I guess he fits right in. Although this one isn't funny, this is sad.

Before I can jump in, Joel does.

"Fallon, please do not say that. We already talked about you not saying you can leave, and now I want to add this to the list. Because you deserve everything you're about to get and more, nephew. We all love you."

Fallon stares down at his hands, picking at the black nail polish that's lasted all week, mumbling a quiet "thanks." I know he's feeling uncomfortable with all the attention right now.

I subtly move my arm until it's touching his, trying to imbue some of my newfound calm into him. He helped me earlier, and I need to do the same. "Open the weird blanket gift," I suggest, nudging his smaller shoulder with my bicep.

"Do it!" Sofie shouts with enthusiasm.

Fallon stands up and reaches for the beige throw blanket draped over his gift, Joel helping to lift the other side straight up. Underneath appears to be a vintage record player but is completely modern and digital, with Bluetooth and the ability to stream music through the high-quality, built-in speaker system. I also know it cost fourteen hundred dollars and that Dad helped Joel get it to make Fallon's birthday special. He was more than happy to do so.

Fallon swoops all his hair back, holding it on top of his head, his face open and honest, vulnerable. "I. . . Wow. Uncle Joel, Alejandro. Thank you."

It's more than he usually says, and Sofie is once again awesome at moving the night along with her energy and enthusiasm. "Here, open mine next!"

Fallon opens a small box wrapped in metallic blue wrapping paper, pulling out a gift card.

"It's for the local music shop downtown. They have really cool clothes there too! A lot of vintage band tees. I think you'll be able to find a bunch of good stuff. So, I went a little extra and got you a hundred-dollar gift card."

"And after Sofie told me about the clothes they have there, I got you another gift card. So now you have two. For records and for some cool T-shirts. Happy birthday, Fallon," I tell him, staring up from my seat.

"Thank you, guys," he says simply, but Sofie beams from ear to ear.

"They serve coffee and do open mic nights on Saturdays. I go with Jamie and Cole sometimes. We don't sing, but some of the girls do."

"And I go a lot too! I'm going to be a barista at their events as soon as I'm old enough," Sofie informs him proudly.

Fallon hums his approval, and she hands him another present. We go through this process several more times as Fallon opens various items like a new photo frame for his room, socks, a couple new video games I recommended to Joel, and a new Acadia Lake Prep hoodie I got him from the school store. Joel said Fallon's uniforms will arrive tomorrow and to help him go through all the options. But I told him to mainly order button-ups and blazers. No one wears sweater vests.

"I don't know what to say. Thank you all." Fallon's voice is slightly raspy, and he's short for words again.

"Well, we're not done. There's a couple more, then we can finally enjoy Georgina's special ice cream cookie."

"Aye, lad. I only share me cookie on your birthdays."

That fucking awkward pause happens again, and I'd swear she was blood-related to us, except I'm not Irish. At all.

A burst of giggles explodes from Sofie, and she presses a hand to her lips, attempting to stifle them.

"That's. . ." More peals of laughter, pure joy tucked into every word as she chokes them out. "That's what she said."

"I suppose I asked for it there, didn't I? Ye little brat," Georgie teases with a warm smile, causing the skin around her eyes to crinkle.

"You walked right into that one," Alejandro concurs. "No one could have saved you."

Sofie laughs again, and so does everyone else. Except for Fallon. He's chewing on his lip ring and picking at his nails, like he's thinking about laughing, but maybe he can't remember how.

Joel stands from his spot on the couch and claps his large hands together, making a noise louder than he probably meant to. "Sorry for that sonic boom," he chuckles. "But let's get back on track with presents. One second."

I have no idea what else he's going to get. I thought this was everything.

Joel returns with a black guitar case and a worn-out-looking white envelope.

He sets the case down on the coffee table and hands the letter to Fallon.

"This was your dad's guitar. And he wrote that letter. Asked me to give it to you when you turned eighteen."

Fallon's trembling hand reaches out, but his face is blank, expressionless. He takes the paper from his uncle's grasp as if on auto-pilot. Fallon slowly and carefully opens the envelope, slipping the notebook paper out.

He unfolds it, his eyes scanning the words and stopping after what's probably just a few sentences. He glances up from the slightly crumpled paper, eyes locking onto mine as they swirl and storm with the deep emotions he normally keeps locked down. His face is usually an expressionless mask, but the pure agony shining through right now absolutely guts me.

"Fallon. . ." I whisper, unsure what I can do to help him. Maybe giving him this letter on his birthday wasn't the best idea, even if it was his father's wish. I glance at Joel and see the regret in his concerned gaze. He's thinking the same thing. This was a mistake, which is made clearer when Fallon abruptly stands from the couch, not even opening the guitar case.

"I can't," is all he says, but the words rip from him in a way I've yet to hear, and it's like a punch to my gut. He folds and stuffs the letter into his front pocket before he runs from the room, the back door slamming shut not even thirty seconds later.

The sound spurs me into action, and I jump from my seat, not wanting him to get far. He shouldn't be alone right now. He doesn't even know the property or the lake and woods. I slip my shoes on and grab my letterman jacket.

"I should have known better," Joel says in a defeated tone, but I know my dad and sister will handle his feelings. I just need to be there for Fallon. He has no one else right now, and I won't let him pull away. If he needs to talk, I'm ready to listen. And if he just needs to cry, I'm ready to hold him. And if he wants to fight, I'm ready to let him rage against me.

My feet pound down the wooden stairs of the back deck. The intense emotions flooding my system over this boy cause more adrenaline to shoot through me. My legs move faster, arms pumping wildly.

I need to make sure he's okay.

I don't like the thought of him being out here alone. In the wilderness, upset.

I know Fallon bottles things up and compartmentalizes his feelings, to put it mildly. He cuts his emotions off, and I'm worried it'll become too much when the pressure builds.

Something like tonight is all that was needed to tip him over the edge. And there he goes. Alone and vulnerable and possibly lost. In the woods. Or shit, the lake.

Panic sets in at the thought of him taking a boat alone at night. I head there first, my long legs eating up the distance across the lawn. But my fear is quickly dashed away when I spot a small shadow hunched over at the end of the dock.

Fallon.

CHAPTER THIRTEEN

FALLON

I had to get out of there. I couldn't sit with all of those eyes on me, like a thousand spiders crawling across my skin. I bolted. I don't care how it looked; I had to go.

And now, I'm sitting at the end of the dock, staring into the dark oblivion of Acadia Lake. The bright moonlight reflects off the shimmering surface, the stars twinkling around it. The obsidian waters try to lure me into their depths like a sailor lost to a siren's song. I lean forward, wondering if I can see my reflection in the darkness.

"What are you doing?!" Footsteps pound across the wooden planks behind me, and the sharp voice makes me jump. I start to waver on the very edge of the dock.

Ryder reaches down just in time and grabs me, wrapping his big arms around my torso and hauling me backward against his chest. He sits there with me on his lap, breathing heavily and resting his face in the crook of my neck.

He doesn't let go.

"What are you doing?" he repeats, calmly this time, but still out of breath.

My heart is racing, pounding against my ribcage angrily, demanding to feel something. But I don't want to.

"Blue. . ." The anguish in his tone catches me off guard. "Let me in." Then he presses his mouth to my ear like he did earlier. "Just a little."

I'm a mess. I'm a wreck. He'll just leave. Everyone does in one way or another.

The numbness is wearing off, and the regret is heavy. I lean back into Ryder's hard chest, wiggling the folded letter and my new stash box out of my front pocket.

How can a single letter be so precious, yet so devastating at the same time?

I hold it up, the small white square tormenting me. "Will you keep this? Don't read it, please. I couldn't get past the first paragraph," I admit.

He takes the note from my grasp, our fingers grazing and my breath hitching. "It's too painful to think about. The memories," I tell him.

"Of course I'll hold it for you. And you don't have to tell me anything, Blue. It's your birthday. But if it makes you feel better, feel free to unload. I'm here either way." He snuggles me closer, and I shiver at the contact.

"You cold?" he asks, and I guess I kinda am. It's not spring yet, and we're in northern California. It's definitely chilly.

Without waiting for my response, Ryder shrugs out of his letterman jacket and drapes it over my shoulders, letting it engulf me. He's a massively tall basketball player, and I'm just me. The kid who likes to dye his hair and write music.

We don't fit.

"Put your arms through," his voice is smooth, and my body listens, slipping them into his jacket. I let his lingering body heat seep into my bones and chase the chill away. The smell of his cologne has me turning my head and subtly sniffing at the collar. Bergamot and something spicy. Something *Ryder*.

I light up my birthday blunt and try not to worry about my dead dad's letter burning a hole in Ryder's pocket. Or my mom who abandoned me. Or the letter 'C' embroidered on my chest while I wear the captain of the basketball team's jacket. Or that we came in our underwear. Together.

I'm not prepared to think about that right now. *Any of it.*

The smoke flows through my lungs, absorbing the effects of the weed and numbing my mind and body. I relax into Ryder, closing my eyes and basking in the darkness.

He squeezes me tighter.

I don't want to be upset or relive painful memories, but he deserves to know a little.

"My dad got sick when I was twelve. Cancer. And I got angry. I wasn't there for him. I couldn't grasp the idea of no one helping him when he went into hospice. All those doctors around, and they just let him *suffer*? He died without me being there. It's not something I can ever fix or change." I have to live with this regret for the rest of my life, and it's why I prefer to be numb. But of course, I don't tell Ryder that part.

Ryder remains quiet, so I continue on. "I know my dad's guitar is in that case. I always thought my mother sold it for drugs or booze. I had no idea Uncle Joel had it this entire time." I pause for a moment, realizing I'm grateful for that fact. "I'm glad he had it so she couldn't get her crazy hands on it."

"I hear you about crazy mothers, dude. I'm sorry. And

I'm really sorry about your dad too." Ryder hugs me even closer, if that's possible, and I melt into him, his words soothing something inside of me. "I think you should consider talking to someone about it, or at least your uncle. I don't know all the details, but I do know there's nothing you should blame twelve-year-old Fallon for. You can always talk to me too. Okay?"

His words hit hard, and I can only nod and take another hit, finishing off my birthday blunt.

Nothing he says can change the fact that I wasn't there for my dad in the end. He was sick and dying, and I was too scared, too upset at the world to spend time with him.

That's enough talking for now.

Ryder squats down. "Here. Hop on. I'll give you a piggyback ride." He doesn't point out that I ran out here with no shoes or socks on, just like he didn't mention that I had no coat. Instead, he offered his own and is now offering to carry me.

"I'm fine," I mumble, not wanting to be a bother. My bare feet are cold and sore. I wasn't thinking. I hesitate at the edge of the dock, reluctant to step into the sandy grass that leads into the backyard.

"Just hop on, Fal. It's no biggie."

I accept his piggyback ride and press my chest to his back, wrapping my arms around his neck. Ryder stands, scooping me under my thighs and guiding my legs around his trim waist.

My dick is rubbing against the hard muscles of his back, and I understand now why grown men don't give each other piggyback rides. Dicks get in the way, and boners would be mortifying. As if the thought alone encourages it, my cock fills as Ryder bounces along the backyard with me clinging to his back.

"Don't drop me."

"You weigh a buck forty max. I won't."

I huff, a little indignant at his comment about my weight.

"I like your size," he corrects. "A lot."

My dick throbs, pulsing embarrassingly hard against his back. I throw his own words back at him. "Sorry. Just an automatic response to stimuli."

He laughs at that, "Touché."

We continue on, the backyard a long expanse of rolling hills that are perfectly landscaped, surrounded by ancient pines and towering redwoods. It's nothing like Philly. The moonlight enhances the surreal aspect of it and the pure, raw beauty of nature. I wouldn't want to get lost out there.

"So, if you're feeling up for it, we should at least go back and have your ice cream cookie. I've been excited for you to try it, and I know Sofie is too. You don't have to open the guitar," he adds.

"Okay," I agree, not wanting to upset my uncle and his new family. They've been nothing but accepting and giving toward me.

"Okay," he echoes, backing me up. "Let's do this." Ryder hitches me higher up his back, my dick rubbing against him harder, rougher.

"Ry," I warn, pressing my hips firmly into him so he knows exactly what I'm warning him about. Need I remind him of how easy it can happen for me when I'm around him?

"Sorry," he chuckles. "I'll try not to bounce so much. You can't go in there with a hard-on. Georgie will call you out and never let you live it down, no matter what just happened."

"Shit," I say, because wow, that's harsh. But then again, she did say that Ryder wet the bed until he was ten.

"She has no filter. Says it's an Irish thing." He shrugs his massive shoulders, even with the heavy weight of my body on his back and my arms around his neck.

"Put me down, then." Not sure my dick will go down otherwise.

"Not yet. Let's get to the deck first."

I don't argue, just resting my chin on his shoulder as we bounce along the backyard to his massive home.

When we get to the deck, Ryder lets go of my legs, and I slide down his back until my feet touch the cold cement stepping stone.

"Should I apologize to everyone?" I ask, unsure exactly how I came across earlier when I ran out of there.

"No. Never. Not for your emotions."

I swallow thickly at his vehemence. "I'm ready," I tell him, smoothing my jeans. I start to take his letterman jacket off.

"Keep it. For now. It gets pretty cold at night."

"Okay," I don't put up a fight. I like it, and I like the way it smells. I like *him*.

"Okay," he echoes, and we stand at the bottom of the steps in the dark and what feels like the wilderness. At least compared to where I come from.

"They can't see us down here."

"Huh?" His pale green eyes are glowing, reflecting the moonlight and distracting me from all rational thought.

"I'm going to kiss you now, Blue."

"Okay." Fuck. Why can't I think of anything more eloquent? But he doesn't seem to mind the parroted response when he lowers his full lips to mine, pressing them firmly against my flesh. We don't have a lot of time before someone else comes looking for us, I'm sure.

I loop my arms around his neck, and he runs his hands down my back. I jump and wrap my legs around his waist, his big hand splayed under my bottom.

He walks us backward or forward, fuck, I don't know. My head is dizzy, and my mind is spinning. He pins me against the hard, stone exterior of the house, but the warmth of Ryder's jacket and the searing hot press of his lips keep the bitter cold away. I'm burning up inside; the one emotion with no leash flares to life the only way it knows how to when I'm around Ryder.

Lust blazes bright, and I kiss him deeper, rolling my tongue against his own. I press my heels into his ass and use the leverage to grind into him.

I don't know what I'm doing, but I don't care as I continue to hump him and chase the high I've so desperately needed since I woke up.

He pulls away. "They'll come looking soon."

"I know," I pant. Double blue balls are going to kill me.

I chase his mouth, taking his kisses.

Ryder gives my bottom a firm squeeze before lowering me, never breaking the connection between our bodies or lips.

After a few more nibbles and licks, he pulls away.

"We gotta stop."

I agree, so I take two steps back, breaking the spell.

Ryder holds one palm out flat. "Let's go inside for real this time. I want you to try to enjoy the rest of your birthday, and let's start with Georgie's giant cookie."

We both pause, and it's like he just asks for it. They all do this. The outrageous statements.

I snort at his antics, always trying to get me to smile or laugh. I'm starting to wonder if it won't be long before he succeeds.

Ryder bursts out laughing at his joke and slings a heavy arm around my shoulder, steering us back toward the stairs and the rest of my birthday party.

Ryder's lounging on the loveseat, his long legs sticking off the end ridiculously. He's playing some fast-paced, *Tetris*-looking game on his phone, his long slender fingers tapping and sliding across the screen.

New thoughts swirl in my mind, things I've never desired before. Not until Ryder Cruz.

How would it feel for those long, lean fingers to trail circles across my bare skin, teasing me as they work lower and lower—

"You can keep that in your room," Uncle Joel tells me after everyone retired to bed except him and Ryder.

I shake the lusty thoughts from my mind and try to understand what he's saying. The confusion must show on my face.

"The guitar," he clarifies.

"Okay," I agree. It *is* mine. I don't expect him to store it in his closet. Uncle Joel's house isn't that big.

"I'll take your gifts home, though. Enjoy the rest of your birthday, nephew." Uncle Joel squeezes my shoulder as he walks by, thankfully understanding I'm not available for a hug now. Everything is just too raw. "Goodnight. Happy birthday, Fallon."

"Thank you," I mumble. "For all of it."

His big hand gives me another firm squeeze. "Love you, kiddo."

He walks away, not expecting or waiting for recip-
rocation.

As soon as Uncle Joel disappears up one side of the
grand staircase, strong arms wrap around me like they
always do. "Ready for bed, birthday boy? You can have the
bunks to yourself, or you can share the king with me. Your
choice. No pressure either way. It's just sleeping." He
penguin-walks us toward the stairs, toward his room.
Because regardless of which bed I pick, I am one hundred
percent sleeping in Ryder Cruz's bedroom. I'm sure most of
the girls at school would be jealous.

It has me wondering. . .

"Do you like girls?"

His answer is swift, and there's zero hesitation. "No."
Then he licks my ear, still wrapped around me like a cuddly
koala. My whole body shivers involuntarily.

So he's gay?

"Where are you sleeping tonight, Blue?" he whispers
dangerously, doing that thing where he presses his mouth
directly to my ear. Electricity shoots through me, jolting my
cock, and attempting to jump-start my heart.

"In your bed," I answer breathlessly.

I need more. I need to take my mind off of everything.
My face throbs with the memory of fists coming at me, and
my eyes burn at the thought of what that letter might say.

Does he blame me for not being there?

"Stop thinking. Let's go upstairs and lemme make you
feel better."

It's like he can read my mind, knows my desires. I'm
desperate for him, for his touch. I want to feel something. *I
need to forget.*

CHAPTER FOURTEEN

RYDER

"It's still your birthday. Let me give you one last present," I tell him, encouraging him to say yes.

I've been holding back my desire to be with a guy for years, and now that I have this amazing person right in front of me, I need to put my hands all over him. My lips. Maybe drag my tongue across his—

"Okay." Fallon's quiet response cuts off my deviant thoughts, and I straighten up, focusing on the boy in front of me.

I grab his hand and lace our fingers together, pulling him upstairs. I've never had anyone in my bed before. Not even Cole or Jamison. I have bunk beds, so they've never needed to.

My mind is a jumble of nerves, and I shake unnecessary thoughts of my best friends out of my head. When we get to my room, I shut the thick wooden door and lock it behind me.

I let go of his hand and walk over to my sound system, turning it on and connecting my phone. I select my sexy playlist, not that I've ever used it with anyone, and let the sensual sounds of "Wicked Games" by The Weeknd slowly pour from the speakers.

When I turn around, Fallon is perched on the edge of the mattress, his blue hair covering one eye, expression unreadable.

That won't do.

I stalk forward, crowding him onto the bed as I peer down into those stormy blue eyes that hypnotize my thoughts. I force him to lean back. He stares up at me, the moment intense and the music matching.

"I'm going to make you feel good. Just let me. Okay?" My question is vulnerable, and his answer is no different.

"Please, Ryder." The emotion swirling in his eyes and words is a stark contrast to the blank expression I usually see.

I brush his hair back roughly, peering down at him. I curl my hand into the soft strands, fisting them and tugging a little, causing Fallon to close his eyes and whimper. I let go, enjoying the control he lets me have. "Lie back."

His eyes pop open, but he listens, slowly leaning back on his elbows, staring at me with a hooded gaze. He's high from the blunt, and his pupils are blown.

I crawl on the bed after him, straddling his lap.

"Arms up."

Fallon listens, and his submission is a beautiful thing.

I slip the hoodie and shirt off in one go, and he rests back on his elbows again. I peer down at him, and my cock fills at the sight of his lean, slim body. His toned muscles are trim, and he has zero body fat, causing every ridge to stand out in stark relief. "Fuck, Fallon. You are so goddamn hot."

I'm not sure it's possible, but his pupils dilate even further, the black taking over the blue like some kind of sex-crazed demon. I seize the opportunity and undo his pants until he's lying before me in his tight, black boxer briefs. His pale skin is flawless. His body is petite and sexy.

Still on top, I slip my fingers into the waistband of his underwear. I give him a questioning stare, and he chews on that lip ring, his Chapstick shimmering and making me even hotter and ready for what I'm about to do.

He nods once and lifts his hips. I curl my fingers into his boxers, my skin cool against his warm flesh, and pull them down. His erection springs free, bouncing between us, and I'm glad he's such a chill person because I am freaking out inside right now.

He's so fucking sexy. Not overly large, but he's proportionate to his size, and I'm dying for a taste. His cockhead is swollen, the skin shiny and pink. I slowly reach out, giving him time to stop me, and wrap my hand around him. I squeeze firmly as I begin to stroke him.

I had plans to swallow his cock whole, but Fallon surprises me and speaks up, voicing his wants. I'm a goner, so I'll do whatever he asks.

"Aren't you going to let me see you too?" He slides his hands under my hoodie, running them along the ridges of my abdomen and up to my pecs, brushing across my nipples and making me shiver.

He curls his hands over my shoulders and squeezes, kneading the muscles. Fuck, it feels good, and it's making me so goddamn horny. When his hands trail back down, he stops at my nipples and squeezes both, pinching them hard, and *holy shit,* I like it. I moan out loud, closing my eyes as my dick throbs painfully in my jeans.

"Take them off," he tells me, and I scramble off the bed, quickly and shamelessly getting naked as he lounges back on his elbows. His adorably pink cock stands proudly between a patch of neatly trimmed dark blond curls, and I yank my briefs down, letting my erection spring free. I'm nine inches when fully erect. I've measured.

Fallon's cock twitches as he stares at me, eyes nearly closed with need and a heady desire. The lust in the room is heavy, the air thick with it.

I crawl on top of him, staring down as our cocks graze. "I've never been with anyone," I tell him before we do this.

"Me neither," he confirms what I already suspected.

It doesn't ruin the moment or slow the momentum when I kiss him deeply, tangling my tongue with his and sucking on it, causing him to moan into my mouth. Fallon spreads his legs wider, and I settle in between. I can't stop kissing him, but I need something from my bedside table.

"Scoot up," I instruct, and he slides up the bed with my help, careful not to agitate his bruising.

I rummage in my drawer until I find the small bottle of lube I use to jerk off and quickly pour some into my hand as another song by The Weeknd comes on. "High for This" filters through my speakers as Fallon spreads his legs even wider, neither of us knowing exactly what we're doing. We just go with what feels right, what feels good. I lean over him on one forearm and peer down as I slot our dicks together and stroke us once.

Oh fuuuuck.

Fallon groans, and my eyes roll into the back of my head. The slippery, slick feel of his cock against mine has me wanting to instantly unload my nuts as I give us another firm tug.

"Not gonna last."

His words echo my exact thoughts as I continue to stroke and twist and twirl my slippery hand over both of our cocks. Fallon locks his legs around my waist and begins to thrust into my hand, forcefully rubbing our cocks together, and holy fuck, that's it.

I'm a goner.

I pull back, jacking myself off fiercely as I shoot loads of jizz all over his chest and abs. His cock too.

Fallon is rock hard, his dick an angry red color, demanding release. I scoop up my cum as he lies before me, vulnerable and relaxed.

As he should be around me.

I press two slippery fingers against his taint, teasing him and testing his reaction. He closes his eyes and pushes his bare feet against the bed, trying to make me touch him where we both want. I chuckle, excited for future possibilities, but I'm not sure he's ready for that yet.

I return to his cock, stroking fast, while I rub my other hand all along his inner thigh, massaging him, making him feel good like I said I would. He's so comfortable, so open with me. He closes his eyes, letting out a long, low moan as his hips thrust up in one last move, spurting load after load onto his stomach and my hand.

"Fallon."

His eyes pop open, glassy and bloodshot.

I lift my hand to my mouth, his cum dripping between my fingers. I stick two of them into my mouth down to the knuckles, dragging them out.

His throat bobs as he swallows thickly.

I release them with a pop, grinning wickedly. "Happy birthday."

Once I'm certain Fallon is asleep, his soft snores sounding like an adorable little puppy, I sneak out of my bed and over to my jeans, grabbing Fallon's dad's letter. I respect his wishes, not opening it and keeping it safe instead.

I pad over to my mahogany jewelry box with the little glass doors that house my St. Christopher chain and the few nice watches I own. I open one of the small drawers and lift the false bottom, tucking Fallon's letter there for safekeeping.

He opened up, just a little, like I asked him to. I wasn't sure of the circumstances of his dad's passing, but now that I know he got sick and Fallon feels like he wasn't there for him, it makes me hurt for him.

He carries all of this blame and self-hatred because of it. Add in an unsupportive, absentee mother, and my stomach turns thinking about how alone he's felt for the last five or six years. I hope he talks to Joel about it. He can't go on like that.

I turn around and peer at the boy occupying my every thought and all of my worries. He's fast asleep on his stomach, arms tucked under his pillow, mouth slightly parted. Slivers of moonlight pierce through the closed blinds and illuminate his creamy, unblemished skin. The bedding is pushed down to his knees, and the delicate curve of his bare ass tempts me.

His looks captured me, his aura ensnared me, and now his soul calls to mine.

He barely speaks, yet I'm fascinated by every word. He's the most interesting person I've ever met, regardless of the fact that his uncle and my dad might get married.

I tiptoe back to him as quietly as I can and brush the blue hair out of his face, peering down at the serene look on his delicate features. He's usually so somber, so indifferent.

Smudges of black eyeliner darken his under eyes, along with some bruising. I pull the sheet and comforter up to his neck, tucking him in and making sure he's warm.

I can't sleep right now. Not after everything that happened tonight. The good and the bad. My mind won't turn off, won't settle. It's exhausting.

Fear takes hold of me; its grip is so tight I can hardly breathe. I need him closer to me. Need to feel him.

I crawl back into bed, even though I'm restless and antsy. I tug Fallon to me, cocooning his smaller body with mine and attempting to relax.

"Ry?" he mumbles, half asleep.

"Yeah. Shh. I just need to hold you."

Fallon sighs contentedly and settles into me. I let his deep, rhythmic breaths attempt to lull me to sleep.

I can't change what happened tonight. I can only move forward.

CHAPTER FIFTEEN

RYDER

A nother week of school passes in a blur of basketball and studying. I've had to focus on getting to the championship while keeping my grades up, so I feel like I haven't seen Fallon in a while. And we haven't stayed over at his uncle's place all week. Dad's been at his new restaurant in LA handling some kind of major meltdown, and Georgie and I have been holding down the fort here.

I hope he doesn't think I'm trying to ghost him. Most nights, I've passed out after basketball, homework, and dinner. But now that I have Fallon in my life, I want to make his *friendship* a priority too.

"There's another party this weekend. Wanna go?" I ask, dipping some fries into ranch and shoving them into my mouth. It's Friday, and the cafeteria is bustling with gossip and excitement before the weekend. The playoffs start next week, so it's going to get wild like it always does.

"Probably not after last time," he says dryly.

"Fair point, but I got you, really. You know you can trust me. I won't let you out of my sight. You'll have to piss in front of me too. And I won't close my eyes. I'll just keep them at eye level."

He snorts like he always does. "Stop. I'll go."

Score!

"Sweet. Alright, well, just to warn you, it's a Jefferson High party this time."

He doesn't react, which isn't unusual, but I feel the need to clarify. "The public school."

Nothing.

"Dustin the cunt will be there."

His normally guarded eyes dart up to mine, flashing brightly for a moment. He's angry.

"No takebacks. You have to go with me." It's immature, but I want to hang out with him, and all of my friends will be at the JHS party on the lake.

It's technically public property down by the shore, but it's put together by the girls over at Jefferson every year before the playoffs start. It can be fun, but they always get drunk and giggly and pressure me to hook up. Especially Cassandra. It makes me uncomfortable. And never works.

"There's a bonfire," I tell him, mistaking his silence for disagreement.

He reaches over and dips a handful of his own fries into my ranch cup, humming his approval when he tries it. I smirk; everything tastes better dipped in ranch. Wait 'til he tries pizza.

"Said I would go," he mumbles around a mouthful.

That was easy. "Okay."

"Okay," he echoes.

"I need to run to my place after school to get ready, but I'll drop you off, then come back and get you before the party."

Fallon just nods, continuing to dip his food into my

ranch. I normally don't like double-dippers, and I normally wouldn't be too happy with someone eating my precious ranch, but Fallon can get away with anything as far as I'm concerned.

"Did I hear *party*?" Cole asks as he drops his tray in front of us, plopping down and bumping the table, causing our drinks to rattle.

"Yeah. We're going to the Jefferson party tonight."

He grins wide, his hazel eyes twinkling and his shaggy light brown hair looking extra messy. My eyes dart to the cafeteria entrance as Gracie Sinclair casually struts in, subtly fixing her uniform skirt and smoothing her long auburn hair. She's a cheerleader and Cole's on-again-off-again girlfriend.

"Seriously?" I complain. He spirals into recklessness every time she gives him a scrap of attention and then takes it away. I hope it lasts longer than a lunch-period hookup this time. I swear this happens once a month, and it's probably overdue.

"She was begging for it, Ry. You know I'm a pleaser," Cole tips his head back and cackles loudly, drawing attention like always. Gracie's eyes dart to our table and narrow. It doesn't look good for Cole.

I sigh, expecting the worst from him tonight after the death glare he just received. There's no point in bursting his bubble now. I'm sure she'll corner him before next period. Jamie and I have learned to stay out of Cole and Gracie's relationship drama.

"Laughing at your own jokes again?" Jamie asks, taking his seat next to Cole.

"Nah. Not jokes. Just realities. My girl can't stay off this dick."

"Dude. How many times have I told you not to kiss and

tell? You shouldn't talk about Gracie like that," Jamison chastises.

"We didn't kiss! Unless you count oral."

Cole can be a pig; there's no denying that. Jamie and I try to help him be better. I glance at Fallon out of the corner of my eye to gauge his reaction, but it's useless. He's completely shut down.

Fallon is a fortress with steel shutters, reinforced doors, and a panic room in the basement. He continues eating his lunch, ignoring the drama around him, which I like.

I like it a lot.

"Not even two minutes after you walked in, all mused up, you're laughing with your friends, like a hyena on acid, in the middle of the cafeteria. Then Gracie walks in, looking the same. I saw it all from the lunch line, Cole. You look like an asshole, and I'm telling you how it is." Jamie is frank, but he cares. He always tries to help his friends, especially if there's some sort of self-destructive behavior going on. Cole's parents are never around, and he has no one but Jamie, me, and the team. And sometimes Gracie.

"Shit. Whoops. Guess you're right. I'll just make it up to her tonight." He wiggles his eyebrows obnoxiously, then mumbles, "If you know what I mean," out of the side of his mouth. I roll my eyes at how ridiculous he can be. And exhausting. Jamie can be on drunk Cole duty tonight. I'm going to have my eye on Fallon.

"It's on the shore again," I inform them, giving Cole a warning glance. Last time, he got drunk and attempted to take the jet skis out. They weren't his, and they weren't mine, either. We weren't at our docks, but his intoxicated brain couldn't understand that. It was a fight to get him away from the heavy machinery.

Cole holds his hands up. "I'll be good. Promise."

Jamie rolls his eyes, a small smile curving his lips. The two of them have been friends longer than us, practically since birth, because their parents are best friends. "You're clueless if you believe yourself, dude," Jamie replies dryly, and Fallon snorts.

Score one for Jamie!

"Hey! Don't all three of you gang up on me! No fair. Gracie did too. *Dang*. Everyone hates me today."

"We love your crazy ass, and you know it." I pick up a fry and toss it across the table at him, but he leans forward, catching it in his mouth instead.

Cole throws his arms up in triumph, making a scene like always. I glance at the cheerleader's table where Gracie and her friends sit and don't miss her massive eye roll. He's outrageous, yes. But she's too hard on him and kinda mean.

"Let's rideshare so we can all get fucked up," Cole declares loudly as Mrs. Lee walks by, giving us a stern and disapproving glare.

"Whoops." He lowers his voice by fifty percent but repeats himself. "As I was saying, let's Uber so we can all get fucked up tonight."

I glance over at Fallon, searching his face. "Cool with you?"

He lifts a shoulder, continuing to eat his lunch.

I turn back to Cole. "Sounds good, dude."

"Yeah. I'm cool with whatever," Jamie agrees. "I don't want to drive."

"Same," I add.

"You got weed? I'm almost out," Fallon asks Cole, speaking softly.

"I got you, don't worry. It's gonna be a good night. We'll show you a proper Acadia Lake party and make up for what happened last time 'cause that was bullshit. You'll see. It can be fun, and the public school kids can be chill. Most of them."

I get an uneasy feeling in the pit of my stomach, hoping we have a good time tonight.

The bonfire burns bright, orange flames dancing against the dark waters of Acadia Lake. The waves lap against the sandy shore, adding to the chill vibes. Some parts of the shore are made entirely of pebbles and stones, making it a bitch to walk on, especially when you're drunk. But this is the spot. Always has been.

"Drinks," Cole declares loudly over the rock music blaring from the open truck doors where everyone parked.

We head to the huge plastic tub filled with ice, and Cole and Jamie drop off our twelve packs, grabbing a cold one for each of us. These parties are public school style and work on donations, which is sort of genius if you ask me. You can't drink without dropping off more than you plan to consume.

"What do you want? They have a few different kinds of beer and some wine coolers. That's it."

"Whatever."

I reach into the ice bath and grab the most palatable beer available, tossing it to him and forgetting he's not one of my teammates a second too late.

He fumbles with the slippery can but doesn't drop it.

"Shit. Sorry."

"It's fine." He pops the top of his beer, holding the can away from his body when it foams over. He takes a big slurp, and his tongue darts out to lick away a lingering droplet.

I force my gaze away. I can't get caught staring. *We* can't get caught. Whatever this is.

All I know is that remembering his smaller frame dwarfed in my letterman jacket does all kinds of primal, caveman things to me. Which is *exactly* why I'm wearing the jacket tonight and not him. I can't risk getting drunk and seeing him in it. I might toss him down in the dirt, in front of the fire, and claim him for everyone to see.

I take a swig of my beer, pushing thoughts of Fallon wearing only my letterman jacket away. Thoughts of him on his knees in my letterman jacket, bent over in my letterman jacket, and on top of me wearing my letterman jacket.

Shit.

I chug the rest of my drink and grab another before we move to the fire. Fallon eyes me curiously, but I shrug, unwilling to share my dirty fantasies with him.

Jamie and Cole slip away to find the other guys, and I grab the best seats for us—two folding lawn chairs—and set them up with a lake and a bonfire view. Kids are sprinkled all over the shore and clustered around the fire in small groups.

"Mason's so drunk, he can't even play his guitar! We've got no live music, so now Gracie, Alexis, and I can't sing," Taylor, the head cheerleader with white blonde hair, whines as she plops down next to us. Her two friends pile on top.

I glance at Fallon, unwilling to call him out in a crowd of people but also dying to see him play. *Hear* him play. I catch his gaze and nod encouragingly.

I know he's introverted, but he also loves music and songwriting. This would be good for him. Push him out of his comfort zone and make him open up more.

"I play," he says quietly, the crackling and popping of the fire drowning him out. Before I have to speak up and repeat what he said, Gracie registers his words.

"Wait, what? Oh my God!" She nudges her friends. "He plays guitar! What's your name again? I love your hair!"

"Fallon," he mumbles shyly. He seems unaccustomed to female attention, and for some reason, that makes me want to fluff up my feathers and get him to notice me instead.

"Yes! Fallon, with the save! She was going to pout all night, I just know it. Now I might get some!" Cole leans over the back of my chair and whisper-shouts into my ear. He unfolds his chair, setting up shop right next to us, on the other side of the girls.

Fallon accepts the guitar from Mason's best friend, Ezra. "Thanks," he mutters with a rough voice, his blue hair hiding half his face. He begins to tune the guitar, strumming chords while tightening and loosening the strings.

"Do you know any Taylor Swift?" Taylor asks ironically, her long blonde hair and blunt bangs adding to the argument.

In a rare show of public emotion, blood rushes to his cheeks, and he mumbles, "A few." Gracie and Alexis squeal, and Fallon's blush deepens in the flickering campfire. I like it. I like him. I *want* him. *So fucking bad.*

"You pick. I know everything. Test me," she encourages.

Fallon glances over at me, then back to the girls piled together on the fold-out lounging lawn chair. "'Sad Beautiful Tragic.'"

The girls are speechless for a moment.

"Taylor's Version," he adds confidently, and my lip quirks. Fucking adorable.

"Yesss! One of my favorites. So lovely. Ready when you are, new friend." She winks at him, but Fallon doesn't acknowledge her, just ducks his head and starts strumming a slow, beautiful melody. A song I've never heard before.

Taylor's soft, honey-sweet voice flows out effortlessly and, combined with Fallon's acoustic guitar skills, is captivating.

They sound amazing, like they've practiced together for years. It's incredible. Everyone nearby seems to think so too, because a crowd gathers.

I expect Fallon to bow out after one song because of the attention, but then he starts to really get into it, tapping his foot and bobbing his head. He hums in the background, harmonizing with Taylor, and I'm completely speechless. I knew he liked to write, but his voice, even just a hum, is fucking special. Raspy and a little scratchy, it offsets hers brilliantly, and the performance ends way too soon.

Everyone is quiet for a moment, shocked by what we just witnessed.

"Ho-ly shit! That was jizz-in-my-pants amazing!"

Aaaand Cole's tipsy.

"I'm next!" Gracie shouts.

"Oh, can't we do a duet, Grace? I don't want to miss out before he gets too drunk like the rest of the guys," Alexis whines.

I glance at Fallon and see him guzzling his beer before accepting another from Cole and wiggling the little stash box out of his front pocket.

"Good point," I tell them.

"Okay, fine. I guess you're probably right. Um. Let's see." Gracie taps her pointy nude nail against her lips before beaming at Fallon. "Hey, Fallon. Do you know any Ed Sheeran?"

He lights the blunt he just placed between his lips,

stoking the cherry to life before answering her with a quick nod.

Gracie and Alexis both name a song, but Fallon doesn't know either. He hits the blunt two more times before offering it to me, but I pass it to Jamie. I'm not big on smoking, so I take a swig of my beer before it turns warm and tastes like piss.

"'Photograph,'" Fallon says, and it takes me a second to register that he's naming a song.

"Oh yes! I love that song so much! Alexis, let's alternate verses. I'll go first. You sing the chorus, and I'll harmonize with you."

"Sounds good! Ready, Fallon?" Alexis asks him, sweeping her long braids over her shoulder and tugging her hot pink cropped jacket tighter around her slim waist.

"Yeah," is all he says, but his eyes are half-lidded now. He looks like he's about to fall asleep or fall out of his seat, but instead, he begins strumming away. The melody is calming, and the lyrics are raw as Gracie starts singing low and breathy, building her voice before Alexis joins in for the chorus. Fallon doesn't sing since there're already two of them, but he glances at me several times in between. I watch his fingers slide up and down the strings, fascinated and dying to feel his touch on my body again. I take a big swig of my cold beer, hoping to cool the raging fire building inside. I can't get a boner at the bonfire. That's weird.

Just as the song ends, cheers and claps erupt from everyone enjoying the mini concert on the shore.

I wonder if he'd ever sing for me?

The thought has me chewing on my bottom lip, thinking about how sexy it would be if he did it in just his underwear. My eyes drag over his body, practically undressing him.

Jamie clears his throat, lifting one eyebrow in a 'be care-ful' way. He comes over, squatting next to me and tipping his beer back. "You're staring at your possible future step-cousin again. Like you want to push him down into the dirty sand and mount him like a horny dog. Cool the come-fuck-me look, 'kay? Or you're going to out yourself."

Jamie's words are blunt yet spoken with zero judgment. They're also sobering as fuck. I need to be more careful. I can't risk basketball, and I don't want to deal with any pressure from Dad to be myself. Or any bullshit from my mother.

My best friend knows what I need and has another beer ready for me after I chug my current one.

Fuck.

I want Fallon, but I don't think I can have him. At least not in public.

"Another song!" Taylor shouts, but a raindrop plops on my hand and then another. I stare at the lake, squinting and barely making out the tiny ripples in the water as each rain-drop makes contact, peppering the surface with little bullets.

"Ahh! It's raining so soon! The party just started!" The girls squeal, worried about their hair and shoes, and Ezra grabs the guitar from Fallon. Everyone makes a break for their cars, and we tag along with Ezra, not waiting for an Uber.

"Move it to my house! Spread the word! We aren't ending the annual kick-off party early! A little rain won't stop us!" Cole shouts, and I guess his parents are out of town again. Not surprising.

"You an academy kid?" Jackson Evans asks Fallon with eager excitement, and my hackles rise. He's known for being *very* friendly to *everyone*. I left Fallon alone in the kitchen for two minutes to use the bathroom, and I come back to see Jacks looming over him, one hand on the wall above his head, caging him in. I know Fallon's uncomfortable with it, even through his expressionless mask.

"Hey, Jackson! How you been, man?" I ask casually, grabbing a bottle of water from the fridge. "I see you've met my friend, Fallon. He's Coach Rivers' nephew," I inform him, hoping he backs off. I don't need to puff my chest out, Jamie's words circling back to me, but fuck do I want to. I want to drag Fallon upstairs to an empty bedroom, pull his pants down, bend him over, and bury my face in his ass.

Fuuuuck me.

I swallow thickly and crack the cold water open, guzzling half of it to cool my heated thoughts. I'm getting too drunk and apparently too horny.

I don't have to worry about Jackson much longer because Raphael, one of my teammates, comes bursting into the kitchen in a drunken stupor, demanding we make a victory cake.

"Our school colors. Just to fuck with all the Jefferson kids," he snickers, either not realizing Jackson is right here or not giving a fuck.

Before I step in and stop the inevitable mess and definite fire hazard of Raph's drunken, manic idea, a commotion at the front door distracts us both.

Dustin and Rich stroll through the open-plan living room, and I clench my jaw hard, nearly cracking my wisdom teeth.

Why would they come here?

Cole struts into the living room next, a beer in hand and a look of pure delight etched across his face.

Fuck, this can't be good. Even with Jamie hot on his heels, ready to stop whatever rash decision he's likely to make.

"Dustin Flynne." Cole's tone is full of accusation.

"I was invited," he answers cockily.

Cole scoffs, "To *my* house? I don't think so. When I said the party could move here, that didn't include you." Then he leans in close, but I'm right next to them, ready to intervene if needed. "Get the hell out of here, you fucking predator. You've attacked two of my friends. One being a fourteen-year-old girl. Get out of my house. Before I call my dad and get my own ass in trouble just to serve you yours."

Shit. I hope he doesn't do that. Mr. Jensen is scary, and also the district fucking attorney.

Dustin pales, as does Rich.

"Does that apply to me too? I didn't attack anyone." Rich holds his hands up and steps away from his so-called friend.

What loyalty.

Dustin narrows his eyes at his friend but doesn't speak up, likely realizing he would have done the same thing.

"I did not *attack* Sofie. Don't be ridiculous. I like her. I want to take her out. We were both drunk, and it was nothing. And I beat the shit outta your little girlfriend with the pretty pink lips because he fucking deserved it. The freak."

I step forward, along with Jamie. All three of us crowd Dustin and Rich. "That's my little sister. You will *never* take her out. It wasn't nothing. Would you have kept going if Fallon hadn't walked in? *Huh?* You fucking creep." I shove him hard, and he stumbles back a few steps, his back hitting the kitchen island, making him wince.

Good.

"And don't you ever speak about any of my friends again. You're the freak. Sick fuck," I sneer through tightly clenched teeth.

"You're overreacting. All of you. Bunch of pussies." Dustin throws his hands up. "Forget it. I can't keep fighting. My dad's been on my ass," he mumbles the last part. "I'm outta here."

"You too, Rich," Cole adds in a sharp tone, pointing toward the front door. *"Leave."*

Rich huffs but doesn't put up a fight, leaving with his friend. As long as Seth isn't here, we can all have a good night.

CHAPTER SIXTEEN

FALLON

After Dustin and Rich leave, tensions settle, and my buzz finally kicks in. I'm not sure if I'm on my sixth or seventh beer, but I've kept pace with Ryder, Jamie, and Cole all night. They're well over six feet, and I'm not sure I'm even five-nine, so I feel the effects a little stronger as I stagger down the hallway toward the bathroom.

"Where are you going?" Ryder follows me, running a hand along the wall to steady himself.

"Need to piss," I answer. "I'm 'bouta break the seal."

"Said you weren't leavin' my sight."

"Funny." He's being ridiculous again.

"I'm serious."

"You're not watching me piss. What the hell, Ry?" I brush the hair out of my face with a flick.

We're in a standoff in front of the bathroom door. He towers above me, stepping into my personal space even more and crowding my body with his much bigger one.

"You're drunk. People might see us go in together,

Ryder," I whisper. I'm not drunk enough to let him make a stupid decision he'll regret later. "Wait here."

He huffs, turning around to lean against the wall opposite the bathroom door, folding his arms across his chest and waiting.

I roll my eyes and snort, slipping into the bathroom and locking the door behind me. I catch my reflection in the mirror, cheeks flushed with a hint of a smile on my lips. Ryder did that. He *always* does that. He threatens to make me feel and lose control of the tight grip I've had on my emotions for the past five years. He makes me want to *talk*, to tell him things. *Everything.*

It's dangerous.

I'm not sure I can handle another person I care about leaving. My smile falters, and I let the numbness settle back in, doing my business in a rush and leaving even quicker.

"Hey! Where are you going? What happened in there?"

Drunk Ryder is a little pushy, apparently.

"Nowhere and nothing." I need some air and to smoke something after re-upping with Cole earlier.

I push through the crowd of drunk teenagers dancing in Cole's living room, the music testing the limits of my eardrums. I lose Ryder as I weave through people, taking advantage of my smaller size. I escape to the back patio, the party now a muffled cacophony pulsing through the walls.

The rain is coming down in heavy sheets, but there's a large covered porch with comfortable-looking furniture, a kitchen area with a massive grill, and a hot tub. There are even a couple of space heaters.

I'm on a mission to be warm, so I flip one on and sit at the table next to it. I can instantly feel the warmth seeping through my hoodie and into my bones as I break up some weed.

The sky is angry and violent, trembling with an intense energy that I feel. My nerves are shot, and my hands shake as I run my tongue along the edge of the wrap, sealing the bud inside. Thunder booms loudly, and a bright flash of light illuminates Cole's backyard for a fraction of a second.

"What are you doing?" I jump in my seat, nearly tearing a hole in my perfect roll.

Shit.

My heart pounds a staccato rhythm in my chest, and the adrenaline coursing through my veins attempts to push the numbness away.

How did he sneak up on me unnoticed?

"Seriously, Blue. You tryin' to lose me on purpose?" His perpetual smile is nowhere to be found.

I shrug. Maybe a little, but I needed some peace and quiet. Some space. And the rain is soothing, like a sound machine.

"You gonna smoke with me?" I ask him, changing the subject.

"Nah. I'm good."

I shrug and spark it up, closing my eyes and inhaling as thunder rumbles and another flash of light pierces through my closed lids. All the beer I had sloshes heavily in my stomach as I adjust myself on the cushioned seat to get more comfortable.

"Why'd you run from me?"

Jesus. He's not giving up. I exhale loudly, the cold air making the smoke stand out against the inky backdrop.

I decide to be honest. Or maybe all the alcohol and weed swirling around in my system decides it for me. "Thought about you leaving. Freaked out for a second."

"Me leaving?"

"Yeah. Everyone does."

Fuck.

Why did I say that?

It sounds pathetic. I press the blunt to my lips and pull for as long as I can, sucking in the smoke and holding it tight.

I can't look at Ryder. There's no way I can handle the emotions he wears so freely.

"Blue. . ." His tone is soft and hesitant. Careful.

The smoke bursts out of me in a massive plume. Violent coughs rip from my throat and burn my lungs.

Fuuuck. Bad decision.

It was too big of a hit.

By the time I'm done hacking my lungs up, I can barely hold my eyes open, and I'm not sure if I can even speak.

I slouch down further into the cushioned seat, my eyes drifting shut.

I'm completely baked.

A soft hand caresses mine, taking the blunt from my grasp.

"Shit. Coulda set m'self on fire," I mumble, unsure if he can understand me. It sounded right in my head.

"Fallon."

I open my eyes wide, or maybe it's just a sliver. "Hmm?"

"Who's left you?"

My inhibitions are lowered or maybe obliterated because I slur out a string of people who have left me in one way or another, starting with my dad and ending with my mom.

That warm hand touches me again, this time pressed to my cheek. "I won't be one of them. And neither will my family or your uncle. You're stuck with us, Blue. Awkward jokes and all. Let's get you up to the bedroom I always stay in. I keep clothes and shit here since I crash a lot after basketball. We can get more comfortable."

He used to stay here? Has he done things with Cole?

"What? No! I mean, yes. I mean, no!" Ryder scrubs a hand down his face in drunken frustration. Guess I asked that out loud.

"Yes, I used to stay here. Before you. And no, of course not. I have never done anything with Cole. He doesn't like guys and doesn't know I do."

"M'kay. Sorry," I slur on a hiccup, and Ryder chuckles, looking over his shoulder quickly.

"Come here. You're fucking adorable when you're drunk." Then he lowers his voice. "And your lips are extra fucking shimmery tonight. Dammit, Blue."

Even in my drunken state, I can hear the lust in his voice. The desire.

"Take me upstairs, Ry. Want you."

"You're too fucked up. I won't take advantage of you, but give me a kiss."

Ryder squats down in front of my chair, and I lean forward, an automatic response at this point. He pinches my chin between his thumb and forefinger, pressing his lips to mine and gently tilting my head to the side to kiss me deeper.

"More," I whisper-moan into his open mouth.

"We can't. You're torched."

"M'not. M'horny." My lips throb from his kiss.

Ryder chuckles, "Actually, you just proved my point. You're wasted. Let's go upstairs to bed, though. The guys won't think twice about us crashing here. They know I'm looking out for you, so you'll stay in my room."

Ryder stands to his full height and holds a palm out. I place my smaller hand in his, and he tugs me to my feet. I waver slightly, stumbling into his chest. He wraps his arms around me, pulling me in and whispering into the top of my head. "You good, Blue?" His tone is gentle and kind.

I nod, the alcohol and weed hitting me even harder now that I'm standing. Ryder keeps his arm around me as he steers us toward the patio doors.

He can't be seen with his arm around me. I panic and tear away from him, pushing through the door and tripping over the molding.

I crash into a hard chest instead of the hard floor. Strong arms band around me in a grip that's too tight and not at all friendly.

"Well, hello, pretty thing," a harsh voice taunts as I stare up into cold eyes, my vision wavering.

Ryder comes barging in the back door after me, and the cruel face before me speaks again.

"Hey, Cruz. Your girlfriend threw herself at me, dude. Better watch that. She's pretty, too."

Seth's calculating gaze scans my face, then darts over to Ryder, a hateful smirk forming on his lips.

"You've got a little something there, Cruz. . ." Seth wipes his lip with a thumb, then peers down at me again. "And you too, *little one*." He swipes that same thumb below my bottom lip, tugging on it and coming away with a smudge of sparkles.

Ryder growls behind me, stalking forward. "Don't fucking touch him. You're just like your scumbag friend, Dustin."

Seth cackles wildly and shoves me at Ryder. I stumble, feeling like a baby giraffe on

new legs as I stumble over to Ry.

He catches me, tucking me under his arm. "Keep your mouth shut, or I'll send an anonymous email to your coach and attach the surveillance video from my doorbell cam. I deleted it from the app so my dad wouldn't see, but you're an idiot, Seth. I know you TP-ed my house and egged my dad's car last month. You're not subtle, douchebag. It's on camera, along with half your team."

Seth pales at that, and Ryder swipes at his mouth, wiping away any lingering shimmer. "Whatever you think you know, you know nothing. Got it, Seth?"

"Yeah, whatever." He eyes me up and down. "Like I said before, to each his own. Enjoy your weird, *gay love*."

Ryder steps forward like he wants to do something about it, but I grab his arm. "Don't. Not 'cause of me." He sighs but listens as Seth cackles and strolls away.

Luckily no one else seems to have noticed, or maybe it's just me who's too drunk to notice. I step toward where I think the stairs are, and the room tilts to the side.

"Let's get you to bed." Ryder's thick arm wraps around my shoulders, keeping me upright and steering us where we need to go. I can barely pick my legs up anymore, the darkness of oblivion calling to me. "Almost there, Blue. Just a few more feet."

Time fast-forwards, or maybe I pass out because the next thing I know, I'm on top of a bed, my shoes and hoodie off.

"Jeans," I mumble, pressing my hips up.

He chuckles low in his throat, and the sound has my dick plumping up. "Right. Who the fuck can sleep in jeans? Not me. Let's get you outta these."

I don't smell cheap booze anymore. Instead, something woodsy and spicy infiltrates my senses. Something uniquely Ryder Cruz. He engulfs me, his golden brown curls begging me to touch their silky, soft strands. Those pale green eyes are so alluring. I'm surrounded by him, and I fucking surrender. Hands up, take my virginity *now*.

Ryder pops the button on my jeans, then drags the zipper down ever-so-slowly. He pulls them off, and I lift my hips so he can shimmy them down my thighs and legs, leaving me in a tight black T-shirt and my new boxer briefs.

He keeps his eyes on mine before he gives in, allowing his gaze to track my body hungrily. Ryder's tongue darts out, licking his lips, and his stare lingers on my growing erection.

I can't help it. Knowing he's watching me encourages it, and he chuckles.

"I'm not taking advantage of you tonight, Blue. It's cuddle time only. Get under the covers." I watch as he slips out of his clothes, leaving him standing before me in tight gray boxer briefs. His impressive package is tempting me, making me impatient for more.

"Please," I beg.

This is so unlike me.

Foreign. Needy. *Desperate.*

Ryder switches the bedside lamp on and slips under the covers, pulling me into him and curving around my smaller frame, spooning me.

His voice is soft and tender, warming the nape of my neck. "You're too drunk."

I wiggle my ass against him, my thoughts wandering to what it would feel like for him to touch me there.

I turn my head and mumble into the fluffy pillow. "Yeah. And drunk blue balls are the worst."

Ryder chuckles sadistically behind me, lightly dragging his fingers across the strip of exposed skin between my undersized tee and my underwear. "You have blue balls? How do you have blue balls?"

Feeling emboldened by the alcohol, I flip in his arms and lift a leg over his, grinding my hard-on into his thigh. "I was thinking 'bout you fingering me and fucking me."

Ryder chokes on nothing, his grip on my hip tightening while he coughs. "Shit, Blue. Holy shit. You can't just say stuff like that. *Fuck*." His curious hand wanders around my hip to my backside, squeezing firmly. He kneads my cheeks, getting me even harder. I rock against his thick thigh, my dick as hard as steel and leaking.

"M'not too drunk to come," I mumble into his mouth as I steal a kiss.

"You're kinda forceful when you're wasted," he pulls back to tell me, giving my ass a firm squeeze.

"And you've been kinda pushy too. So what?"

Ryder chuckles at that. "True. Guess I'll take off your underwear now."

I moan, excited to get what I want. He lowers my leg and rolls me to my back, peeling my underwear off and pausing to watch my dick bounce free.

He hasn't put his mouth on me yet, but I can see the desire in his eyes. Ryder leans forward and swipes his tongue across my sensitive head, collecting the pre-cum oozing from my slit.

Oh fuck, I've never had anyone's mouth on me before.

"You haven't?" he asks before swirling his tongue from root to tip, causing my hips to jolt.

I said that out loud, and I don't even care. I shake my head frantically. "More."

He peels my underwear the rest of the way down my legs, and I help kick them off.

"Leave your legs bent. I'll be right back."

I keep my feet flat on the bed, completely naked, my ass somewhat vulnerable, and my dick rock hard.

Ryder comes back from the en-suite with a little bottle in his hand, and the confusion must show on my face.

"Lube," he says, answering my unspoken question. "You wanted *more*, right?"

I swallow thickly but nod. I do want more. I want to know how it feels. *If I like it.*

He tosses the bottle to the bed next to us and kneels between my legs as best as his big body can manage. He licks my cock slowly before swallowing me down in one go.

I cry out, and my hands instantly grasp his curls and keep his head pressed between my legs. Where he belongs. *Fuck*, where he belongs. With my feet flat on the bed, something takes over as I thrust a steady rhythm into his open mouth, practically fucking his face.

Ryder pulls back, choking and gasping for air. "Shit, Blue," he chuckles. "That was fucking hot."

I chew on my lip ring, nodding eagerly. I'm lost for words again but ready to let the sensations take over.

Ryder begins sucking me at his own pace, and I slowly rock my hips with him, closing my eyes and enjoying the new feelings and the easy pace.

Shit, this is good.

I grab his hair again as tingles race down my spine, and my balls draw up. I'm on the verge of coming when Ryder pulls away with a *pop*, squeezing the base of my cock hard so I don't accidentally nut with a weak, half-assed jizz when he's not even sucking me.

"Nooo. Ry, whaa—?"

"Shh," he cuts me off. "I gotchu. It's gonna feel so good, okay? Just trust me. I'll take care of you. Promise."

I nod again, ignoring the near-painful pulse in my cock as I'm denied release. I keep my eyes squeezed shut, just wanting to feel something for once and allowing myself to.

Ryder scoots forward on the bed until his knees press against me. He scoops under my ass and sets me on his lap, my hips angled and my knees still bent. He pushes them back even further.

"Hold them."

I grip under my knees and pull back, groaning when I expose myself even further to him.

I hear a bottle click open, and then a cool, slick finger traces my crease, circles my hole, and teases my taint. My breathing picks up, and I moan long and loud.

Oh fuck, that feels amazing.

"Relax for me, Blue. Take a deep breath, okay?" I listen on instinct, my chest rising. "Now let it go." As I release my deep breath, the extra oxygen relaxes me further, and Ryder slips the tip of his finger into my ass. I feel myself tense up at the unfamiliar intrusion.

"You're doing great. So good. Relax your body for me, Fal. I want to feel you on the inside." I whimper at his dirty words, and his finger slips all the way in, his knuckles grinding against my rim. I suck in a sharp breath at the feeling of fullness.

"Baby, breathe," Ryder whispers gently. I didn't even realize I was holding my breath.

He pulls his finger back and then pushes forward again.

"Oh fuuuck," I whine as he shoves it in again. The feeling is so foreign, and the rush of new sensations bursting through me is overwhelming, but I can't stop now.

With my eyes closed, Ryder slowly begins to fuck my ass with his finger.

"You like it, Blue?" he whispers. "Like my finger in your ass? Do you want another?"

"Mhm. Y-yeah. More."

I feel Ryder move like he's reaching for something, and

then I hear the click of a lightbulb. Bright light illuminates my closed eyelids, and I squeeze them shut tighter.

"I need to see this," he whispers in awe, and I groan in both desire and shame. I'm on complete display for him.

Ry slows his pace, slipping a second finger in and causing me to whimper, the stretch nearly burning.

"You okay?" he asks, always careful with me.

"Yeah. J-just a little tight." He takes my breath away, and I can barely think.

"I can see that. Your little hole is stretched to its limits. We're gonna have to practice more. Two is your max for now."

I groan in utter embarrassment, the humiliation turning me on even more, loosening me and lessening the burn.

"Open your eyes. Look at me, Fal."

I squint my eyes open, blinking rapidly as the soft glow of the bedside lamp temporarily blinds me.

When we make eye contact, Ryder does something inside me—something with his fingers—curving them and pressing on my inner walls. He finds a spot, and I cry out, feeling like he's stroking my cock from deep inside my ass.

"Ungh!"

Unfamiliar feelings wash over me as Ry nails that same spot, stretching my hole as he lowers my hips to the bed and thrusts harder and deeper. He leans down, swallowing my aching cock whole.

I cry out again and come instantaneously. My dick erupts in his mouth, and my hole pulses around his fingers, clenching them tightly. The orgasm goes on and on, feeling like I just came five times in a row.

"Oh. Fuck," I say breathlessly, letting my knees drop to

the bed. I hiss when he slips his fingers from me. Not because it hurts but because of the loss. I feel empty.

Ryder's eyes flash to me in concern. "Pull your knees back again. I need to check you." I don't listen right away, not sure I'm comfortable with such scrutiny, so Ry pushes my knees back for me.

"Hold 'em."

Then he leans down to take a closer look.

"Ryyy," I whine, mortified by his inspection. "I'm fine."

"You're a bit red and puffy, but nothing a little cum won't fix."

"Wh-what?" I sputter.

Did he just say cum?

CHAPTER SEVENTEEN

RYDER

I don't even know why I say it. It's ridiculous, and Fallon's wide eyes make me question whether I should go this far with him right now. But I just had my fingers in his ass and my mouth on his cock, so I don't think it's too far a stretch to come on his asshole.

I pull my cock out of my underwear and press the blunt head to his shiny, red hole. He looks tender and slightly open, and it takes everything in me not to surge forward and just cram myself in there. But I'd never hurt him, and he's definitely not ready.

"You know I've never been with anyone, so you trust me, right?" There's an unspoken question there that I know he picks up on. We're both virgins, so I'm skipping the condom and coming on his ass.

"I trust you, Ryder." His eyes are sincere, and his words are impassioned. My stomach flips knowing he has such wholehearted trust in me. I don't take his words lightly. Not at all. Not after everything he's been through, and when I'm sure I don't even know the half of it.

My eyes blaze with heat, scorching a trail along his

body as I devour him. "Flip over," I command, and he scrambles to release his legs and roll over.

He lays flat, so I reach under, grabbing his hips and lifting, causing him to grunt at the manhandling. I press one hand between his shoulder blades.

"Keep your shoulders down and your ass in the air for me, baby." I don't know why the endearment slips out again, but it sounds right. Sounds perfect, actually.

Fallon obeys, spreading his legs so I can crawl in between. I squirt more lube in my hand and stroke myself as I rub my dick up and down his crease and over his slightly swollen pucker. I can't wait to see what his hole looks like after I fuck him. But no matter how badly I want that, it can't happen tonight. He's not ready.

I stroke faster. My stomach is coiling tight, the pressure building.

"Stick it in. Fuck me, Ry. I want you to." Fallon arches his back, opening his hole up even more. The tip of my cockhead just barely breaches him, and he cries out. I stay on pace, holding steady, and jerk myself off against his tender hole. It takes absolutely everything in me not to surge forward and impale him on all my nine-plus inches.

"I wanna fuck you so badly," I grit out. "So badly."

"Do it," he whines, but we're both still drunk, and I'm not hurting him.

"Not. Tonight." I press down harder on his shoulder blades, forcing his smaller body to bend to my will even more. His ass tips up further, and I trail my hand down his back, caressing his hip and pale cheeks. I run my thumb along his taint and continue my assault against his hole.

"Ryyy," he whines again and shifts slightly, and I hear the telltale sign of jerking off as he begins to stroke himself.

"Gonna come," I warn, then move my thumb to press

into his asshole slightly, tugging it open a little more as I shoot my load. I keep my head against his opening, grunting as I attempt to fill him up without actually penetrating him.

Fallon is a shaking, shivering mess as I pull my spent cock away. His asshole is even redder now, puffy and sore, and my cum oozes out of him, dripping down his crease. I scoop it up with two fingers and stuff it back in.

"*Ungh!* Oh fuck!" He continues to stroke his dick while I finger his ass. It doesn't take long until his muscles squeeze my fingers like a vise, and he comes *again*.

As soon as he finishes, I slip my fingers out and take a second to admire the utter mess I just made of him. I squeeze his cheeks and push them together before spreading them again.

Fallon lets his hips fall to the bed, lying in his own spunk. "Uhh. No more. Too sensitive."

I chuckle. "Let's hop in the bathroom. We need to clean you up."

"I've got it." Fallon jumps up, wincing slightly, and my brow creases in concern.

He wraps the sheet around his waist and scurries to the bathroom, the shower turning on right after.

Fuck.

I hope he's not shutting down again.

I wake to the overpowering smell of bacon and groan, realizing we passed out at Cole's last night after getting really, really freaky. Shit. I guess I get a little dirty when I'm drinking.

My stomach turns at the thought of Cole's breakfast

hangover special of three packs of bacon, two pounds of sausage, and plain toast. His house is going to smell like grease for a week.

I nuzzle further into my pillow and Fallon. After he came back from the bathroom last night, I took my turn. By the time I came back, he was passed out.

A loud knock on the bedroom door startles both of us, making me roll away from Fallon quickly. "Breakfast of champions in five! Let's go, boys! Time to eat and rally!" Cole shouts way too loud for first thing in the morning.

By the time Fallon is fully awake and registers his surroundings, I'm back on my side of the bed and settled innocuously.

"Breakfast's ready," I tell him obviously.

It's a little awkward. Why is it awkward?

I need to fix this!

"Smells like more meat on the menu, although we both sorta had our fill last night, if you know what I mean?" I wiggle my eyebrows at him, still lounging on my side of the bed as if I've been here all along.

He snorts and rolls his eyes. "I'll pass on Cole's meat," he mumbles.

Jokes! He's got jokes!

Double fucking score!

I burst out laughing. Can't help it. "Dude, it's a fucking sausage fest down there. And bacon. Pounds of it. Cole's gonna give himself gout."

"Let's go home," Fallon says softly, and my heart flips, beating upside down and inside out.

I swallow thickly, knowing I never lost him.

"Yours or mine?" I ask, unsure which he means.

"Wherever you are. And everyone else." He says it so

matter-of-factly, but this is huge. He sees us as family. As his home.

We won't let him down, either. None of us. And we won't leave. *Ever.*

But I'll tell him these things later.

"I'll text my dad, see where they're at," I say casually, not making a big deal out of his words. Even though the open vulnerability in his tone both breaks and heals my heart simultaneously. He's been so closed off since the beginning, but I've noticed small changes already, and this counts as a big one.

I crawl out of bed and check my phone, texting my dad and ordering an Uber. By the time I'm done, Dad lets me know they're at my house.

"We're going to my place. Uber's here in fifteen if you want a quick meat snack before we hit the road."

He huffs out a breath of air, slightly different from his usual snort, but I also get a little twitch of his lips as one side tugs up for a fraction of a second.

Fucking score!

That was definitely a smile. There's no denying it.

"My house was TP-ed again," Joel informs me the second we walk in the front door, not even two steps into the foyer. He's frowning, his features tight, as he leans against the wall with his arms crossed.

Goddamnit Seth.

My hangover brain completely forgot about his accusations last night. He thinks he has one over me, finding Fallon's shimmery Chapstick on my lips? But the dumbass gave me even more ammunition by TP-ing Joel's house. *Again.*

He has no proof about Fallon and me, but I'm starting to question whether I care anymore if he did. Will it even matter if everyone knows I'm gay? Am I just being paranoid about staying in the closet like this? Will the private college I'm attending in the fall drop me if they know I'm gay? I've dreamed about playing ball in Southern California since I was eight.

I wasn't ready to gamble on these questions before Fallon, but the more I'm around him, the more I don't want to hide. I'm caring less about what others think and more about what I want. And there's no doubt that I want Fallon Rivers.

"This rivalry between you guys and Jefferson is normal to an extent, but what's been happening this year isn't healthy. It's hazing, and it's bullying. And it seems to go both ways—"

"I don't—"

"I didn't say you, Ryder. This all just needs to end. Text the guys at Jefferson and try to make amends. Then message the team chat. You're the captain, Ry. Help me get a handle on the boys. We need to focus on the game. Play-offs start Monday."

I don't need to make amends with anyone. *They just TP-ed his house,* among a slew of other offenses, half of which he has no clue about.

He eyes me dubiously, giving me a disappointed dad look that's magnified times two when my actual dad strolls over.

"Mijo. Are you both hungover?" His dark brows crease as his eyes scan us. "I hope you didn't drive."

I sigh internally. "No, Dad. Uber."

"Playoffs are Monday, no?"

This time I sigh out loud. I just want my bed. "Yes, Dad. It's fine. That's next week, and today is today. I'm fine."

I just said I was fine twice, but fuck, I am! I love them, but Fallon and I don't need a double-dad-grilling right now.

"If anything else happens, the coaches will have to get involved."

The coaches? What the hell does that mean?

Fallon is silent the whole time but stands by my side in support. He may not have basketball to worry about, but they're not too happy with either of us.

"Go get some rest. Both of you," Joel says with a tired sigh.

"Our bean bags were delivered this morning!" Sofie shouts in excitement as she jogs down the stairs in her unicorn pajamas and bunny rabbit slippers, curly hair bouncing with each step. We all love the ones at Joel's place, so Dad got Sofie and me our own. It's the softest shit I've ever felt, and the best thing is it's oversized, even for me. I can't wait to try it.

"Hey, Sofie!" I call out, and she runs over, wrapping her arms around my middle and hugging tight.

"Missed you, big bro."

"Same." I squeeze her tight. "So where are these bean bags at?"

"In our rooms. Mine is rainbow!"

"Sick, dude!" I reply in genuine excitement. I love to encourage everything that makes her who she is. If that's mythical creatures and colorful shit, I'm all for it.

She releases me and surprises everyone when she does the same to Fallon. Since he's not much taller than her, their hug is small and adorable, just like they are. My stomach flutters when he reciprocates, giving her a little squeeze before they separate.

"Missed you too," she whispers, but I hear. It makes warmth bloom in my chest and hope sprout in my soul. Hope that he'll be happy. And hope that we can be together. The two of us and all of us. A family.

He'll be loved, cared for, protected, and fucking *nurtured*. Everything he's lacked for the past five years. But that changes now.

"Come on," Sofie says with glee, tugging Fallon's hand and grabbing mine, pulling us toward the stairs.

"Bye, Dads!"

I chuckle and follow along until we're in her bedroom, staring at an enormous rainbow tie-dye bean bag that could probably swallow her whole.

"Watch!" She lets go of our hands and runs toward her bean bag, diving for it in a monster belly flop.

"Oof."

A bunch of muffled giggles ring out, and she sinks into the fluff, practically consumed by the massive thing.

Sofie rolls over while Fallon and I watch the show from her doorway. "I wasn't ready to wake up before you came home. I might just stay here a bit. Enjoy my Saturday morning. Pass me my iPad and tuck me in, please?" She flashes her eyes at me, and I cave, playing fetch with the fluffy throw blanket she keeps at the end of her bed while Fallon grabs her sparkly pink iPad. We both tuck her in like it's the most normal thing we've done all weekend. And shit, maybe it is.

"Goodnight," I say without thinking, and Sofie giggles. "I mean, good morning? Whatever. See you later, Sofie. I need a nap."

"Enjoy your bean bag! You guys might have to wrestle

for it or something. It's really comfy." She snuggles further into the mammoth thing and practically purrs like a kitten.

I eye Fallon, smirking. I'd wrestle him for fun, but we can share too.

We close the bedroom door, leaving her to most likely fall asleep watching random cat videos online.

My bedroom is more down the hall, and as soon as I open the doors, my eyes zero in on a dark blue fleece-covered bean bag.

"Would ya look at the size of that sac," I admire out loud, in complete awe. Somehow mine is even bigger than the others. I can't believe they did that. This had to be custom-made. Good thing my bedroom is the size of two because this thing is damn near the size of a car.

Fallon snorts a laugh again, and I smile widely, proud that I continue to make him feel *something*. That's what matters. Because when the time comes for him to read the letter from his father that's burning a hole in the bottom of my jewelry box, I already know he'll need to confront his emotions head-on. But now isn't the time to think about that.

"Nap?" I ask because even though we dodged Cole's meat, we ate his muffins, dipping out before ten. So I'm full and exhausted. I know Fallon is too. "We can share."

His steely blue eyes dart to the bean bag, then back to me. "Okay."

"Okay."

I need to decide what I want. We haven't even talked about what this *is*. But I had my fingers in his ass last night, and now we're about to spoon on a king-sized bean bag. We should probably talk soon. And it's going to be me that initiates the conversation, that much is clear.

I wake to Fallon missing and the soft sounds of an acoustic guitar strumming a few rooms away. I slip out of bed and tiptoe down the hall. The closer I get, the more haunting the melody becomes. Beautiful, but with an edge. Restless. It's absolutely amazing, and I know it has to be Fallon with his dad's guitar.

I peek around the doorframe of the bonus room, observing him in silence. Fallon sits on the edge of the couch, playing with his eyes closed, completely lost to the music. And then he starts to hum. Low and edgy. I give him a little whistle to cheer him on but startle him instead, and he misses a chord, the guitar screeching.

"What are you doing, Ry?"

"Listening to you play. Amazingly, might I add."

Fallon ducks his head, mumbling out, "Thanks."

"You're amazing," I repeat *again*. "The way your fingers dance along the strings? Fuck, it's the sexiest thing I've ever seen. Keep going, please."

Fallon combs his fingers through his blue and black hair, the dirty blond roots starting to show. When I first realized that he's a blondie under there. . . *Oof.* Yeah. I think I'm gonna need to see that natural look sometime.

"Do you sing?" I'm pretty sure I know the answer to that already.

He nods once. "Yeah. And write."

It's impressive. "I'd love to hear something if you want to share. Pretty sure everyone at the bonfire wanted more," I say with a chuckle.

He eyes me, considering his options. "Okay, just a little." He chews on his lip ring and taps his fingertips against the body of the guitar. It's nearly as shiny and blue as his brightly colored hair.

I know Joel had the guitar cleaned, tuned, and restored before giving it to Fallon. And my dad bought a brand new case. I still need to take him to the record store. Sofie will want to come too.

"Okay. This is one that I've felt most comfortable with for a while. It's the chorus and part of the first verse."

Fallon starts the haunting melody that pulled me from sleep, adding lyrics this time. His soft, raspy voice is soothing yet abrasive. Calm yet a raging storm. He sings about the sheer destruction of his soul. Painful memories. Loss. Regret.

Holy shit, it's heavy.

But the melody is even more beautiful, his words pouring from his heart like a tidal wave, sweeping me off my feet.

His soul is so real. So raw. *So authentic.*

Fallon ends his vocal performance but continues strumming, finishing the song with just the guitar. He's still getting used to speaking and opening up more. This is huge progress, and I don't expect more.

I grit my teeth, thinking about how alone he's been and wishing I could have been there sooner. But I'm here now, and I'll pull him out of the fog. He's already starting to feel again. I can see it. Fuck, I just *heard* it.

"Holy shit, Blue. That was fucking incredible. Your voice is curl-my-toes and come-in-my-pants sexy."

He's chewing on that lip again, and I quickly glance behind me, then back to him.

"They left. Went for lunch," he says, reading my mind.

"Yeah?"

Fallon nods slowly, and I dart forward, leaning over the

guitar on his lap. I claim his mouth eagerly. I can't get enough of him.

We continue to kiss, and I slip my tongue into his mouth, rolling it against his own. Pulling away, I carefully pick up his guitar and set it on the coffee table, reaching for him next.

"Come here." He places his hand in mine, and I switch so that I'm sitting on the couch, and Fallon settles onto my lap.

"Mmm," I moan, nuzzling into his neck and hugging him tight. Strawberries and fresh soap. Drives me fucking wild.

"You showered?" I ask, sucking on his skin delicately, not enough to bruise the flesh and give him a hickey, but enough to make goosebumps sprout across his soft skin. No hickeys allowed in this house. Sofie or Georgie would call us out in a second.

"Yeah. I did a lot of things while you were asleep. I was writing. Thinking a lot too."

"Thinking about. . ." I'm distracted by his smell, his taste, his *everything*. I kiss Fallon's jawline and nibble his ear, eliciting a round of delicious shivers from him.

I press my mouth to his again, sealing us together in an urgent kiss.

He said no one's home, so as soon as he tells me what he needs, I'm giving it to him.

CHAPTER EIGHTEEN
FALLON

Ryder's kissing me with such intent, like he wants to consume every atom of my being. I run my hands along his broad shoulders, unable to stop myself. His body is made of hard muscle and sharp contours, and my body tingles with awareness. I can feel his cock hardening, and my own starts to fill.

"Think I'm gay," I pant into his open mouth.

Ryder breaks the kiss, pulling back. His eyes are inquisitive yet lust-hazed as he scans my face. "Yeah?"

I nod. I have to be.

There's no other excuse for what's been happening since I moved to California and met Ryder. I'm completely gay.

"Yeah," I confirm.

"That's awesome, dude. Me too."

I wasn't worried about his reaction. It's Ryder. And even after so little time, I know that means easy acceptance, enthusiastic loyalty, and a blinding smile. And he doesn't disappoint when his lopsided grin slowly eases into a full-on, dazzling as fuck Ryder Cruz smile.

He's beyond attractive and oozes charisma. I don't deserve him. But I think I'm going to let myself have him. So, when he asks his next question, there's zero hesitation on my end. We're on the same wavelength, our frequencies aligned.

I want this.

I want him.

Ryder doesn't stop touching me as he speaks softly, trailing those long, slender fingers down my cheek before thumbing my lip ring like he always does.

"I've been thinking too, Blue. A lot. *Every day.* About you. About *us*. I want you to be *mine*. My boyfriend. Will you go out with me?" His smile is slightly hesitant now, and that won't do.

"Yeah. Fuck, Ry." I kiss him again. *My boyfriend.* "Yes," I hiss into his mouth as he grabs my waist, pushing his hips up and pulling me down at the same time. He's hard. Really hard.

I thread my fingers through his soft curls and grasp on, kissing him hungrily. Deeply. I want Ryder so badly. I try not to think about anything else, living in this moment with him. I push the demons away, the ones telling me I'm not good enough for him.

Ryder stands, one hand pressed to my back while the other splayed under my ass. I release my grip on his hair, wrap my arms around his neck, and lock my legs around his trim waist.

We continue to make out, our mouths practically fused together as he stumbles down the hallway back to his bedroom.

He pulls his lips away, panting like he just got off the basketball court. "Bean bag?" he asks, eyes half-lidded.

I press my lips back to his. "Mm-hmm," I moan into his

open mouth as he squeezes my ass and walks us to the oversized bean bag. He deposits me there, going back to close and lock the door before whipping his shirt over his head and yanking his basketball shorts and boxers down in one go.

His massive cock springs free, and I scramble to my knees, not an easy task in this giant, squishy thing.

I've never done this, sucked a cock, but I'm ready. I lick the underside of my boyfriend's shaft, tonguing at the slit. He tips his head back and groans. The long column of Ryder's throat is a beautiful and mesmerizing sight.

I continue to show his length attention until a loud chime makes both of us jump, and he chuckles.

"That could be a delivery, but I'm in no state to sign," he deadpans, and I can't help but snort and roll my eyes, giving his cock a quick teasing lick.

"I'll get it. You stay here. Naked and ready," I tease him.

Lust gleams in his gaze. "Yes, sir. I won't move a muscle or put a stitch of clothing on until you tell me. Promise." He holds his fingers up like a Boy Scout or something, which I'd be surprised if he wasn't.

I roll my eyes at the giant dork, my lip twitching on its own accord.

"Saw that, Blue! I'll definitely be getting a smile now that you're my boyfriend. My boyfriend's definitely gonna smile. No doubt."

Yeah. He's probably right. Maybe it won't be so bad feeling again.

I wander down the stairs, my head in the clouds thinking about everything we did last night and that I now have a *boyfriend*. Not a girlfriend. That never really felt right. I don't think it's just a Ryder thing, either. I definitely like boys.

I'm not focused and am unprepared to open the front door to a beautiful woman with curly golden blonde hair and an olive-green stare. Her eyes are bright, but her smile is forced. I instantly recognize her.

"Hello, there. Are you a friend of Ryder's? I'm his mother, Penelope." She holds out a dainty hand, nails tipped in white, the rest a pale pink. I politely shake her hand, even though she's not around for her son or her daughter, and I don't know if I'm supposed to just let her into Alejandro's house like this.

"Nice to meet you," I mumble on autopilot.

Ryder mentioned that he related to having a crazy mother. My good mood is dampened because now I'm worried about him.

I wouldn't be okay with my mother showing up, asking to see me unannounced. He won't be happy. And I probably shouldn't leave her unattended to find him, either. I chew on my lip ring, unsure of what the right thing to do is.

But I don't have to worry long because Ryder comes downstairs in basketball shorts and a white T-shirt with the sleeves cut off. The holes are so big I can see his nipples, and I lick my lips, remembering how sensitive and responsive he is.

His smile falters when he sees her, and I hate it. Ryder Cruz should always be happy and smiling. The world is a darker, more fucked up place when he's not.

"Mom. What are you doing here?"

No hello, no hi, nothing. Straight to the point.

He's not messing around.

"Ryder, do not speak to your mother that way. Aren't you going to introduce me to your friend?"

He just grunts and flicks his eyes my way. "This is Fallon Rivers."

That's all he says.

Not 'Fallon Rivers, my boyfriend,' or even 'friend.'

My stomach drops, and I can feel myself crawling back inside my safe place. The numb place that has no feelings. No emotions. No worries.

That sure didn't last long.

The shutters are drawn, and I can feel Ryder staring at me with concern. I know he didn't want to come out because of basketball, so I don't even know why I'm acting like this. Of course he doesn't want to tell her. I'm being irrational.

"Rivers," she sneers. I'm taken aback, but my face remains a neutral mask. "As in *Joel* Rivers? Husband-stealer?"

What. The. *Fuck*.

"Mom. Stop. Don't do this. Please."

"Do what? Honey, I'm only stating the truth."

Ryder's mom pushes past us. Her rude and brash behavior reminds me of my own mother, currently locked up in Philly.

"She never used to be like that," he says quietly when she disappears into the house that's not even hers anymore. "I need to call my dad. Warn him that she just showed up again."

"She does this a lot?"

"No. And that's part of the problem." Ryder's whisper gets even quieter. "I'll tell you more later, but she left town when Dad came out. By herself. Sometimes we don't even see her for a whole year, but then she'll just show up out of the blue. And she's always rude. Even to Sofie, but I'm not sure Sofie even sees it. Mom takes it out on us even more than my dad."

That's really messed up.

"What she said about your uncle isn't true, by the way. Joel and my dad hadn't even met when he decided to live his truth and tell her he wanted a divorce. She just has it in her head now." He sighs deeply before pressing the phone to his ear.

"Dad. Hey. Yeah, everything's fine. I know I never call. Yes, I know I could text, but it's urgent."

Ryder pinches the bridge of his nose and closes his eyes, taking a big breath before firing off a string of perfectly fluent Spanish.

Oh. Holy shit.

That was hot.

I shouldn't be surprised. And yet I just wasn't expecting it.

Ryder's eyes pop open and lock onto mine. I can hear his dad through the phone speaking rapidly, urgently. Ry says something else, sounding a little angry and a lot sexy. I chew on my lip ring, and his eyes zero in on it, darkening further.

Ryder switches back to English. "Just prepare Sofie the best you can, Dad." He ends the call, stuffing it back in his basketball shorts. He pulls off his backward Acadia Lake Baseball cap and rubs a hand through his curly hair. "This is fucked up and the last thing I want to deal with on the day I start dating my boyfriend."

"It's okay, Ry," I tell him. "You can talk to me later. Vent. Whatever you need." There's nothing left for us to do in the foyer, so I follow Ryder as he stalks toward the kitchen in search of his mother. And probably a snack too.

Ryder's mom is sitting at the white marble island veined in gold—ostentatious-as-fuck and probably chosen by her.

Looks nice, though.

Penelope thumbs through a *Teen Vogue* magazine on the counter, sipping a glass of red wine and looking very at home somewhere that's actually *not*.

"Sofie will be home in an hour. I have that time frame to convince you to leave. You can't just show up when you want. It always causes a setback for her." He leans a hip against the counter, arms crossed tightly. Defensively.

"Oh, don't be ridiculous. My daughter wants to see me, even if my son doesn't." She purses her lips, flipping her curly hair over her shoulder.

"Yeah. She does want to see you. More than once a year. You aren't around to deal with the aftermath when you leave. It wrecks her. You can't come and go from Sofie's life. Either stay or leave for good. You can't keep doing this."

"Don't tell me not to see my own children, Ryder." She takes a sip of wine, continuing to flip the magazine pages.

A vein in his temple pulses, and his nostrils flare slightly. He's irritated and rightfully so. Ryder storms into the pantry, grabbing a bag of salt and vinegar chips and making loud rustling noises as he opens it as obnoxiously as possible. He shoves his hand in to grab a massive handful before cramming said handful into his mouth and crunching loudly as he stalks toward the exit.

I'm a silent observer. A witness to the awkward encounter between my boyfriend and his *mom*.

"Don't make a mess!" Penelope shouts.

"Not your house!" Ry counters, and I feel so uncomfortable standing here, trapped in her gaze like a moth to the flame. I should fly away because following the light only leads to getting burned.

"Do you not talk, *little boy*?"

Jesus. She's nasty. Nothing like sweet Sofie or my kind, loyal boyfriend. He said she wasn't always like this, and I can relate to that. Sometimes people change, and it's not always for the better. My own mother is sadly a testament to that.

I don't give her the satisfaction of an answer. Ryder quickly returns, circling his massive hand around my wrist and tugging. Her bright eyes dart down, but she doesn't comment, and we slip away successfully.

CHAPTER NINETEEN
RYDER

I pull Fallon into my room, shutting the door and locking it behind us. I don't trust her not to barge in without knocking.

"God. I hate when she does this. Just shows up unannounced. Throws the whole house into chaos. Sofie gets depressed for like a month afterward. I can't see her like that. It's not who she is. And I hate that our own *mother* is the cause." I take my hat off again, tossing it to the desk and scrubbing a hand through my curls.

Fallon calmly walks over and reaches up, grabbing my wrist to stop the nervous gesture. He threads our fingers together and tugs me toward my bed. We both sit on the end, and he doesn't let go.

"Ry. I'm so sorry. For you and especially for Sofie. She doesn't deserve that."

"She doesn't," I agree. "I'm just glad she has Georgie around. And that she's nothing like my mom." I can't help but snicker, remembering the burnt end of the shepherd's pie that she served my mom the last time she was here.

Georgie said it was worth every second of the verbal scolding she got for it when Dad wasn't around.

"Georgie's cool. I need more ice cream cookie cake. Whose birthday is next?"

I chuckle, letting him know that Sofie turns fifteen next month. We're going all out with a party at the skating rink and keeping tradition, so a giant ice cream cookie of Sofie's choice will be on the menu. Which probably means a peanut butter cookie with double chocolate chunk ice cream. Not my favorite of the usual combos we've circulated over the years. Sofie calls it a reverse Reece's cup.

"I can skate," Fallon says.

"Oh, really? Rollerblades? Skateboards?"

"Both."

"Nice. I can rollerblade too. We'll rent those at her party and run the entire rink. Show the freshmen what's up. It'll be cool." My smile is forced. We both know I'm avoiding the subject of crazy mothers.

"Well, I guess I need to explain that." I motion toward the door and my horrible mother beyond.

"You don't need to explain anything you don't want to, Ryder." His eyes search mine with an intensity that pours from his core, offering only support and a calm acceptance.

I close my eyes for a moment and appreciate the serene silence of being around Fallon.

I take a deep breath and slowly open my eyes, needing to explain things. "I *want* to tell you. Want you to know." I clear my throat, having trouble getting the words out. It's not easy talking about one of the worst things to happen to our family, leaving scars on everyone, especially Sofie and maybe even me.

Fallon speaks up. "I'll go first." His voice is a little off.

Void of emotion, like he's preparing to recite boring, factual information detachedly.

"My mom became a different person after my dad died. She turned to alcohol, drugs, men, anything really. I was twelve when it started, and I had to learn to fend for myself. She slowly lost everything. We barely had food in the house. I usually just ate peanut butter and jelly sandwiches with maybe milk and cheese on the weekends if she had a good Friday night at the club. Eggs if I was really lucky."

I swallow thickly at his confession. No wonder he scarfs everything down; he's been starving for five freaking years! I'm shocked into silence, and maybe it's a good thing because Fallon continues undisturbed. I know it's hard for him as he continues in a flat tone, eyes focused on the black nail polish he's chipping away at.

"Her boyfriends used to come and go, changing so often I couldn't even remember their names. They were never nice, though. So it didn't matter. They liked to insist I was all sorts of things I'm not, aiming a barb at whatever color my hair was at the time. Her last boyfriend's name was Johnny. I only remember his name because he was probably the worst. Greasy, slicked-back hair, never showered. His BO used to linger in the trailer for hours after he was gone. My mom was always too high to realize it. She was running low on money about two months ago, and Johnny was there. He stormed into my room and started tearing my stuff apart for anything of value so they could get their next fix. He found my guitar case under my bed and took it to the pawn shop. Probably sold it for a day's worth of crack or heroin. I'm honestly not sure. It could be both. I tried to stay away after that, and I guess I shut down even more. She did nothing to stop him, probably doesn't even remember, and that's why I give no fucks that she's in prison now. For how long, I don't know and don't care."

"Where is he?" I growl out. I'm not a violent person, but I'd like to get my hands on that fucking scumbag.

"Prison," Fallon answers swiftly, and I visibly relax.

"Good."

Fallon nods once sharply, and I think he's done talking about it, but there's one more question I need to ask.

"He never hurt you, did he?"

Fallon tenses up, and so do I, holding my breath and waiting for his answer.

"No."

"None of them? In any way?" I need to know how deep his trauma goes. His well-being is important to me.

"Not physically or anything like that," he murmurs, ducking his head further. I know they fucked him up emotionally, and I'm beyond pissed about that.

"Come here, baby," I say gently but with urgency. A desperation I can't contain. We both need a fucking hug for having shitty moms.

Fallon crawls onto my lap, straddling me, and wraps his arms around my neck, lowering his lips to mine for a brief, tender kiss before pulling back. I tuck a lock of blue hair behind his ear, murmuring soft words and reassurances to him.

"I'm so glad you crash-landed into my life, Blue. And thank you for opening up and letting me be there for you like you need. I promise you can trust me." I kiss his neck, right behind his ear, making him shiver.

"I didn't tell my mom you're my boyfriend earlier because she said horrible things to my dad when he came out and wanted a divorce. He wanted to remain friends because he still cared deeply for her, but just like your mom, she changed. Became a different person. Although Georgie tells me she was always nasty and condescending."

I sigh loudly, wishing she would just be a normal, nice mom who loved her kids and did crafts and baked banana nut muffins every weekend. I swear to God, if I ever have kids, I'm going to spoil them with time, attention, and *lots* of baked goods.

"I don't even know why she comes around. I guess for Sofie. Not me. She knows I hate her. I won't forget what she said about *homosexuals* and, therefore, *me*. She doesn't deserve to know that part of my life, that side of myself. And I don't want you to be a target of her hate. I won't risk that either."

"I understand, Ry," he whispers softly, squeezing my neck tightly. "I can be your secret."

My stomach drops at his words, not liking the sound of it. *At all.*

"You're not a—"

My words are cut off by a loud, harsh knock on my bedroom door, and we scramble apart even though I know I locked it.

I straighten my clothes, and Fallon moves to the gaming chair in front of the multiple computer monitors on my desk and starts *Command and Conquer*.

I open the door, and my mom sticks her head in, peering around dubiously, eyes landing on Fallon. Her perfectly arched brows scrunch ever-so-slightly, but it's hard to tell with all the Botox she gets.

"Yes?" I say rudely, but I don't care. It's not fair that she disrupts everyone's life when she shows up.

"Well, darling. It seems you've gotten your wish. I just got an email from a dear friend of mine, Roger. He invited me on a lovely Caribbean cruise. I head out tonight, so I need to leave. But maybe I'll plan a trip for the three of us when I return."

She won't.

"Or I'm sure Roger would be more than happy to take the three of us," she muses, eyes sparkling. I don't want to be anywhere around her gold-digging, old-man-fucking ways. And Sofie isn't going to be around that either. Dad will not allow it.

"No thanks," I tell her bluntly, folding my arms across my chest and shuffling over to block her view of the inside of my room and Fal.

Mom huffs. "Always so difficult, Ryder. Just tell my daughter I stopped by to see her. I miss her."

No way in fucking hell.

"Bye, Mom. I'll see you out." As I step out of the doorway, she darts a curious glance over to Fallon again and then back to me. Luckily, she doesn't comment, just follows me when I shut the door and head for the stairs.

Time to get her out before everyone gets home.

And it's a sweet fucking relief. Penelope Schneider-Cruz is the Wicked Witch of the West, and I'm glad she's out of here before my innocent little Dorothy gets back. She doesn't need that mindfuck a month before her birthday. She deserves to be happy. Excited. We all do.

Not twenty minutes after Mom speeds away in her tiny red Ferrari, the rest of the family loudly piles in through the garage door, laughing and debating something ridiculous per usual.

Fallon and I are in the living room, flipping channels, acting casual. I texted my dad that Mom left, off to her next parasitic relationship, but he didn't respond, so I'm not sure he saw it. And not that I care what happens to *Roger*, but she'll use him until he's a shriveled-up husk and then move on to the next unfortunate bastard. It's been her M.O. for the last five years, and we don't want Sofie exposed.

"Bro beans!" my little sister exclaims as she skips into the living room and plops on the couch between us, giggling.

"Hey, sis."

"Fallon," she coos, looping her arm through his and resting her head on his shoulder. "How are you, my new favorite person slash possible future step-cousin? Your hair is looking extra blue and extra floppy today."

"Sofie," I huff in disbelief, laughing at her outrageous attempt at a compliment. She's trying to use her quirky charms on him to butter him up for something she wants.

She just giggles, ignoring me. "You'd tell me if you knew where my surprise birthday party was going to be, right?"

"No," he deadpans, and I laugh when her mouth drops open in shock.

Sofie sits up straight and narrows her eyes playfully. She crosses her arms and huffs out an air of disbelief. "How rude."

I chuckle more, shaking my head at the two of them together.

Dad, Joel, and Georgie stroll in next, taking in the scene on the couch.

"Sofia Eleanor! Stop trying to coerce answers out of people, cariño. We already told you there is no party. Surprise or otherwise."

"Lies!" Sofie pouts even more, then turns pleading eyes to the only other woman in the room. "Georgie, this isn't nice. A girl needs to know these things! I only have a month! I won't know what outfits to plan. What make-up. What type of shoes to wear. How to do my hair. Please! Time is running out!"

My little sister is so dramatic, but we love her regardless.

"Aye! Stall the ball, missy. Don't ye worry about it; it'll be grand," Georgie says with her no-nonsense approach.

"But you're all teasing me. I don't want a surprise party. I'm not ten anymore!"

"Fine!" Dad exclaims, throwing his hands up. "You want to plan your own party?"

"Can I?" Sofie's eyes sparkle with hope and excitement.

"Of course, darling," Joel agrees, placing an arm around my dad's shoulders and pulling him close. "If that's what will make you happy. Right, honey?" He gives my dad a little squeeze, prompting him to agree.

"Yes, whatever you want to do, cariño. I guess you're not my little princess anymore."

Sofie jumps up, squealing. "I'm so excited! I need to get my iPad and start shopping right away! Can I have an eighties theme? No! No! Nineties? Way cooler."

"We did already book the skating rink for the Saturday after your actual birthday. We dropped off the deposit last week, and it's non-refundable. So I hope skating sounds fun, sweetie. But other than that, yes, you can plan whatever you want." Joel's tone is always warm and steadfast. Reliable. Just like him.

"I've hired Darcy again, so you can work directly with her to make your vision come to life," Dad adds.

Sofie spins around in a perfect pirouette, then nails the latest dance from social media. I burst out laughing again. So over the top.

"This is a present in itself! I can't wait to choose my

color aesthetic! I have so many ideas already. Can you send me Darcy's number? I want to text her my ideas right away."

Oh, poor Darcy. Whoever she is. Wherever she is. Unfortunate soul.

Sofie's phone chimes with the contact from Dad, and she scurries for the stairs. "Thanks, Dad! And thanks for brunch, Joel! I'm off to plan!"

As soon as Sofie disappears and her thumping up the stairs ceases, Dad turns to me. "Tell us what happened. Where's your mother now?"

I recount everything that happened, and Dad visibly relaxes, slouching back in his seat and into Joel's embrace.

I glance away, usually a little uncomfortable with their open affection, but now jealous that I can't do the same with my boyfriend sitting quietly next to me.

"That woman is an awful gobshite," Georgie supplies quite unhelpfully. "I'm sorry, lad, but yer mam's got my stomach in bits every time she pops back into my sweet little Sofie's life."

Georgina is protective over Sofia and me, having helped to raise us. I'm realizing that she's always been more of a mother to us than our own ever was.

"Let's just be grateful Penelope left before we got back. Sofie is so excited about her party now, and I don't want to ruin that. She doesn't need this," Joel says reasonably.

"I agree. Everyone also needs to know that Mom threatened to come back and take Sofie and me on a cruise with her and Roger." I snort because it's ridiculous and so not happening.

I'm eighteen, so I can make my own decisions, but things are a little trickier when it comes to Sofie. Mom still has partial custody, and Dad hasn't wanted to take her to court and make a big fuss, upsetting Sofie.

"I'll call Howard. I think it's time I go for full custody. We can't keep going through this. Howard seems to think if I explain the psychological stress and confusion this places on Sofie, we won't have any trouble being granted it. Not to mention the fact that she hasn't seen you in over a year."

"Do it, Al. What the feck have you been waitin' for, ye dope? That woman has no business influencing my Sofie with her unsavory life choices."

"I won't put it off any longer. This has to stop," he mumbles the last part, and Joel squeezes him. "Tesoro, come with me to my office for support?" Dad asks Joel.

"Of course, honey."

"Well, I'm gonna retire on home as well. There's a mystery casserole in the refrigerator, and I wrote the cooking instructions on the foil. Follow it, please. Don't ruin me hard work, lads."

I chuckle, excited for another Georgie mystery casserole special. They're always delicious and some version of shepherd's pie with meat and potatoes in a savory gravy.

"See ya later, George. Thanks for everything."

"Ye cheeky get, ye." But she smiles kindly, knowing I'm only teasing when I call her George.

Fallon's been quiet this whole time, just observing. Now that everyone's gone and off to their own afternoons, we can spend the rest of the day in my room *together*.

Just me and my boyfriend.

CHAPTER TWENTY

RYDER

Two weeks.

I've had a boyfriend for two weeks, and we've successfully hidden our relationship. When all I really want to do is show him off and tell everyone that I'm gay and Fallon is mine. I'm too close to winning the championship, though. I can taste it. And I just can't risk it or add any unneeded scrutiny.

We're playing the Jefferson Jaguars, and things haven't cooled down in the slightest since the toilet paper incident. Tensions are higher than ever. Seth has not-so-subtly reminded me what he thinks he knows about Fallon and me. I keep reminding him that I have proof of him vandalizing a school employee's home. Twice. Shuts him right up every time.

And two days ago, Cole let a donkey loose in the JHS gymnasium. Just free to roam, shit, and enjoy the massive amounts of hay he generously sprinkled over the hardwood court.

It was a mess, but the donkey enjoyed himself, and Cole did too. As did the rest of the academy. The Jaguars, not so much.

Knowing the prank war has been escalating, I heard Coach Patterson made his team clean up the gym themselves, with no help from the custodians. And picturing Dustin, Seth, and Rich bitching the entire time, looking and smelling like jackasses, brings me so much fucking joy.

"PETA is gonna be on our ass if this gets out!" Joel shouts in the authoritative tone that usually only comes out when we play like shit.

"The donkey is fine! He's back at the petting zoo. No harm, no foul. That dude lived like a donkey king for the night. And that was not a confession of guilt! Just a statement of fact," Cole adds, and Joel rolls his eyes.

"Regardless, these pranks have to stop, guys," Joel tells the locker room at the end of our last practice before the weekend. "We'll have four more practices next week, then the championship game on Friday. We're going to scrimmage hard and focus on our individual weak spots. But until then, I don't want you to think you've got the weekend off. There will be no relaxing. Only trust building."

What?

The room is so dead silent you could hear a pin drop. Everyone's as confused as I am, holding their breath and waiting for our coach to explain.

I know the guys were looking forward to blowing off some steam before the most stressful week of our high school basketball careers. Parties, hooking up, drinking, and probably doing stupid things are a given.

"You're all wondering what that means." Joel pulls a stack of pamphlets from his back pocket and walks around the locker room, tossing one to each of us.

Camp Dakota: Trust and Team Relationship Building.
Is he shitting me?

A chorus of groans echoes within the stark gray concrete walls and metal lockers. I shift my feet, squeaking my Jordans on the shiny floor as I lean against the lockers. I've already showered and changed into gray joggers and a new white hoodie.

I glance at the clock on the wall. It's getting late, and this new development is ruining my plans for the night. I was looking forward to making out with my boyfriend, maybe even taking it further than we have. We've been keeping pace, holding steady and enjoying sucking each other off while I train his hole to take me—

"Ryder."

Shit.

"Hmm?"

Joel's eyes bore into mine from behind his glasses, silently telling me to pay attention.

"I said, as team captain, I'm going to need you to head to the campsite early. As in right now, after school."

I close my eyes and drop my head, letting it bang loudly against the metal lockers. That may not be the most mature thing to do, but I'm not thrilled to spend my weekend doing trust falls.

"Is this a punishment?" one of the juniors asks.

"No. But both teams have been harassing and humiliating each other for too long."

He continues, pacing in front of us with his hands clasped behind his back. "This behavior is unacceptable. Coach Patterson and I have both decided this trust-building weekend is imperative. You'll be separated from the Jaguars but partaking in the same exercises. You *all* need this. I know many of you live on the lake, but you'll be on the non-residential side, deep into the forest, so don't let it fool you. You *will* be camping, and you *will* be roughing it.

There will be trust-building exercises, obstacle courses, and sportsmanship classes. Camp Dakota is challenging and fun. And yes, there will be a test at the end. And you will need to pass it to play in next Friday's championship game."

With that comes another round of groans, and I join them this time.

"That's how serious this is, guys!" Joel shouts over all the bitching and moaning around me.

"Coach Rivers," I say, raising my voice over the crowd. The guys immediately simmer down, listening to what their captain says. "It can't possibly be a good idea to be at this camp at the same time." I'm trying to sound reasonable because what Joel and Coach Patterson are asking seems completely unreasonable and risky.

"Well, something needs to be done before a prank worse than a donkey happens. These actions have no business in high school basketball, and Coach Pat and I decided an intervention was needed before something happens that we can't come back from. There are counselors on staff at Camp Dakota who'll camp right along with you. You guys aren't working with the Jaguars, but you're not in this alone, either. The counselors are great at what they do, and they'll help rebuild the trust within this team. Things got out of hand, but we can end the season strong. And with integrity. What do you say?"

He's trying to amp us up like he does before our big games. Some guys nod a little, and it's ridiculous how quickly they change their tune.

Jamie slides over to me. "We can't trust any of this."

I close my eyes, sighing deeply, before opening them and watching some of the younger guys talk excitedly with Joel.

"I know," I say, continuing to stare straight ahead. "Come early with me?"

"Bet. I wouldn't leave you to the wolves, dude. There's no way Seth, Dustin, and Rich won't try something if they know our team is there too."

Shit. He's right.

"Have my back?" I hold my fist out, and Jamie knocks his into mine.

"Always, bro." He leans closer. "You gonna have Fal come?"

Jamie knows we're dating. He figured it out after the very first time he saw us together. Perceptive mother fucker.

It shouldn't be too hard to convince Joel that camping would be better than Fallon staying home alone. "Yeah," I whisper.

"That's kinda dangerous."

I turn toward my best friend. "You don't think he should?"

"I'm not sure, dude. It's not my call. But it's risky for a few different reasons. You two have chemistry, and now that you're together, it's even easier for some people to pick up on. Like me. And maybe Seth."

"They don't control me, though, Jamie."

God. I'm so close to just telling them. I *want* to tell them. Or better yet, show them. Just kiss him right in front of their faces with the campfire roaring behind us. All cozy and shit.

"You've come this far, Cruz. Don't get reckless now. I have enough fires to put out because of Cole. Focus on the game first. You only have a week to get through."

Jamie, always the voice of reason.

Too bad, though. Because my boyfriend is *definitely* coming.

We cross into the Acadia Nature Preserve through the giant blue and white sign that people like to stop and take touristy photos by. The lake glistens to our right, the afternoon sun sparkling like diamonds sprinkled across the surface. It's nearly blinding to look at but breathtaking nonetheless.

Like I thought, it wasn't hard to convince Joel to let Fallon come. He always wants to do what's best for his nephew, so I assured him that having Fallon on the camping excursion would be good for him.

He knows we've become fast friends and that I genuinely care about his well-being. It needs to stay that way for now. Because besides being unsure how coming out would affect my basketball career, college career, and a possible shot at the NBA, I'm unsure how Joel would feel about me dating his nephew, specifically.

"Hey. You didn't want a pic with the sign, did you?" I say to Fallon.

"Funny," he deadpans.

"My bad. I can go back? For our future scrapbook."

"Stop it." His lip twitches.

Score. My charm is fucking irresistible.

"Because as soon as Sofie finds out we're dating, we are one-hundred-and-ten percent getting a 'Sofie Shipped It Scrapbook.' And dude, you don't even wanna know what that is." I shudder at the glittery monstrosities she creates for her favorite fictional couples. I cannot even imagine what she'd create for the two of us.

"I think I'd like to see that, actually. Let's go back. Get a photo."

Is he for real?

"You're shitting me."

"I'm not. Turn around. Go back to the sign. Maybe someone will be there, and we can get one together."

"Who are you, and what the fucking hell did you do with my broody little boyfriend?"

Fallon snorts. "Do not call me that."

"What? My broody little boyfriend?" I glance over at him and catch his narrowed-eye glare before checking behind me and making a quick, illegal U-turn.

I chuckle, already pulling into the small parking lot at the entrance to the Acadia Nature Preserve. The monument sign is taller than I am by at least a foot, but Fallon hops onto the base and hoists himself up. I give him a boost with a hand under his ass and a quick squeeze for good measure.

"Ryder!" he whisper-shouts, flicking his head toward the family piling out of the red minivan that parked next to my truck. "Stop. Before I pop a boner."

I snort at his comment. One little ass squeeze, and he's fighting a hard-on. I fucking love how responsive he is to my touch. "Be careful up there, Blue. I'm gonna see if they'll take a pic of us."

I jog over to the family and ask the woman if she'd take our picture. She's friendly enough but a little preoccupied with two fussy toddlers. "Rhett, come here!" she hollers into the van.

A fifteen or sixteen-year-old boy climbs out of the back with a Nintendo Switch. "Yeah, Mom?"

"Take a photo for this nice boy, please. I need to get your sisters' snacks." She digs through a giant tote bag and pulls out all kinds of crackers, cookies, and fruit pouches, making me hungry. My stomach growls loudly, and I instinctively place my hand over it.

It catches the woman's attention, and she eyes me speculatively. "You hungry?"

I smile politely and nod enthusiastically. "Always, ma'am. It takes a lot to fuel a body this size."

"I bet it does. Here. Hold this out." She hands me an empty grocery bag, and I listen, holding it open like a kid on Halloween.

"Trick or treat," I say with a big smile, and she chuckles, tossing in bags of fruit snacks, chips, little packs of crackers, and even some mini powdered donuts. She goes back to her van and opens a cooler, pulling out four grape juice boxes.

My favorite.

She drops those in my bag as well.

"Thank you so much, ma'am! Wow." These are some good fucking snacks.

"You're welcome, hun. Hopefully it holds you over for a little while. Wouldn't want to get lost in the redwoods without any supplies. We just went into town for a snack run while the hubby stayed back to guard the fort. But anyway, make sure you boys stay safe."

"You too. And thanks again for all the snacks." I hold the grocery bag up in silent cheers.

She nods once, going back to her toddlers as the teenager strolls toward me.

"Sup? Name's Rhett. You want a pic?" He holds his hand out, silently expecting me to place my phone in his palm.

"Yeah, dude. Thanks. And my name's Ryder."

"Sure thing."

Fallon is still perched on top of the sign, and I smile, thinking about everyone that just drove by in the last five minutes. Their photo included an emo boy with blue hair sitting on top.

Sounds like an awesome pic, so I snap one of just Fallon before handing my phone to the kid.

I jog over and stand next to the sign, smiling as Rhett snaps photos. "I'm in photography," he tells us. "So these should be pretty close to professional quality."

Yeah. Okay. Sure, kid.

But I say, "Nice, dude!" instead.

"Look out!" he shouts back, and I'm confused for a split second before a heavy weight lands on my back.

Oof.

I stumble two steps before I regain my balance and grab his knees.

Strawberries and fresh linen surround me, and I laugh freely, Rhett taking candid photos of us the whole time.

A low, rumbly laugh filters into my ears, and I'm stunned. It's amazing. Incredible. I need to hear it again.

Louder. More.

Obsession is too light a word. My insides are raving, and my dick is filling.

Fallon laughs again, and a shiver races down my spine. The rough sound is toe-curling. It's like being in the presence of a rare, beautiful flower that only blooms once every century.

He gives me a quick squeeze before letting go and hopping down.

Rhett comes running over with a giant smile on his face. "These are awesome! Look!" He shoves my phone in my face, and I rear back to get a better look.

I take it and flip through the photos, angling it so that Fallon can see.

"These are so good, Rhett. You were right; these *are* professional. You got major talent, little dude."

They really are good, and there's no point in not pumping him up. Rhett beams back at me, a slight rosy tint filling his cheeks. "Thanks, man!"

"Rhett, hun! Time to go before your father starts to worry!" his mom shouts.

"Coming!" he hollers back before turning toward me again. He pulls his beanie off and runs an awkward hand through his shaggy brown hair.

"Uh. You got Insta or something? Maybe we could take more photos later? Like for my class or something?"

I glance at Fallon and catch the tiny little smirk on his lips before he hides it by chewing on his lip ring. I can feel the happy energy radiating from him, and if surprise-attack piggyback rides and getting hit on by a nice little fifteen-year-old is what does it, sign me up for that shit every fucking day. Because this vibrant aura of his right now? It's positively angelic.

"Sure, dude. What's your handle?" I ask the kid.

Rhett spells it out for me, and I follow him. "I'll tag you in the pic. Give you photo cred and all that."

"Thanks!"

"Rhett! Let's go!" his mom hollers for the second time.

"I gotta go. Nice to meet you guys!" And then he's tugging his beanie back on as he heads back to his mom and little sisters.

As soon as he's gone, I turn toward my broody little boyfriend. "You smiled. You laughed. You rocked my fucking world, Blue."

Fallon rolls his eyes and snorts, gracing me with another little smirk.

Score!

"Holy shit! Another! My heart can't take it." I clasp my chest dramatically. "And that raspy little laugh of yours? Curls my toes, dude." I glance around and squint my eyes down the road. It looks like no one's around, and no one's coming.

"Come on," I say urgently, grabbing his hand and tugging him toward my truck.

He knows what I want. What I need. We both scramble into the vehicle and lock the doors. My windows are dark, so no one can see in.

"My lap. *Now.*"

Fallon straddles me, whimpering as I waste no time spearing my tongue into his mouth, taking charge and owning this kiss.

I pull back, needing him to hear something. To believe it.

"You're allowed to be happy, Fallon. It's beautiful when you are, and I don't just mean the physical. Although trust me, baby. You've got that in the bag too. Your joy is infectious, and your soul is unique. You're worthy of happiness. Worthy of love. And worthy of attention. Fuck, Fallon. I need to hear you laugh and see you smile every fucking day. *Please.*"

I'm hanging on by a thread. The passion swirling inside is urging me to take him here and now. But I don't want either of our first times to be cramped in the backseat of my truck, no matter how large the cab is.

"I'll try," he whispers against my lips, and that's all I can ask of him.

I reward him with a soft kiss, and he weaves his fingers into my hair, tugging on my curls.

"Thank you," I breathe into his mouth, rocking my hips up into his and making him groan.

We get lost in the moment, making out and grinding against each other in the front seat.

"We should stop," he says, trying to be the voice of reason for both of us.

"We should," I agree, running my hands down his ribs and squeezing his hip hard as I pull him down. "Wanna fuck you so bad, Blue."

Fallon whimpers, and his words are barely audible. "I want that too. I'm ready."

I groan, so turned on yet extra annoyed that we're forced into this trust-building weekend. Because there's no way I'm taking his virginity in a tent in the woods with a bunch of pranking douchebags nearby.

It doesn't mean blowies are off the table, though.

"When we win the championship," I whisper, kissing my way across his jaw and over to his ear, pressing my lips directly to it. "I'm going to celebrate by claiming your tight little hole and filling you all the way up with my cum."

"Ryder, shit," he whimpers. "Are we coming in our pants? 'Cause fuck, I'm gonna."

I chuckle, lifting him off my lap and depositing him back in his seat, to our displeasure. "We can't show up with jizz pants, dude. Maybe we can suck each other off when the tent's set up. My dad got us some fancy-ass kind that's basically a little house with a zipper door."

Fallon presses the heel of his palm to the boner straining his jeans. "I didn't know being gay and having a boyfriend meant having near-constant blue balls. Damn," he whines some more, and a low laugh rumbles out of me.

Every day he opens up a little more and shows me more of who he really is under all that sadness. That *grief*. It weighs on him, and I want to help lift it.

The letter resting in my jewelry box back home is

taunting me with its potential to harm or help. I know it will be devastating for him; there's no doubt about it. No matter what his dad wrote in that letter, reading words written for eighteen-year-old Fallon, it's fucking heavy. But I know he'll feel much lighter once he does. The reality won't be as burdensome.

And I'll be there for him when he's ready. This letter is important, but I won't push it. I'm looking forward to the day he can truly be himself. And I can too.

After basketball. Maybe.

CHAPTER TWENTY-ONE

FALLON

I've never been camping before, and I don't think this whole trust-building thing is a good idea, let alone actually accomplish anything. But Ryder wants me there, and Joel says it would be good for me too. I don't play sports and don't need to trust any of these people, but I'll go anywhere to spend time with my boyfriend, even if it's camping. It could be fun to mess around in a tent.

"Let's get settled and pick our spot before anyone else gets here. They have little plots of land for tents that're separated by the trees for privacy. Some have a firepit or picnic table. We definitely need to get one of those. You brought your guitar, right?"

"Yeah."

I've been practicing again. Been thinking about that letter a lot, too.

"Will you play for me tonight? Sing for me?"

"Just us?"

His lip twitches and that dazzling smile blooms. "Just us, Blue," he confirms.

With a sharp nod, I agree. I don't mind serenading my boyfriend by the campfire.

"Sweet!" he cheers, happy as ever. His enthusiasm is growing on me.

The deeper we get into the preserve, the denser the forest becomes. Trees tower above us, their thick trunks and massive height blocking the afternoon sun.

We follow the winding path, and Ryder flips his headlights on, illuminating the road in front of us. He reaches his long arm over, resting his hand on my thigh and giving me a squeeze before leaving it there. I like it. The weight of his hand, his strength. It's comforting. Reassuring.

A small wooden sign marks the entrance to *Acadia Lake Campgrounds*, and Ryder flips his blinker on, turning in. The lot is only half full, a couple families and another young couple milling about. Hopefully two dozen rivaling high school basketball players won't disturb their vacations. I take a deep breath, already anticipating the worst.

"What? What's wrong?" Ryder picks up on my mood shift.

"Nothing. Just hoping nothing goes wrong. For our sake and the sake of all these poor, unsuspecting people. I wouldn't want to be around a bunch of teenagers if I were them."

Ryder winces. "Yeah, this is probably just a bad idea all around. I hope we don't kill each other being in such close proximity. Because I know it's going to be tempting."

I nod, agreeing while I reached for the new hiking backpack Joel got me so I could pack all my stuff in one convenient bag. I don't really like accepting things from him because it makes me uncomfortable. But I don't have enough money for camping gear, and I'm only here for Joel and Ryder.

"Let's go claim our spot. You gonna be able to get out of the truck okay, babe? That bag's nearly the size of you. And the drop? Please don't sprain your ankle before the weekend even starts."

"Har, har," I deadpan. "I think we've established that I do not need a step stool. Thank you very much."

Ryder's smooth laughter bubbles out of him. "Well, regardless, be careful. You're kinda small, and that drop is kinda big."

We both get out of the truck, and I leave the heavy-ass pack on the seat while I climb down. Before I can even grab it, Ryder reaches over me with his big body and grabs my pack like it weighs five pounds. He slings it over his shoulder, a matching bag in forest green on his other side.

"Can you grab the tent from the back? And the cooler if you can."

The tent is pretty big but packaged securely and weighs less than my pack. And the cooler has a handle and wheels, so I pull it after me as we head toward the Camp Dakota Adventure Bus.

"Hey, guys! I'm Dale. Are you public or private?" he asks with an overzealous smile, bright orange hair, and clipboard in hand.

This is going to be a long weekend. I'll probably just be a silent observer and *not* an active participant.

"Private. Ryder Cruz. Team captain. Here to get settled in and claim the plots for my team."

"Great! That means I'll be your counselor. Bryant is taking on the public school. One tent and two campers per campground. These are smaller plots for singles and couples. There are a variety of firepits, seating logs, picnic tables, and other small amenities unique to each. Bathrooms and showers are communal and marked with several signs on the trails between campgrounds. You won't miss it. We also have some here." Dale motions behind him at a large brown building.

He hands us each a map and itinerary. "Here's the schedule so you know when there are mandatory exercises, optional discussions, mealtimes, and evening gatherings. We at Camp Dakota look forward to providing a fun, safe, and adventurous excursion to build trust, teamwork, and leadership."

"Great, thanks," Ryder says with false enthusiasm, but I don't have the social energy required to interact with someone as peppy as Dale. He is a step above my processing power at the moment.

This weekend should be interesting. I'm not required to do any of this. I'll do what I want, but I don't need to push myself like the rest of them.

"I don't play ball," I respond in a scratchy, quiet voice, grasping the tent bag tighter and refusing to take the papers from his grasp.

"Oh. You're Coach Rivers' nephew. No problem. But please, here. You still need this information. It has safety precautions as well." His smile seems genuine, but he reminds me of one of my mother's exes, and my brain won't get past that.

"Okay," I mumble, rolling the papers up before sticking them in my back pocket.

"Alright, boys. Take a left at the first fork in the road. Keep traveling left, and you'll reach your school's section of the campground. The public school is to the right. Separated. Everything is isolated and private, so we'll meet regularly as groups. To talk about issues and try to work them out. Discuss things you've learned and how our activities apply to the building of trust."

Fun.

I'll pass.

I plan to stay zipped up in our tent and write music or, if I'm lucky, find some quiet solitude. . . *and write music.* Maybe the map in my back pocket will come in handy, and I can find my way to the lakeshore.

There's beauty in the repetitive patterns of nature. And just like the melodies constantly swirling in my head, these patterns are never perfect. But they're beautiful. Unique. Something worth noting. Something worth showcasing. Something worth appreciating.

Something worth remembering.

And now I'm itching to write. Desperate to pull my colorful Sharpies out and scribble my thoughts on paper before they turn into actual feelings. All I know is that whatever I do on this weekend camping trip, it most definitely will not be trust falls and obstacle courses.

I'm not much help, but with Ryder's size, it takes him no time to set up our tent. It looks like a little canvas shack, the size of a small bedroom. Some windows unzip, allowing air to flow through the mesh, and the front door is a little more structured than a typical tent flap, but we still just have a zipper.

He took his shirt off, working up a sweat, even though it's chilly. His tall, tan, and toned body is so alluring. The grooves of his abdomen and the lines of his obliques draw my eyes in, instantly plumping up my dick from the mere sight of him.

I have no reason for how clueless I was about the fact that I like guys. I guess I've just blocked everything out.

Every single feeling, even to the detriment of learning who I am. But I'm trying now.

Ryder helps, even unknowingly. From the very beginning, light and safety radiated from his every pore. I can't help but let my guard down around him. It's powerful and heady, giving into my desires and giving into Ryder. I *want* to give him everything if he'll take it.

Take *me*.

My whole body tingles with awareness, and my cock gets harder. I'm still horny from earlier. I press the heel of my palm into my straining erection and hop up from my place at the picnic table.

I stalk toward Ryder as he bends over, hammering the last stake into the ground. I run my hand up the hard muscles of his back, enjoying the feel of his sweat-slicked skin.

"You done?" I grunt. No one's around. It really is secluded. We can definitely fuck around out here.

I let my hand travel the length of his back and curl around his shoulder, squeezing and kneading the muscles there. He groans before standing up slowly, my hand slipping away.

"Yeah, Blue. I am. You want something?"

I chew on my lip ring, nodding slowly, glancing at the boner tenting my jeans.

"Whatcha want?" His eyes turn hooded as he stares down at me. His voice drops an octave, and my heart rate kicks up a notch.

"I want to see the inside." I tilt my head toward the oversized structure.

Ryder grabs my hand and tugs me toward the door, zipping it after us.

I can stand, but Ryder has to duck, so he pulls me down to the sleeping bags and pillows he placed side by side.

Ryder wastes no time, sealing his lips to mine and coaxing my tongue out. His hand travels down my body, cupping me over my pants and squeezing gently. I gasp into his open mouth, pressing myself further into his sweaty chest as I straddle his lap.

We fit perfectly like this, and I want to rub myself all over him like a possessive cat. I run my hands across his pecs and over to his nipples, grabbing on and squeezing gently.

Ryder moans into my mouth, "Mmmm. Fuck, Blue. You're getting me so hard. Lemme suck you first."

Ryder's hands scramble for my jeans, desperate to free me from their grasp. It doesn't take long before I'm lying completely bare in this canvas tent in the woods, allowing Ry's hungry gaze to traverse my trembling body.

But I'm not scared. I'm fucking needy and horny and. . . "I need your mouth on me now, Ryder. *Please.*"

He peers up at me between his golden brown curls, giving me a sexy wink before trailing soft, teasing kisses down my torso until he gets to my leaking cock.

I'm so rock hard, my tip angry and red. One suck and I'll probably explode in his mouth.

"It's not gonna take long," I warn, and fuck, I feel like I'm always telling him that. I need to work on my stamina.

He gives me a cocky little smirk before he licks a long stripe from my balls to my tip, sucking on the end.

Hard.

"Oh, fuck!" It's almost *too* much. The sensations are almost too strong. But I force myself to lie there and take it.

My hips start to buck wildly into Ryder's mouth. He pops off, holding me down with both hands, the pressure and restraint turning me on even more. My cock pulses with desire.

"Stay still and be quiet while I blow you, baby. We can't make a mess. We're too far from the bathroom. I'm gonna suck every last drop of cum from your cock and swallow it down. All of it."

He keeps both hands on my bare hips, pressing me down into the ground while he deep throats my entire length, pulling back to lick down to my sac.

I can't move, but my body is trying to squirm, the feeling turning me on even more. The next time Ryder takes my entire length into his warm, wet mouth, I detonate without warning.

He chokes on my cum, not expecting an unwarned volcanic eruption down his throat. Jizz dribbles out his mouth, down his chin, and plops onto me, making a mess.

Whoops.

A raspy-sounding laugh bursts out of me, its rough edges tickling my throat for the second time in hours.

Ryder's eyes open wide, blinking slowly. And then a slow grin tugs at his full lips before he leans forward to clean me up with his mouth. He swipes his tongue across my body, licking every drop of cum from me, making me shiver.

"My turn," I declare, giving him a devilish smile. I'm not sure what's come over me, maybe it's all the fresh air, but I'm feeling good. Feeling happy, maybe. And I haven't even broken out the weed stashed in my backpack. I'm hoping it's a sign of a good weekend to come.

CHAPTER TWENTY-TWO

RYDER

Cole and Jamie arrived shortly after we got settled, claiming the closest campsite to ours. They don't have a fire pit, but they have a nice wooden table with four sawed-off stumps for seats and a charcoal grill. We can cook dinner over there and roast marshmallows over here.

After setting up the tents, we all meet with Dale and his Camp Dakota counselors-in-training—Mindy and Sam—by the big number one marked on the map.

"I have some unfortunate news," Dale says with a sigh, and my hackles rise. I glance at Jamie, a bad feeling settling in my gut.

"Bryant, my fellow Camp Dakota counselor, has been taken out by a nasty case of food poisoning. He won't be able to camp with and coach the Jaguars."

"What does that mean?" I ask because he just needs to spit it out.

"Mindy and Sam aren't old enough to be full-fledged counselors, nor do they have the proper training and certifications. I cannot allow them to work with the public school alone. I'm going to have to manage my time and both schools."

I groan and scrub a hand down my face because Dale has lost touch with reality if he thinks this will work, or maybe he doesn't even know about the pranks.

It isn't long before the rest of my team and the Jaguars show up, forcing Dale to repeat his unfortunate news. After another debate and a lot of bitching, we all decide to do the exercises and move on with our weekend.

If only things were ever that easy.

The first challenge is a team obstacle course in the forest. Even though we aren't competing with them, we beat the Jaguars; not only can they not get along with us, they can't even get along with each other. They argued non-stop; we could hear them from the ground. I'm sure it was justified, but Dustin was shoved off twice.

Number two on the map is a classic game of tug of war. Although with this many giant teenagers, it got a little rough. Seth and I faced off in the lead spot on opposite sides of the mud pit. It was only appropriate for the team captains to take the brunt of the loss on this one.

They need more than one weekend away at trust camp to fix their team issues. And really, it's too late anyway. There's one game left. It was always going to be a pipe dream for them. And maybe even for us.

My attention to detail is always spot on, so I wait for Seth to ever-so-slightly adjust his grip and yell 'Pull!' to my entire team. We yank them forward so hard and so unexpectedly that Seth flies right into the mud.

Face first.

He even takes the second person on the rope right along with him. Dustin lands right on Seth, his weight further pressing the team captain into the mud, causing him to sputter and choke on dirt.

Cole immediately burst out laughing, and there's just something contagious about his laughter. I join soon after until the entire length of our rope laughs at the public school idiots in the mud.

Yeah, our sportsmanship isn't exactly going to get an A plus, but we're still completing the challenges. So all Dale could do was sigh and call it an early day so the losers could shower their shame off before mealtime.

Dinner is assorted foil packets, catered by none other than Georgie. There's white fish in butter sauce and Italian sausage with peppers and onions. But I'm choosing teriyaki chicken with pineapple and bell peppers. No doubt. That shit is bomb! I'm pretty sure Georgie made it just for me.

At the very end of the table are shrimp dinners with potatoes and corn on the cob in Cajun seasoning.

Thinking about their little legs swimming through the water, their speed and zig-zag, and their beady little eyes, I gag, dry-heaving while I reach for the chicken dinner instead.

Jamie side-eyes me like I'm about to yak all over the food.

"Shrimp," is all I say, shivering in disgust.

I grab two packets for myself and two for Fallon, one sausage and one chicken. He's still trying to catch up from being malnourished for the last five years. And me, well, I'm a big guy who needs a lot of calories to maintain my energy and body. Cole and Jamie also grab two, and we head to their campsite to grill our dinners according to Georgie's convenient instructions.

Fallon is already there, perched on one of the sawed-off

logs, scribbling in his little green notepad and chewing on the end of a Sharpie.

I stand there for a beat too long, no less fascinated by his mouth than yesterday or the day before.

Jamie sidles up next to me, subtly nudging me with his elbow. "Let's go, lover boy," he whispers teasingly. "Time to cook dinner for your man."

I chuckle at my best friend's joke, making my way over to set the food on the wooden table while Jamie grabs the charcoal.

I missed Fallon today. He stayed back, opting out of today's trust-building exercise. Don't blame him. I would have passed too, if it was an option.

"Hey, Fal. How was your day?"

He lifts a shoulder in response. "You?"

"Awesome 'cause Seth, Dustin, and Rich looked like complete tools. Wish you coulda seen it," I say with a wide grin as I picture Seth face-down in the mud with Dustin on top of him. "Mud facials."

He looks up from his notepad at that, giving me a curious expression, but doesn't ask.

"Did you spend the day writing?" I probe, trying to get more answers out of him and wondering if he'll sing me something later tonight. Just the two of us around our fire pit, like we talked about.

"Yeah. Found my way to the lake and took my guitar. It was nice."

I nod, agreeing because it *is* nice out here.

"After dinner, wanna play something for me? I've been thinking about it all day."

"I will, yeah. Dunno if I feel like singing, though. But I can play for you."

"I'll take it."

I'll take anything he gives me.

Saturday morning greets us with a cacophony of mockingbirds and woodpeckers. The distant sound of water running and the wind blowing through the leaves soothes a part of me that I didn't know needed soothing.

Ten minutes into lounging, I'm drifting back into that warm, comfortable space, hovering on the edge of sleep. Bliss. It might be bliss. Especially when I'm curled around my sweet and broody little boyfriend.

The calming sounds of nature are interrupted by a shrill bell and Mindy's accompanying high-pitched voice. "Breakfast!"

I crawl out of bed, Fallon stirring next to me. I unzip the tent and stick my head out, squinting into the brightness. The early morning sun shines through the trees, bathing the hillside in beautiful shades of crimson and gold like a stained glass window.

My stomach growls when the scent of warm baked goods wafts to my nose. A giant picnic basket sits on the ground outside our tent, and relief washes through me that I don't have to race over to the mess hall and grab breakfast before it's gone. I lug our basket into the tent, immediately opening the top and peering inside.

Fresh chocolate chip muffins, croissants, bagels, jam, butter, cream cheese, prosciutto, and smoked salmon, along with a pitcher of orange juice and plastic cups.

There's a note on rainbow tie-dyed stationary that I immediately recognize from home. And judging by the food in this basket, I'm guessing Georgie was at it again.

Oy! Me boys winning the games! I'm so proud! Keep up the

*hard work and enjoy some of me fluffy muffs! Warm and moist
and there's plenty to go around! So I'm letting ye share!*

Enjoy,

Your Georgie

Oh, God. How can the awkward innuendo come
through on paper? It makes me cringe. Hard.

"We should take it to the other guys before we open
everything." I grab one croissant and then another, tossing
it to a sleepy-faced Fallon. He catches it easily and shoves
half of the bread into his mouth, chewing with his eyes
closed.

I chuckle at his adorable blue hair sticking up in every
direction.

I take a bite of my own croissant, examining the map.

"Number three is by the river. . ." I trail off, glancing up
and making eye contact with my now wide-awake
boyfriend.

"I can't swim," he tells me, dusting the lingering pastry
flakes off his sleeping bag.

"I won't let anything happen to you. And it may not
even have to do with water."

He takes a deep breath and rakes a hand through the
dark side of his hair, closing his eyes and shaking his head.

"A river is different from sitting on a dock or at the edge
of the lake. I have control, then. My body decides whether
or not I enter the water. But a river is turbulent, volatile,
aggressive. It can't be trusted."

Damn. That was kinda deep. And hot.

"The Acadia River has Class Four rapids, so I can't
imagine we'd take that route." I'm trying to make him feel
better, but we're here to test our limits and trust.

"Not helping, Ryder."

Fallon has bowed out of the other challenges so far, and

I kinda hope he sits this one out as well. I'm not so sure it's a good idea, actually.

"Uncle Joel said I should try one of the exercises, and I already skipped yesterday. Don't wanna let him down."

"I don't know, Blue." I'd be worried about him the entire time, unable to focus on the task myself.

"Think I'll do it." His steely-blue eyes are determined, and I know I can't push this.

"Okay. Let's do this. I'm wearing swim trunks under my pants and a long-sleeve dri-fit tee, just in case. But I really hope we're not actually getting in the water. It's way too cold for that shit."

Fallon's slim body looks so sexy in his deep blue skin-tight, long-sleeve shirt. It accents both his eyes and his hair. Combined with the black cargo pants and hiking boots, he looks like a sexy, emo mountain boy, and holy fuck I'm already thinking about swallowing his cock again.

I clear my throat. "Let's head out before I get a boner over how hot you look in blue."

The number three trail leads us to the next spot on the map, a massive zipline that crosses the water.

The Acadia River carves its way down the mountain and feeds directly into the lake, causing the water to be cold.

"Oh, this is insanely awesome," I say aloud, and Cole instantly agrees. After sharing the breakfast basket with the team, we made the hike out here with him and Jamie.

"Fuck yeah, Dale! A zipline? You're winning today, brother. I'll go first!" Cole jogs ahead, bumping fists with our camp counselor, apparently his new best friend.

Dale chuckles at Cole's enthusiasm. "I'm glad you're

excited, Cole. Let's wait for everyone else to get here and discuss this morning's activity."

After ten minutes of impatiently standing around, the public school kids finally show up, and Dale begins his spiel.

"Today is all about the challenge of personal choices that can also affect the group. You are a team, not individuals. So you need to work as a team to get to the finish line. Sounds simple, right? Well, sorry folks, it's not. It won't be the Jaguars vs. the Knights today. That would be too easy. Nope, you'll be mixed up. I decided to take advantage of the situation and make things a little more interesting. Each stage of today's challenge will have an easy choice and a hard choice. Beware that the easy choices come with unknown time penalties, and your time won't stop until the last person on your team crosses the finish line. So choose wisely and help each other out. Keep in mind that it might be best to choose the harder route and assist each other along the way. Even if it takes longer. The winners get campfire treats tonight!"

He's ignorant if he thinks that's what's truly at stake here.

Dale claps his hands and rubs them together excitedly. "Alright. Time to get started. I'm going to split you up and give you thirty minutes to talk over what you think your potential weaknesses and strengths are. Maybe formulate a rough plan of attack. You can choose to jump and swim or zipline across easily. Your own decisions. Remember that your individual choices affect the whole."

As if the universe hates me, Fallon, Cole, Jamie, and I are placed on a team with Seth, Rich, and fucking Dustin.

We form a loose circle and voice how we want to handle this first obstacle, agreeing to tackle the rest as they come.

"Swim," says Jamie.

"Swimming for me too," Cole states.

Luckily Fallon is before me in the rotation, so I'll let him take the lead on this one and do what he does.

"Zipline," is all he utters, and the three public school guys immediately jump down his throat.

"No way! You heard Dale. It's not good to take the easy route. We'll get penalized, and that's selfish," Rich whines like the little bitch he is.

"Fallon can make his own decisions," I say with a bite to my tone. "And I'm ziplining too." Pretty sure they won't question me on it. We don't owe them an explanation, and they don't need to know Fallon can't swim if he doesn't want them to.

Rich scoffs, throwing his arms up in the air. "You pussies are going to be the reason we lose."

I'm not engaging. And I won't let him pressure us into choosing something Fallon isn't comfortable with.

"Don't listen to them." I lean down and whisper into his ear. "We do this together."

"Okay!" Dale shouts. "Zipliners, grab your harnesses from me, and let's get this challenge going!"

"I'll get them for us," I say to Fallon, and he heads toward the cliff's edge, waiting by one of the cables.

Only a couple other guys are taking the zipline and none from the academy. It doesn't matter, though. I do what my boyfriend does.

Before I even make it over to Dale, I hear a loud shout, followed by a splash.

A cold wave of dread washes over me, tiny icicles creeping down my spine.

I spin around and race toward the cliff, my heart galloping like a herd of wild horses.

I shout at Cole and Jamie because I don't see my fucking boyfriend where I left him.

"Where's Fallon?!"

No one answers.

Jamie and Cole dash after me, echoing my thoughts with more vulgarities.

My eyes find Dustin's, and a cruel smirk forms on his hateful face.

"He wanted to go first. Decided to swim after all." He holds his hands up in mock surrender.

All the blood drains from my face as fear squeezes my heart in a death grip. It's like a blizzard sweeps through my insides, freezing every cell, nearly immobilizing me.

"He can't swim, you fucking *idiot*!" My voice sounds like it's coming from someone else.

I frantically push through the crowd of public school cunts, and make a break for the cliff's edge. I don't even hesitate. I dive off, even though this is a jump-only spot. There's no time.

The impact is startling, the cold water rushing up my nose and causing my muscles to stiffen. I open my eyes underwater, searching through the murky depths for my boyfriend. My heart is hammering against my ribcage, and my lungs burn as they warn me to take a breath.

Fuck! Where is he?

I can't see anything!

My hand snags on something, and I grab the fabric, pulling him to me and desperately swimming toward the surface.

I break through the dark water, and we gasp and cough for air. The sound of his breathing is a fucking balm to my soul.

I can't lose him. I just found him.

I band my arms around him, speaking in soothing tones so he stops panicking. "I got you. It's me. Just relax. Don't panic. I'll get us to shore."

I don't know why I just told the panicking boy not to panic, like that's actually a thing.

He doesn't hear me anyway, thrashing against me as I try again.

"Blue, I got you. You're okay. I got you."

I start paddling against the current toward the other side of the shore, straining my muscles and gritting my teeth as I kick with all my might and desperately clutch my boyfriend to my chest.

"You're okay, Blue. You're okay."

I chant the words for his benefit as well as my own.

"Hurry up! Before you slow our time down even more!" Dustin hollers back at us like a fucking asshole. Seth and Rich are right behind him, casually backstroking and laughing.

Pricks!

Jamie and Cole catch up to us, keeping pace and helping Fallon and me make it to the other side of the river.

As soon as my feet touch solid ground, relief washes through me. This part of the river has Class Four rapids, and you never know when you can get swept away.

I glance back at the cliff's edge where the rest of the teams stand, staring in disbelief.

Yeah. I can't believe he just pulled this shit, either.

They're trying to provoke me. Get me disqualified. Make me lose. Push me until it affects my basketball game.

And the fuckers are getting close.

Because, of course, I don't see Dale, Mindy, or Sam as I scan the cliff. They didn't see anything, and they're going to think we all *chose* to swim.

So if Dustin isn't getting punished by the authorities, I'll have to do it myself.

Fallon stands not long after me, but I hold his soaked shirt because he's small, and this river is wild. The loose pebbles of the riverbed slip beneath our shoes as we wade toward dry land.

"Fallon. Talk to me."

"I'm fine."

He's not. He's shivering, and not just from the cold. But I don't argue with him.

"There are dry clothes over here!" Cole shouts, and I jog over, seeing the picked-over pile that Dustin, Seth, and Rich left behind. We're all supposed to be on the same *team* today.

God, I hate them.

"I'm done. I'm out. Fuck this," I say, completely fed up, running a hand through my wet curls. "I'm just gonna chase those fuckers down and take 'em all on."

"Like hell you are, dude!" Cole yells at me, peeling his shirt over his head. His normally shaggy hair is slicked back and dark.

Jamie hands Fallon a towel and throws one at me.

"Be smart, Ry. That's not smart. For many different reasons."

"Did you see what they did?!" I shout in my best friend's face, letting my overwhelming feelings get the better of me.

"Yes, Ryder. We all did. But you don't need to go running into the fucking woods, guns blazing!" he yells back. "You'll be killing our season. Your dreams. *Everything.* Don't do it."

"He's right. Let's finish this," Fallon says with a fluffy white towel wrapped around his shivering shoulders.

"What?" I ask in utter disbelief.

Is he serious right now?

"No fucking way, Fallon. You nearly drowned!"

God, why am I shouting so much?

I don't *shout* and especially not at my friends. This is exactly what those assholes wanted, and it pisses me off even more.

"I'm fine," he repeats, but his teeth are chattering.

"He said he's fine and wants to keep going," Cole encourages. Of course he does; he just wants to win everything all the time.

"Just beat them on the court. Completely wipe the floor with them," Jamie adds with his voice of reason.

I stare at Fallon, wanting to wrap my arms around him. Help him change. I want to warm him with my body heat and press my naked skin to his. But I can't. I can't do any of that. Because I'm not out. And it sucks.

I'm okay, he mouths, imploring me with his blue-gray gaze.

I take a deep breath and release it slowly, lifting my dri-fit shirt and peeling it over my head. Our new T-shirts have Camp Dakota printed on the front.

"Guess we're gonna keep going," I give in, unwilling to disappoint my team. I'll get my revenge on the court later.

"Oh, look at the pretty, pretty princess. Will you be my cheerleader? Or has Cruz already locked that weird shit down?" Rich taunts cruelly before I "accidentally" elbow him right in the fucking mouth.

Bastardo.

He immediately throws his hands up, muffling his curse, before spitting a mouthful of blood onto the outdoor concrete court Cole found behind the showers. It's perfect for this early morning scrimmage, and I sneer in disgust at Rich's bloody spit on the pavement.

Andy, one of the juniors, is acting as our ref and blows the whistle, but it was worth it. They can take their foul shots. They're still going to lose.

"Fucker!" Rich yells, his teeth shining crimson, and I smirk.

I glance at Fallon sitting on the sidelines, which is just another log. He's got his headphones in, so he didn't even hear that homophobic bullshit. Not that Rich knows anything. He's just trying to egg me on and get me to hit him or any of them. I realize that now. It won't work, though. The guys and I just spread the fouls out so no one gets ejected. We already discussed this.

"Why are you all so obsessed with Fallon, huh? That's what's weird, dude. And unwanted. Go the fuck away."

Rich sputters a little, walking over to the free-throw line. He assumes his position, and Andy tosses him the basketball. The teams line up on either side. Flustered by my comment, Rich misses both shots.

I can't help but be the one asshole to laugh, and Andy side-eyes me like *I'm* the freaking bad guy here. Ridiculous, but whatever.

They've done nothing but target Fallon since they met him, simply because he's different and to get at me. To affect my game. But nothing can affect my game, and I show them this when I score the next four three-pointers effortlessly.

Call me Steph Curry!

These Jefferson kids are a complete joke.

Cole, the bulkiest of us all, shoulder-checks Dustin as

they lunge for a ball that I "accidentally" tossed toward the sidelines.

Dustin grunts at the impact and goes flying into the vegetation at the edge of the court. Andy blows his whistle, signaling the other team as out of bounds.

I burst out laughing at the ridiculousness of the situation as his fucking legs stick out of a bush like this is some sort of comedy sketch.

"Oh shit! I wish I had my phone!" Cole says, howling with laughter and most definitely planning on spreading this little mishap around both schools.

I glance at Fallon again, and he's already staring at me. His dark eyes are intense and unyielding. Asking me a question without verbalizing a word.

Are you doing all of this for me?

I give him a little wink before focusing back on the game and scoring as many three-pointers as possible. Obnoxiously so.

They're starting to get flustered and defeated, unable to block me more than ten percent of the time. If this game counted for their stats, it would be a joke.

I'm guarding Seth as he attempts to dribble around me, but I keep bumping him with my chest and forcing him back. He gets annoyed and lashes out.

"You gonna get more sparkles on your lips after this, Cruz?" he taunts cruelly.

"Shut up," I hiss, bumping him hard enough to make him trip over his feet. He falls back on his ass with a pained grunt. The concrete is more unforgiving than our usual hardwood.

"Stay down," I add with my golden boy smile, wondering if it's too late for me here at Camp Dakota. I'm on the verge of saying fuck it all. Fuck everything.

But then I glance at Fallon sitting on the stump, tapping his foot and scribbling in that fucking notebook like always. The silent strength he projects in the face of his fucking bullies. His attackers. *Our enemies.* Showing them he isn't fazed by their reckless pranks and narrow-minded views. So, I'll stay strong too.

All I need to do is pass this bullshit trust camp, and I can sweep the floor with them in the championship.

CHAPTER TWENTY-THREE

FALLON

I don't know why I'm sitting by the water again after what happened earlier today, but things are getting hazy, and I guess the lake just doesn't scare me. The stillness of the surface has a calm serenity to it. Or it could be the numbness washing over me as I take another hit of the blunt I rolled before sneaking out of our tent.

Either way, it's midnight, and I'm too tired to fall asleep. It doesn't make sense, but it happens. And I'm sick of counting sheep.

I hold the blunt between my lips and strum a few new chords I've been hearing in my head all afternoon. I alternate between smoking and strumming until the roach is too small to hold, and I flick it into the lake.

I duck my head down, curling in against the wind and letting the music steer me in the right direction. The melodies roll through me, and I release any residual feelings leftover from this afternoon's bullshit. I welcome the peace of nothingness.

I can't let Ryder ruin what he's spent his whole life building. He just has to let it go. We all do. The counselors didn't see shit, so they don't know shit, so they won't *do* shit.

And that's really all there is to it. End of story. Nothing new.

There's rustling in the woods behind me, but I don't even blink. I must be more fucked than I thought.

I peer over my shoulder and watch with half-open lids as Ryder appears from the forest's edge with a blanket wrapped around his head and shoulders. My lip quirks. Even through the numbness, he has that effect on me.

I stop playing, resting my guitar on my lap.

"Don't stop. You said you'd play for me," he whispers somewhat vulnerably.

I did say that, so I continue with the chords I was strumming earlier.

Ryder sits next to me and closes his eyes, bobbing his head to the melody. "What song is this?"

"It's nothing," I mumble.

"It's something. I mean, I'm hearing it with my own ears right now at this very moment."

Funny.

"Just some chords I've been working on."

"Music you composed?"

I lift a shoulder. It's not that fancy.

"Did you write lyrics?"

My eyes automatically dart to the notebook beside me and his follow. I *always* have words.

"Right. Of course you do. Well, if you ever need a listening ear, I'm your guy."

I set the guitar back down next to me and sink into Ryder's arms, letting him wrap the blanket around us, further cocooning me in his warm embrace.

With the numbness in full effect and Ryder surrounding

me, this is turning into a peaceful and, dare I say, relaxing night.

I'm not sure how much time has passed, but my eyelids start to droop.

"Fal," Ryder whispers. "Let's head back before we're too tired to walk. It's almost one."

I force my lethargic body to move, and Ry laces our fingers together, tugging me along with him.

"Come on, sleepy face."

I give him a dopey half-smile. The weed, lack of sleep, and massive adrenaline crash from this afternoon are finally catching up to me, making me feel drunk.

I stumble on a rock.

"Whoa. I got you," Ryder says, pulling me into his side and wrapping us in the blanket again. He practically takes my weight, steering us back to our tent.

I'm moments away from passing out, so I sigh with relief when I see the glowing embers of the leftover fire.

"Bed," I grumble, and Ryder scoops me up, bridal style. I rest my head against his hard pec and let the darkness call me home.

I'm yanked from sleep, a harsh flashlight shining in my face as rough hands grasp my biceps. I'm disoriented, sluggish, and confused.

"Ry?" I don't know why I say it. He would never grab me like this.

"Nope. Not the big, gay giant." The voice is cruel and the tone grating. He's right in my face, but it's too dark to see. It sounds like Seth, though. The ring leader. His bruising grip travels down my arms, giant hands encircling my wrists and wrenching them behind my back without mercy.

I can't help but cry out at the abrupt and unexpected pain, making a chorus of ruthless laughs ring out around me.

"Let's put a bag over his stupid face," another voice sneers behind me. It's early morning, not even light out, and Ryder left for his run an hour ago. He has the big 'trust' test this morning, and we'll hit the road before ten.

I must have drifted back to sleep. And now, here I am, alone and vulnerable and half-naked.

The next words spoken freeze me to my core.

"Shame, though," a third voice says with zero emotion. "He's prettier than some of the junior girls. I'd probably let him suck me off."

No.

The thought has bile rushing up my throat.

"Dustin, that's the gayest thing I've ever heard. I'm going to pretend you didn't just say that. Put the fucking bag over his head, you moron."

Dustin.

"You're disgusting like I've said before. Fuck. *You.* I wouldn't touch your dick if my life depended on it. You'd have to kill me first. *Pig.*"

Dramatic, I know. But, *fuck* him.

The slap comes out of the darkness, violently whipping my head to the side. My cheek stings, but I don't make a sound. Seth still has my arms pinned behind my back. There's nothing I can do if they wanna jump me. They're gonna jump me. It wouldn't be the first time. The trailer park where I lived in Philadelphia wasn't a nice place. Neither was my school.

"Okay. Okay. Enough, D," Seth says unsympathetically, beginning to loop a rope tightly around my wrists.

"What the fuck are you doing?!" I start to struggle.

No.

"Just think of it as another trust-building exercise, Fallon, since you decided you were too good to participate for most of the weekend. Like you're better than us just because you came from a trailer park, and now you go to a fancy-ass school. Yeah, I know you came from nothing back in Philly. Dead dad, whore-of-a-mom on drugs. Blah, blah, blah. Your sob story wasn't hard to figure out. You're pathetic, and now it's time to man up. Trust yourself. Trust that you won't let yourself stay lost and die out here. *Pussy.*" Dustin cackles mercilessly, walking me in circles and farther into the forest.

After I'm disoriented, he shoves me forward, and I trip on a root or something else sticking out of the ground. I fall forward, unable to brace myself with my hands tied behind my back. I hit the hard dirt with an unforgiving force.

I grunt at the impact as pain splinters through my shoulder, shooting down my arm. I grit my teeth, unwilling to give them the satisfaction of hearing me cry out.

My heart hammers against my ribcage, panic taking over. Bad memories batter against the walls surrounding my emotions, but I shove them away, refusing to remember how the prick who sold my guitar also used to push me around.

"See ya later, Fallon. But not until Ryder fails *Camp Dakota* and ruins his chance of playing in the championship looking for your pathetic ass." It's Seth. They're desperate to win, and they know they can't, so they're trying to sabotage him. I can't let that happen.

"Here's some water and a few granola bars. Don't say we didn't try to help you."

Small pebbles and dirt hit my skin, and I roll away, trying to avoid them kicking at the ground around me. I won't let Ryder lose and these assholes win. Because of me. No fucking way.

My shoulder throbs, but I don't care. As soon as I hear their obnoxious voices disappear into the forest, I stand gingerly, shaking off the hood and trying not to further agitate my shoulder.

Fucking pricks. Completely remorseless for absolutely *everything*.

They don't know my thumbs are double-jointed, though. I pull and tug with my left hand, the least important one if things go wrong, and the coarse fibers scratch against my sensitive flesh.

I grit my teeth, groaning as my tendons stretch and my thumb folds inward, slipping through the tightly bound rope.

Sonofabitch, that hurt.

I whip my arms around, rotating my sore shoulder up and around in circles, testing the integrity. I don't think it's out of the socket, but I rub the tender joint. My thumb feels like someone bent it the wrong way, so I massage that, too. I can still move it, so nothing's broken. All in all, I'll live.

I need to find my way back to the campsite before Ryder freaks out and misses his test. That can't happen. He has to beat them fair and square. No suspension, nothing.

I can't tell anyone what just happened.

Ryder needs to win the championship first.

It wasn't too hard to find my way back to the tent, even though the sun's still not fully risen. I attempt to brush the dirt and debris off my skin in case Ryder's already back from his jog. But I can't really explain the no shoes and no clothes situation.

Sleepwalking?

Desperately needing the toilet?

Running out of water?

No, that one won't work. I think the cooler was full last night.

"Fallon!" Ryder's deep, concerned tone pulls me from my inner crisis.

Shit. He's back. And I didn't have my alibi fully decided on.

"What are you doing out here in your underwear?" He rushes over to me, hands traveling over my body, checking for injuries.

He cups my cheek next. "What's this red mark?"

I pull my head away from his touch. He can't know. He can't risk suspension from school—from the team—*and* his college scholarship. I'm not worth it. This championship means everything to him. He's spent four years working toward this goal, and I won't be the one to ruin it for him.

I'm torn from my spiraling thoughts once again. "Blue, did someone *hit* you? Why are there scratches and dirt all over you? Why don't you have shoes on? Clothes?" His tone is worrisome, gentle.

Too many questions. Too many words. Too many thoughts.

"Why aren't you answering me?"

I'm shutting down.

"Talk to me, *please*," he begs.

"I. . ." I choke, making a weird hiccupping noise.

My words won't work right now. I'm not sure I could speak even if I knew *what* to say. What excuse to tell him.

"Come here." Ryder envelops my smaller body with his giant frame, curling his considerable bulk around me and making me feel secure. Safe. Cared for.

I sink into him, the pain of everything making it too much to hold myself upright. So, I lean on my boyfriend instead.

Fuck.

The walls I've erected are delicate at best at this point. Paper thin at worst. One wrong breath and the emotions will come flooding out, and I'll be swept to sea, left to drift alone. Like always.

"Where were you? What happened?" he tries again.

"Nowhere and nothing," I whisper into his sweat-soaked chest. Ryder needs to drop this, for everyone's sake.

"It was Seth and those pricks, wasn't it?"

I don't answer. The memory of his rough touch makes me want to scrub my skin raw.

Ryder lets me go and steps away, pacing in front of the tent, running a hand through his damp curls.

"Fucking bastardos," he mumbles under his breath. "Don't let them come between us, Blue."

I amble toward the tent like a zombie, the numbness creeping back in. "Go take your test, Ry," I say flatly.

I think I need to be alone.

He glances at the time on his phone and curses in Spanish again. "I've gotta shower before the test, but this isn't over, Fallon. I mean it."

I ignore him, crawling inside and zipping up the flap.

"Don't shut me out. *Please.*"

I can't help it. I do.

CHAPTER TWENTY-FOUR

RYDER

That dead look is back in Fallon's eyes, and I fucking hate it. It's like we're back to day one when he was prickly and wouldn't talk to me. I can barely concentrate, my thoughts scattered, focusing solely on my boyfriend and what could have happened to him.

Is he really okay?

Why won't he talk to me?

He's so small, and the thought of anyone roughing him up again has me fuming. I should have been there, not out running. Always worried about myself and basketball.

Fuck!

But I won't let him shut me out and lock his feelings away like he's trying to. He's made too much progress.

Luckily, the final test is the team obstacle course in the trees. And even though I'm distracted, Cole, Jamie, and I nail it on the first try. I'm sure we'll be the fastest group of the morning. No doubt.

We have to show good sportsmanship and watch everyone else. But I'm secretly dying inside, desperate to get back to Fallon. I don't like that vacant stare, and I *hate* that I left him like that.

When Dustin, Seth, and Rich saw me waiting by our instructor, right on time and first in line, they did a double take, mouths gaping comically.

They huddled together, discussing *something* while their eyes flicked over to me. Not subtle in the slightest. And they're doing it *again* right now!

"What the fuck are those idiots doing?" Cole asks, standing next to me and witnessing the whole thing.

"Dunno. Probably planning something."

Or maybe they already carried out their plan. Something clearly happened.

But why would Fallon hide it from me?

"They're looking shifty as fuck, and I don't like it. Watch your back, Cruz. Fallon's too."

Fuck. I wish I had been.

Cole storms away to cheer on our teammates trapped in a rope net about twenty feet up.

"Did something happen?" Jamison's calm, easy tone settles some of the nerves bubbling up inside of me about what the fuck happened to Fallon.

"I don't know, Jamie. And that's what's got me on edge."

"How do you not know?"

"Well, *something* happened. Fallon came hobbling back to the campsite in his *underwear*, Jamie! Not even socks! And he has a red mark across his cheek. But he won't tell me anything. He shut down. Completely. That was right before I came here. Perfect fucking timing." I run a rough hand through my messy curls, getting tangled and yanking hard.

"Fuck!"

What did they do to him?

"I'm going to ask them what they did," I say with a cool detachment, ice running through my veins and slowing my heart.

Maybe I'm a little numb, like how Fallon probably feels right now after they did whatever they did to him.

I *know* they did something. *Bastardos.*

I take one step forward, and Jamie grabs my shoulder *hard*, grounding me. "No. You're not. We've got thirty minutes tops. That's it. Half an hour before we can leave. Go our separate ways and see them one last time when we hand them their fucking asses on the court. Okay?" He gives me a little shake. "Don't start shit right now, Ry. You won't get to play on Friday. Don't you understand why Fallon didn't tell you about whatever happened to him? It's his way of protecting you. Don't you get that? He knows how much basketball means to you. And because of how much you mean to him, he stayed silent. So respect his wishes, and just finish this out. Stay right here, next to me. Watch Cody, Andy, and Mitch finish. Rather pathetically, actually. Look." Jamie ticks his head toward the trees, and I snort a laugh at the way Cody is currently hanging horizontally through the net, clinging on for dear life.

"Why they think over six feet tall teenagers need to be doing obstacles in the trees is beyond me," Jamie adds dryly, and I crack up. It's fucking ridiculous when I look at my huge friend trying to get his size fourteens out of the holes in the net.

When the public school idiots catch me laughing and smiling with my friend, they scowl, and Dustin hollers, "Hey, Cruz! Where's your pretty little friend with the make-up and sparkles? Did you see him this morning? Rather cute when he has a sleepy face, huh? The black eyeliner smeared under his eyes and that blue hair sticking up everywhere. I can *maybe* even understand why you—"

"Enough!" Jamie shouts, cutting Dustin off.

He's trying to goad me, but I know Fallon is relatively okay. I just saw him. He's not lost in the woods or bleeding out in a ditch somewhere.

"Where's all that toilet paper that went missing from your school, Dustin? Seth? Because if you add theft to the list. . ." I whistle between my teeth obnoxiously. "You're seriously fucked."

I shrug Jamie off and step toward them. "So, say one more thing. Do it. Say one more fucking thing!" I shout in Dustin's face, nearly stepping on his toes.

We're the same size, and it'd probably be an even fight. Even though I've never punched anyone before, I might start now.

Jamie pulls me back. "Beat them on the court, Ry. Not here."

Seth barks out a cruel laugh. "Keep dreaming, rich boys. You ain't beating shit."

God. I can't fucking *stand* them.

A whistle blares, and we all glance up on instinct. Our teammates finally make it to the end of the obstacle course, and we're done. Free to leave and head home.

"You all did a great job this weekend, and I think we've seen some real progress. Although we can't expect you to change overnight. But in any case, I hope you've learned some valuable life lessons to carry with you. And everyone is cleared to play in the championship game! Congratulations!" Dale ends with a shout.

"Let's go, Ry. Let's check on Fallon," Jamie whispers, and I nod, turning without a second thought to those public school fuckers or this trust camp. I need to focus on my boyfriend.

"Stay out here," I tell Jamie quietly, heading toward the tent.

"Fallon. You awake?" I say gently, unzipping the door slowly so I don't frighten him. But there's no answer.

I glance over my shoulder at Jamie, and his worried eyes mirror my own.

I step into the tent, flinging the blankets and sleeping bags around.

Fallon's not here.

"Shit! He's gone!" I shout.

"What do you mean gone?"

"He's not here! But his backpack and all his stuff are," I answer frantically and on edge.

Did they get him again?

"His guitar is gone, look." Jamie points toward the open guitar case.

"He went to play," I murmur, thinking hard about *where*.

We make eye contact, and it comes to me. "The lake."

"Let's go. I'll help you find him." Jamie nods his head toward the exit, his voice calm and reassuring.

We sprint into the woods, and it doesn't take more than ten minutes of jogging to reach the lakeshore. It would take longer to walk, but I don't have time for casual strolls. I need to find him.

We hear Fallon before we see him. The same haunting song he loves so much pours from his dad's guitar. The melodies are a tormented, jagged sound that scrapes at the soft underbelly of my emotions, giving me a taste of the hurt he's felt for years. But I'll take it. *All of it.*

When he finally comes into view, his head hangs low, and his vibrant blue hair is a mess across his face, matching the bright shade of his dad's guitar. It's all so fitting that goosebumps erupt across my skin as he hums that tune that stirs my soul.

"God. He's amazing," I voice my thoughts aloud in complete awe.

"Yeah, that's some serious talent, dude. He could go places."

"Yeah. Thanks for helping me find him, Jamie."

"Of course, bro. Text me if you need anything else, but I'm gonna head home. It's been a hell of a weekend."

"We won't need anything. Enjoy your Sunday." I pat him on the shoulder before we do our signature handshake, and he disappears into the forest behind us.

I focus on the breathtaking sight before me. The sun glistens off the sapphire waters of Acadia Lake. The trees are ancient, and the water is deep. It brings a certain beauty, and so does Fallon, sitting in stark contrast against the muted colors of nature. He's so vibrant, even when he's sad. His soul calls to mine, and I join him on the old wooden bench, careful not to scare him.

He slowly finishes playing, turning those deep blue eyes to me.

"That was incredible," I whisper.

"Did you pass?" he asks.

"Yeah, Fal. I passed. Now tell me what happened to you. I know those fuckers did something." I reach out and trail my thumb over his cheek and down to his lips, tugging on his piercing, entranced as always.

"Can we just go home, Ry? Please?"

Fuck. When he looks at me like that, I can't say no. I just want to scoop him up and squeeze him to my chest. Maybe rut against him until we both come in our pants again.

"Yeah, Blue. We can go home." I hold my hand out, and he places his smaller one in mine. I squeeze tight, lifting him to his feet and taking the guitar, slinging it over my back. He doesn't need to carry anything when I'm around. I'm a gentleman.

I rest my arm over his shoulder, tucking him close as we head back to my truck. We're both ready to get home and put this trust-building bullshit behind us.

I decide to walk Fallon inside. He was quiet the entire ride back, but he needs to tell me what happened. He can't keep ignoring me.

"How was the test?" Joel asks, strolling out of the kitchen with my Dad and Sofie on his heels.

The camp counselors were the adults running the show; Joel and Coach Patterson only stopped by for support and dinner.

"It was fine. Everyone passed. Still don't trust half my team, though. And definitely not the Jefferson douchebags."

"Mijo!" Dad reprimands me, and Sofie giggles. He would change his tune real quick if he knew all the shit they did to Joel's house, to Fallon, and especially to Sofie.

I just need to get through one week of practice, then one final game. That's it. Just ream them at State, and then I never have to be concerned with the juvenile bullshit of high school sports again. I hope college will be better, and maybe I won't even have to stay four years. The NBA is my endgame.

I glance at my coach and possible future stepdad. "Sorry, Joel," I say apologetically. "I'll keep the guys in line. No more pranks."

"I'm holding you to that as captain, Ryder," Joel says sternly, his coach hat firmly in place.

I nod once. "Won't let you down."

I already told Cole to knock it off before he gets me kicked off the team or out of school. He's adding fuel to the fire every time he retaliates.

"We're going to run this stuff upstairs," I hold Fallon's guitar case and my extra gear bag up. "But we'll probably go back to our place and relax for the day."

"Oh, but can't we hang out later? After you take a nap or whatever you're going home to do together?" I nearly choke on my own spit at Sofie's innocent comment. "Pretty please, bro beans? I miss you both!"

I glance at Fallon. We're both exhausted, but it's hard to say no to her. He gives me a subtle nod of approval.

"What do you want to do later?"

"Late lunch at the country club! Fallon would love the food." She shuffles over to Fallon in her fluffy rainbow socks, latching onto his arm and peering into his eyes. "I've been wanting to take you, possible future step cuz."

I groan internally, not liking hearing that about the boy I've fallen for.

"Not the country club," I whine.

"I want Fallon to try the she-crab soup! It's not about you."

"I thought you missed me and wanted to hang out," I counter.

"I do. But what I really meant was I want you to take us

to the country club so I can eat she-crab soup with Fallon. They only have it on Sundays. You know that." Sofie pulls out all the stops, pouting and flashing eyes that match mine back at me.

I can't say no to her. Even though I hate the smell of seafood.

Looks like we're going to Acadia Lake Country Club today.

CHAPTER TWENTY-FIVE

FALLON

After we dropped our stuff at my place, we took quick showers before leaving for Ryder's house. Luckily Joel bought me some dark gray slacks and black dress shirts in case I needed to look presentable outside of school. I'm not sure what dress code a fancy-ass country club enforces, though.

"Do I need a tie? Blazer? I didn't bring any." I'm stalling, relaxing on Ryder's giant bean bag. I don't give a shit about ties or blazers. If they don't let me in because of my outfit, fuck them. No, I'm just trying to avoid the inevitable conversation about what happened at the lake.

I could hide my cheek from Joel and Al with my hair, but I'll be sporting a small bruise for a little while, courtesy of Dustin. But I don't want to tell Ryder. He needs to focus on basketball. On the championship. On his *dream*. Not on me. I'm not important.

"Talk to me, Blue. I want to know what they did to you. Everything. I need to know. I hate not knowing. It's worse wondering what you went through when I wasn't there to stop it. It fucking kills me. So please, Fal. Tell me, no matter how much I don't want to hear it."

I blink to break the hypnotic pull of his stare. My chest squeezes tight. The weak, needy part of me thrives on his attention and care.

With a heavy sigh, I explain what happened. How they pulled me from sleep, disoriented and sluggish, tied my hands, put a bag over my head, and slapped me around. All to sabotage the big game. To get Ryder to miss the trust test, thus failing and not being allowed to play in the state championship game.

It's whatever, though. They didn't succeed. Not even close.

"I'm not a violent person, and I've never fantasized about murdering someone before, but holy fuck! I'm going to kill Dustin. That's it. That's all that's left to do. No other options. He needs to die."

"Stop. Ry. Come here." He needs to calm down. He can't get worked up because it's exactly what they want.

He stops pacing and plops down next to me, making me roll into him. I brace my hand on his chest, peering at him.

"Don't play into it, Ryder. Don't let them win. Just beat them on the court." That's all he needs to do.

"You're right." He rubs a thumb under my eye, right over where I know the mark is. "Their plan was weak anyway. Because apparently, my boyfriend is a hot little Houdini, escaping in thirty seconds flat. My sexy fucking magician. Actually. . ." Ryder trails off, and his eyes glimmer with mischief.

"My broody little magician," he says, grinning wide, showing me all his teeth. His beautifully straight, perfect, gorgeously white teeth.

"Stop."

"My broody—"

I cut him off and roll on top, pinning his arms above his head. But only because he lets me. He smiles even bigger, if that's possible. I think it might be for Ryder Cruz.

He likes it when I'm on top, but that doesn't mean he doesn't take control. He slips out of my grasp, cradling my face and leaning up to kiss me, nibbling on my lip ring like always.

"I'm going to fuck you on this bean bag one day soon. For now, I wanna take my time. You've been through hell this weekend, Blue. But you're so fucking strong. I'm 'bout to reward you, okay?"

Lost for words, all I can do is nod.

"Arms up." His voice is a low, sensual rasp.

I listen on instinct, wincing when my shoulder stretches uncomfortably. It's sore as shit, and Ryder doesn't miss a beat.

"What's wrong? I thought you said you weren't hurt."

"I'm not."

"What was that face you made, then?" He won't give up.

"I don't make faces. I only have one. Mine."

Ryder's frown quirks up at that. "And I like it a lot. It's a nice-looking one. I just don't like to see it in pain." His smile drops again, brows creasing. "You hurt, Blue? Tell me. Please."

"I'm fine, Ry. For real. Okay? Just a little sore."

"Do you need ice?"

"No."

"A heating pad?"

"No."

"Ibuprofen?"

I sigh heavily. "No, Ryder."

"Dick?"

"No—"

Wait a second. I narrow my eyes on him. *Tricky.*

"Yes to the last one," I murmur, and he chuckles. Wanting dick, or anything sexual, really, is a new development in my life, but it feels right. Everything with Ryder feels right.

He trails his big palms up my stomach, causing me to shiver. My belly hollows out, and my skin pebbles. I'm already hard, and he's barely even touched me.

"You like it?" he asks softly.

"Yeah." My voice is low, scratchy.

He continues his exploration, circling my belly button with his pointer finger and making my stomach flutter. My breath hitches at his teasing touch.

He trails those gentle fingers higher, grazing over my nipples. I keep my gaze locked on his. Hypnotized by his words, his touch, and his mesmerizing stare.

"I'mma win the championship for you, Blue. Steal the trophy from those fuckers, crush their dreams, and stomp on their hopes. They deserve less than nothing for how they've treated you and a possible restraining order because Dustin seems to have fixated on my sister *and* boyfriend. It's not normal. *He's* not normal."

I keep the blowjob comments Dustin made to myself, deciding not to divulge every sordid detail to further antagonize Ryder. He's not an angry person, but he's walking a fine line of restraint. He's a hair's breadth away from laying Dustin out and possibly losing everything in the process. He doesn't need this negativity or stress during the most important week of his high school career. He just needs to get through it so he can retaliate on the court.

His gentle touch skims over my sore shoulder, and I

lean down to claim his lips to take his mind off what happened to me.

His mouth takes command, rolling his tongue against mine and stoking a fire inside me. A flame that was never lit until Ryder came into my life. And now we burn bright—hot and heavy—as I grind against him in my soft gray joggers.

"I wanna do something. Will you let me?" He pants into my open mouth.

I pull back, peering at him quizzically. "What is it?"

"Trust me, right?"

"Yeah, Ry. I trust you."

His small, vulnerable smile turns into a fully wicked grin. "Pants off. I need you naked."

I snort and roll my eyes, "Of course you do."

"Damn straight. And you're gonna love it."

I climb off Ryder's lap and pull my joggers and underwear down in one go. My already hard and weeping cock springs free, bouncing as I step out of my clothes.

Ryder's hooded gaze zeroes in on my groin, and he licks his lips like he's starving for a taste. My dick pulses, twitching and begging for his attention.

His giant hand engulfs my cock, giving me a firm squeeze before softly trailing his fingers down the sensitive underside ever so slowly.

I tip my head back and groan loudly, knowing we're the only ones home and wanting Ryder to hear me.

He leans in, pressing his nose to the base of my cock and inhaling deep. "Mmm, you smell like strawberries and fresh soap. All the fucking time. Drives me wild." He rubs his cheek against my shaft, the slight friction teasing me mercilessly.

"Fuck. Lick me," I rasp out.

What is he waiting for?

"Nah." But he gives me one long swipe of his tongue from base to tip, kissing my crown with soft lips. "Not here."

Ryder reaches around and squeezes my ass, slipping a finger between my cheeks and caressing my hole. "Here," he whispers somewhat cautiously.

Oh, holy fuck.

Lost for words.

I chew on my lip ring, nodding my head with half-lidded eyes as I stare down at him crouched before me.

"Get on the bed. Hands and knees."

I scramble to obey, not giving my brain a chance to catch up with what's about to happen. Ryder remains fully clothed, and something about that gets me even hotter. I stare at him over my shoulder, and he stares back, the lust thick between us.

"I think you'll like this," he murmurs, running a sensual hand up the curve of my spine. I arch into his touch, sticking my ass out further.

"Is your shoulder okay in this position?" he asks, rubbing the tender muscle gently.

"Mhm. It's fine," I murmur, ready to feel his tongue on me.

The bed shakes slightly as Ryder maneuvers into position. "Widen your knees."

I comply, spreading my legs further while he caresses my body. My dick is rock hard and leaking pre-cum.

"That's it. Like that. Perfect." He presses his thumb against my hole, the foreign pressure causing it to twitch. "Your asshole is *perfect*, Blue. Just perfect."

"Ryyyy. . ." I groan, hanging my head in both shame and arousal.

And then his thumb is replaced with a warm, wet tongue, and my groan turns into a sharp cry of surprise pleasure.

Holy fuck, that felt incredible.

He strokes me with his tongue, adding his thumbs to tease my rim. The sensations are overwhelming, overstimulating, and completely and utterly mind-blowing.

"Ryder," I rasp, lowering my shoulders and dropping my forehead to the bed. My legs are shaking. I need more, yet it's also entirely too much. He stiffens his tongue and works those thumbs, spreading my hole until it slips in.

Face-down in the bed, my moans are near-animalistic, muffled wails. It's embarrassing, yet I can't stop. My dick is leaking, and I reach underneath to stroke myself.

"M'gonna come. Gonna come," I chant into the sheet, my breath coming out in hot pants.

Ryder can't answer me with his tongue shoved in my ass, and the dirty thought pushes me over the edge. I jerk myself faster, the orgasm racing down my spine. My muscles lock, and my ass pulses around Ryder's tongue as I empty my nuts on the sheets below.

Ryder slips his tongue out, and I fall flat to the bed, right into my load. I lie here, letting the waves of bliss roll over me, and take a deep breath, sighing my contentment.

Ryder chuckles, giving my butt a playful slap. "Feelin' good?"

"Mhm," I confirm, my eyes starting to droop. I watch as Ryder slips into his en-suite to clean up. The sink runs, and the soothing sound puts me to sleep.

I hear the door click shut, and my eyes pop back open when I feel Ryder's bulk weigh the bed down behind me. I already know what he wants, so I tip my ass up, ready to let him come on me.

CHAPTER TWENTY-SIX

FALLON

The parking lot is filled with Rolls Royces, Bentleys, and other rich-ass cars I never would have seen at the trailer park in Philly. Not in a million years. If I did, it would have been on its way to the chop shop or up on cinder blocks in the street, picked apart in minutes like piranhas feasting on prime rib.

The clubhouse, well-maintained grounds, and the bright green golf course all boast wealth and luxury.

The valet at the podium rushes over with a big smile when he sees us pull up, and we hop out, not wasting a moment.

"Hi, Kenny!" Sofie says enthusiastically to the pimply, ginger-haired boy who takes Ryder's keys.

"Hey, Sofia," he mumbles shyly, blushing bright red before turning back to Ry.

"Ryder, you ready for the championship? My mom said I can go this year, and I'm so excited! I know you're gonna dunk on Seth. Please tell me you're gonna dunk on Seth?"

Cute. My boyfriend has a fan.

"Heck yeah, dude. Dustin first. Seth can have my sloppy seconds. Rich can get thirsty thirds."

Kenny chuckles, still slightly pink. "Well, I can't wait to watch you serve them. In whatever order. I know you'll kick ass and bring the trophy home for us."

"Thanks, dude." Ryder fist-bumps the kid before we head toward the massive doors blocked by another person sitting at *another* podium.

Fancy.

I don't fit.

My hands twitch with the need to adjust my borrowed tie and tug at my collar. The man at the door stares me down like I have a dick and balls drawn on my forehead instead of a little eyeliner and tinted Chapstick.

Whatever.

Wonder how he'd feel if he knew where Ryder just had his tongue. And how much I fucking liked it.

He clears his throat uncomfortably as if he can read my dirty thoughts. "There's a dress code. No make-up."

Huh?

Before Ryder or I can say a word, Sofie speaks up. "Bernard! Every woman in there has make-up on. I have freaking make-up on!"

"It's Barry," he replies coolly.

"Right. And is that not short for Bernard? Anyway, back to the point! Half the people here wear make-up, and my dad pays for a membership just the same. This is our guest." Sofie loops her arm through mine in solidarity, not needing Ryder or me to step in. She can apparently handle grown men for us. Put them in their fucking places.

Priceless.

"You're rude and insulting. Step aside, sir," she finishes in a very serious tone. Her Cruz family smile is nowhere to be found. This is serious-Sofie we're dealing with, and I don't think Bernard should fuck with her.

I can't help the snort that escapes me or the crooked smile tugging at my lips.

Her spunk and defense of me wash away some of the lingering anxiety of being tied up and left for dead in the woods.

I push it away. Push it down deep.

Bernard starts to sputter, gobsmacked by this little whirlwind of a girl. I would be too. He has no excuses left when she pushes past him, tugging me along with Ryder following behind. I glance over at my boyfriend, his lips tight with restraint.

As soon as we're past the entrance, Ry can't hold it in any longer. He explodes with an obnoxiously loud laugh that has the older patrons eyeing us with disdain as they eat their Sunday lunches.

"Can you guys believe the nerve of that man? Saying that? Gah!" Her growl isn't intimidating in the slightest; she just sounds like an angry kitten.

"Well, you put him right in his place, little sis. That shit was epic. Nearly the highlight of my day. Not quite, though." Then he winks at me. I nearly choke on my spit and trip over my own feet, thinking about what we did earlier.

Ryder just laughs again and steadies me. With a Cruz sibling on either side of me, we go through the country club to wherever Sofie takes us.

"My favorite table is by the giant bay windows in the back. I'm seating myself after Bernard's rude behavior," Sofie declares with her usual tenacity. Ryder chuckles, and we follow along, clearly not wanting to get on her bad side.

The exclusive lakefront restaurant has a wall of

windows, crystal clear glass stretching from floor to ceiling. The view of Acadia Lake is stunning.

Yet another place I don't fit in. But it doesn't really matter anymore. Ryder and Sofie are inserting me into this lifestyle whether I want it or not.

I've come to the conclusion that I want anything that Ryder does. And I want to *be* anywhere he is.

So Acadia Lake Country Club, you better fucking get used to this hair and this face because I'm starting to realize that I really am here to stay.

"Oh. My. God. This soup! It's so incredible. Right, Fallon? You like it, don't you?"

I nod eagerly, taking another slurp of the warm, orange-colored soup. I can't disappoint her even though crab is my least favorite seafood, and I don't even fucking know what a she-crab is. It kinda freaks me out, and I'm not sure I want to know.

Ryder somehow voices my own thoughts. "Yeah. But what the fuck even *is* a she-crab?"

"Don't worry about it. Just let Fallon enjoy it. I think it's Southern or something." She darts her eyes to me and then back down to her bisque, taking a dainty slurp before dipping her toasted bread chip in.

That doesn't leave me with too much confidence, but I've learned that sometimes it's better not to ask questions.

"Glad I'm not eating that shit." I give Ryder an unamused look before dipping my own cracker thing into the soup and crunching on it. "No offense," he adds.

"Don't listen to him, Fallon. My brother's a hater. Just enjoy. It's basically a delicacy."

Ryder snorts, chomping on his burger before dipping his fries into ranch even though we're at this fancy-ass place with linen tablecloths and napkins.

I eye his food with jealousy, way hungrier than just a bowl of this weird soup. I should have ordered something else too. I just didn't want to run up Alejandro's tab. I grab my Coke and slurp half of it to fill myself up more.

Ryder's foot nudges mine from under the table, his long leg easily stretching the distance and getting my attention. He holds his burger up in silent offering, asking if I want some without voicing it out loud. I glance at Sofie. She's busy in her own world, eating her soup, sipping her raspberry lemonade, and scrolling through Instagram. We're sorta tucked in back here, away from everyone else, so I lean forward and open my mouth wide. Ryder's pupils dilate, and he quickly feeds me a bite of his messy, oversized chili cheeseburger. A large plop of chili lands in the middle of the table on the stark white linen.

"I didn't know bromances involved feeding each other. Guess you learn something new every day," Sofie says plainly, not even looking up from her phone.

Shit. Called out.

Ryder quickly cuts a quarter of his burger and puts it on my little soup plate in a much more reasonable attempt at sharing.

"I didn't say you had to stop. It was cute," she says with added pep.

"Sofie. . ." Ryder warns, but we're sort of asking for it, forgetting our surroundings like that.

"Just teasing, bro beans!" she tells Ryder, then bumps my shoulder. "Just kidding, cousin beans," she murmurs, and I snort at her ridiculousness.

We continue eating in silence, and I also finish off Ryder's fries.

"I want dessert," Sofie declares. "The display case was amazing today; I don't even know what to choose. Let's go look again."

As we peruse the selection of cheesecakes, pies, and crumbles, I can't help but overhear the hostess fretting over their guitarist canceling for the evening.

"Chauncey wasn't supposed to cancel without twenty-four hours' notice, and Mr. Russo will be here any minute! I'm going to lose my job. He won't care," she sniffles.

"I can play," I speak up, forcing myself out of my comfort zone. Even though I'm tired after this weekend, I should probably get used to playing publicly if I want a shot at this music thing.

She blinks tear-filled eyes at me. "Wh-what? Really? You can? Y-you will?"

I glance at Ryder, and his eyebrows have disappeared behind his curls.

"Yeah. Just give me fifteen?" I need to figure out a way to sneak the joint in my pocket. I need to calm these nerves creeping in.

"Oh. Thank you. Seriously, you're a lifesaver. And you've got thirty. Just go to the stage and say you're subbing in for Chauncey. The band will get you a guitar, and you can decide what you want to play. It'll be an hour set, and be sure to see Jenn the bartender before you leave. I'm Haley if you need anything in the meantime or a drink in between songs. Anything."

"I'm good. I'll just have some dessert to go."

"Whatever you want. On the house."

She looks at me expectantly, like I'm supposed to tell her my order here and now.

Okay.

"Uh. Tiramisu and apple crumble."

"No cheesecake? The triple fudge is what we're known for." She seems extremely eager for me to try it. I can't say no.

"Okay, sure. And that too."

"You got it." She winks and a smile spreads across her face. It's nice. She's pretty. But I feel nothing. Nothing at all.

I glance quickly at Ryder, and my stomach flips at the tender look in his eyes. Like he's *proud* of me. And I haven't even played yet. It makes me uncomfortable yet turns me on a little, too. An awkward feeling, for sure.

"Looking forward to seeing you up there," Haley says before hurrying away to seat the people that just walked in.

Was she flirting with me?

Whatever.

"Look at you, Rockstar! I'm gonna find a front-row seat. I can't miss this." Sofie wanders away, leaving me standing with my boyfriend in front of a glass display of desserts.

"I need to smoke," I blurt out, the anxiety taking over. The negative thoughts are telling me I'm just a screwup and I'll only fail.

"You don't need that, Blue. You got this. I've heard you. You're amazing." Ryder glances around, lowering his voice. "I wish I could kiss you to take the nerves away."

"I wish you could too," I murmur, hating all the hiding but understanding why he's not ready to be out. We just met, really. "But I still need to smoke, or I won't get through an hour-long set. No way."

I see the flash of disappointment in his eyes, and a twinge of pain hits me deep, like when he told me not to get drunk in front of Sofie, and I sort of did anyway.

I don't like it, but I step away from him and head for the

back exit. Thirty minutes is plenty of time to go to the shore and smoke a joint.

I feel itchy and restless, like my skin is too tight for my body, and I can't stay still. I anxiously tap my painted fingertips against my thigh as I power-walk to the exit.

I need to calm the storm that's raging.

When I reach the shore, I spot a large rock and wander over, digging the joint and lighter out of my pocket. I perch on the edge, not wanting to get dirty or sandy.

As I attempt to light up, a deep voice startles me, and I fumble the lighter, dropping it right into a small puddle of lake water.

Fuck! Just my luck! There's no point in fishing it out. It's fucked.

"Shit! Sorry! Here, borrow mine."

The kid from the party is here. Jack or something. I'm not feeling particularly social, but I need a light, so I take it from him. He lets our fingers brush awkwardly, and I pull my hand back quickly.

"Thanks," I mumble.

"Fallon, right?"

"Yeah." I wish he'd fucking go away. I need to get my head in the game because I'm about to perform in front of a restaurant of people for the first time, with a band I've never rehearsed with, no less.

I flick the lighter on, quickly sparking my joint and handing it back to him. I inhale deeply, letting the THC filter through my system and relax me. I close my eyes and try to *wish* him away. Yeet him with the strength of my mind. That would be pretty sick.

Yep. Instantly stoned.

My wish is granted in the form of a six-and-a-half-foot tall basketball player.

"What are you doing, Jackson?" Ryder asks in an irritated tone, folding his arms across his chest. His biceps stretch the sleeves of his button-up deliciously.

I try not to stare, probably failing, and take another hit.

Jackson sticks his hands in his pockets. "Just offering a light to a friend in need. What are you doing, Cruz?" he counters. I can see the flicker of uncertainty in Ryder's eyes before he turns his gaze on me, ignoring the guy altogether.

"You're on in twenty. Finish up so you can speak with the band."

He's right. I take another pull or two. I offer it to Ryder, who shakes his head, then to Jackson because I'm too nice, and he takes it.

"You're playing at Acadia Landing?" he asks before taking a hit. His tone is curious, and his eyes light up with interest. The dirty blond man bun on his head is loose and messy, but his outfit is crisp and put together.

I shrug and glance at Ryder. "Is that what it's called?"

"Yeah, it is." He turns to Jackson. "He's subbing in for the guitarist at the Landing. For a whole set. So fuck off, Jacks. Let him concentrate. Did Seth send you?"

Whoa. That sorta came out of nowhere.

Jacks holds his hands up in mock surrender. "Ryder. Chill out, dude. What's your problem?"

Ryder does need to relax before he blows his cover by going all caveman over me. Even though I like it. *Really like it.* I'd let him throw me over his shoulder, actually. Take me to bed. Maybe we can try that later.

Shit. I'm stoned.

Jackson passes the joint back to me, but I definitely don't need anymore, so I stub it out on a rock, dipping it in a puddle for good measure. I'll toss it on my way back to the restaurant.

"Ryder, let's go. I gotta get ready to play," I mumble, trying to sound casual and not like I'm falling for him more every day. These feelings unnerve me, but at the same time, I know it's right. A jolt of warmth rushes through me at what we did earlier today.

"You singing?" Jackson asks.

He's still trying to have a conversation with me?

God.

My eyes dart to Ryder's irritated face.

"Uh, not tonight. And I really gotta go. See ya."

Or not. Hopefully not.

Ryder gives Jackson a final once-over before he glances at me. He turns and stomps away, leaving me behind to make it seem less suspicious.

"I'd watch you if I could, but I don't have a club membership. The public school kids just sneak on the golf course to smoke sometimes. But good luck, or break a leg, whatever I'm supposed to say." His smile seems genuine, but if Ryder doesn't trust him, I don't either. I wish everyone would just leave me alone. I really don't need anyone except Ryder. And my new family.

"Thanks," I mumble, ducking my head and slipping past him, hurrying after Ryder. I let any lingering thoughts of this pointless interaction slip through the fog. It's time to let the creativity take over, and I'm ready to get my hands on that guitar and play with a real band for the first time.

CHAPTER TWENTY-SEVEN

RYDER

I'm sick of hiding and sick of other people hitting on Fallon. Guys *and* girls. He's clueless to it all and doesn't see it or doesn't care. And that bothers me. He doesn't really seem to care about anything except maybe music and, hopefully, me. The more time I spend as Fallon's boyfriend, the more I'm willing to take the risk. The risk that my university will drop me, the NBA won't want me, and my mother will abandon me. *Again.*

Fuck. It could happen. All of it. Easily.

The last chord of Fallon's guitar strums, and I look at the giant nautical clock on the wall. His hour-long set should be over now, and I'm feeling so fucking proud of how he stepped out of his comfort zone to play in front of people.

Fallon sets the guitar down and bumps fists with the band members, murmuring something before hopping down and letting the keyboard player take over with soft, soothing piano music.

Sofie jumps up from the table before I do, nearly spilling her raspberry lemonade as she runs to congratulate Fallon.

"Fallon! Oh my God! You were so good! I can't believe you can play like that," Sofie squeals, throwing her arms around him and squeezing tight. I forgot she hasn't heard him play yet. I don't think Joel or my dad has either. He's amazing and deserves to be heard by everyone.

Fallon looks a lot more comfortable with the embrace than he did a few weeks ago. It's that Cruz family charm coming at him from all fronts. He just can't deny it, so we're making progress.

Score!

"Thanks, Sofie," he mumbles in that quiet, raspy voice, squeezing her before stepping away and running a hand through his two-toned hair.

"I need to find Haley and get the money, a drink, and my dessert. Been a long weekend."

"It sure has. Let's do that and go home, kids." I sling an arm around Fallon and my sister to cover the fact that I wish I could just openly touch him however and whenever I please. I want to hold his hand, hug him, kiss him, flirt with him. Shit. I'm really starting to question staying in the closet. Fallon makes me want *everything*. All the time. I'm not sure if I can hold out for another week, let alone my entire basketball career. It's not realistic.

I know what I want to do now.

"Dad?! Have you seen my game day kicks? I'm gonna miss the bus!"

Fuck, where's my lucky pair of sneakers?

"You're not going to miss the bus, mijo. You're the team captain, and the head coach is standing right here." My dad pulls Joel into his side and gives him a big kiss, making that obnoxious smooching sound. I glance away, wishing I could do the same with Fallon.

"Gah! PDA, guys! How many times do I have to tell you?" Sofie jogs down the stairs holding my sneakers by the shoestrings. "You left these in the bonus room, and I tossed them into the closet 'cause they stink." She juts her arm out at me, turning her head away and wrinkling her nose, but she just looks cute. Especially dressed in our school colors with my number twelve on her cheek and her hair in pigtails.

I snatch them from her, chuckling as I sit on the bottom step. "Funny. Except they don't." I slip my shoes on, pulling my classic, striped crew socks halfway up my calves and praying for luck in tonight's game.

Another week has passed, and I've hardly had a moment to myself, let alone to spend with my boyfriend. Besides a few quick handies and a blowie on Wednesday night, it's been school and basketball only.

I passed out after finishing dinner and homework all week, so I'm looking forward to the season being over and getting a breather.

Fallon comes down next, dressed in a black hoodie with *Acadia Lake Knights* on the front in metallic silver. Joel must have gotten that for him. He looks good. *Really good.*

His nails are freshly painted, his eyeliner is extra dark, and the *shimmer*. The fucking shimmer on his lips is extra bright tonight. I can't wait to see them wrapped around my cock later.

I stand quickly, grabbing Fallon by the elbow and halting him on the last step. Everyone else is grabbing their jackets and wallets and isn't paying attention to us. "I'm gonna win the championship for you, then take you home and fuck you, Blue. Get ready 'cause it's happening tonight. I can't wait to see you impaled on my cock, riding me."

I need to chill before I pop a boner in my basketball shorts. It wouldn't be easy to hide in the silky maroon fabric.

"Ryder," he hisses, trying to subtly adjust himself in his ripped black jeans.

I chuckle, stepping down to grab my jacket.

"Let's roll, kiddos!"

Sofie groans. "Joel, you're only fifty-one. Don't sound so old." She rolls her eyes, flipping her braided pigtail over her shoulder, glitter streaked across her cheeks in silver and red designs.

"Sofia Eleanor! You just aged me two decades. I'm barely thirty! And don't you have a birthday coming up too? You sure that's a smart play?"

"Are you threatening me, possible-future-step-father?"

"Sofie," I snort. "Stop."

Then I turn my reprimanding glare to *Coach Rivers*. "Don't encourage her, Joel. We need our heads in the game and our asses on the road."

"Yeah. Yeah. But she's just so cute!"

"I'm right here. And I'm about to be fifteen. I am not cute!" She throws her arms up dramatically, huffing out a breath.

"You are," Fallon insists with a little smirk, and I love seeing his playful side. He doesn't show it enough.

Sofie narrows her eyes, ready for a comeback, but we just don't have time. And Georgie beats me to it anyway.

"Alright, everyone. Get yer arses moving. Let's not be late for Ryder's big game."

We hustle out the door, ready to head to the academy.

Joel and I will ride the school athletic bus with the rest of the team, and Dad will follow behind with Fallon and Sofie.

After the team dinner, Dad and Joel are leaving for San Diego, and Sofie is staying at Katie's for the weekend. So Fallon and I will have the houses to ourselves. And we're staying at my place.

"I forgot something in my bag," Fallon mumbles, turning and running up the stairs.

I narrow my eyes at his retreating back. He better not be bringing drugs or a flask or some shit. I thought we already went over sneaking and drinking around my family.

"Set the alarm and lock up when you're done, mijo. We'll be in the car."

I use the opportunity to my advantage and chase him up the stairs, barging into my bedroom.

"What are you doing?" I ask somewhat suspiciously.

Fallon spins around with his hands behind his back. "Nothing," he mumbles. "Why are you creepin' on me, Ry?"

I huff out a laugh and step forward, crowding him into the wall. His duffle bag is on the floor between us, unzipped and gaping open. I glance down but don't see anything but his usual black clothing.

He's hiding something.

What the hell?

"Whatcha got there?"

His arms are crossed behind him and pressed against the wall.

"Nothing," he repeats.

"Liar. Show me."

With a deep sigh, Fallon brings his arms back around as I step back, revealing a medium-sized gift wrapped in silver paper with a maroon bow. Our school colors.

I ask another question that I think I know the answer to.

"What's that?" My throat is a little thick.

"A present. For when you win the championship."

"*Fuck.* Blue." I grab him and squeeze him to my chest, banding my arms around his smaller body in a tight bear hug.

"What is it?"

Fallon snorts before lifting his chin for a kiss. "Enough with the questions, Ryder. Not telling you."

"Fine. I'll just make sure I win so I can open it."

I lean down and press my mouth to his for a quick kiss. We really need to get going.

"I'm returning it if you lose. So no pressure."

The snark!

I tip my head back and belt out a loud laugh because he's hilarious when he's completely himself around me.

"Not a chance. I'm not worried. We got this." Although I'm not entirely sure if I'm telling him or myself that.

I sidestep Seth, my sneakers squeaking against the shiny hardwood floor as I dribble down the open court. There's no one to stop me, so I dunk it. Just because I fucking can. I'm in my element, and the crowd goes wild, their cheers echoing off the high ceilings.

We're playing at the college just outside town, and the place is packed. Tickets were sold out, and I'm here to show all of California who the Knights are. We're mopping the floor with these Jefferson High idiots.

I'm not going to taunt them, though. I'm no poor sport, no matter how terrible they've been to people I care about.

Dad always taught me to be the bigger person, so it's ingrained in me.

But Cole. Well, he's a different story.

"Yeah, buddy! Let's goooo!" he hollers, jumping up and down. His shaggy brown hair is pulled into a small top knot that bounces with him. He looks obnoxious as fuck, but Jamison reprimands him quickly before he gets our team a foul. Not that it would matter. A few free throws won't affect anything. We are one hundred and ten percent winning this championship.

They can't come back, and they know it with only five minutes left.

Seth throws the ball to Rich, who tries to dribble down the court, but I can tell he's stressed and flustered at how they're blowing this whole thing.

I'm not sure what their deal is. They usually play better than this. I throw my hands up as he attempts a three-pointer over my head. I block it, knocking the ball to my teammate Clarence who takes off toward the opposite basket.

At half-court, he's stopped by Dustin, who attempts to swat the ball away. When that doesn't work, he straight-up trips my boy. Clarence sprawls to the floor in a pile of long, gangly limbs.

The ref blows his whistle, and I rush over to make sure he's okay. He sits on his ass, hissing as he examines the floor burns on his knees. His top layers of skin are gone, and the flesh is raw and red.

Ouch.

Those fuckers.

Poor Clarence. He hasn't even been mixed up in the pranks or drama. He's only a junior, which is probably why

Dustin targeted him. They know I hate when people pick on the underdog.

I lean down and grab him by the bicep, Jamison on his other side. We help him stand, and he grits his teeth as the skin pulls. He can't play like this. He's gotta sit the end of the game out.

That's so fucked.

Two trainers rush out and grab him, ushering him to the locker rooms for medical care.

But Dustin just doesn't want to stop.

"Your little cheerleader is in the crowd, I see. He doesn't have much school spirit except for the hoodie and a little face paint. Or does that spirit come later? Maybe in the bedroom?"

What the fuck is his fascination with Fallon and me?

It's not normal. *He's* definitely not normal, and I'm starting to wonder if he's possibly hardcore repressed. Because he shouldn't be so hyper-focused on the two of us. I can only think that he's gay and maybe hates himself. I might feel bad for the guy if he wasn't a grade-A predator and spiteful asshole.

"Those sparkles? Bet they'd look nice on my dick."

I forget where I am for a moment, rage sizzling in my bones. My vision goes black around the edges, and I start to lose my mind and lunge for him.

Jamie's calm presence is needed and appreciated when he bear-hugs me, preventing me from smashing this prick's face in and getting ejected from the game and possibly even school.

"Don't do it. His future is going down with this game, and he's trying to take you with him. Don't let him, Ry. You're smarter than this. You're the winner. You've got everything." Then he whispers directly into my ear. "Including Fallon."

Fuck! He's right. I don't need to play into this and look like the aggressor in front of the entire crowd.

Cole speaks up for me. "Shut your mouth, you narrow-minded prick. We're trying to play basketball here. Not sure what *you're* trying to do. Lose? Well, congrats. You're doing a great job!"

The tunnel vision clears, and I step in as team captain. "Okay, enough!" I turn to Dustin, sneering in disgust. "Fuck off, Dustin. Your jealousy is showing." Then I turn to my own team. "And you guys," I say to my boys. "Let's go check on Clarence. We've got an injury break because someone's hurt."

"Not jealous of shit. You all got lucky tonight," he mumbles and walks away.

Yeah. Right. Not jealous at all.

I've been fighting hard not to look at Fallon this whole time, not wanting to give us away. But I give in and flick my eyes up to the crowd, where I know my family is sitting.

And there, right behind him, is fucking *Jackson*. He should be sitting on the public school side, not behind Fallon. He's not doing anything, but I'm already irritated, on edge, and ready for these last few minutes to go by so we can get our trophy and go home.

I swipe the sweat from my brow, waiting for the medics and Joel to finish helping Clarence to the locker rooms. I'm taking his foul shots.

After I make both baskets, the game continues, and I can't help but glance up to the bleachers as much as I can now that I know Jacks is up there. Probably trying to talk to my boyfriend.

I'm sick of it all.

He's fucking mine.

I score a handful more points, and before I know it, the final buzzer blares as I let off one last three-pointer.

Swish!

The ball goes in, and the crowd goes crazy. I glance at the glowing red numbers on the scoreboard, just to be certain. But I already know. We fucking won! We swept Jefferson and beat them by seventeen points tonight, bringing the trophy home for the Knights.

My eyes scan the stands, sweat dripping down my brow. I can't wait any longer. This is it. The world needs to know that Fallon Rivers is mine.

In a split-second decision that feels so right, I climb the stairs two at a time. The crowd cheers for me, already on their feet.

"Ryder! Ryder! Ryder!"

The sound is deafening, and my heart beats wildly, but there's no turning back now. All I can focus on is my boyfriend, how much I love him, and how badly I need to show it.

He's sitting there while everyone else stands, towering over him and whooping loudly. My smile grows. I think he's typing out lyrics in the notes on his phone.

His lack of enthusiasm is the most endearing thing ever. Something about his aloofness and bored, uninterested face just does it for me. And the shimmer.

Fallon's eyes dart up and widen when he finds me towering above him. His dark blue eyes turn hooded when I lean down and cradle his face between my palms in front of *everyone*.

I just don't care anymore.

This is me. This is us.

Take it or leave it.

I seal my lips to his, pressing our faces together hard. They need to know he's mine.

I can't extinguish the fire that burns between us. It's wild, out of control, and overwhelming. It's *everything*.

I pull back slightly and whisper in his ear. "Can't wait to celebrate tonight."

I turn to Sofie next, who has tears in her eyes, and I just fucking *know* we're getting a scrapbook. She jumps up and throws her arms around my neck. I catch her waist as she dangles there. "Love you, big bro, and I'm so, so proud of you." She kisses me on the cheek, and I set her down before swallowing the lump in my throat and turning to Dad.

"Mijo. Is this what I think it is?"

"Yeah, Dad. Talk later?"

"Of course."

He gives me a big embrace, whispering similar sentiments in my ear as my sister, further solidifying how much I love this family of ours, Joel and Fallon included. "I'm so proud of you and the man you've become. Congratulations on all of it."

"Thanks, Dad," I mumble, needing to get back to the court.

I take one last look at Fallon, flashing a huge grin, and he gives me a small one in return that makes my stomach flip. His smiles are something special and rare. Just like he is.

I cannot wait to finish the ceremonies, eat dinner, and go home with just my boyfriend. The boyfriend that everyone now knows I have.

I expect my phone to blow up; it probably already has. But I'm turning it off for the whole weekend. I can deal with school gossip on Monday.

For now, I'm going to celebrate my win and enjoy being gay and out with my boyfriend.

I jog down the stands and back to the team, where I'm greeted with loud cheers and quite a few hugs. Being accepted and welcomed back with open arms has an annoying lump forming in my throat that I'm forced to swallow past.

Cole gives me a big squeeze and whispers into my ear, "Bro, that was some serious game! Like top tier, romantic shit. Now I'm gonna have to try harder every time I wanna get Gracie back." He laughs and wanders off toward the cheerleaders.

I shake my head at my friend and glance at Jamie, who gives me a wink before making his way to the locker room.

"Love you, kiddo. Talk later?" Joel whispers quickly before he's swept away to do an interview with a local news station.

Everything's happening so fast, but it feels good to be free from this burden. I'm done hiding who I am. I head to the showers and change into my school suit. Time to accept my awards so I can go home and claim my real prize.

Fallon.

CHAPTER TWENTY-EIGHT

RYDER

"It's just us now," I murmur against his lips as I drop my gym bag by the front door. "Wanna go to my room?"

"Yeah, I'm gonna shower quickly and get comfortable."

"Come out naked."

Fallon snorts. "No."

"In your underwear?"

"No."

"Underwear and socks?"

"What is this? Some kind of reverse strip poker? I don't understand you sometimes, Ryder Cruz."

I chuckle, and Fallon loops his arms around my neck. I lean down, and he jumps and wraps his legs around my waist as I stand. We start to kiss as he clings to me like a koala, and I make my way toward the stairs, splaying my giant palm under his butt. I can feel his erection against my stomach.

As soon as I place my foot on the bottom step, Fallon peels his lips away from mine.

"Wait. I'm too heavy. You can't carry me up that many steps."

"You're not. And I can. I'll help you shower too, if you want. I'll take care of you in any way I can, Blue. You need to start understanding that, okay?"

"Okay," he murmurs back, nuzzling his nose into the crook of my neck. "You smell good."

I chuckle, continuing up the stairs and straight to my bathroom. I set him on the white marble countertop and flip the shower on, letting the room fill with steam.

I turn around and stare at his sexy little self sitting by the sink, his blue and black hair hanging in his face. An intense energy exists between us, vibrating against my skin and making my heart pound when he looks at me with that half-lidded stare that's only for me.

The tension is palpable. I stalk toward him, cradling his face and kissing him deeply. I coax his tongue out, stroking it with my own and caressing the soft skin of his cheeks with my thumbs.

I break the kiss, both of our chests heaving.

With our foreheads pressed together, he meets my gaze. His breath fans against my lips, teasing and tempting me. *I need him.* I need him so fucking bad I can't even suppress my feelings any longer.

"I love you," I whisper against his mouth softly. Barely audible over the shower behind me.

He doesn't move a muscle. Doesn't react. But I know he heard me.

"You can't."

I pull back, staring at his expressionless face. "Why not?"

"I don't deserve your love. Or any love," he mumbles the last part. Whatever he's talking about, I know it has to do with his parents abandoning him somehow, and it breaks my heart. But I know that it fucking feels like shit.

"You do deserve it. And you have it. The whole family's too, including Georgie. Everyone loves you. So whatever you're thinking, or whoever's making you think these things, they're in the past. My family and I are your people now. Your future. *Your family.* Okay?"

"Okay," he agrees reluctantly, looking down and picking at his nails. But I need to make sure he heard me.

I put a finger under his chin and lift his face to mine. "I want you to hear it again. So you can start to believe it. 'Cause it's not changing anytime soon. *I love you.* I love you so fucking much, Fallon Rivers. And I'm ready for the whole world to know it. I can't hide it. It's who I am. You're built into my *soul.*"

"Ryder. . ." he whimpers, his chin quivering as he glances to the side.

It's too much for him. I know it is. He can barely process it, let alone reciprocate.

"Come here, baby." I pull him into my chest, banding my arms around him tightly. "You don't need to respond right now. Just try to let it sink in, yeah?"

He nods into my shoulder, and I realize that's all I'm going to get right now.

"Shower?"

He nods again, and I help him undress, slipping his hoodie and T-shirt off first. I step back and admire his slim frame and his flawless pale skin. Fuck, he's sexy.

"Hop down."

I wrap my long fingers around his waist and help him off the counter. I trail a soft touch down to his jeans and flick the button open. I slowly pull the zipper down, dragging the moment out and teasing us both.

I crouch before him and tug them down with his boxers. His cock bobs free, already pink and glistening with pre-cum. I lean forward and swipe my tongue over him before telling him to get in the shower.

I just had one, so I don't need to get wet unless he wants me to.

"Need help?"

"No," he murmurs, grabbing his cock at the base and squeezing. "Just kinda worked up, is all."

I laugh loudly. "Well, hurry up then. And I can help you with that."

I slip back into my bedroom, shedding my clothes on the way to the giant, oversized bean bag. I've been dreaming, or more like fantasizing, about fucking him on it. I plop down and fold my arms above my head, settling into the soft beans and getting comfortable.

Ten minutes later, Fallon emerges, his blue and black hair dripping down his bare chest and soaking into the towel around his waist. My dick fills rapidly as I take in the sight of my sexy, broody little boyfriend.

He reapplied his usual eyeliner but not the Chapstick.

Fallon stalks toward me, his eyes half-lidded as he takes me in, long legs stretched out before me and my hard body waiting for him. He pauses in front of me and drops his towel.

He's already hard, just like me, but he drops to his knees and runs his soft hands up my thighs, squeezing and kneading my quads.

"Shit. That feels so good." The relief to my muscles causes my dick to twitch in front of him.

Fallon takes the hint and presses a soft kiss to my crown before licking down my shaft. "Blue. Oh God." His mouth is amazing, his tongue soft and wet. He slides me into his mouth as far as he can, nearly choking himself. He bobs a few times, dragging his metal piercing against my sensitive flesh, and pops off, spit hanging from his swollen lips. But no sparkles.

"Oh. Fuck. Put the lip gloss on. The shimmery one."

He glances up at me, chewing his lip ring, a slight blush on his cheeks. His eyes are practically iridescent with lust. He scrambles off the bean bag, and I stare at his ass as he walks away.

I reach down and tug on my cock, imagining being inside of him.

Fallon ambles over to his bag, purposely bending over and exposing himself to me.

The little tease.

My cock throbs, and I squeeze the base, waiting for him to come back and suck me with those sparkly lips.

I hear the pop of a cap, and then he's back on his knees before me, stretching those beautifully plump and shimmery lips around my cock. I flex my hips, trying to temper the need to thrust into his mouth. He's not ready for that, and I'm too big for him to swallow.

"Fuck, baby. Look at you. So sexy. So hot. Let me fuck you. I need to."

Fallon whimpers around my cock, the vibrations causing a chill to race down my spine and through my balls. I shiver as I race toward the edge. "I'm gonna come."

He encourages me, massaging my thighs and caressing my balls as he licks and sucks with more enthusiasm than he normally shows.

I detonate, coming with a roar as my cock spurts into the back of his throat, causing him to make a choking noise. The sick part of my brain likes it.

He pulls off, sucking me clean and only leaving sparkles

behind. His lips are swollen, Chapstick smeared across his chin, and I yank him closer and kiss him hard.

"I fucking love you," I tell him, not caring that I won't hear it back. "Let me make you feel good now, Blue."

Fallon nods, and we switch positions. Except he's on his hands and knees with his head down and ass up, presenting himself to me.

"Such a beautiful sight," I praise, rubbing a hand along his cheeks and down the center, through his crease and over his hole. It twitches at my touch, and memories of my tongue there come rushing back to me. Tonight, it'll be my dick in there.

I grab the lube from my bedside table and flick the cap open, squirting the cool gel directly onto him and then on my fingers. I rub it in as Fallon moans, dropping his head and pressing back against me, trying to get me to slip inside.

"Ryder, please. I need to feel you inside me."

"I know, baby, I know. Be patient." I circle his hole with my index and middle fingers. Around and around. Teasing him. His hole pulses against my touch, his body begging for me and desperate for stimulation.

My finger easily slips inside with the slightest pressure, and I push forward until I'm knuckle-deep. Watching it disappear in and out of his ass makes my cock weepy and desperate.

I add another finger, scissoring them. I've been working him up to take my cock, and he loves this part. Loves the feel of the stretch.

"More. I can take more."

I scissor my fingers wider, staring at the obscene sight as I open his asshole wider.

I quickly slip a third finger in while his body offers no

resistance and fuck him deep and hard. Making room for all three of them.

He's stretched wide, and he moans loudly and pants urgently. His face is pressed into the bean bag, and the slick noises of my fingers fucking him without mercy cause more pre-cum to ooze out of me.

"Are you ready for my cock?" I ask, needing to make sure he wants it. This is new for both of us. Regardless of how much *research* I've done.

"Y-yes," he pants. "Fuck me, please, Ry."

I slip my fingers out, and he cries at the loss. "Shh. It's okay. C'mere."

I flop onto the bean bag, lying on my back. I grab Fallon's hand. "Straddle me. I want you to ride me."

"I don't know about this, Ry." He looks shy and self-conscious. That won't do.

"You'll be in control this way. How deep and how fast you take me for your first time. Try it?"

He chews on his lip before nodding and swinging a leg over my hips. I squirt more lube into my hand and stroke myself. I know his ass is open and ready. He just needs to relax and not tense up.

I grip the base of my cock, holding it steady. "Lower yourself slowly. Once you get past the initial stretch, I'll glide right in and fill you up. It'll feel so fucking good. I promise."

Fallon braces his smaller hands against my chest, pressing on my nipples deliciously as he leans his weight on me. I grab his hip, helping guide him, holding my dick with my other.

"Relax and just sit down on my cock. Let me in." My head presses against his open hole, slipping in slightly, and I can already feel the tight grip.

Fallon whimpers but doesn't say anything. His body is trying to pull me in, so I flex my hips, giving the gentlest counterpressure. I slip past that first ring of muscle, causing him to cry out and squeeze his eyes shut tightly. I pause, not going further than an inch or two.

It's fucking torture.

"You okay, Blue?" I grit out, trying to hold steady and not plow into him. I'd never hurt him.

"Y-yeah. Give me some more. I'm ready. I can take it."

Fuck. That's so sexy.

He sinks down fully as I push up until I'm fully bottomed out, and we both groan loudly. His dick is rock hard and leaking between us where he sits on my lap, impaled on my length. My brain short-circuits at the sight of him.

He presses his weight on my pecs, using his upper body strength to lift up and sink down repeatedly onto my cock. I bend my knees, press my feet against the floor, and thrust up into him.

The beans crunch beneath us as our bodies slap together and grunts fill the air. He rolls his hips and grinds into me on every other thrust in a surprisingly sensual move. Then he pinches my nipples, abusing them into tight little buds as I pound into him.

Oh. My. God.

Fuck!

"Shit. Shit. Shit," I chant. I can't come this soon, I can't.

I lift Fallon, pulling out quickly, causing him to whimper. I flip us so that he's on his stomach.

I tap the side of his thigh. "Bend your knee to the side a little, and tip your ass up for me." Fallon struggles to get to his elbows, sinking into the giant bean bag. I lean over and whisper into his ear, nibbling at it. "Just lie down. Okay? I got you, now. It's your turn to relax."

I grab the little bottle from the ground and spread his cheeks, squirting more lube directly onto his open, slightly puffy hole.

Shit. I did that. Stretched him open with my dick.

That is so fucking hot.

I use my finger to rub it around his rim and then slip it inside, causing him to moan and arch his back more, sticking his ass out even further. I need my dick back in there immediately.

I remove my finger and press the head of my cock back to him, pushing forward in one solid thrust. Fallon cries out, gripping the fabric above his head, and I freeze.

"Shit. I'm so sorry. You okay, Blue?"

His chest is heaving as he presses his face to the soft bean bag.

"I'm fine," he rasps out, voice rough like he just woke up. "I just need a minute."

"You sure?" My dick is pulsing, my nuts begging to bust, but I'd never move if it caused him pain.

"Yeah. I'm fine. Now fuck me, Mr. MVP."

The little shit.

"No, you did not just say that with attitude when I have my dick up your ass, baby."

Oh fuck, his snark is going to do me in. I pull out and give him what he wants, thrusting back in with a little more force.

Since he asked for it.

Fallon groans long and loud when I grind my pelvis against his ass. I'm all the way in. And it's fucking *deep*. His breathing picks up, as does his moaning, and he pushes back against me when I begin to set a steady rhythm.

His breaths are punched out of him with each unforgiving thrust of my cock. His shiny black nails squeeze the bean bag as I relentlessly pound into him. I can feel the sweat drip down my temple onto Fallon's back as I lean over him, trying to get a better angle so I can hit that spot inside him. I grab his thigh and bend his knee higher, allowing me to get deeper.

"*Ungh!* Oh fuck, Ry. Right there. Right there."

Found it.

I don't stop. Instead, I lean over him further, pressing more of my weight down and squishing his smaller frame as I fuck him into the bean bag.

Fallon grunts softly with every thrust, and it's so fucking sexy. I ease back to watch my dick go in and out of his beautifully stretched hole. It's fucking fascinating and so goddamn sexy. I grab onto one hip as I rub my hand up his back, caressing and massaging his smaller muscles as I fuck him a little less gently.

"Oh shit. Ry. I'm gonna come on the bean bag," he grunts out.

Fuck! I didn't even think about the fact that this was gonna get messy. I can't get jizz on my new custom-made bean bag. But I can't stop. There's no way. No way in hell can I stop pounding into his tight ass right now. Not until I come.

Without stopping my movements, I grab the championship T-shirt he had custom printed for me. I put it on after showering in the locker rooms.

"Come on this," I grit out, tossing it to him, unwilling to slow down.

Fallon takes it and shoves it underneath him, grabbing his dick and stroking himself in time with my thrusts.

Fuck, that's hot.

He's so hot.

"I love you. So. Fucking. Much." I punctuate each word with a hard thrust into his pulsing ass, and he cries out, coming hard. His muscles squeeze me tightly, and my nuts draw up, spurting load after load into his clenching ass.

I fall, draping myself over his smaller body while we're still joined together.

"I love you," I repeat, nibbling on his ear, ensuring he knows it. *Believes* it. And I'll keep telling him every day.

CHAPTER TWENTY-NINE

FALLON

R yder collapses on me, and I'm surrounded by his huge body, his cock still deep inside me. I feel safe. Sheltered. Secure.

He tells me he loves me again, but I struggle to feel worthy.

I think I can feel it too. Love. Through the numbness that still lingers. I know it's there. I'm just not ready to say it.

And Ryder, being the amazing person he is, doesn't pressure me or expect anything in return.

He pulls out, and I whimper at the loss, my ass feeling tender. I stand up slowly, careful not to get any jizz on the bean bag. I wince at the soreness as Ryder's cum oozes out of me and slowly drips down my leg.

"You okay, Blue? Should I look?"

"No," I rush out, hustling to the bathroom to clean up in privacy.

"No, you're not okay?" Ryder comes over quickly, his long legs eating up the distance as his glistening cock hangs thickly between his legs.

"No, you shouldn't look," I huff out a little laugh. "You've done enough tonight, Mr. MVP."

A loud laugh pours from Ryder's mouth. "Your T-shirt predicted the future, Blue. I am indeed MVP *and* State Champion. Too bad you just jizzed all over it."

I let out a raspy chuckle. I can't help it. His smile. His laugh. His jokes. His kindness. And those curls. Fuck, his curls. All of it. It makes me want to be happy. To tease him and be teased back. To love and laugh. And I'm starting to feel like it's more possible all the time.

I hurry to the bathroom before more of Ryder's cum drips from me onto the carpet. Cleaning up quickly, I find Ryder lounging in his king-sized bed with a bowl of candy.

I carefully climb onto the bed. It's high off the ground, and my ass is fucking tender. I try to hide the wince, but I know Ryder is watching my face for every reaction.

"Fallon."

He sounds stern, but really I'm fine. "Ryder, it's nothing."

"You sure? You'd tell me? I got cream if you need it. The directions say it's soothing."

"Yeah. I'm fine. Really. What are you eating?" I nod toward the giant plastic bowl of little colorful candies.

"Sour jelly beans. The only acceptable kind. Here." Ryder grabs a handful, and I open my mouth, allowing him to pour them in. "Even the yellow ones are good. It's pretty amazing. When is yellow *ever* good?"

I nod my head. He's not wrong. These are delicious, not too sour.

He nudges the bowl toward me, and I shove another handful into my mouth while Ryder selects a basketball show on Netflix. Something else I've never experienced because Mom didn't pay for cable or internet, let alone a streaming service.

I eat a few more handfuls before Ryder sets the bowl on his nightstand, and I snuggle deeper into his side, throwing a leg over.

"You tired?" Ry asks, kissing my head as he squeezes me tighter.

"Mhm," I hum with a raspy-sounding voice. It's been a long day for me, and I know it sure has for Ryder.

"M'kay," he mumbles, clicking the TV off. "Me too."

The darkness is comforting as silence envelops us. We have the whole weekend and the whole house to ourselves. And I'm looking forward to something for the first time in a long while.

Saturday passes too quickly in a blur of blow jobs and Georgie's mystery casserole. Another amazing version of shepherd's pie. Ryder has kept his phone off, and we told Uncle Joel, Al, and Sofie to contact us via my cell if they need us. No one else has my number, so no one can harass me.

I'm not looking forward to Monday, but at the same time, I just don't care what any of them think. This is me. This is fucking *us*.

Sunday comes, and it's still a little chilly even though spring is nearly here. I slip Ryder's letterman jacket on, tucking my nose into the collar and inhaling deeply. Bergamot and spice, my new favorite smell.

We pull into Katie's driveway, and Ryder honks the horn, not bothering to ring the doorbell.

A girl who looks familiar and our age steps out of the

front door in tiny sleep shorts, an oversized T-shirt, and bare feet. She gives Ryder the finger, and he tips his head back with a loud laugh. I guess it *is* only ten in the morning. Maybe she was sleeping.

"Ah. Kelsey. What a gem. She loves me, though. Honest."

I snort. He is utterly ridiculous. Ryder's charm knows no bounds. Even his goofy, off-the-wall jokes are endearing and lovable. Fuck. *Lovable.* There's that L word again. I can't seem to escape it, and maybe I don't need to.

Sofie slips out from behind Katie's sister, I guess, and hustles over with her Hello Kitty suitcase bouncing along the driveway behind her. She climbs into the back.

"Sup, Sofie?" Ryder asks, tipping his sunglasses down to look at her in the rearview mirror.

"Nothing. What are you guys doing today?"

"Thought we could go to the record shop," Ryder says.

"Spend my gift cards," I add, hoping she'll help me with some clothing choices. I might get a few new vinyls too.

"Ooo! Yay!" she exclaims, always full of energy and enthusiasm. "Can I help?" she asks.

I turn around in my seat and give her a small smile, catching her off guard and silencing her for once. "Yes, please."

"O-okay. Cool," she stumbles over the shock before giving me a megawatt smile like her brother's.

I turn back in my seat and relax while Ryder drives us to the small music shop they love so much.

Sofie flips through the classic rock albums, trying to help me decide between Lynyrd Skynyrd or Pink Floyd. Ryder has his long arms wrapped around my smaller frame from behind while I lean back into his hard chest.

None of us are really paying attention. We're just having a good time, looking for music and T-shirts.

"So you really are gay? Not just getting your dick sucked 'cause you won the championship and can make anyone do what you want?"

I didn't even hear the bell ring. Where did they come from?

"Shut your mouth around my little sister."

Ryder pulls Sofie and me behind him, standing tall.

"Aww. Look at big, bad, *gay* Ryder Cruz protecting the weak and innocent."

"You're a jerk, Dustin! I've told you to stop messaging me. You're not coming to my birthday party," Sofie yells at him, never afraid to voice her opinion.

"You stalking my little sister?" Ryder crowds into Dustin, who just brushes him off to walk down a different aisle like he's afraid to talk shit too close to Ry.

"Nah, I'm over that little girl. I'm into real women."

Sofie throws her hands up. "Then leave! Stop messaging me on Insta and just. . . GO. AH. WAY." She sounds it out loudly and slowly. Dustin's face turns red, but he doesn't say anything. His hateful eyes dart to me next, running over my body quickly, and I see a hint of something in his gaze. Something I don't even want to examine.

"Yeah, just fuck off, dude. Okay? Your team lost. I'm gay. Leave my sister alone. Done. End of story. We don't have to ever see each other again. So please, let's make that happen."

I snort at Ry's tone, and Dustin's eyes narrow, but I couldn't care less. He can fuck all the way off. Like Ryder just said.

Dustin huffs out an annoyed breath. "I don't have to

take orders from you just 'cause you think you're better than me."

"My team won. I'm definitely better at basketball."

"He's a better person too," I add. "You're a shit human."

"And you're just a make-up-wearing fagg—"

"Hey!" the old man behind the counter shouts. "Not in my store!" He storms over and stands in front of Dustin, pointing toward the door. "Out."

"You can't kick me out, old man."

"I can and I will. Hate speech isn't tolerated here. You will not verbally assault paying customers. Now leave, young man."

I see hurt flash through Dustin's eyes before being replaced with his usual cruel stare.

"Whatever. Stay away from me with your gayness, and I'll stay away from you," he sneers like the homophobic asshole he is.

"Perfect! Absolutely perfect! You've got yourself a deal, Dustin Flynne. Now, please. Fuck all the way off."

Dustin turns on his heel and storms through the front door, letting it slam and bang closed loudly.

"Ridiculous. I'm sorry, young man. I'm happy to have you both in my store, especially state champion and MVP Ryder Cruz." The old man shakes Ryder's hand enthusiastically.

"Thank you, Paul, really. We need more people like you in the world," Sofie agrees, making Paul blush.

"Oh, it's nothin'. Just common decency. You kids know where to find me when you're ready to check out. And if any of you like to sing or play music, I'm having a little talent show here. There'll be a prize at the end, and some of my old record exec buddies will be here, looking for new talent."

"Ooh! Ooh! Fallon! You have to sign up!" Sofie shouts in excitement, bouncing on her toes.

I've been thinking about putting myself out there. Ryder makes me want things I've never dreamed of. Love. Success. Music. Happiness. And even basketball. I see all of these things in my future with Ryder, and more importantly, I actually see a future. I can visualize things now, instead of just a deep, dark cavern where my dreams and aspirations should be.

"You should, baby," Ryder murmurs, a rush of warmth flooding me at the public endearment.

"I'll do it," I say before talking myself out of it.

"Eeeee!" Sofie squeals, clapping her hands together and doing a twirl. Luckily no full dance move this time.

"It's two weeks from this weekend, so you've got time. We're looking for interesting covers. Show us your creativity with up to three songs. The flyers and sign-up form are by the door, so you can grab more information on your way out. I look forward to seeing what you've got to show us, young man."

"Thanks," I mumble, grabbing my last album choice and heading for the clothing area. I'm ready to go home, listen to my new albums, and mess around with my boyfriend before Joel and Al get back to town. Not that we'll let that stop us. Especially not now that we've had sex.

He's unleashed a beast in both of us, and I want nothing more than Ryder's huge cock spearing me open every night. The change is startling. I've never even been interested in a person before. Absolutely no one. But now I can't get thoughts of Ryder out of my mind.

CHAPTER THIRTY

RYDER

Another week of school passes, and it's such a relief that no one at the academy cares that I'm gay. No one even bats an eye. They just care that we beat Jefferson High, completely sweeping the floor with those assholes. Cole was a little surprised, but nothing phases him, and Jamie, of course, has always known. Gracie, Taylor, Alexis, and the other girls practically swooned at my 'grand display of romance' when I climbed the bleachers and kissed Fallon in front of everyone, claiming him and declaring my sexuality in one fell swoop. Two birds with one stone. No doubt.

I added a state championship patch to my letterman jacket. Fallon wears it to school every day, despite it getting warmer. There aren't any dress code violations against such things, even though it's usually girls wearing the oversized jackets of their boyfriends, not small emo boys with blue hair. It's a school-issued piece of clothing, so even though a few of the older teachers sneer at us, none of them can say anything.

It feels good to have a break from basketball, even if it

won't last. I got accepted to my dream college just outside of LA, and apparently, they also don't care if they're about to have their first gay player. Gay Latino player. I'm not the norm. I know this. And it's fine. I can be an outlier.

With my future secured, basketball on pause, and my sexuality public, I need to have the talk I've been avoiding with Dad. Well, not really avoiding per se; it's more like neither of us has had the time.

After they returned from San Diego late Sunday night, Joel had to get caught up with work, and Dad had things around the house to manage, as well as his other restaurants. He hasn't slowed down for a minute, let alone to talk.

But now, it's Friday night, and he's relaxing in the movie room downstairs with Joel. They're in matching plaid pajamas, drinking wine.

"Oh. I can come back later," I say, slipping into the hallway.

"Ry!" Dad calls out, so I amble into the room once again. "Come sit and talk to me. I've been meaning to talk with you since last weekend."

Joel moves to leave, but I stop him. "No. You should stay too. We're all family, right?"

"Right," he confirms with a small smile and a tight nod.

"I'm sorry I didn't tell you I was gay," I blurt out unexpectedly, even to myself. I stare at Dad with wide, nearly panicked eyes, blinking rapidly. I run a hand through my curls, scratching my head at why I did that.

Fallon is upstairs napping after a long week of school, so I figured I'd have this talk with Dad on my own since he's not very chatty with other people anyway.

"Ryder," Dad says with a strained voice. His dark brown eyes soften even more than usual, and he pats the couch cushion next to him. "Come, mijo. Sit. Please."

I listen to my dad, feeling like a little kid again instead of a young man ready to graduate and move away from home to play ball in college.

"Don't ever apologize for who you are or how long you keep it to yourself. You don't owe me an explanation, and you never did. It's your life, and you have to live it at your own pace. When you're ready. Not others. And I just need to tell you again how proud of you I am. Not only for winning the championship but for your bravery in coming out in the absolutely spectacular way you did. You made this old papa bear proud, mijo. I'm always proud of my children, but Ryder, this was something special."

"It was very special, and I'm so proud of you too, Ry. As your coach, your friend, and—"

"My possible future stepdad," I supply, cutting him off and repeating what Sofie always teases them with.

"Yeah, that." A grin tugs at his lips as his curious eyes dart to my dad next to him.

"Mhm. I've heard it from you all, and I'm working on it."

"Al, honey!" Joel gasps with a hand to his chest, making me laugh. For being such a big, athletic basketball coach, he can be super stereotypically gay sometimes.

"Don't say that in front of Sofie," I warn. "Working on Fallon's and my scrapbook has begun, and let me tell you," I pause with a crooked smile, "this one involves a lot of black lace, purple, pink, and teal. So actually, it's pretty awesome."

Joel and Dad laugh, steering the conversation back to asking me how coming out and school have been.

I let them know that everyone at the academy has been great and supportive, and at this point, my only real nerves involve Mom and when or if I'm going to tell her.

She's not on my social media, so it wouldn't be hard to hide and just not announce it. We never talk, and I don't really want to. She's toxic and would only have negative things to say.

"I'm not going to tell her," I say, deciding on the spot. "It's not that I'm hiding. More like she doesn't deserve to know that part of me or even be included in my life. She lost that privilege a long time ago, and I don't plan on ever reinstating it. I'm an adult now. I don't owe her anything, least of all an explanation about my sex life."

"Yes, that's exactly right," Dad agrees, as does Joel.

"And she'll only accuse you of making me gay," I tell them.

Dad scoffs and rolls his eyes.

"You know it's true, Dad."

"Yes, sadly, I do."

"That's a ridiculous notion," Joel adds.

It is what it is at this point. We've known she was unreasonable for a long time.

"Okay, it's settled then. I'm not telling her, but if she finds out, I'm not denying it, either."

She probably won't find out, though. She's selfish and is only concerned about keeping up with herself and whatever man is paying for her expensive lifestyle that week. I wonder how poor Roger is fairing and whether she's drained him dry yet.

"I'd like to discuss something else with you while you're here, Ry," Joel says hesitantly.

"Yeah?" I always get a little nervous when my dad wants to talk, and Joel is no different.

He clears his throat. "The sixth anniversary of my brother's passing is coming up at the end of the month, and

I thought it would be good for Fallon to visit his dad's grave in Philadelphia. Has he read the letter yet?"

I feel bad for divulging the information, but Joel only cares, and I need to make sure Fallon is okay, which he *isn't*. I know it deep down.

He still hasn't said I love you.

At least he's not sneaking weed and alcohol all the time now like he used to. And I even see little glimpses of happiness beneath the mask he always wears.

"No."

Joel rubs the scruff forming on his chin. "That's what I thought. Do you know where it is?"

Shit. I feel like such a snitch.

"Yeah. He asked me to keep it for him."

"Keep it for him?" Joel's brows scrunch together behind his dark-framed glasses.

I nod slowly, not willing to explain any further.

"Okay. Well, would you feel comfortable bringing it with us? If Fallon agrees to go? I think it would be really healthy for him to read it. He hasn't told me how he feels about everything, but I think he's harboring some guilt for not being around toward the end."

That's the fucking understatement of the century.

"I'm not asking you to divulge any more of his secrets, but this is my nephew, so please take care of him if I can't be there to help. He's been through so much, Ryder. He needs people behind him."

"I know," I repeat solemnly, crossing my arms and rubbing my biceps like I'm cold. I'm feeling mildly uncomfortable even though I know we all just *care*. So much. We just want him to be happy. And healthy.

"I'll bring it. And I'll find the right time to ask him about the trip. It should come from me."

"We can help him together. As a family," Dad adds.

"As a family," Joel repeats.

Sofie walks by the movie room, stopping and popping her head in. "Family?"

"Yes, darling. We were just saying how we're all a family, Fallon included."

"Aww, Joel! You're so corny. But that's okay. You're still my favorite possible future stepfather!"

"Get in here, you little brat!" Joel hollers back, and Sofie giggles, skipping over and jumping right on top of the three of us, causing us to grunt, even though she barely weighs a hundred pounds.

"You're crushing my bones, cariño," Dad teases, making Sofie laugh harder, and I grab her bare feet, ready to make her submit.

"Ry! Please don't tickle me! Please! You can have all the corner pieces of Georgie's casseroles for a month! A whole month, Ry! Just please don't!"

I would have stopped because of the begging, but I'll take control of the crispy corner pieces, too. Sofie and I have fought over them our whole lives.

"Deal." I release her foot, and she rolls off us, plopping onto the floor with a thud.

"I thought you just said we were a family! This is treachery!"

I snort, heaving myself off the overstuffed couch and stepping over my overly-dramatic sister. I'm ready to go relax with someone more chill. These people run on full energy from start to finish.

I need mellow.

I need Fallon.

CHAPTER THIRTY-ONE

RYDER

"Y ou nervous?" I ask as Fallon leans over the sink and lines his eyes in black.

"Maybe a little, but not really. I've played these songs so many times. It's more about the vocals. Putting myself out there and being vulnerable publicly."

"Well, I'll be there, so you won't be alone. Jamie, Sofie, and Cole too. I also think Gracie, Alexis, and Taylor are performing. If not, they'll at least be there. We've all got your back. So you've got support, okay?"

I come up behind him as he continues to lean over the bathroom counter to finish his eyeliner. When the pencil is safely away from his eyeball, I grab his hips and grind my semi against him. Seeing his ass bent over in those tight black jeans has blood instantly rushing to my dick.

He re-dyed his hair last night, so the black is extra dark, and the blue is extra bright. His jeans have holes everywhere, and his shirt is a skin-tight black mesh that shows off his tiny pink nipples. The multiple silver chains hanging from his pants add to the rockstar vibe, and holy fuck do I want front-row seats to everything Fallon Rivers. I want to kneel before him and worship at his altar.

He is a God. A future legend.

"Fuck, you look good tonight, Blue. Can I blow you before we leave? I'll be quick," I beg, whispering into his ear. And it's not unusual at all lately. Me begging to suck him off. I can't get enough of his sweet cock in my mouth.

Fallon spins around, chewing on his lip ring, and nods.

I drop to my knees and slowly unbutton his jeans, peeking up at him from under my lashes. His eyes are hooded and as mysterious as the deepest, darkest trenches of the ocean.

I pull him out of his boxer briefs, leaving his pants around his thighs, and shove his soft dick into my mouth. I love to feel him grow bigger and harder inside my mouth. I squeeze his balls gently and slip my fingers further down, caressing and massaging his taint.

"Fuck, Ryder. Lower." He tries to spread his legs, stopped by his pants around his thighs.

I pop off of his growing erection, chuckling at his neediness. "We don't have time, and it's too messy. Lemme just swallow your cum real quick."

Fallon whimpers, squeezing his eyes shut while I suck him down again. He presses his hips forward, and I reach around to rub his ass cheeks and encourage him to fuck my mouth.

He starts to thrust, and soon enough, he's nearly gagging me, holding my head still while he utterly uses me. I slip a finger between his crease and start to rub circles against his hole, and that does it. With a quiet grunt, Fallon explodes, releasing load after load into the back of my throat, nearly choking me.

He's panting heavily when he releases my hair. I suck

every drop off before tucking him back into his underwear, pulling his pants up, zipping and buttoning them.

I stand, wiping the corner of my mouth. "Gonna go brush my teeth real quick before we leave," I tease, and he bursts out with a raspy laugh that curls my toes. He shakes his head at me.

"You better go do that, Mr. MVP."

I smirk, loving when he teases me with that nickname.

Sofie, Jamie, Cole, and I sit at a small, round table with a black linen tablecloth and a tiny battery-powered candle. We have Cokes while Sofie has a coffee.

She and Jamie are sitting awfully close, but I trust him, so I don't question it. *Yet.*

Fallon and the girls in our friend group who like to sing are back in the employee lounge, getting ready for their turn on stage.

Thirty minutes after we arrive, the lights dim, and Paul walks on stage, adjusting the mic to his height. His bald head gleams under the spotlights.

"Good evening, everyone! I'm excited to start tonight's concert! As you all know, we have a grand prize and a few special music executive guests sitting in the back." Paul uses his hand like a visor, pretending to gaze off into the distance. "Ah! Right there! Mickey, Sal, and Ronnie. Three of my old buddies, who have some really helpful connections down in LA. And the grand prize. . . is five thousand dollars!"

The crowd cheers at that, and I'm a little surprised it's so much money. This is an awesome opportunity for Fallon. One he wouldn't have had back in Philadelphia. And speaking of Philly, time is running out. I haven't had a chance to bring up the trip and ask him if he wants to go, and I don't know... *grieve?*

It just hasn't felt like the right time.

Paul starts again as the clapping dies down. "We've got a talented line-up of aspiring musical artists, so let's show them some support!"

The small audience claps loudly, and Jamie sticks his thumb and index finger into his mouth for a loud whistle.

"First up, we have Taylor Roberts performing Taylor Swift!" The crowd chuckles kindly and claps as Taylor walks on stage with her guitar and cowboy boots.

She does great, as does Alexis, Gracie, and a few older musicians I don't know.

"And next up, we have Fallon Rivers, singing an acoustic cover of "Creep" by Radiohead."

Fallon calmly climbs the stairs to the stage, adjusting the mic to his height.

His dad's acoustic guitar hangs on his back, the black studded strap across his chest. Once the mic is situated, he pulls his guitar around and takes a deep breath, strumming a gentle melody.

When Fallon's raspy, breathy voice starts to sing, the melancholic lyrics flow effortlessly from his mouth. It's slow and haunting. Mesmerizing. Devastating. Special. *Everything*. He is fucking everything to me. And when I glance around, I see that he's enraptured the entire room.

There's only silence and maybe some watery eyes.

His strumming picks up, and the chords turn optimistic, hopeful, and beautiful. Just like him.

Holy fucking shit.

I'm stunned speechless, like everyone else. Except he's singing *at* me, making my skin tingle and my dick harden.

The words pour from his heart and bleed from his soul. I squeeze my eyes for a beat, fighting the emotions that his vulnerable voice elicits from me. I can feel his gaze on me, burning into my flesh and igniting my insides.

My eyes pop open, and that intense, steely-blue stare bores into me, open and unguarded. He uses music and lyrics to express himself, so I listen, ensuring I hear what he's trying to tell me. My heart melts listening to him so raw, so exposed. Telling me and the entire room how lost he feels.

I'll show him where he belongs tonight—in my bed and underneath me. God, I can't wait to be inside his tight body again. I need to tell him I love him. *Again.* All the damn time. Every day. Until he believes it. Until he *feels* it.

When the last chord echoes from his guitar, before the crowd even has a chance to register that this masterpiece of a performance is over, Gracie hops up the steps in a bright blue mini dress and matching eyeshadow. Her auburn hair is curled into a complicated updo, and she sits on a small stool that Fallon set next to him.

When did this happen?

She smiles at Fallon and winks. Her pale, shimmery lips nearly match his.

What the hell?

Fallon starts strumming his guitar, and Gracie starts singing "Stitches" by Shawn Mendes. Only it's a remixed cover, unique to their styles. Her soft, airy voice matches Fallon's, who comes in next, picking up the pace and the volume. It's different from his first song but no less amazing.

They slow it down again toward the end, adding the soulfulness I'm recognizing as his brand. He whispers the next bit, Gracie harmonizing with him, patting her leg and bobbing her head. They go back and forth, switching off for the last chorus, then coming in strongly, harmonizing again beautifully.

When the fuck did they practice this?

Are they in Advanced Music Study together?

That's the only thing it can be.

Fallon finishes the song, his words escaping in a hopeful whisper.

His stage presence is captivating. He's coming out of his shell yet still being himself—the same slightly lost boy I met all those weeks ago but with confidence and strength. He's not there completely, but I hope this trip to Philadelphia will help. If he agrees. I still need to ask.

Every single person in the record store stands, cheering, clapping, and whistling.

I have a weird moment of clairvoyance, wondering if this is only the beginning. The very start of his career as a fucking *rockstar*.

Because that's the only place this is headed.

Paul scurries onto the stage, taking the mic as Fallon and Gracie rush back to the lounge. "Alright, alright, calm down, folks. That was something special, wasn't it? Wow, just wow! The judges and I still need to deliberate, so in the meantime, enjoy coffee, soda, and an assortment of finger foods catered by the lovely Ms. D from Mary D's Bakery. Right down the street!"

As soon as Paul's done talking, I sneak away to congratulate my boyfriend. I already know he won. Everyone knows he won.

I find him in the employee bathroom, washing his hands and fixing his eyeliner. He spots me in the mirror and spins around, bracing his hands on the sink behind him. His pale skin peeks through the black mesh, inviting me.

I click the lock shut and stalk toward him, crowding him into the sink.

"You were fucking hypnotizing up there, Blue. You had the whole place spellbound. I was fucking entranced. Nearly drooling. I need to fuck you. Say I can fuck you tonight, baby?" I nip at his shimmery lips, tracing his piercing with my tongue.

"Yes. Please," he rasps out, closing his eyes as I trail my lips and tongue up his neck, making him shiver.

"Okay." I squeeze him through his jeans. "Let's go collect your prize first 'cause there's no other winner but you, Fal."

He chews on that lip again, and I tug him after me, slipping out of the bathroom and pulling him to our table. Gracie is perched on Cole's lap, smiling and laughing. I think they could make it. If they both actually *try*.

I sit down and pull Fallon onto my own lap before he can take the seat next to me. There's no reason we can't. Fuck everyone else.

He settles his smaller frame into me, his back to my chest, and I squeeze his hips, ready to get home and get inside his tight little body. He's so fucking tempting in this little mesh top, tight jeans, and all these chains. My dick starts to fill, and I press him down on me, letting him feel it.

"Ry!" he hisses, grasping my hands that are squeezing his hip possessively and unreasonably.

"Fallon Rivers!" Paul yells with genuine excitement.

Shit! I wasn't even paying attention.

I was distracted by the hot little ass on top of my crotch.

Fallon slips off my lap, and I immediately tuck myself under the tablecloth, hiding my half-chub. I glance up and make eye contact with Jamison. His dark eyes sparkle with amusement, and I roll my own, not really caring if he caught all that. It's his own fault he's so goddamn perceptive.

My broody little rockstar hustles up the stage, accepting his oversized check. I slip my phone out and snap a few photos of Fallon on stage holding his massive, five-thou-sand-dollar-winner's check.

This is fucking amazing!

Cole laughs loudly. "It's like he won the lottery or something. Price is Right? I don't know, but it's fucking hilarious!"

Gracie slaps Cole's arm. "Shut it. You wish you just won five thousand dollars. Jerk face."

"No. No. It's hilariously awesome, I mean! Chill, woman! Fallon's my boy."

"That's more like it because Fallon and I will probably end up on tour together one day. It seems inevitable, right?"

"Yeah," I agree. "That would be pretty awesome. And Cole and I can be on the same NBA team." I sigh, wishing that could all come true.

I focus on the stage and watch Fallon shake hands and speak with three old dudes, taking business cards and giving them small smiles. He's so out of his comfort zone, yet he's doing absolutely incredible.

I'm so proud of him, and I'm going to give him my own reward tonight.

With my mouth *and* my cock.

"Will you go to Philadelphia with Joel, my dad, and me?" I ask, trailing soft fingertips along his spine, lightly caressing his heated skin after I made love to him.

Fallon's back tenses at my question. "When?"

"The weekend after Sofie's party," I answer.

He narrows his eyes, obviously recognizing the date. The anniversary of his dad's death.

"Why?"

Shit. The hard part. But there are no secrets between us, so I'm nothing but open and honest.

"To visit your dad's grave."

Our gazes meet through the darkness, and the silence is deafening. Intense. It echoes throughout my entire body.

Fallon maneuvers to his elbows. "Will you be there?" he whispers with a vulnerability that stabs me in the heart.

"Of course, baby," I murmur back. "Come here."

Fallon crawls on top of me, both of us still naked, and lays flat against my bigger body. I band my arms around him, squeezing tight.

"I'll always be there for you. No matter what. We do it together."

"Okay. Together."

I burrow my face into his soft hair, kissing the top of his head.

"Forever," I murmur.

CHAPTER THIRTY-TWO
FALLON

Sofie's fifteenth birthday party went off without a hitch, and everyone was happy to celebrate the amazing person she is. I never imagined I'd get so lucky to have someone who's like a little sister to me. It's a relationship I never knew I needed or wanted, but here we are.

Jamie and Sophie looked awfully close, in my opinion, and Ryder definitely gave his best friend a few curious yet non-hostile glances. I've been wondering for a while what, if anything, is going on there. I know Sofie has a crush on Jamie; most girls do. And he treats her with care and respect. But that's really an understatement. He honestly treats her like a queen.

I'll leave it up to Ryder to decide if he trusts his best friend with his sister.

Now, it's officially spring. Signs of life and growth surround us. It's a season for regeneration. Yet for me, it means death. Cold, uncaring *death*. It means six years since I lost my father. My best friend. Six years since I abandoned him to die alone in a hospital bed.

The words are harsh, and the truth is unsettling, jarring even. But no matter how much regret I carry or how much the pain has begun to break through the mental fog, nothing I do or say will ever change the fact that I wasn't there for him. That I couldn't handle it, and I left him before he ultimately left me.

"We're almost to the hotel," Ryder whispers, nudging me awake from where I fell asleep on his shoulder in the rental car. Although I haven't exactly been asleep, more like stuck in my head and letting my negative thoughts consume me.

"We're going to freshen up after the long flight and settle into our rooms. We have adjoining suites, so just knock if you need anything, boys," Al says kindly from the passenger seat. "We can meet for lunch at the hotel restaurant after and decide what's first on the agenda. If there's anything in the city you want to do for fun or show us, Fallon, just let me know."

"Not really," I mumble. I'm not here for a vacation or for fun. I actually don't even want to be here. I don't want to think about Dad. Or Mom. Or how I'm all alone. Well, I *was* all alone. Now I have Ryder and Uncle Joel and all of these other people surrounding me. Supporting me. Loving me.

I swallow past the lump in my throat, knowing it will only get larger as the weekend progresses.

"Nothing?"

I shake my head. I hate being here. The memories, the negative thoughts. Questions about where Mom is and if she even loves me. It's all too much.

Alejandro's dark brows furrow, creasing the skin around his eyes even more than normal.

"Alright, well. Think about it." I can tell he wants to say

more, but it was a long flight. We're all a little tired and well aware that things could get emotionally charged soon.

I don't have the energy to pretend to enjoy myself. And I'm not here to sightsee. I just can't do it.

As if sensing my mood, Ryder's big palm settles on my thigh, squeezing gently.

I glance over at him, and he mouths, "It's okay."

I sink into my seat and close my eyes for a moment longer, trying to halt the emotions threatening to bubble up. I know I agreed to this trip, but I'm not one hundred percent certain I'm actually ready for this. I haven't been to my dad's grave. *Ever.* Didn't even go to his funeral.

I'm a shit person sometimes.

There's nothing else to say.

A vortex of self-hatred is forming so strong that if it sucks me in, I'll be spiraling for days. All of this will be for nothing. I'll have wasted everyone's time, and maybe they'll end up leaving me like—

"Fallon."

My uncle's voice pulls me from the brink, and an odd sense of déjà vu washes over me. I feel like I'm back in that social worker's office when he came to retrieve me all those weeks ago.

"Hmm?"

"We're here," Ryder says, repeating what Joel probably said a few times.

"M'kay," I mumble, running through a list of names. Guys that I might be able to call for some weed. Or maybe even some pills.

I need it to stop.

I don't want to feel these things. I'd rather go back to feeling less than nothing if I have to.

"Fallon, you okay?" I meet Ryder's concerned stare, so earnest and compelling.

"Yeah," I lie. Although I'm sure he knows. It's obvious I'm not.

His brows furrow and his lips tighten, but he doesn't call me out.

"Let's get the bags while they check us in."

I nod, moving on autopilot.

Ryder hops down, grabbing me by the waist and lifting me out of the rental SUV, even though it's lower than his truck and Joel's Bronco.

I head toward the front of the historic hotel. The brick is worn and distressed, but the colonial-style columns are painted a bright white. With five stories and adjoining wrought-iron balconies, it has a sort of hundred-year-old, old-world charm.

I might appreciate such things if I wasn't so focused on survival right now. Because that's what this trip feels like. Like I'm in a capsized life raft in a life-or-death struggle, and I've got the unfortunate feeling that I'm going under.

I grab a luggage cart by the front entrance and wheel it back to Ryder, helping him load our bags.

He pushes it over to Joel and Al as they smile and laugh at the receptionist lady.

I won't ever be that happy.

I just can't.

"Okay, kiddos," Joel says with a somewhat forced smile, trying to make light of a heavy trip for the both of us.

"Here's a keycard for each of you. Al and I are in room four-sixteen, right next door."

His worried eyes flick to my boyfriend for a moment. "Take your time and get settled in. We'll bring the cart with us and knock on your door."

Ryder grabs our two duffle bags, looping a thick arm through them. "Nah. I got it."

"I see. Well, text me or the 'Dad chat' when you guys are ready to meet for lunch and discuss our plans."

By plans, he means when I'm ready to go to the cemetery. To visit my dad's grave. The one I left for dead.

It's the entire point of this fun little weekend getaway.

Fuck.

I'm not good company.

I'm buckling under the weight of regret. The weight of not being there. Seeing his grave—proof that I can never change things—might be more than I can handle.

A soft touch skims between my shoulder blades, and a low voice murmurs in my ear. "Let's go, Blue. We can lie down for a bit."

My feet move on their own. One in front of the other until we reach our hotel room door. Ryder uses the keycard and opens it to a clean, fresh suite with two king-sized beds and a city view from what appears to be the top floor. I'm not sure. I can't even remember riding the elevator.

I slip my shoes off and then my jeans, pulling the covers back and climbing into the still-tucked-in sheets, letting them cocoon me.

"Want me to get in there with you?"

"No. Just gonna nap," I mumble, hating that I'm blowing him off. But I'm two seconds away from letting myself slip into oblivion, the only peace my mind can get when I'm in one of these moods. I need to take the relief where I can.

The last thing I see before I close my eyes are Ryder's concerned ones staring back at me from the end of my bed.

I take a shower after my two-hour nap, and the combination of sleep and warm water has me feeling a little more human. Especially after I ate a full sleeve of mini powdered donuts from the vending machine down the hall. Ryder also procured a bucket of ice, two cups, and orange soda. Both of our favorites.

"You feeling better, Fal? You look better."

I flick my eyes to Ryder's intense stare, then away. "Yeah. I was really tired. Makes things worse."

His eyes soften as he ambles over, standing at the end of the bed, peering down at me with love and concern. A tenderness I wish I could fully reciprocate.

"Since you're doing better, I was hoping we could talk. And just hear me out, okay?"

"Okay." He's making me nervous, but I trust him.

I spread my thighs for him, and he shuffles in between, cradling my face with his giant palms and peering into my eyes. So intense and so determined. I can't look away, even if he wasn't holding me in place. I'm entranced by his charisma, his allure. I'll say yes to anything, so when he tells me he brought my dad's letter and wants me to read it before we go to the cemetery, I hear myself say, "Yes." But whether I mean it or not is a different story.

He doesn't give me a moment to take it back or think about what I just agreed to and slips away, digging through his bag and coming back with the folded letter. So small, yet capable of catastrophic damage.

Ryder stands before me again, holding his hand out; the letter is tucked between his index and middle fingers.

My limbs move without any input from me, as if knowing what I need before I realize it myself. I grab the note and unfold it slowly, still perched on the end of the bed with Ryder's larger-than-life presence towering over me.

My eyes scan the letter, trailing back and forth rapidly. I choke on a gasp, making a strangled sort of sound. I quickly press a fist to my mouth to stop any more pained noises from escaping.

The emotions boil over while I'm simultaneously numb and in sheer agony.

Despair rushes out of me in waves, and if I wasn't already sitting down, I'd be knocked off my feet.

It's overwhelming.

Devastating.

"*Oh fuck.* I can't do it, Ry."

He leans forward and presses a soft kiss to my forehead. "You can. You're so strong, baby. Strongest person I know." He murmurs the last part, and if Ryder Cruz, state champ and MVP, says I have strength, then I have no choice but to show it.

My gaze blurs as my eyes fill with tears. I blink them away, desperate to finish reading this letter and be strong. For Ryder. For myself. For *Dad*. No matter how much it hurts, I want to read his message. Follow his advice. A stabbing pain tears through my ribs, the anguish tangible.

Fallon. My dearest son. I know you were afraid. I know you were angry. And I hope now that you're older, you can give that scared little boy a break. Maybe even some support. I don't blame you for not wanting your last memories of me to be in a hospital bed.

It's okay to be scared. It's okay to be unsure. But it's never okay to blame yourself for the past. I know you're an emotional soul, an old soul, and I worry for you and your future. I want you to follow your dreams and not let anything hold you back, especially not my passing. Please, Fallon, don't let it.

I'm leaving my lucky guitar with you. To bring you success and positivity. This guitar has been with me since I was your age. My father gave it to me when I was eighteen. It's a vintage Fender acoustic guitar. In our favorite color, blue. Well, I hope it's still your favorite color. But if you like hot pink or something less traditional, that would be cool too!

I snort at his corny joke, even in a letter. It's so good to see his words. Hear his voice in my head. God, I miss him.

I hope your mother's been there for you. Your uncle too. You are so special, and I never want you to regret anything. I know how much you love me, but it will never be more than I love you. Until we see each other again one day, I will be watching over you. Love always. Dad.

A tormented sob rips from my throat, and I slap a hand over my mouth as keening cries attempt to tear free. Six years of built-up suppressed feelings. Six years of hating myself. *Blaming* myself for everything. And like a dam bursting, I have no hopes of stopping the flood of emotions pouring out of me.

I know there's more to the letter, but I completely break down, releasing the numbness and accepting the pain bubbling out. But also the love. So much love.

The love and acceptance pouring from my father's letter are like a balm to my soul. He doesn't hate me. He never did. He *understands*.

"I d-don't know what's h-happening," I gasp out between heaving breaths and choked sobs. I thrust my arm out at him, the paper trembling. I can't talk about this. He just needs to read it for himself.

"It's okay. Let it all out. It's the only way."

He's right, and I trust him more than anyone else. I just need to let this out.

I sob as Ryder scans the paper rapidly. His eyes glisten with unshed tears the closer he gets to the end.

"There's no blame," he whispers. "Your dad understood, Fallon. It wouldn't have been easy for anyone, let alone a twelve-year-old child. He loves you. Always. Unconditionally."

He's right.

Fuck, he's right.

Ryder envelops me tightly, pulling my face into his chest.

"Let it out, baby. Let it out."

After a few more minutes of uncontrolled crying, my wails become gentle whimpers. I need to share more. I feel raw, like an exposed wound being cleaned with alcohol. It hurts now, burning with a fierceness hotter than fire. But it's necessary. It's for the best.

I pull back, putting space between us. "I was in a shit place when I got to California. Every movement and every moment fucking exhausting. I was lost, just existing. No focus. No motivation. No *dreams*. No life." The confession pours from me, and my words land like an ax, heavy and brutal.

I feel like I'm stumbling over my thoughts, but Ryder reaches out and grabs my hand, giving it a squeeze, allowing me to continue while also reassuring me.

"I didn't really care where I went or what happened to me. I abandoned Dad, and I wasn't enough for Mom. Wasn't enough to keep her happy. I lived through years of being told by her asshole boyfriends that I was worthless. An easy, unmoving target. They knew I wouldn't fight back.

Talk back. It was too easy." I turn my head and lift my arm, wiping my nose on my shoulder and sniffling loudly.

"You *are* worthy. You *deserve* to be loved. I'll show you. Every day. For as long as I need to, Fallon. I love you so fucking much." Ryder gently nudges me to the bed, and I fall back.

He climbs on, lying next to me with his hand tucked under his cheek. He reaches out and brushes a leftover tear from the corner of my eye.

Desire, need, and *love* blaze within me, heating my skin and forcing me to finally voice what I've been feeling for a while now.

"I. . . I love you too, Ryder. So fucking much. You're the one person on this planet that holds my happiness in his hand. And that scares me, Ry. It scares me so much."

"I'm not going anywhere. Ever. So be prepared to be happy for the rest of your life, Blue."

He lowers his full lips to mine, pressing hard like he wants to be as close as possible.

I want that too.

I think I need it.

CHAPTER THIRTY-THREE
RYDER

I pull back from the kiss, and his steely blue eyes search my face before darting down to my mouth. I tell him I love him. Let him see the words on my lips. I'll tell him every day until he truly feels it.

He closes his eyes for a moment. A single, silent tear leaks from one eye. "I need you," he murmurs, his voice breaking on the last word.

I lean forward and kiss the tear away. "I got you, baby. I got you."

I scramble off the bed and rush to my duffle bag, digging through my toiletries until I find the small bottle of lube I packed.

The hotel beds are on a platform of sorts and at the perfect height for my hips. An idea strikes me.

I toss the bottle next to Fallon and lean forward, grasping the waistband of his sweats and peeling them down with his underwear. I grab his hips and yank him to the edge of the bed, causing his breath to hitch. I smirk. He loves it when I manhandle him.

Fallon isn't completely hard yet, so I lean down,

pressing my face to his groin and inhaling deeply. He smells like fresh soap and Fallon. My favorite smell.

I suck his soft cock, letting it harden inside my mouth until he's fully erect.

"Fuck, Ry," he mumbles before pulling his T-shirt over his head. I do the same, removing my pants too.

"Pull your knees back for me, Fal."

I'm serious-Ryder right now, and his cock jumps at the command. He grasps under his knees and pulls back, exposing his ass to me.

My pupils dilate at the sight, and I chew on my bottom lip, contemplating what I want to do next. A shiver races through me at the thought that I can do *anything*.

I grab the lube and squirt a generous amount onto my fingers before running them through Fallon's crease, making him moan and pull on his legs. I continue to just tease and caress, not penetrating him.

His cock is leaking and twitching.

"Ry. Please."

Deciding he's waited long enough, I reward his patience by pressing into him with one finger, his body easily pulling me in.

His eyes roll into the back of his head as he groans in relief when I begin to pump my finger into his ass.

"More."

I slip another finger in, scissoring them to help get his body ready.

I curl my fingers up, pressing that spot inside him, and he cries out. His knuckles turn white as he squeezes his legs hard enough to force back the impending orgasm.

I don't want him to come yet, so I slip my fingers out.

"Fuck. Ry. Wha—?"

"My cock. You need it. And I need to be inside you," I

whisper, lining myself up with his twitching hole. I push forward until my cockhead slips past the tight ring of muscle, and Fallon cries out.

He slaps two hands over his mouth, releasing his hold on his legs and resting them against my chest. I grasp his hips and press in slowly. The sounds of Fallon's muffled groans spur me on until I bottom out.

I caress his hip lovingly. "You okay?" I pant.

His dark blue eyes pop open, and he nods, keeping his hands over his mouth and his legs against my chest as I thrust into him.

The muffled noises make me feel like we're doing something wrong and are trying to hide. My dick pulses with excitement, growing even larger inside of him and causing his asshole to clench around me.

"Fuck, Blue! You're so tight. I love fucking your little hole. Love being inside you." I'm near delirious with pleasure.

Fallon's legs slip off my shoulders, almost going limp. I hook my hands under his knees, using my leverage to yank him toward me as I thrust into him. I set a punishing pace, Fallon's hard cock bouncing between us.

I'm not going to last long at this speed.

Sweat drips down my temple onto Fallon.

"Touch yourself while I fuck you. Gonna come."

I grit my teeth, continuing to plow into him as he jerks himself off.

Not even one minute later, he's crying out behind his palm, covering his shouts as cum spurts between us and his hole clenches around me.

I follow right after him, pulsing inside his tight body and filling him with my spunk.

We're both panting, our bodies sweaty and twitching with aftershocks.

I pull out slowly and watch as my cum oozes out of his open hole. I scoop some up and push it back inside, fucking him and making him moan. "I need to get you a plug. Keep you stuffed."

He groans in embarrassed arousal. "Fuck, Ry. Don't say that."

I pull my fingers out. "Okay. I'll order one when we get home."

He groans again, and I chuckle, gently setting his legs back on the bed.

"Let's get you cleaned up. We have more things to overcome."

I know it sucks, but we came on this trip for a reason. And it can't be avoided any longer.

"Together," I add.

"I'm proud of you today, Fallon," Joel says in a heartfelt tone. I can see the truth in his eyes and know we all feel the same.

We're back from the cemetery, eating room service in Dad's and Joel's suite.

"Me too. I've grown quite attached to you already," my dad says.

Fallon glances up from inhaling his hamburger and fries, offering a small smile before returning to his dinner.

Dad glances at me, I think stunned by the smile. I guess he hasn't seen one of those yet. I give him a blinding grin in return, then Joel, who shakes his head.

I told Joel I'd have Fallon's back and make him my friend, probably even get him to smile.

I didn't intend to also make him my boyfriend. But once we met, there wasn't any stopping the momentum or the chemistry. I'm drawn to him, and he fits into my life like a missing piece, making me want to be brave and live however I want.

"While we're here, I wanted to mention that your mother contacted me from prison, asking to speak to you."

Fallon's eyes dart up from his food, the blood draining from his already pale face.

"I'm sorry if it seems like a bad time, but we're here, and you are an adult now, Fallon. It wouldn't be right for me to keep that information from you."

I can see Joel's point and respect it, even if it's an overload for Fallon.

He tilts his head to the side, anxiously running his hands through his hair.

I want to give him space. I know he needs it, so I reach over and gently squeeze his thigh, letting him know I'm here.

He needs someone to try for him, and luckily he has an entire family to do that now. Joel is an amazing person, and my dad isn't going to let Fallon slip through the cracks without feeling like he's wanted and belongs.

I'm ready to show him too.

"I can handle it for you. Or I can pass her your number. It's in your hands. In your control, Fallon."

"No. I can't see her. It's too much. Handle it. Please, Uncle Joel." His eyes dart away from his uncle's after the plea escapes his lips.

I can't help it. I tug him into my arms, leaving our half-eaten burgers behind.

"I'll tell her you're not ready, but you can contact her if and when you are."

"Was she sober?" Fallon mumbles.

"Sounded like maybe," Joel murmurs truthfully.

"Hmm. I still can't."

I squeeze my boyfriend to my chest, not caring that my dad and his uncle are sitting on the bed across from us. He needs some comfort. This is heavy stuff.

"I don't blame you, kiddo. It's been a rough day."

Fallon didn't break down at the gravesite. I think reading the letter in private was cathartic for him. He released all the pain and could say hello and goodbye to his father at the same time.

It was tragic and devastating but so, so healing.

It'll take time for the wound to fully fade, but the path has been started, and I feel so proud of the steps he's taken to do right by himself.

So. Fucking. Proud.

CHAPTER THIRTY-FOUR

RYDER

It's May now, and prom is two weeks away. Things at school and home have been going smoothly. I haven't officially asked Fallon, but that's about to change with help from my favorite chef and one of my favorite people.

"Think this'll do? Yer oul fella was tryin' ta help. Doin' it arseways. But don't ye worry, I didn't let him ruin yer message."

I only understood half of what she just said, but the mini ice cream cookies spelling out "PROM?" are fucking epic.

I hug her to my side, sticking her right under my armpit like she hates but just fits so well. "It's amazing, Georgie. Thank you."

"Aye! Ye best not put me in yer stinky pit, lad. I know where ye sleep, what ye eat. Everything."

I chuckle, releasing her from my heavy arm and straightening the dot on the question mark. It needs to be one-hundred-and-ten percent perfect for Fallon. He deserves everything and more, and I think this will make him smile.

God, I hope it makes him smile.

He's doing a lot better, and I get his smiles more frequently now. They're fucking addicting.

His hair is neon green now. Still half black, of course. I'm not sure he'll ever change that. It's sorta just a part of him. And he's added a nose stud to his piercings.

"He'll be back from band practice any minute," I say excitedly, doing an obnoxious drumroll on the kitchen counter. "Almost time."

Georgie narrows her eyes on me. "I see. I can take a hint. I know when I'm not wanted. Enjoy yer cookies and yer boyfriend. You better treat him right." She holds her fists up like she wants to box, and I tip my head back, laughing.

"I'll punch myself in the face if I hurt him. It's not happening. Don't worry."

"Think I'll punch ye too. I'm thinkin' Sofie as well, so ye stay in line on prom night. Be a gentleman like I taught ye. Alright, lad?"

"Of course, Georgie." I kiss the top of her gray head before she scurries out of the kitchen with a plate of extra mini ice cream sandwiches for the rest of the family.

She's never made them individually sized. We always make one giant cookie and slice it like a pizza. And it's just for birthdays. But Fallon instantly loved them, so I cannot wait to see the look on his face when I ask him to prom.

The door from the garage opens and in walks Fallon. He finally got his license two weeks ago. Joel and my dad surprised him with a new car, rewarding him for all the hard work he's put into overcoming his past trauma.

A brand new Mustang Shelby GT500, custom painted in

chameleon paint that changes from bright blue to bright green depending on the lighting. It has an all-black interior and is more than perfect for Fallon. I still call him Blue, even though his hair is now green.

He'll always be my Blue.

His dark gaze hones in on the cookies, widening in surprise as a slow smirk tugs at one side of his mouth before that intense stare switches to me.

"Hey," I say, feeling oddly shy about this whole thing.

"Hey," he replies, stepping further into the kitchen from where he froze in the doorframe. He sets his guitar case down, and his eyes dart over to the cookies, then up to me.

"Will you go to prom with me?" I ask, regardless of how obvious a question it is.

He picks up the dot in the question mark and takes a huge bite, moaning at the flavor.

I chose strawberry cheesecake ice cream between homemade chocolate chip graham cracker cookies. Special. Just like him.

"Yes," he mumbles around another mouthful, and I pick one up too.

"Oh. Holy shit. Yes. This new combo is fucking on point. Thank you, Georgie."

Fallon chuckles, and the raspy sound rolls over my skin like a soft caress.

I lean down and kiss the strawberry ice cream from his lips, enjoying the taste of my boyfriend.

"It's going to be fun. Good memories. Happy memories. And the after-parties will be fucking epic," I say, grinning widely before grabbing a second cookie and biting it in half.

"Smile, kiddos!" Joel shouts, pushing his glasses up his nose before attempting to use the new camera Dad got for his birthday.

He wants to take up another hobby in his old age and decided it's photography. But he can't be bothered to figure it out himself so that task landed on Joel.

He holds his eye to the hole and nearly bumps his glasses off.

Sofie giggles from her spot next to Jamie, her lime green dress strapless and floor length. The entire thing is made of sequins and glitter; as she put it, she looks like a mermaid. Her hair is intricately pulled up, tendrils escaping and framing her face.

"I thought you weren't old, Joel? Just use the screen! I want to get to prom before they start closing down. Fallon can't miss his performance, and Ryder's probably prom king. Basically, we're important people, so hurry up please, future stepfather!"

That's another thing that just happened. Dad popped the question to Joel in San Diego at one of his new restaurants right on the marina. He closed the place down for the night, his personal assistant setting up tiny, electric tealights over the entire deck.

The chef cooked their favorite meal and Joel's favorite dessert, strawberry shortcake, with an engagement ring resting on top.

It made my prom proposal look like child's play. But that's fine. Fallon enjoyed ours, and that's all that matters.

Dad and Joel chuckle at Sofie's antics, but Joel takes her advice and uses the camera's screen.

"Oh, much easier. Thank you, darling. And you know I'm not old. Don't tease me."

Sofie is giggling, and the rest of us laugh. Even Fallon is smiling, and I know it's going to be an amazing photo.

Jamie invited Sofie, and Cole and Gracie are currently together. The six of us coordinated to wear shades of green, and the effect looks amazing.

"Oh, Sofie! Look at my baby," a high-pitched feminine voice squeals from the doorway.

Mom.

We're on the back deck at my house. The lake is behind us, and the sun is almost setting. Golds and purples glow around us.

What the fuck is she doing here, and how did she know?

"Absolutely stunning, sweetie." She walks over and stands next to Joel and Dad.

"Alejandro," she says in a cool tone, and I'm ready to get out of here. We don't need this on prom night. We're here to have a good time and make good memories with good friends. At least she won't be able to do this as soon as Dad's full-custody case goes through the system.

"Penelope, what are you doing here?"

She huffs out an annoyed breath. "Well, obviously, I know when the senior prom is. I just didn't expect to see my baby girl here. Looking absolutely gorgeous."

Her green eyes travel over to me, my arm around Fallon's lower back, and I tug him closer, making it clear what's happening.

Her lips pinch together tightly, but she doesn't ask me the question she knows she has no right to ask.

I put her out of her misery, not necessarily wanting to come out to my mother on prom night, but, hey, you win some, you lose some.

"Yeah. I'm gay, Mom."

Her right eye twitches, but she doesn't say anything too rude. But nothing too nice, either.

I'm counting it as a win.

"Are you?"

I nod, rubbing my hand up and down Fallon's arm, her eyes honing in on the movement.

"Since when?"

"Okay, Pen, that's enough. He doesn't owe you any answers."

"He's my son, Al. I think he can at least tell me."

"I did. I'm gay. And there's nothing else to say, Mom. We can be cool, but you left a long time ago, and you get no say in my life or my happiness. Especially not my sexuality. So I'm going to politely say excuse me, but we have a prom to get to."

We got enough photos, so we shout *goodbye* to everyone, and Sofie hugs our mom on the way out.

She still loves her, and so do I, no matter her shitty behavior. My love will never fade; it just changed.

"Be safe!" Joel shouts.

"Have fun!" Dad adds. We slip out the front door and jog over to the ridiculous stretch limo that Cole booked. We laugh as we pile in, not letting any of that drama pull us down.

It's fucking prom night.

Cole sticks his head out of the sunroof, hollering into the air and pumping himself up for the party. He's already drunk, pre-gaming with flute after flute of champagne. He's being outrageous and reckless, as usual.

Gracie tugs at the hem of his tuxedo jacket.

"Get him down, Jamison. He's being drunk and stupid," Gracie says, calling it how it is. It's part of why they're so on again-off again, always bumping heads.

Jamie sighs and leaves his spot cuddled next to my little sister, squeezing Cole hard around the ribs. He falls back into the limo, nearly crying when Jamie doesn't relent.

"Mercy! Stop!"

"Stay inside the moving vehicle. Say it."

"I-I will stay inside the m-moving vehicle," he howls until Jamie stops, then casually sits back in his seat like nothing happened.

"Good. Now drink some water and sober up. We gotta pass the faculty and take photos, *again*. And you know ours will end up in the yearbook. You *know* it. You can't look torched, Cole,"

"Okay, Dad! Damn!"

"Don't *Dad* me, young man," Jamie retorts.

"Okay! Enough bromancing with my date, Cole. We're almost there," Sofie teases.

I made her promise not to drink champagne or drink the punch. Bottled water only tonight. Jamie will watch her like a hawk, so I'm not worried.

We're going to a fancy hotel downtown. The academy rented out the ballroom, and we all rented rooms in addition to the entire penthouse level.

Well, except for Sofie. She's too young, and part of the deal Jamie and I made was for him to return her home by midnight like the princess she is.

He agreed, no problem, showing he respects me, my dad, and especially Sofie. I can only hope she decides to keep him around.

When we pull up to the hotel, spotlights highlight the

old brick facade, and a red carpet greets us when our limo door is opened. The prom committee decided on an old Hollywood theme, and so far, they've nailed it.

We stop for group and individual photos, indulging in every ridiculous prom pose, all for the sake of Sofie's scrapbooks.

Okay. Someone definitely spiked the punch. I mean, I'm not exactly surprised. I warned Sofie not to drink it and told Fallon to lay off before he hit the stage.

Afterward, I ladled him a thermos of the stuff. It's fruity and delicious.

Fallon, Gracie, and Taylor absolutely killed it. Fallon mainly played the guitar with Gracie on the keyboard while both girls sang, but he joined in and harmonized. His raspy voice mingled perfectly with the softer, breathy tones of the girls. The three of them sounded amazing together, as they always do.

Their band, Fallen Grace, it's going places. Everyone knows it after tonight.

I take another sip of punch, popping a pretzel into my mouth to counteract the sweetness.

We're lounging at our group's table, waiting for the prom committee to finish their announcements so we can move on to the after-party.

Alexis clears her throat. "And this year, I'm excited to announce that for the first time ever, we will have runners-up winning Prom Prince and Prom Princess! So, without further ado, let me announce your Acadia Lake Prep Senior Class Homecoming Court!"

The crowd cheers and claps, the energy building with anticipation.

"Your Prom Queen and Prom Princess are. . ." She slowly opens the envelope, a smile quirking her lips at the names she finds.

"Gracie Sinclair and Taylor Roberts!"

More applause and loud whistles fill the space.

"And your Prom King and Prom Prince are none other than Ryder Cruz and Fallon Rivers! Everyone come up here and accept your crowns and sashes!"

I glance over to my boyfriend to gauge his reaction to the title.

New Fallon is smirking. New Fallon may even be laughing inside at the notion of being prom royalty with me.

All four of us make our way to the stage. Gracie and Taylor jump up and down, holding hands and squealing as they both get crowns placed on their heads.

Then Alexis looks at the two of us standing side by side in matching black tuxes with neon green accents and winks.

I understand what she did for us, anointing us Prom King and Prom Prince. *Together.* As a couple. In front of the entire school, sending a message of acceptance and inclusivity.

The crowd cheers as I lean down, allowing her to place the crown on my curls while Taylor and Gracie help with Fallon's.

This feels big. Monumental almost.

Allowing future classes to have same-sex couples win together is progress I didn't even know we needed. I smile wide as Glenn from Yearbook snaps photo after photo, the flash nearly blinding us. But we don't care. The four of us link arms for a group shot, and Fallon even gives a little half-smile.

"Alright. Let's dance!" I shout, ready to get the night going.

The after-parties are when the *real* fun starts.

CHAPTER THIRTY-FIVE

FALLON

The senior class rented out the entire penthouse level, ensuring we could be as loud as we wanted before dispersing to our individual rooms.

And, of course, Ryder and I are sharing.

The after-party is going strong. The drinks are flowing, and the music is bumping.

I took my suit jacket off, tossing it somewhere around here. My tie hangs loosely from my neck, and I'm lounging on the sofa, legs spread, head on the back of the couch, watching my boyfriend dance with one of his girl friends.

I can't take my eyes off of him. His smile is radiant, his personality unknowingly seductive, and with kindness so warm that he glows with an inner light. I'm dazed, completely charmed like a snake in a pot, and Ryder is the man with a flute.

I tip my head back, guzzling the last of my beer but never taking my eyes off him. He's so carefree, and the positive energy radiating from him demands my attention. I was lost to his pull, the attraction slowly drawing me out of the dark pit I was trapped in. Until there was no more denying *us*.

He's fascinating. And mine. *All mine.*

I slam my empty bottle down and stand abruptly. I walk steadily despite the five beers I've had.

We don't have to hide anymore, and I'm done with this afterparty.

I'm ready to get fucked by the prom king.

The alcohol has lowered my inhibitions, so my filter is gone, and my inhibitions are out the window.

I grab Ryder's wrist and tug without saying anything or stopping my momentum. He's half a foot taller, and God knows how much heavier, but he follows obediently, laughing and apologizing to the girl he was dancing with. Taylor maybe. I couldn't tell you. I have a singular vision for one boy with flawlessly tan skin, olive-green eyes, and adorable curls.

"Fallon, what are you doing?" he chuckles. There's no point in answering. He won't hear me over the thumping bass and vibrating crowd. I lead us down the hallway, away from the buzz of the party.

I slip into an empty bedroom and pull Ry in behind me, locking the door and slamming my mouth to his. I need a detour before we find our actual room. Maybe a blowie too.

I bite my lip, chewing on the piercing and thinking hard before I push him against the wall and yank him down by his collar.

Ryder traces my mouth with his tongue, mapping every groove before tangling it with my own. He slides his hands down my back and grabs my ass, squeezing firmly before lifting. I wrap my legs around him, never removing my mouth from his.

He walks us backward and sets me on the mirrored dresser, standing between my spread thighs.

"What do you want, Blue? I booked a room on another level," he pants.

"I-I can't wait. I need you to suck me. Right now. *Here. Please.*"

Ryder unbuttons my pants, and I lift up, allowing him to peel them and my briefs down my ass.

My cock bobs out, already hard and leaking. I have been for a while. Watching him dance got my pulse racing.

Ryder leans down and swipes his tongue from base to tip, swirling it around the head before swallowing me whole.

"Fuck!" I shout, startled by the immediate force he starts sucking me off with.

"Goddamn, Ry. Slow down. I'm gonna blow."

He pops off, taking deep breaths. "Good, 'cause I need you back in our room. Where I have lube. So I can fuck you."

I groan, dropping my head against the mirror, my hole twitching in anticipation. "You can just use spit. It's fine. I need you, Ry." I'm drunk and horny and whiny. I know that's not the smart thing to do. That it'll hurt. But I just need my boyfriend inside of me. *Now.*

"Fuck, Blue. I can't do that to you. I won't hurt you. I'm going to make you come with my mouth, and then we're going back to our room. Where I can fuck you properly."

Ryder dives down again, taking me to the back of his throat and rolling my balls in his palm.

I thread my fingers through his curls, adding light pressure. Ryder hums, and the vibration shoots through my cock and straight to my balls, causing them to draw up. I'm seconds away from lift-off. "Ry. Gonna come," I manage to grit out seconds before I shoot my load down his throat.

Ry chokes and sputters around my length, the back of his throat squeezing my tip and milking me even more.

"Fuuuck, Ry. Your mouth is so good."

He pulls away from my softening cock, licking up every drop of cum before helping to tuck me away and zip me up.

"Let's go. Now." Ryder flicks his eyes down to the massive erection straining against the front of his tuxedo trousers because they're not very restrictive. He looks sexy as sin with his white dress shirt halfway unbuttoned, showing off his firm, tan chest. The neon green tie rests around his neck, and his pale eyes gleam under the recessed hotel lighting.

I scramble off the dresser, nearly face-planting, all too eager to get to our room. And desperate for the prom king to fuck me.

"Ungh!" I cry out unintelligibly from my seat on top of Ryder's lap. I'm thoroughly impaled on his massive cock. The thing is splitting me in two, pressing deep into my guts.

My cock is leaking as it bobs in between us, untouched. I don't even need to be touched as I brace myself on Ry's firm chest, using the leverage to plunge myself up and down, fully sheathing his cock inside of me each time.

Ryder grabs my hips, pressing me firmly down onto his length and grinding his pelvis into my sensitive rim.

I throw my head back.

So. Fucking. Full.

I hold a hand to the front of my stomach and swear I can feel it bulging out as he grinds and swivels his hips into me, stretching and rubbing me in all the right places.

I pinch Ry's nipples, rolling them between my fingers as

he pulls out and shoves back in, nailing my prostate each time.

"Right there, Ry. Right there!" I call out, arching my back so he can get even deeper and press that spot even harder.

"Gonna come. Gonna come," I chant.

He reaches for my cock, but I swat his hand away.

I'm too sensitive, and I don't need it.

I grit my teeth as the orgasm races down my spine and through my balls, drawing every last drop of spunk out of them as I explode onto Ryder's chest. My cock throbs as it releases my load, and my asshole pulses around his cock, gripping it tightly and forcing an orgasm out of him as well.

"Fuck! Fallon! Fuck!" he shouts. "Your asshole is so. . . fucking. . . *tight*." He stares into my eyes, something hot and intense burning between us as his warmth fills me.

"I fucking love you."

His heartfelt declaration causes another mini orgasm to roll through me, soft and languid. Easy and comfortable, like sleeping in on a rainy Saturday morning.

My love and desire for him are never-ending, all-consuming, and inescapable. Burning bright and never fading. He's opened my eyes to colors I've never seen before and introduced happiness to my life that I've never felt. Never even dreamed.

"I love you more, Ryder Cruz," I say with a fierceness I feel in my bones.

I've never felt anything so strongly in my life.

I *crave* him.

His soft cock slips free, our connection broken, and I whimper at the loss.

He bands his arms around me, pulling me to lie on his

hard chest. My sticky cum smears between us, and his left-over seed oozes out of my hole.

It's messy, but neither of us cares.

"Can I ask you something? Even if it's not the right time?"

It's after midnight on prom night, and we're both slightly intoxicated, but my brain says, "Yes, of course," anyway.

"Will you come to college with me? Well, I know you're not *going* to college, but will you come with me? I can't be apart from you. I have to live in the dorms the first year, but we'll figure it out. I can't be separated from you. I just can't."

Ryder squeezes me tightly, and relief washes through me. I didn't know what to expect after graduation in a couple weeks. Where I'm going or what I'm doing. All I know is that I want to be with Ry, and I want to pursue my music. Maybe even stay with the band—with Gracie and Taylor. And now that he's out and not hiding who he is, any college or team that accepts him or drafts him is also accepting the lifestyle.

"I'd follow you anywhere, Ry. You brought me back from a void of nothingness and no feelings. Now, I'm so full of love. And not just yours. *Everyone's.* Friends. Family. *Our family.*"

"We can follow our dreams and find happiness together, baby," he whispers. His touch both warms me and sends a chill down my spine.

"Together," I echo, grinding myself against the hard ridges of his abdomen, ready to go again. Ready to show him how much he makes me *feel*.

"I love you," I murmur, truly *feeling* everything.

"Forever, Blue."

EPILOGUE
RYDER - THREE YEARS LATER

"Fallen Grace is on in an hour! I gotta leave, Ry!" Fallon whines from where he's bent over our couch in the penthouse loft we now call home. True to his word, Fallon followed me anywhere. It just turns out it wasn't very far.

I got drafted by my dream NBA team, and now we're in LA, not even two years after I started playing college ball.

"Do you want me to remove my cock from your ass, then?" I deadpan, giving him the dry humor he normally serves me.

Fallon cries out as I adjust the angle of my pumping hips and nail his prostate.

"No! Just. Keep. Doing. That!" he grunts with each one of my thrusts.

His hair is hot pink now but still half black. It's longer than it was in high school, and I grab hold, wrapping his hair around my fist as I continue my punishing pace.

It still doesn't take us long; quickies are kinda our thing. And I prove my own point when Fallon comes without even touching his own cock. I continue to nail his prostate, milking him for every drop.

His spasms trigger my own release, and soon we're both lying nearly comatose on the living room floor.

"You're gonna be late," I murmur into his neck, sleep calling me home.

Fallon rushes into the bathroom, nearly tripping over the pants around his ankles, making me chuckle.

"Where are you playing tonight?" I ask, scratching my stomach absently. I'm sprawled out on our couch, enjoying my post-sex and post-nap relaxation.

We're in the off-season, and I have two more weeks before practice starts again.

"Just this little dive bar on the Sunset Strip. Gracie's agent booked it."

Another thing that conveniently lined up. Cole got drafted to the same team in LA, and he and Gracie have surprisingly been going strong since high school. The four of us have become close because of it.

Sofie graduates high school this year and will be attending culinary school here in LA, as well. Jamison is unfortunately on the other side of the country in New York, but his contract is up, and he's looking to get traded. I've been pressuring my coach to snatch him up, and I'm convinced it worked.

The poor bastard has been pining after my sister this whole time. If I have the power to help bring two people together, then so fucking be it. I'll do it.

Dad and Joel officially married last year at Dad's newest

restaurant in San Francisco. Alexis is in school for event planning with dreams of becoming a wedding coordinator, so Joel gave her the opportunity, and she more than proved herself.

"Want me to come? I can wear a disguise?"

Fallon snorts, thinking about the long, straight black wig I sometimes wear, hiding my recognizable curls. He says it doesn't work, and I'm better off sticking with a baseball cap.

"My agent got me a new wig. This one is blond. Looks more realistic."

He side-eyes me, questioning the validity of that statement and having every right to. Sandra is pretty shit at picking out wigs, but I told her not to spend less than three grand on this, so there's no fucking *way* it looks fake.

We'll see, I guess.

"I think Cole's coming. You can coordinate your disguise with him."

My eyes light up as a million ideas pass through my head, including every possible superhero costume.

I see the instant regret in his eyes and tip my head back to cackle.

"I promise we won't embarrass you and Gracie too badly. Like, it won't be career-ending or anything. For either of us."

"Oh gee. Thanks for the reassurance there, boyfriend," he deadpans, but I see the sparkle in his eyes. And I love it more every time I see it. I'll never take it for granted.

Fallon was so lost when we met, and I had no idea if I could find him. Now, every time I get a glimpse of the happy soul underneath the serious, damaged façade, more of his truth seeps into me. He's found the person he was always meant to be and the person I will continue to help him be. Fallon is wise beyond his years and amazing beyond this earth. He's something else. Something angelic. Precious.

I'll be his guiding force always.

And forever.

ACKNOWLEDGMENTS

First, thank you to my amazing readers for your continued support! It really means so much to me that you love these boys and root for them as much as I do. Every review, comment, and recommendation is truly appreciated, and I look forward to writing more loyal boys in the future.

A huge thanks to my awesome ARC team. Y'all are so supportive and creative with your posts, and I'm lucky to have you! I smile every time you share something and hype up my stories.

My beta readers, Elizabeth and Shannon, thank you for reading *Lost Boy* so last minute and giving me the validation I always need. Having you both there to talk things through was so helpful, and I value all of your ideas and opinions!

Molly, my favorite editor, you continue to take my words and stories and help me develop them to their full potential. You are invaluable and so very appreciated for your hard work!

Silver, my cover designer—the way you make my thoughts come to life will never cease to amaze me. I love that we've been on this journey together since the beginning, growing and doing all the things! You are so talented, and every detail of our intense, lost boy Fallon is just perfect!

A big thanks to Chaotic Creatives! Ari, I'm so glad you're my PA, thank you for all of your help with this book. You've been a lifesaver! Britt, my awesome proofreader, I really appreciate the last minute help and seriously adored your comments. I'm so happy you love Ryder and Fallon!

Lastly, to Elizabeth Dear, T. Ashleigh, and Cora Rose, your support and encouragement, both personally and professionally, means more than you know. Thank you.

ALSO BY CHARLI MEADOWS

The Loyal Boys

Cali Boy

Bad Boy

Lost Boy

Unlucky 13

Shattered: A Black Diamond Novel

ABOUT THE AUTHOR

Charli Meadows is an obsessive reader, avid Bookstagrammer-turned PA, and now an author herself. Lover of all things romance, she plans to write a little bit of everything but make it sweet and spicy.

You can usually find Charli working her boring corporate job or at home playing video games. When she's not reading, writing, or daydreaming about books, that is.

Subscribe to my newsletter!
Join my Facebook Group!

Printed in Great Britain
by Amazon